The Vigilance of Sι

Novel by Patricia O'Donnell

The Vigilance of Stars

Novel by Patricia O'Donnell

For information contact:
Unsolicited Press
Portland, Oregon
www.unsolicitedpress.com
orders@unsolicitedpress.com
619-354-8005

Cover Art: Kathryn Miller
Editor: S.R. Stewart

ISBN: 978-1-947021-81-5

"He was blessed with an eternal childhood,
with the givingness and vigilance of stars"

(Anna Akhmatova, "Boris Pasternak")

"Oh please don't go—we'll eat you up—we love you so!"

(Sendak, *Where the Wild Things Are*)

Contents

for Molly and Grace O'Donnell

Chapter One

Kiya, half-awake since 4:00 a.m. on her narrow bed, makes herself wait until the sun is above the horizon before allowing herself to get up and pad into the bathroom. She opens the foil package carefully, pulls her pajama pants down, and sits on the toilet. This is the second time she has taken the test, so she knows how it works. She lets go a stream, then tightens the muscles inside herself to stop, and puts the stick between her legs before she lets loose again. *Mid-stream,* it is called, the warm urine streaming over the narrow stick. In the middle of the stream, in the middle of her life. Kiya closes her eyes, letting the water out, and imagines herself thigh-high in a stream up north casting a fly rod, the line curving a graceful arc into the rushing water. She will catch something this time, a small slippery fish.

She has not tried for this, but birth control—even the best, most effective kind of birth control—does not always work. As the light of the sun makes its way between two buildings on Commercial Street, glancing off a bit of bright water to land on her still sitting on the toilet, she stares at the stick in her trembling hand, sees one blue line, then another, crossing it. She does not know if the feeling inside her is physical or emotional or even metaphorical, but something bright and painful blossoms within her, causing her to lie down on the colorful hooked rug and curl around, hugging herself. It is desire, desire for whatever is already inside her that she feels. Lying on the rug alone in her small apartment with the morning sun touching her shoulders hesitantly, Kiya sees the future break open and start growing inside her. It is something she would not have dared to ask for, but knows instantly she will not refuse.

✵ ✵ ✵ ✵

There is a time in the evening when it is neither day nor night, neither light nor dark. Divisions dissolve. Peter sits by his open-second floor window, picking on the banjo. The light in the room is a gray that softens everything, makes it hazy, and the sound as it floats through the room and out the window seems more substantial to him than the walls. If he half-closes his eyes, if he unfocuses, it's as if he can loosen the structure of himself, of his body and his mind or whatever makes him *him,* and he becomes part of the leaves whispering in the dusk, the sound of the music lifting and falling on the floating air.

Eventually, Peter lays his banjo on his bed and turns on the lamp, and light blooms into the room. Night now, dark outside the windows and light inside, and he lives inside his body again. He is Peter King, tree-climbing arborist, banjo-picking Philosophy BA. He thinks briefly of Kiya, wonders again if and how they should break up. He doesn't want to hurt her, but he's not ready to be a part of someone in a structured way, linked by a ring or a promise. That kind of commitment is not for him, not yet anyway. There are places to go, things to do; he isn't sure what they are yet, but he's just twenty-six, and when he thinks of commitment, he thinks of doors closing, of a hallway narrowing in rather than opening up. He doesn't think he's what they call polyamorous, like his previous girlfriend decided she was; he doesn't want to love many people at one time. Just one is enough, one is all he can handle, but not for long. The leaves of the trees are thick and heavy outside his window; he hears them rustling in the breeze, and the sound reminds him of the melody he was picking out. He pulls a journal towards him and opens it. The words to a song come to him and he wants to capture them, try them out: "The road is here, and it's a long ways away. I'm there, I'm here, I'm lost on the way." He pictures a little drumbeat, snares, banjo breaking in.

Later, he picks up a book and leafs through it—one of his philosophy books from college—and puts it down. The evening is open; there's a show he could see, a band from Nova Scotia that he likes. He could call Kiya, but he doesn't. He opens his computer, checks Instagram, watches a bit of *Breaking Bad,* an episode he's seen before. He shifts his shoulders and stretches his arms above his head, working out tension there from holding the chainsaw all afternoon, cutting into branches. The minutes slip away, getting late to make it to the show. In the mirror above his dresser, he sees himself, a young white American guy. Nice-looking, he supposes, for what that's worth. He thinks briefly of his father, that mystery figure who sometimes appears in his imagination like a shadow. What would his father say to him; would he tell him to get serious about his music? Or go to grad school, or get a better job? He wonders, again, if there is something in particular he's supposed to do with his life.

✳ ✳ ✳ ✳

Late flowers bloom in the nursing home's small front garden, catching the sleepy afternoon sunlight: tiger lilies, hosta, pink hydrangea. Maddie King pushes a button next to the gate door and opens it when a buzzing noise sounds. In the lobby, a few people sit bundled into the corners of the couches or propped in the stuffed chairs, faces upturned to the large television set on the wall as if the sounds of the man and woman talking to one another on the screen are the voices of God. A woman standing behind a desk smiles and waves her on. Maddie walks down the hall, stopping at the fifth door on the right. It is ajar, and she knocks hesitantly, and then pushes it open. "Hello?" she says, her voice a question. "Are you here?"

He is propped in the reclining wheelchair by the window, dressed and ready for her visit. Every Tuesday and Thursday she comes by after work, without fail for the past six years.

Alex turns his head and looks at her as she enters, but she does not know what he sees. She keeps her voice quiet; loud noises seem to bother him. "Hello, Alex. How are you today." His hair, graying strands mixed with the brown, is neatly combed and parted, and he has been shaved. His eyes move in her direction, and his mouth twitches, in what she thinks is a smile.

She gives him a hug, careful of his tracheostomy, and sits in a chair next to him. She takes one of his hands in her lap, unhooks the Velcro splint and takes it off. She massages his hands with her two hands, pulling and rubbing gently, talking to him all the while. "It's warm outside. Maybe we should go for a little walk in the garden." She puts the splint back on his hand and takes it off his other hand. "They're redoing the floors in Ricker Hall today. If I smell weird, that's why. The stuff they put on it stinks." Finished, she puts his hands back on the arms of his chair gently and looks at him. His eyes look in slightly different directions, one over her left shoulder, the other one at her face. "My handsome guy," she says. When she looks at him, she sees the face she used to see, angular and clever, animated, always joking. That face is fuller now and shiny, duller, but it's still him.

She pulls a library book from the cloth bag. She has tried all kinds of books; she read two Harry Potter books to him before she decided to try something different. She doesn't know if it is because she reads these new books differently, or because he understands more in them, but he seems more focused on her recent choices: books for young children. *The Velveteen Rabbit, Harold and the Purple Crayon, Green Eggs and Ham.* He keeps very still when Maddie reads these books, staring at the wall as if he is contemplating the metaphorical significance of Harold's boat. His hands seem to relax from their clenched position, and she takes that as a good sign. Sometimes his eyes fall on pages she holds open on her lap.

Maddie brings *Where the Wild Things Are* once every few weeks. It was Peter's favorite when he was small, and some of the pages still have his crayon scribbles. She likes to imagine that it's Alex's favorite also. Halfway through the book, she looks up to see Alex staring at the wall, his face calm and relaxed, his mouth slightly open. She waits to see if he will look at her, and when his eyes shift in her direction, she smiles. There is something of the child in his face just then, the wild child. She begins reading again. "But the wild things cried, 'Oh please don't go - we'll eat you up - we love you so!' And Max said, 'No!' The wild things roared their terrible roars and gnashed their terrible teeth and rolled their terrible eyes and showed their terrible claws, but Max stepped into his private boat and waved goodbye."

She looks up to see Alex's eyes, faded blue, staring at the wall as if into his own blue horizon.

Chapter Two

Kiya steps from the shower and, naked in the bathroom, towel-dries her hair furiously. It sticks up in pale yellow spikes like those of a child. She blinks at her reflection in the small misty bathroom mirror; her skin is pink and damp, and her eyelashes are stuck together with tears as well as water from the shower. She smiles, loving herself.

Her hand wanders toward the medicine cabinet, opens it and hovers absent-mindedly above the small bottles on the second shelf. She picks one up, turns it over and reads it in the morning light. She opens it and shakes out the small pink pill into her hand. *No,* she whispers, and puts it back. She touches her stomach lightly, trying to picture what is inside there, floating; she will protect it.

An hour later she runs up the stairs to Umojo, rated the best hair salon in Portland, Maine, for the past three years. Kiya has worked there for two of those years. She hangs her jacket in the closet in the high-ceilinged room. "Hello, dear," she sings out to Clyde, the colorist.

"Aren't we glowing this morning," he says, looking at her. Clyde is tall, skinny, and gay, though he has told her often that he has a crush on her. "What makes you so happy? Have you gotten rid of that new boyfriend?"

"No, I'm in love," she says. It is indubitably true, though who exactly she is in love with, Kiya can't say for sure. "I'm in love with Peter, and with you too. And with that sunshine." It is true, she is in love with the way the sun pours through the tall windows. Late summer, the time of warmth and peace in Maine. "And my life."

"Be careful, dear," Clyde says, looking at her knowingly before turning away. "It's dangerous to be happy. It just leads to unhappiness. You know that."

It is silly that his words make her feel instantly dampened, quieted. He is joking, but he is also saying the truth. In Kiya's case, his words are more truthful than he knows. Her feelings can switch in a moment, and they often do; the sun goes down as quickly as it rises. With an effort, she throws her shoulders back and runs her fingers through her hair. "Tell me something," she says decisively to Clyde. "I have to know." When he turns to look at her, alert, Kiya asks, "Do you think I wear too much eyeliner?"

With her first client, Kiya is unfocused, dreamy and silent. The woman looks not exactly dissatisfied, but not happy, when Kiya gives her the hand mirror and swivels the chair so she can see. She has graying hair and hoped to be made beautiful, but she is disappointed. "Fine," the woman says. "This will do."

This will *not* do, so Kiya goes to work. She erects a barrier, a wall surrounding the part of herself which is secret. She has had experience erecting similar barriers; she is knowledgeable in the field of interior construction. She channels the sunlight for inspiration and makes herself shine. Her next client, a taciturn mid-thirties businessman who seems embarrassed to be seen caring enough about his hair to come to an expensive salon, sits stiffly in his chair, blinking. She moves around him in the hair-cutting dance, combing, lifting, and massaging mousse onto his head. He smiles finally, and closes his eyes when her fingers brush small bits of cut hair from his forehead. He glances at himself in the wall mirror when he leaves, and gives her a nice tip.

At her lunch break, Kiya goes to the coffee shop next door, where she orders a bagel and green tea. Sitting alone at a table by the window she checks her cell phone for messages. The only one is from her mother, who doesn't seem to remember that Kiya holds a job and works during the day. She always sounds surprised that Kiya doesn't pick up. "Hope everything is okay," she says on the message, her voice trailing off, worried. Kiya sighs and drops her head, steeling herself to return the call. She loves her mother and she understands why she acts the way she does, but still, it takes all her strength to tap call. When her mother answers, her voice confused and worried, Kiya channels the sunshine again, this time into her voice. "Hello, Mom! I'm fine; I was at work. How are you?"

She is rewarded by hearing the lift of relief in her mother's voice, by hearing her give the little laugh that lets Kiya know that her mother knows that she's been silly. "I was just worried, you know . . . "

"Yes, Mom. I know." A truck rumbles by outside the window and Kiya pauses to let the sound fade away. "I'm having a good day, a really good day. How about you?"

After talking with her mother, Kiya finishes the bagel and is still hungry. She considers biscotti but buys an apple instead, a shiny red perfection. She ponders its gleaming surface, wondering what invisible germs it hides; to be safe, she dips the tip of her paper napkin in the cup of water and rubs it over the apple, wiping it clean. She will be careful of what she puts in her mouth, in her body; her body is a house, a temporary residence. A railway station, as it were.

After lunch, she usually smokes a cigarette on the street as she walks back to the salon. Today she pulls the pack out, looks at it, and shoves it back into her bag. She won't throw them away, not just yet, but she won't give in to the urge. The thought of smoking one makes her feel queasy, anyway. The sky above the city is sunny, with a few small floating cumulus clouds. She passes the small group of homeless people that hang out in the corner of the square in front of the mural. A middle-aged white man wearing a dirty jacket with a Patriots logo catches her eye. "Hey miss Ki-yelle!" he shouts. "How you doin' this fine day?"

She gives him a thumbs up, and shouts "Good! How about you?"

The man turns in a slow circle, arms lifted, looking up at the blue sky. "How could I not be happy?" he shouts. "This sky—and you!" She laughs. The man hunches over to take a drag from the cigarette he holds in one hand, squinting against the smoke.

Peter would be happy if Kiya quit smoking. He's wanted her to. Her steps slow, as she tries to imagine what Peter will say when she tells him. They began dating only two and a half months ago. He'd just broken up with his girlfriend—well, to tell the truth, he was in the middle of breaking up with his girlfriend when they started hanging out. She tries to think of what he will say, and then suddenly doesn't want to think about it anymore. Which is just as well, because she is back at the salon. There is certainly no rush about things, she muses as she climbs the stairs. She takes a deep breath, feeling the muscles in her legs, feeling the slight heaviness in her abdomen—a fullness, like period weight. No rush at all.

✵ ✵ ✵ ✵

Peter climbs into the bucket and puts on his ear protectors. He prefers climbing trees to going up in the bucket, but it's not his decision. And there is the thrill of being lifted, of rising into the sky, into the high branches. The first lift of the day is exhilarating, like rising in the Ferris wheel. Peter starts the saw, hearing it roar through the ear protectors. He steadies its shake and lifts it, feeling the power in his arms, fighting to control the quivering machine they hold. It chews through one branch, then another. This is the type of work he likes: trimming branches on a sunny day, making trees stronger, rather than cutting down healthy trees. He thinks of his mother at her cabin by the lake in the western foothills: he wants to cut down that white pine there, afraid it will come crashing down on some cold winter night. He thinks of Kiya, who he will probably see tonight. There is something about her that he likes; something he can't quite figure out. It has to do with her pale skin, and the way she can be so serious at times, and the way her smile breaks through so unselfconsciously and warms up everything around her. It makes him feel good to be near her at those times.

Yet she makes him uneasy. He's in his mid-twenties, he should have figured women out by now, but he doesn't know if he should trust her. That charm of hers is flickering, up and down; it could start a fire, or it could go out completely, and he isn't sure what would happen then.

A sudden shout from Gary below and he realizes he's gone too far, cut too much on that last branch. He pulls away, moves lower, begins again, using the saw more carefully now. He has his own issues, he knows, his own things he doesn't talk to her about. He cuts carefully, moving from spot to spot, in a rhythm that reminds him of music. He hears something in the back of his head, a tune corresponding to his rhythm as he cuts and to the sound the saw makes, muffled through the ear protectors. He wonders if he could make a recording of tree-work sounds and splice them into a song. It would be muted, to not overshadow the guitar, banjo, and violin he imagines.

Peter stops, pushing his helmet and glasses back. He takes a break, looking up at the sky, at the blue that reaches inside his head. It is a perfect color; it soothes him, making him feel for that moment as if everything will be all right.

* * * *

Maddie kisses the thin gray hair on top of Alex's head before she leaves. It's her usual gesture, done so often these years he's been in his wheelchair or in his bed that it has nearly erased the memory of the kisses they shared before. Alex was in his late 50's when he suddenly became ill. They had been a couple for several years; Maddie had been contemplating selling her cabin on the shore of Parker Pond and moving into his big house in town. He was not feeling well one evening, and when she came by to check up on him the next morning he was feverish and groggy, with a severe headache. She drove him to the hospital and held his hand as he walked into the emergency room. Maddie was on her way to work, so she didn't stay. She kissed him goodbye and left him in the waiting room. How she wishes she had stayed. That was the last time he walked, the last time she heard him talk. He became un-conscious in the waiting room and didn't open his eyes for two months.

After the diagnosis of acute encephalitis, after it became ap-parent that his condition would not improve, Maddie told herself she was glad to stay in her own house. The lake house was small and needed a new roof, but she could wake up every morning to the sun coming over the lake, the sun glancing off the water. It had been her maternal grandparents' house, which her parents had taken her to when she was a child. Later, her son Peter grew up in this house. She remembers her mother sitting in that rocker, smil-ing at her. She can almost see her grandmother and grandfather at the sink, one washing, one drying. The shouts young Peter made, playing in the water, still hang in the air if she listens. She can come home from work at the college, or from the nursing home, take a glass of wine and a book and sit on the dock for as long as she wants, looking at the blueness of the water. No one is on the lake today, no one in the cabin next door. The still blue water reflects the light; the air holds the smell of sun-warmed pine. It is perfectly silent, and she is still for one illuminated empty moment.

The book she is reading is about the psychoanalyst Wilhelm Reich, who moved from Germany to Rangeley, Maine, not far from this lake. Maddie's mother was a fan of Reich's theories and a friend of the man himself. When Maddie was young, she lived in Illinois with her mother and father. Years before Maddie was born, before her mother even met Maddie's father, she had cancer. Her mother traveled to Maine to be treated by Reich in his laboratory, staying in this house, and she believed that Reich cured her. The cancer went away then, before it came back twenty years later and killed her. After her father's death, with both her parents and her grandparents gone, Maddie moved with her young son to Maine and back into this house.

Reich believed human beings were united with the universe through orgone energy, or sexual creative energy. Maddie opens the book and reads: "If we are open to orgone, especially as it relates to sexuality, we are in contact with the energy of the earth. To be cut off or separated from orgone energy is an illness which denies that which would heal."

The sunlight is less bright than it was a few moments ago, and a breeze kicks up bits of white froth on the tops of waves. The water's surface doesn't seem peaceful now but is moving with a restless, uneasy energy. She puts the book down and stands, rubbing her arms. She is in her fifties, is tormented at night by hot flashes, and she doesn't feel particularly in contact with the sexual energy of the earth. That is for others, for her son, working on trees and breaking up with one girlfriend after another. It was for her once, that feeling of oneness with another person, with the earth, with herself, resting post-orgasm in his arms. Doesn't there come a time, she wonders, when sex doesn't matter so much, isn't important—or at least not the most important thing? Can't one be open to orgone energy in other ways? She wants to argue with the author of the book, and with Wilhelm Reich, and maybe with her own mother, dead too soon to have gone through this passage herself.

She hears the spit of car tires on the gravel lane past her camp, turning in next door. She hears doors opening and closing, and after a moment, the sput-sput roar of an electric lawn mower starting. Maddie lets her breath out in an exasperated sigh. The man owns a quarter acre of green out in the wilderness, miles from a town, at the end of a lane where no one will ever drive past, and he has to use an electric lawnmower. She picks up her book and her glass and stomps up the wooden steps, slamming the door behind her in a satisfying way.

* * * *

Evelyn, 1955

Evie unrolls her sleeping bag in campgrounds in Ohio and in upper New York state on her way from Champaign-Urbana. Following her parents' advice, she has chosen campgrounds in advance and paid a fee so that her mother and father will know she is not alone in the country, that there are people around watching out for her. The first night she slept in her pup tent but her second night, under a cloudless sky. She unrolls a pad, to offer some protection against the hard ground. It is a small thrill for Evie to lie in her bag with her face open to the night sky, watching the stars wheel through the trees above her. She can see the lights and hear the sounds of people camping next to her. When they finally turn off their lantern, the darkness is deep around her. A light, fitful wind rustles the leaves of trees. The air smells of earth and growing things, and faintly of something roasted—hot dogs? She hears small rustlings in the underbrush, and then, surprisingly near and so loud it makes her jump: the hooting of an owl. "Hoo, hoo, to-hoo, Hoo, hoo, to-HOO-ooo," a barred owl. She remembers her father whispering at their back window as they listened, telling her it was saying, "Who cooks for you? Who cooks for you-all?" She hears murmurs from the site next to hers, sounds of children giggling; they have heard it too. She waits, and then hears the reply from farther away; "Hoo too, to-hoo."

After the owls quiet down, probably connecting and doing whatever it is they do, it is a long time before Evie can sleep. The incision on her back, and the longer one in her armpit, hurt where the stitches were removed. The ache is lessening every day, but the worry and anxiety are still there. She is aware of the remaining lymph nodes in her left armpit, and the ones in her neck, and wonders if she feels anything there, if small cells have escaped from the melanoma and lymph node before they were cut out of her and have raced their way to nearby nodes where they are happily, energetically proliferating.

The sun will wake her early, and she worries about being tired while driving; she has nearly 400 miles to travel the next day. She convinces herself that it will be all right if she spends another night on the road—no one is waiting for her, after all—and pulls her extra pillow over her head. She arranges her left arm carefully to the side.

She soon forgets about the pillow, about the stars above her and the owls, whooshing through the night; Evie forgets about her incisions, about skin cancer and the possibility of an early death. She is in her parents' camp, she has made it, but someone is there already; it is Eric, the guy she used to date in college. She is both happy and not happy to see him, and then they are in the canoe on the lake, and in the uneasy rocking of the waves, Evie is asleep.

Chapter Three

After work Kiya drives to her mother's house. Regular visits reassure her mother. She finds a parking spot in front of the house on the narrow street that slopes down to the bay. Since the divorce, her mother has rented an apartment on the ground floor of what used to be a sea captain's house. Kiya wonders if the landlord doesn't say it's a sea captain's house just to explain why the rent is so high. The crumbling ornate woodwork, the iron doorbell that turns and the widow's peak on the roof at least hearken back to an earlier time. She slips inside the entryway and knocks on her mother's door at the bottom of the stairway. She hears her voice; "Who's there?"

"It's me." When she receives no answer, she adds, "Kiya."

"Oh!" her mother says, opening the door. She looks surprised, pleased.

Kiya leans in to give her a hug. "You look so pretty," she says. In the slanting light coming through the tall western windows, her mother does look beautiful in her blue sweater, her graying blonde hair pulled back into a thick ponytail. Her eyes, surrounded by fine lines, soften as they look at her daughter.

"You do too," her mother says. "You always do look beautiful." Her expression grows serious as she touches her daughter's face.

Kiya pulls away, smiling. "I know. Except for the eye makeup."

"I just think you'd be SO much prettier . . ." Her mother's voice trails behind her as she walks into the kitchen. She runs water into the teapot and opens a cupboard, bringing down a tin box. "What kind of tea do you want today?"

"Earl Grey, I think." They sit at the kitchen table, following the choreography of their routine. Kiya and her mother will each have one cup of tea, sitting at the table in front of the kitchen window overlooking the small, cluttered backyard. Kiya will rest an elbow on the flowered tablecloth and lean her cheek into her closed fist; her mother will sit across from her, hands cupped around the tea, blowing into it. Kiya will begin by talking about her job, about how the day went—in the telling it will always be a good day, with particular attention paid to moments when she thought something was going wrong, and then surprisingly, miraculously even, it turned out to be okay, or better than just okay, wonderful—and they will laugh, and marvel, and then there will be a silence. Her mother's face will grow serious and she will make a sound, a little humming noise, and say something like "I still can't believe it. I just can't believe he's gone." Kiya will make a little noise in her throat signifying agreement, and they will fall silent again. She is referring to Kiya's brother Andrew, who took his own life nearly three years ago. They don't have a conversation in which he isn't mentioned, or referred to.

At one point a year ago Kiya thought enough was enough; she was ready to move on, to talk about something else, or at least to stop talking about Drew all the time. She brought it up to her psychiatrist, and they agreed that if her mother wanted to continue talking about her son's death, Kiya shouldn't stop her. So now she listens, and doesn't say much, until her mother is able to let it go. Perhaps her mother thinks Kiya needs to talk about it, because towards the end of the conversations she will take Kiya's hand, saying something like "You poor girl."

"It's all right," Kiya will murmur. "I'm doing fine." Her mother always seems relieved after they have "the conversation," and is able to smile and laugh with Kiya. By then the sun is down behind the buildings, and Kiya can stand up, stretch, give her mother a hug, and tell her she will stop by again in a day or two.

As Kiya leaves the building she remembers, with a sense akin to guilt, she has something special going on. It is her secret, like the first times as a teenager she smoked dope and would come home still high. Only this secret will bring her mother happiness, will make her smile, she is sure. Thinking about it makes her feel both warm and weighty, light and heavy at the same time. Light with a giddy excitement, heavy with the significance of what is happening. Another life, curled inside this one.

* * * *

Peter hears the thumping of bass over the noise of the shower

14

and knows that his roommate is home. When he comes out, a towel wrapped around his waist, both his roommate Ryan and their friend Matthew are sitting on the couch. Matthew is picking at his guitar along with the music from the computer, one long curl hanging in front of his face. "Hey," Peter says.

"Hey!" Matthew's head jerks up. "Peter! Are we gonna play some music, or are we not!" Matthew has been saying for months that they should get together and work up some tunes.

"Yeah, sure man," Peter says, wiping his head with a second towel. "Not tonight, though. I have plans."

"You always have plans, man. I'm starting to think you don't like me. Or you don't think I'm good enough as a musician. If that's the case you can just tell me, man. I can handle it."

"Nah, that's not it." Peter shakes his head. "You're a great musician." Matthew *is* good; he plays with several groups in town. If anything, Peter doesn't think he is up to Matthew's skills, but he doesn't want to say that. He knows he should have self-respect, which means letting Matthew figure it out for himself. "Maybe tomorrow," he says.

There is something different about Kiya tonight, but Peter can't put his finger on it. When he came by her apartment to pick her up, he thought at first she was high, the way she giggled then became so serious, then giggled again. By the time they get to the restaurant, he decides that she isn't high, she is Kiya; that is the way she is.

It's a place they haven't been to before, and they spend a long time over the menu. Kiya orders a glass of wine, but barely sips it. "What's the matter with the wine?" Peter asks.

"Nothing," she says. "I'm just not in the mood." She picks up the last piece of bread and dips it in the oil.

Peter looks in the basket, then looks at her. "You ate it *all?*" She sheepishly hands the piece to him.

When Kiya's food is gone and Peter is eating the last of his, Kiya leans forward, crossing her arms in front of her. Peter can't help but look at the smooth roundness of her breasts, pushing out of the scoop neck of her knit top. "So your mother lives on a lake up north."

Peter nods, wondering where this is going. "Well, north of here, yeah. In the foothills."

"Do you visit her very often?"

He shrugs. "I see her every few weeks. I've been meaning to visit. I haven't been up there for a while." He has the uneasy feeling that he shouldn't have said that.

"I'd love to go with you sometime." Her eyes are shining, and he does not know how to say no.

"You asked her to go visit your mother with you? Whoah."

"What do you mean, whoah?"

"I mean, serious step, man."

Peter leans back on the couch, inhaling the joint Ryan passes to him. "I know, right? I didn't ask her. I just didn't say no."

Ryan holds the smoke in, then lets it out as he speaks. "Kiya's a nice lady, and she's hot, don't get me wrong."

"You think she's hot?" Peter looks at Ryan, one eyebrow raised.

"Yeah, sure, she's hot. Hot enough. I'm not going after her or anything. Because she'd go for me, you know?" He flexes a bicep, watching a tattooed rose rise as the muscle rounds. "She would totally go for me. What I mean is I like her, but I don't know if you want to get that serious about her. Kinda quick."

"Right." Peter stands up and stretches in the dusky living room, lit by the light of the TV with its sound muted and the watery glow of Ryan's aquarium. The fish all died long ago but he keeps it full of water and the light on because he likes the way it looks. "I'll keep that in mind. Just one afternoon visit to mom, that's all we'll have."

       ✳ ✳ ✳ ✳

On the way into work, Maddie buys a quart of blueberries.

She works in the Sciences Department. Whenever anyone calls her "receptionist" she corrects them to "Administrative Assistant," saying reception is only a small part of her work, but she truly doesn't care. She's been there longer than any other staff in the department and longer than most of the faculty, and she doesn't care about a title anymore.

She washes the blueberries and puts them out in a bowl on her desk. Jeff, a biologist, sticks his head in, exclaims over the berries. "Nature's goodness," he says, popping one in his mouth.

"They're magic," Maddie says.

"They're nature," Jeff says. "Not magic."

"Nature is magic," Maddie says.

The Department chair, Ron Grey, wanders from his office into Maddie's, hands in the pockets of his baggy pants. His curly gray hair frames his face in a type of halo, and he wears a look of perpetual astonishment. "What's this about magic?"

"Maddie says blueberries are magic," Jeff says.

"Maddie is the magic one," Ron says. "We all know that."

Maddie can't help it, she blushes; 54 years old and she blushes when Ron says something nice to her. She swivels her chair around, facing her computer, hoping they won't notice her pink cheeks. She assumes a scolding tone; "I don't have time for your foolishness. Take it on out of here."

Ron reaches into the dish and scoops up a few berries. He drops them into his mouth, one at a time, then says "Oh all right, Wilhelmina. Madeline Wilhelmina."

"No!" Jeff says. "Really? Is that your name, Maddie?" His smile is wide.

"Yes. But I never want to hear you say it."

"It means 'Willing to protect'," Ron says. "That's Maddie."

"Out of here," Maddie says. She makes a shooing motion with her hands, but smiles over her shoulder. Jeff is chuckling, and Maddie is rewarded with a warm look from Ron before he goes back to his office.

She knows nothing can happen between her and Ron; nothing can or will happen, but still, when she dresses in the morning she wonders if he will like the way she looks; she powders her nose

17

and puts lipstick on before she comes in on the days she knows he will be there. Ron has been divorced for several years from his second wife. In the evening as Maddie cooks her dinner, stir-frying vegetables on the range, she goes over the things they spoke about, looking for hidden meanings in the things he said to her that day. She reviews the things she said to Ron, searching for anything that made her sound stupid or naïve, or as if she has a crush on him. She admires him, that's all; he is honest and intelligent and funny. So what if he has a wicked cute smile, she thinks as she dumps the veggies into a bowl. She has no desire to get together with Ron, or with anyone. Her first true love is dead in a car crash, her second true love is staring at the wall in the nursing home, and she is done with all that.

After dinner, she reads the book about Reich. She wonders whether orgone energy is flowing around her, wonders if that's what the faint light coming off the lake is; she wonders if it's still inside her, connecting her deepest urges to the earth, the sky. She is wondering, again, why her mother insisted on giving her Wilhelmina for a middle name, and why her father went along with it, when her phone dings with a text. She picks it up from the table in the corner next to the window, the only place in the house with good reception. It's Peter. "Thinking of coming up this weekend, with a friend."

✵ ✵ ✵ ✵

The next day Evie packs up early, in spite of her late night, and is on the road by 8:00. She stops for lunch at a drive-in restaurant in a small town in Vermont, eating a cheeseburger at a picnic table next to the road. She wipes her face with the paper napkin and orders a second cup of coffee with cream and sugar, drinking it from the white stained mug while she watches cars drive slowly by. A man wearing a battered hat driving a noisy pickup looks at her car, her parents' old blue Dodge with the dent in the fender, and at her, a stranger in this town. She will make it to the cabin by dinnertime.

There is still light when Evie drives down the bumpy lane. The radio fuzzed out in static when she reached Vermont, and she drives in silence, windows partly cranked down. The air is cool, with that Maine freshness she remembers. The first sight of the lake flashing through the trees always fills her with happiness, reminding her of the excitement she felt as a child when they finally made it. "We're here, we're here," she'd shout, bouncing up and down on the bench seat in the back. Her father taught high school in Illinois, and they spent most of every summer at this camp that her mother's parents had bought decades ago. They are to join her here in July, a month from now. Until then she has the place to herself, with certain tasks to complete: cleaning the interior, painting the clapboard exterior, and—though her parents didn't say this—pulling herself together.

Evie sits still for a moment, hands resting on the wheel, gazing at the cottage. The grass is high and weedy, with mossy spots, but it looks as if the house has weathered the winter well: the clapboard exterior and roof look solid. She can see blue water on the far side of the house.

The camp interior is cool and shady, as always. Evie hauls her suitcase into the main bedroom. She flips the electric switch in the back room to turn the electricity back on, but before doing anything else, she unlocks the back door and steps outside. She steps carefully on the rocks at the water's edge and looks out across the lake. The shadows of trees behind her stretch long into the lake, but there is still sunlight in the middle and on the far shore. The air feels charged to Evie, full of energy unlike the quiet, humid air of the Midwest. Urbana, Illinois is a quiet town, heavy with trees, and with straight even streets, which always turn at a ninety-degree angle; it makes her feel sleepy even to think of it. The air in Maine, and the water, make her feel alive.

She sits on a smooth rock on the shore and pulls out a package of Marlboro cigarettes. She bought it at a gas station in Vermont; her parents don't know she smokes, so she will have to finish it before they arrive. She'd started last year at the university, her senior year. Eric would light up and offer her one. After they broke up, she kept on smoking; it helped her relax, and she needed that. It had been a horrible year, really; first the itching on her back and the discovery that she had a melanoma, followed by the surgery, the discovery that it had spread to a lymph node; then Eric breaking up with her; then, Grandpapa's sudden death. She still

19

cannot think of the last year without the threat of tears behind her eyes. She hates to cry. To ward off tears she squints, shakes her head, and laughs at herself. She lights another cigarette, trying to ignore the faint trembling of her fingers.

Chapter Four

Riding beside Peter in his old with the top down, Kiya gives herself over to joy. The sky is so blue that the few clouds only make it look bluer. They are on the way to a lake, which would make anyone happy, and she is young and beautiful, and she has a joyous secret. It has been a week since she learned she was pregnant, and a week since she's taken her meds, and she feels absolutely fine. She's taken antidepressants since Andrew died. She's grown to be dependent on medication, she thinks, but she feels much better not taking it. They aren't really her, they don't allow her full personality to be alive. What she really needed was this pregnancy, the knowledge that she was carrying new, precious life.

She steals glances at Peter's profile while he drives, and it occurs to Kiya that she truly loves this man. He has kind eyes, that was one of the first things she noticed about him; kind eyes, and a sweet smile. He is tall and his shoulders fill out his shirt nicely, his clean dark blonde hair hanging over the collar of his shirt. He catches her looking at him, and gives her a quick smile. She smiles back. Who would not love him? She looks out the windshield, humming along with the radio under her breath.

After nearly two hours of driving, they are on the single-lane camp road twisting through overhanging trees. Kiya catches glimpses of water glimmering through the trees. Peter pulls up in front of a small cape with weathered gray shingles. Kiya gets out and stretches, just as the door to the cabin opens. A woman stands in the shadow of a small porch, looking. Conscious of being observed, Kiya steps forward. "Hi, I'm Kiya." She holds out her hand with a big smile, something she never did before she worked at Umojo. "Professional, hip, and warm," Clyde used to say. "That's our brand."

The woman is nervous, Kiya realizes. "I'm Maddie. Nice to meet you." They shake briefly, Kiya aware of the woman's palm that holds hers in a way that seems questioning, assessing. Kiya sees an expanse of water behind Maddie, a splendor of blue with white sparkles. They pass through the kitchen into a small, comfortable living room, with wide windows looking over the water.

Maddie shows them the guest bedroom, across a narrow hallway from hers. A neat double bed covered by a quilt, "A Starry Night" in a frame on the wall.

"This used to be Peter's room," she says. "It had posters on the wall then. Beatles, Johnny Cash. Who was that other one?"

"White Stripes. And Johnny Cash was giving the finger." Peter puts his backpack on the floor. "What do you mean, it's still my room." He gives his mother a smile, and she holds out her arms.

"C'mon, you, give me a hug," she says. He hugs her in the way grown sons hug mothers—arms around their shoulders, bodies arched away so they don't touch. Their bare arms look alike, Maddie's muscles an older female version of Peter's.

Peter has told her that he has no siblings, and that he has never seen his father. Now that she is standing in front of the grandmother of her baby-to-be, Kiya wishes she'd asked more. Were his parents married, for example? Were they together long? If she knew more, she might be able to ask questions that made sense. Genetics, she thinks, and rubs her abdomen gently. Maddie glances at her gesture and then looks away.

They take iced tea on to the deck overlooking the lake. "Oh my god," Kiya says, her voice hushed. "This is so beautiful." The lake spreads in front of them, only one other house visible behind a screen of trees.

"We have kayaks if you want to take a ride," Maddie says, pointing to the fiberglass boat upside down next to the lake. "There are two others in the shed. The water's too cold to swim, but it's great for a ride."

"Later. Right now I just want to get to know your mother." Kiya smiles, but then wonders if she's gone too far; Maddie seems to shrink away slightly, pulling into herself, deeper into the Adirondack chair.

"So how did you two meet?" Maddie asks.

Kiya starts to say, "At a club," then stops herself; "A friend introduced us." That sounds better. It was just three months ago, but she wants to tell Peter's mother that it seems like much, much longer than that; it seems as if she has known Peter for a long time. Sometimes it seems as if she's known him from other lifetimes.

But she can't say that to this pleasant-faced, reserved woman. Instead, she says, "Peter says you and he moved here when he was little."

"Yes, we lived in Illinois, where I grew up. This was my grandparents' camp. We came here almost every summer." She looks up at the trees above her head. "It always held so many memories for me."

Peter sits with long legs sprawled out in front of him, drinking beer from a can. "I don't remember much about Illinois," he said. "I was just four when we moved. Maine is what I remember, playing here in the water. There was a boy who lived over there." He points with the beer can. "He would come over here and we'd catch frogs. We'd follow turtles in the water; try to catch them. We'd go under when loons went under, trying to see where they went. Never managed to do that."

"It sounds like a wonderful childhood," Kiya says. She sips her iced tea, looks out at the lake. A wind ruffles the surface. She thinks of turtles, of loons, of dark things looming underwater, coming close to the surface, mouths open.

Maddie asks about Kiya's childhood. "I grew up in Massachusetts," Kiya says. "My parents moved up to the Portland area when I was in high school. My dad got transferred." Kiya shifts on the deck chair, and feels tension building somewhere inside her body. She sees shadowy rooms, feels something looming, ready to jump out of the darkness. "My parents divorced a few years ago," she says.

"That's too bad," Maddie says.

"No, it's okay," Kiya says. "Really, it's the best thing. Everyone's happier." She smiles, channeling sunlight.

"Do you have any siblings?"

"I did," Kiya says smoothly. She turns to the side, facing the lake, away from sudden frightening things in the darkness, away from Peter's quick look. "Maybe a kayak ride is a good idea."

"I've never done this before." Kiya stands on the dock, holding the paddle before her. She looks doubtfully down at the blue kayak. "I've taken canoe rides, but never a kayak."

"It's easy; you just settle your butt in it, like this." Peter eases himself into the kayak, legs stretched out in front of him. "See? Nothing fancy, it won't tip over or anything." He grins up at her from behind his dark glasses.

"Okay," Kiya says. "Here goes." She steps into the water, holding onto the sides of the kayak. "Cold!" The boat rocks from side to side as she gets in, but soon stabilizes. She pushes the paddle through the water and the kayak moves agreeably, almost as if she knows what she is doing. She floats under a branch of a tree hanging over the edge of the lake and looks up to see white light flickering, shifting on the bottom of the leaves. The sunlight reflecting off the lake makes patterns that look like smoke, or steam, on the bottom of the leaves.

They paddle toward the center of the lake, oars dipping and rising. Kiya looks back to see Maddie standing on the dock watching them. "I like your mother," Kiya says.

"Good," Peter says. He lowers his voice. "Be careful, though; sounds carry over this water like you wouldn't believe."

Peter leads the way toward an island covered in pointed firs. The lake is large and quiet, with only two other kayaks visible in the distance, heading for a different island. The house grows smaller in the distance until it is barely visible. Kiya focuses on the brightness of the sky above her, on the glimmer of the lake, trying not to think of the darkness she sensed lurking in the depths.

On the other side of the island, they step out of the kayaks onto a shore with a small sandy beach beyond some rocks jutting out of the water and pull the kayaks up onto the rocks. Stepping carefully, Kiya finds a flat rock to sit on. Peter stands beside her in knee-deep water. He pulls his tee shirt off. "I'm going to take a swim," he says.

"Won't you freeze?"

"Nah, I'll be quick. It will wake me up." He leans down into the water, pushing away and letting it lift him until he is swimming away from shore. She sees his white back, shimmering under the water. He returns and dries himself with his tee shirt, sitting on the rock next to her. He shivers and lifts his face to the sun. She puts an arm around him, hugging to warm him up. She says,

"What a fantastic place to grow up."

"Yeah, it was fun," he says. "Kind of lonely at times, though." He shakes water from an ear, looking at her sideways. "Did you have siblings? I thought you said you were an only child."

Kiya imagines she sees a large and glistening mass rising from the water, water sluicing off smooth skin the color of stone. The water remains level and smooth, ripples crisscrossing on its surface. She takes a breath and says, "I told you I *am* an only child. I used to have a brother."

She tells the story; how the move away from his high school friends upset her younger brother, who wasn't too emotionally steady to begin with; how his parents' divorce made things worse. How he started using drugs and cutting himself, not acting like himself. How he took his own life by hanging himself in his parents' house, the house his father had just moved out of and his mother had put on the market, on a summer afternoon. She tells Peter everything except how she had come to the house that day without letting anyone know she was coming; how she knocked but no one answered, how she walked in, surprised to find the door unlocked if no one was home. How she wandered into the kitchen and started to make herself a peanut butter and cucumber sandwich when she suddenly stopped. She remembers slicing through the cucumber. The green skin was starting to wrinkle, but its flesh inside was green and innocent. She didn't know what made her stop, didn't know if it was something she heard or something she sensed, but she suddenly lifted her head and felt something clench inside her.

How she put the knife down carefully on the countertop next to her half-made sandwich, how she walked slowly up the stairs calling "Drew?" yet how she knew he wouldn't answer. How she pushed open the bedroom door and saw nothing, how she almost knew what she would see when she pushed open the bathroom door yet how she could never, ever have imagined it—how could one imagine how such a thing could look? His head hanging from the light fixture at such a strange angle, his body turning slowly, hanging so limply, so unlike him, rotating until she saw his face . .
.

25

"My mother found him," Kiya tells Peter now.

"That's why you visit her so often," Peter says softly.

Kiya nods. "That's why." She takes Peter's hand in hers, running her fingers along it, feeling the skin slide over the narrow bones. "She needs me."

* * * *

Peter's roommate Ryan has a book on the shelf in their living room called *The Days Run Away Like Wild Horses Over the Hills*. It's a book of poems, but Peter remembers only the title. He thinks of it in the morning when he wakes, when he pulls the shade by his bed up, letting the light come in. Another day, just like the last one except he is a day older. Sometimes then he feels a sense of urgency, as if there are things he must do in order to capture his life, things he is not doing. He doesn't know what they would be. He gets up, splashes water on his face, eats his morning eggs and drives to work. There the familiar morning greetings, the cool air on his face, the sound of machinery lulls him into forgetting, cover over his sense of urgency with the calm of everyday activity.

He studied philosophy in college because he wanted to learn the secrets of existence. He had a teacher in high school, Mr. Raleigh, who made him feel that the world was a giant puzzle which could be figured out if he would just read the right books, ask the right questions. He did learn some things in college—he learned how to think better, how to work hard. How to drink, how to smoke dope, and how to not take himself so seriously. How to talk to girls, how to make them laugh. And there were times, reading Heidegger or Kant, that he felt as if he were uncovering central truths, ones which would build on others, ones he could never forget. But now, three years out, college seems like a dream, and whatever he learned is only enough to keep him at work, trimming trees.

Or maybe it's his current life that is a dream, up in the trees, the intermittent roar of the chainsaw, then the rustle of leaves, trying to tell him something. Sometimes the spatter of rain on his face, sometimes the sun through leaves. Then it's evening, and he maybe goes out to eat or meets some friends or Kiya, or stays home playing music or watching a movie and drinking beer, then he sleeps and dreams things he can't remember and then it's morning again, and he doesn't know where the days are going in their long, rippling movement over the hills.

✼ ✼ ✼ ✼

A knock at the door startles Maddie. She didn't hear footsteps. It is her neighbor, the man who bought the house next to hers last spring. The lawnmower. She doesn't remember his name. He is somewhat older than her, a solidly-built man with a Downeast accent and shaggy graying hair. "Hello theah," he says through the screen door. She is sure he exaggerates his accent for effect, for humor or drama. He is a frustrated actor, she thinks, his best role that of a canny old Maine hick. Tom, is that his name? Or Glenn? One syllable, she is sure.

"Hello," she says, dashing a hand through her hair. But it is too late for that; it is Saturday, and she is wearing cut-off sweatpants with paint stains and a baggy tee shirt. She pushes open the door but does not ask him in. "What can I do for you?" she asks, and regrets it; too business-like, something she'd say at work.

"Well, I was wondering if you wanted some help sometime getting this dock in." Standing on her top step, he gestures toward the wooden dock attached to the shore, floating on plastic hollow drums. He has thick graying eyebrows above black glass frames, which are too contemporary for the rest of him. *Actor,* she thinks. "You bring it in before it snows, right?"

Something about his attitude strikes her as impertinent, mocking; she reminds herself it's just the Maine way, the edge of humorous sarcasm that lines his words. Of course she brings the dock in before it snows. And it *is* difficult, nearly impossible, to do by herself, but she doesn't know if she wants to struggle with it with this man—Bill? —helping her.

"Thank you," she says. "But my son helps me."

"All right then." He stands there, glancing out over the water, then back at her. She knows she is supposed to say something; she has lived in central Maine long enough to learn the speech patterns, to know that neighbors are important, and she needs to make friends with this one, but nothing rises to her lips. She is stunned, silent, as she stares at the man. "Well, if you need help," he says, backing away, "just let me know."

"I'll do that," she says, and then, "I appreciate the offer."

He nods, a half-smile crossing his face, and turns away. She watches him pick his way past the picnic table, over her tall un-mown grass, stepping around trees and bushes onto his lawn. Something about him, his baggy jeans and slightly shambling gait, seems familiar. She tries to think what that half-smile reminds her of, something from her past, but gives up. She is about to turn away when she hears a voice coming from inside his house: a high voice, like that of a child. She hears the low rumble of the man's voice answering as he enters the screened-in porch, the door slap-ping shut.

✻ ✻ ✻ ✻

Evie has got the water running at the camp, swept the interior of dead insects and mouse droppings, and put bedding on the beds. On cool days she starts a fire in the woodstove in the morn-ing to take the chill off, letting it die out by afternoon. She drives to Mt. Vernon for paint, using the money her parents sent with her, and drags the ladder, brushes, and rags from the shed. After several rainy days, she wakes and the air is warmer, the sun bright. After breakfast, she ties her hair back with a bandanna and climbs the ladder slowly, carefully. She is glad the camp is just one story tall. "Only one story to tell," she murmurs to herself, as she begins to scrape off the cracked paint.

By mid-afternoon, she is tired of scraping, tired of the sun on her head, tired of waving off the black flies. She puts on her bathing suit and gets into the water. It's still cool but feels good. The top layer of water is warmer than the cold, dark layers below. She treads water and thinks about the depths below, and about Wilhelm Reich.

Evie had studied psychology in college, and came across the name of Wilhelm Reich in an article. Something in the glancing, disparaging comments about the psychoanalyst intrigued her, es-pecially the fact that he had worked with Freud but currently lived in Rangeley, Maine, not far from their camp. The more she read

28

about him, the more she was interested. It wasn't his weather experiments that intrigued her—although a newspaper article from a couple of years ago claimed that he made rain fall to save blueberry crops in Maine from a drought—but the idea of orgone energy, and the orgone accumulator box. When she looks into the sky above her head, it is easy for Evie to believe in the idea of orgone energy; it explains the connection she feels with the sky, and it explains why she always feels better next to the water, letting its energy fill her and soothe her.

The next morning Evie takes out her Mobilgas roadmap and opens it up on the kitchen table. She writes down directions to Rangeley and draws herself a little map, just in case. She'd read that Reich lived in a place outside Rangeley he called Orgonon. She has the address but no phone number and doesn't know what she'd say if she called anyway. She just wants to visit; she has to go, she doesn't know why. What would she lose, anyway? Her dignity? Hah. And what could she gain? Evie combs her fingers through her hair, checking her appearance in her small pocket mirror, and folds the map up to carry along in her purse.

Two hours later, Evie is turning the old Dodge onto a road called Dodge Pond Road. She sometimes talks to the car, and now she pats the dashboard, saying "You feel like you're coming home, Dodgie?" She almost missed the sign, hiding in the trees, but saw it just in time. She drives slowly up a road as bumpy and narrow as the road to the camp, and stops where the road clearly is about to become a driveway, leading up to a strange-looking house: it is modern, with rectangles on top of one another like pictures she'd seen of Frank Lloyd Wright houses, yet made of stone. Exterior walls made of large, grey stones. It looks both light, as if it will fly away, and very heavy perched on top of the hill. She stares at it bemused, and walks slowly towards it, leaving her car parked by the road. The house has a look of a fortress, she thinks; a fortress on a hill. A fortress that might be able to turn into an ungainly bird, and fly away.

Halfway up the drive, Evie turns around to look behind her. Through descending layers of green, she sees a lake. Full-bodied clouds scud across the sky, their shadows moving across the land. She is wondering if it is Rangeley Lake, or some other body of water—Dodge Pond? —when she hears a noise from the house.

A man stands on the deck, behind a railing with bright blue trim. The noise was the front door closing. Evie catches her breath; something about him makes her suddenly afraid. "Hello," she calls out and gives a little wave.

Evie has the strange feeling that the man's body—his posture—is communicating things to her. It is saying very clearly that she is an intruder on this property, that he has every right to defend himself and call the police instantly. It is also saying, in slight shifts of body alignment, that he understands she probably means no harm, and perhaps he will not unleash his full wrath upon her.

She continues walking toward the house, slowly, arms wrapped around her mid-section. She stops when she nears the house, and looks up at him. The man has shocks of gray and white hair above a round, red face and is wearing khaki pants and a light-colored shirt. He stands still and gives an impression of great, condensed energy. She knows that he is reading her movements. Evie had planned a dialogue on the way here but now her thoughts have deserted her, and she does not know what to say. "Mr. Reich? I...um...I heard of you..." She lifts her arms and flops them out to either side, in despair at her own ridiculousness.

At her gesture the man, mercifully, allows a small smile to cross his face. He takes a step back and holds a hand toward the door in guarded welcome.

Chapter Five

Doctor Wang looks at Kiya over reading glasses perched on the end of her nose. Kiya can see her go into rescue mode. "It looks as if you are in your second month. I assume you want to have the baby?" Kiya nods. "Are you still taking antidepressants?"

Kiya considers whether to tell the truth, and decides to go for it. "No."

"Have you discussed this with your psychiatrist?"

Kiya considers again, decides this time to lie. "Yes. We're talking about it. She is arranging to have me switched to another antidepressant." Kiya has canceled all appointments with her psychiatrist; the last time they spoke was before Kiya learned she was pregnant.

The doctor nods. "Good, good. Stay in close touch with her, follow her advice. It's important. There is some risk to the fetus if you continuing taking the medication, but there is also a risk for you if you don't take it. Pregnancy and birth are stressful times."

Kiya looks at her hands. She hates this, hates being here, but she will do it for the living being inside her, for their child—for "the fetus," as the doctor says.

"Is the father supportive?"

A burst of anger rises in Kiya at the question. Just who does this woman thinks she is, Kiya's mother? She searches for calm, tells herself it is the doctor's job to ask these questions. "Yes," Kiya says brightly. "We plan on getting married soon. He's very excited about being a father."

Doctor Wang smiles at her. "That's good. Congratulations."

Kiya thinks the doctor does not look totally convinced, but she doesn't care. It's her life, her body. She jumps down from the table. "Are we all done, then?"

She has not been able to tell Peter yet. The right moment hasn't arrived, and though Kiya knows she must tell him, she doesn't think there's a rush. She hopes he will be positive about it, but if he isn't, that won't change the fact that she, Kiya, will be having a baby. Will be a mother. The thought makes little flecks of light in the darkness.

But it is not easy. She works on channeling the sunlight and reflecting it for her clients, for Peter, especially for her mother, but sometimes the walls grow high around her, blocking the light. The worst thing, she thinks, is that when the light doesn't reach her, she doesn't care whether she finds it to channel or not.

Her feet drag on the steps to the house where her mother lives. Her mother loves her totally and wants what is best for her daughter, but does she know how hard it can be to be the one to cheer her up? The only one? She rings the doorbell, takes a deep breath, and prepares a smile on her face as the door opens. She's been doing this all day at work, she can do it for a while longer. Only a little while, and then she can let the smiles drop, can close her eyes and retreat into kind darkness for a while.

"Hi!" she says to her mother. She holds out the bunch of gladioli she purchased at the market. "I bought these for you." She watches the lines of worry ease out of her mother's face, watches the darkness leave her expression, watches her enfold the flowers as if they were her own child.

* * * *

Peter goes to work every day through the autumn, but once the snow starts falling he knows the tree work will die down, and he's not on salary. He thinks about taking a second job. He thinks about doing something else entirely. He wonders whether he should apply to grad school, wonders if he should get training in something new—as an electrician, maybe. He finds it hard to get excited about anything.

One evening Matt came by and they picked out a song, Peter playing banjo and Matt guitar. Peter had written the tune and some words, and Matt added others. Peter thought they sounded good. Matthew wanted to get together again, wanted to build up a repertoire. The thought makes Peter uneasy; what is it for? Why put all that energy into it? Peter doesn't know if he'd want to get up on stage even if someone did hire them. And if they did hire them, they still wouldn't make enough to live on.

"But don't you enjoy making beautiful music?" Kiya asks. They are having dinner at their vegetarian favorite restaurant. Neither of them is into cooking much at home. "Wouldn't it be wonderful just to play for other people?"

"As an egoistic thrill, I might enjoy it. But it takes so much practice and so much effort to get to that point." He shrugs, taking another bite of his soy chicken.

Kiya just looks at him, without saying anything. She has pretty eyes, but just now they look like they are expecting something from him. "What, do you think I'm lazy?" he asks.

She smiles then. "Yes."

He smiles back at her, he can't help it. "Okay, then. I'm lazy."

They lie naked on Peter's mattress, quiet after love. Kiya is staring at the trees outside his window in the darkness, Peter tracing lines on her belly. He pats it, feeling a jiggle, a bounce that wasn't there before. Her hips, her breasts are all fuller than they used to be. His finger traces a faint line of hair from her navel down.

Kiya grows suddenly still, as if listening to his gestures. "All right," she says. "All right. Are you trying to say something?"

He looks up at her. "What?"

Kiya sits up on the bed, resting her arms on her knees. "Are you trying to tell me something about my body?" She is frowning.

"What, are you crazy?" He sits up and brushes hair from his face. "You know I think your body is beautiful."

"Yeah, but it's different. Right? It's different than it used to be." She looks down at herself, at her breasts and her belly in the darkened room, and looks as if she is trying not to cry.

"If it's different, it's still just as gorgeous as it always was." He strokes her belly, one of her breasts. She is right that her body is more full than it used to be, but he is telling the truth when he says he likes it.

She pushes his hand away. Taking a deep breath, Kiya says, "I have something I have to tell you."

33

"And Max stepped into his private boat, and waved goodbye and sailed back over a year and in and out of weeks and through a day and into the night of his very own room where he found his supper waiting for him and it was still hot."

As Maddie reads these words, she smells food in the hallway outside Alex's room and hears the banging of the dinner cart. Perfect timing. She closes the book with satisfaction, and looks at Alex. His eyes are closed, and he hasn't moved since she started reading.

The afternoon had been cloudy, and when Maddie turns in the lane to her house the sky lets loose. She runs into the house with her jacket held over her head. She becomes soaked anyway, as she clumsily unlocks the door.

Inside her living room, Maddie hangs the jacket over the back of a chair and stands in front of the windows. The rain pounds the lake, sweeping across it in sheets. She sees Alex's face in front of her, the grimace of his smile, the eyes which almost meet hers. She used to think that he waited for her visits, that he thought about her when she was gone, even if it was in a vague, non-specific, unworded way. She tells herself that he is happy to see her, that her visits cheer him up. Alex's doctor has told her that her visits are important to him. Alex has no family apart from a brother who lives far away and rarely visits; he has no children, and apart from the nursing home staff and another friend who rarely visits, she is his only connection. But what if the doctor was comforting her, trying to make her feel useful? What if Alex is just making expressions and noises he would make if it were anyone there, someone he doesn't even know, reading to him? Does he really remember her, is there anything left of their relationship?

She opens the refrigerator to see about dinner and closes it. She pours herself a glass of wine and sits by the open window, listening to the sound the rain makes on the water. There is no forgetting about the rain, about its force and power, when she looks out the window.

This morning just after Maddie had opened the office, Susan, the administrative assistant from History, stopped by her desk. Looking around to make sure no one could hear them, Susan had leaned into Maddie's ear and whispered, "Ron Grey is taking Jane to the campus dinner."

"What?" Maddie had jerked away from the unpleasant sensation of Susan's breath in her ear. "Jane Dougherty?"

"Shh," Susan said, looking around nervously. "Yes! Jane told me herself." Jane is a single history professor, never married as far as Maddie knows. She must be ten or fifteen years younger than Maddie, which would make her fifteen or twenty years younger than Ron. Maddie looked at Susan's round face, pink with excitement from her discovery, and shook her head. She waved her hand in the air, and Susan took the hint. "Bye, lady," Susan said and was gone.

The rain pounds harder on the water, and Maddie thinks she hears the low rumbling of thunder. From the house next door, barely visible through the trees, she hears a regular thumping noise, and then a kind of singing, chanting—or is it crying? She sits still, listening. The sound rises and falls in waves through the sounds of the storm, regular and mysterious.

*　*　*　*

The house—Orgonon—is cool and spacious. Evie has an impression of shiny wooden floors, wide windows letting in the light. The man sits at a table in front of a stone fireplace and gestures to a chair across from him. She sits, trying to hide her nervousness, the trembling deep inside. "So," he says. The word is followed by a burst of air, an eloquent sigh. "Who are you, young lady, and what are you doing here?"

Evie knows by the accent who he is, but to make sure, she says "Dr. Reich?" He nods. Another man appears in the doorway, looks at them for a moment, then walks away. "My name is Evelyn McArthur. I have heard of your work, and . . . wanted to meet you."

"You wanted to meet me," he says in his Austrian accent. "And why? What did you think I could do for you?"

35

What indeed, she thinks. The foolishness of her endeavor, the futility of her hopes, overwhelms her. Gather yourself together, Evelyn, she thinks. Don't be a ninny. Don't waste his time any more than you already have. Taking a deep breath, Evie says "I have read something of your work with orgone energy and its healing properties. I believe you might be able to help me."

Evie thinks it is the word "believe" that makes the man's face soften. "The work does require faith," he says. "An openness to possibility is a necessary prerequisite." He sits up straight then and looks at her. "I don't usually treat people here, but tell me what is going on with you."

Evie tells him that she has just graduated from college with a BA in Psychology, and she is now living for the summer at her parents' camp in Chesterville. She tells him about the cancer. "The doctors think they got it all, but they just don't know for sure, no one can know." Her voice starts to shake slightly at this point. "And there were . . . other things," she says.

"Yes, of course," Dr. Reich says and waits. When she doesn't say more, he says, "Well, if you're going to tell me the problem, then tell me the problem."

Though the words are sharp, his voice is kind. "My grandfather died." Here it is hard for her, because she knows that grandfathers die, and parents die, but not so suddenly and not *her* grandfather, not the man she loved so much.

Reich nods, still watching her closely. "Anything else?"

Evie hesitates. She doesn't want to say it because it seems so trivial compared to the other issues, so commonplace. But death is commonplace, she reasons, and that does not make it less painful. "And I broke up with my boyfriend. Or maybe he broke up with me, I'm not even sure." She looks at her hands for a moment. "Yeah, I think he broke up with me."

Reich smiles at her then, a smile of surprising warmth. "All right then. I will see what we can do for you." They agree Evie will return next Monday, to begin a series of treatments in the accumulator.

"Thank you. Thank you so much," Evie says. She stands by the table, uncertain. She knows she has to ask, and she doesn't want to. "What will . . . how much will I owe you?" She has $250 in her savings account.

He stands up also and makes a dismissive gesture. "Do not worry," he says.

On the drive back to the camp Evie feels lighter, as if something has already been lifted from her. The blue Dodge crests a hill too quickly and she feels her stomach rise inside her, then settle down. She can't believe her audacity in approaching the man, and more than that, she can't believe that he actually agreed to treat her. Below her blue water in an unnamed lake catches the sun, and winks at her.

Chapter Six

The words, once said, cannot be taken back. Peter looks at her. The light from the streetlight, broken by moving shadows of trees, plays across Peter's face. "You're kidding," he whispers.

"No!" Kiya says, realizes she is speaking loudly, nearly shouting, and says more quietly, "No. Would I joke about that? No. I really am pregnant." She draws her knees up to her chest and wraps her arms around them. She rests her face on her arm; her skin feels cool against her cheek. She finds the feel of her own skin oddly comforting, as if she has become two people, one of them comforting the other one.

Peter sits up on the bed next to her, pushes hair from his face as if the gesture will help him to think. "Did you take a test?" he asks. "Did you see a doctor?"

"Yes, and yes." She rocks just slightly on his mattress, back and forth. She hears the apartment door open and close, and sounds from the kitchen; Ryan must be home. Kiya clears her throat, allowing the next words to exit. "I'm going to keep it."

Peter continues to stare at her, and suddenly in the shadowy room, he looks like someone she doesn't know as well as she thought she did. "Don't you think this is something we should talk about?" His voice is quiet, and that scares her. She clutches her arms around her folded legs more tightly.

"Well, yes," Kiya says, trying to keep her voice calm. "I do want to talk about it with you. That's why I told you."

"How far along are you?"

"Two and a half months."

"How long have you known?" His voice is still quiet, and feels dangerous to Kiya.

"Peter . . ." She reaches a hand out to touch his arm. "Not long. I had to figure out what I was going to do before I told you."

"Did you know when we went to my mother's? Is that why you wanted to go with me?"

Kiya turns away to look out the window. Cars pass, and a couple walks on the sidewalk below the window. She can hear their voices, but can't make out what they're saying. She doesn't want to answer Peter's questions anymore. "So . . . how do you feel about this?" She picks at a bump on her arm. "What do you think about the idea of being a father?"

Peter sits very still, his head at an angle away from her. He is holding himself very contained, Kiya thinks. After a moment he stands up, reaches down to the floor, and picks up his jeans. He puts them on and pulls the tee shirt from the floor over his head. He shakes his head and looks at her. "I'm going out," he says in a flat and expressionless voice. The door swings closed behind him.

Kiya sits a long time on Peter's bed after she hears his footsteps walk away. She hears music from the living room, but no voices. She looks at Peter's room; the banjo leaning against the wall in the corner; the scratched wooden dresser with a drawer half open; his collection of carved wooden animals. The pictures taped to the walls: Brando, Dylan, some people she doesn't know, all black and white. His wooden bookshelf against the wall, filled with philosophy books, novels, and poetry. She is naked and alone on a man's bed, and the man does not—at this moment—love her. She is certain that he does don't love her at all. He may even hate her. She looks down at her naked body, at her scraggly pubic hair, her tummy bulge, her skin white and vulnerable, and closes her eyes so she doesn't have to see.

⁂ ⁂ ⁂ ⁂

Peter walks to Congress Street and heads downtown, walking without thinking where he is going. He hears snatches of music from cars, from restaurants as he passes, from apartments with windows open. He refuses to let himself think—he will just walk—but he can't help seeing Kiya's face as she said: "I'm pregnant." She was first impassive, as if she didn't need to feel anything about this; then angry; then something in her seemed to crumble and slide apart. What the fuck, what did she expect him to do? The way she said, "I'm going to keep it" in that conversational tone, as if this had nothing to do with him—it made him feel like the top of his head was going to be blown off. He had to get out of that room, had to get away from her. He doesn't know what to think about this, and he won't think about it, not yet.

He hears live music coming from an open door ahead. He stops, looks in, sees a band playing at the back of the room. Discordant, but some irresistible head-thumping energy is going on. He turns in, flags down the bartender for a beer.

"That's weird. She just told you like that? Said she was going to keep it?" The girl—her name is Toni, short for Antoinette—leans both elbows on the table, looking at him. Her hair, black and straight, falls across her face when she leans over. "What are you going to do?"

Peter takes another long drink from his beer. "I don't know, what choice do I have? Be a daddy?" He'd just met Toni tonight and told her his dilemma. What did he have to lose? They were standing at the back of the room watching the band and started talking. When a booth opened up, they took it. She just moved to Portland from Fort Kent, she said, and is staying with her friends until she finds a place. She has a directness that appeals. He never has to see her again if he doesn't want to.

Toni asks him something. They are sitting together on one side of a booth; her friends, a couple who were sitting on the other side, are now dancing. He can't hear her through the noise. "What did you say?"

"I said, do you love her?"

He laughs. "Shit. I don't know." He smiles at Toni. She's cute. "I doubt it?"

Toni shakes her head. "I don't know, but I think you'd have some idea if you loved her. That seems kind of relevant to the situation." She picks at the label of the beer bottle in front of her. He sees the bottom of a tattoo below the short sleeve of her shirt, some letters to a word he can't read. "So how do you feel about being a daddy? You like kids?"

"Kids?" Peter says, looking at Toni as if she were speaking a foreign language. "What's a kid?" The girl looks at him; clearly,

40

she does not think he's funny. She's right, he isn't funny. He's angry and disturbed, and now he's a little drunk. "Sorry, I don't mean to be an asshole. I just don't know what to think. I can't process, I don't know . . ." He shoves her hip, gently, with his hand. "Will you dance with me?"

* * * *

Thursday is sunny, and warm for late September. Maddie drives toward the nursing home after work and then, slowly, drives on by. The fading flowers in front watch her pass. An afternoon like this is rare, she thinks; she owes it to herself to be on the lake. There won't be many more like this. She doesn't want to think of the emptiness she saw on Alex's face the last time she was there, doesn't want to wonder if he is waiting for her to come.

At the house, she unlocks the shed and pulls the blue kayak out. She is standing on the rocks in front of the house, buckling a life jacket, when she hears a car pull up next door. She is pulling out onto the lake when she hears another sound make its way across the water: a regular shrieking noise. She stops paddling and floats, listening. It's the sound a human would make if it were a bird, she thinks, or a bird would make if it were human; cawing, chirping, calling.

She paddles out, hearing the sound fade behind her. The trees are changing color on the shoreline, orange and gold mixed in with dark evergreens. The sky is enormous, blue with white wisps. She reaches to touch the water, which is warm on top, cooler underneath. She lets her fingers skim just below the surface. She lifts her face to the sun, feeling its warmth. There is something healing about it. Sometimes she thinks things over when she floats on the lake, thinks about work, and sometimes—like this time— she is absolutely thoughtless. Her mind is a blank slate, like the sky. It is soothing, this emptiness, and calm.

She paddles slowly back toward her house, watching it gradually take on its features, become visible to her as she approaches. The yellow paint under the tall trees; the small wooden dock; the deck and the Adirondack chairs; the person sitting on the green chair, her folded arms, her short pale hair.

41

Maddie turns the teapot on and stares at the flame, trying to calm herself. It was a shock to see Peter's friend Kiya sitting on her dock—uninvited, unannounced. She didn't even know if she and Peter were still dating. She felt oddly threatened by the girl's appearance, the way she sat there unmoving as Maddie approached, not saying anything. Maddie wondered, briefly, if she should be afraid, if she should stay out on the lake and not come in. "Kiya?" she called out. Then she saw the fear in the girl's face, saw that her arms were crossed in front of her not in belligerence, but in self-protection. She was holding herself in, protecting herself against the world.

Kiya stood up when Maddie stepped onto the dock and walked toward her, and the expression on her face, the way she stood there shivering, made Maddie wrap her arms around her and hold her. They walked inside the house and Kiya sat at the table. "I would love some tea," Kiya said. "Do you have any? Do you mind?"

And so they sit with hot cups in front of them. "I'm sorry," Kiya says. "I know it's rude to show up like this. I've been raised . . ." Here she chokes on her words. "I've been raised better than this." Her face is pale and blotchy, her eyes red-rimmed. When she reaches for the cup, her hand trembles.

"It's all right," Maddie says and sips the hot tea. "I like unexpected visitors." She smiles above the cup, hoping it will put the young woman at ease, help her story come out.

"You're very nice," Kiya says. "It's just . . . I go see my mother nearly every day, and we have tea." She takes a deep breath. "And I can't see her today, and so I thought I would come and see you instead."

Maddie thinks about this. "Is there a reason you can't see her today?"

Kiya's head drops. She is shaking, and Maddie lets her cry. Finally, Kiya composes herself and says, "She's in the hospital."

"What's wrong with her?" Maddie asks.

"She has some kind of infection, and pneumonia also. She's pretty sick." Kiya takes a deep breath and sits up straighter in the chair. "I'm not even sure she knew who I was when I was there this morning."

"Well, that's bad, isn't it? I'm sorry to hear it." Maddie wonders just what is going on, why Kiya is here, falling apart in Maddie's kitchen. Maddie hasn't heard anything from her son for a few days. "Have you talked with Peter about this?"

Kiya shakes her head, silently. Maddie waits. Finally, she says, "We aren't . . . really talking these days. He's angry with me."

Maddie nods and waits some more. When nothing more is forthcoming on the subject of Peter, she says, "What's the prognosis for your mother? Do you know?"

Kiya shakes her head a little. She is wearing a stretchy knit top that is tight over her breasts and belly, more voluptuous than Maddie remembers. Kiya sits up tall and pulls her shirt down, looking at herself self-consciously. Something about the gesture makes Maddie ask cautiously, "Is there anything else you want to tell me?"

Kiya and Maddie talk for an hour, until Maddie, looking at the clock, gets up to make dinner. After they finish eating Kiya helps her clear the table and stack dishes in the dishwasher. Then they stand in front of the windows overlooking the lake. The sky is nearly dark, and the rising moon is half-hidden by long clouds. "Would you like to spend the night?" Maddie asks. "I would worry about you driving home."

Kiya looks relieved. "Oh, thank you for asking. I would be so grateful if I could stay here. I don't have to work tomorrow morning."

Maddie loans Kiya a tee shirt, and Kiya takes the book on Wilhelm Reich into the bedroom. With the bedroom door closed behind Kiya, Maddie falls into the recliner and leans back. So if all goes as it will probably go, she is to be a grandmother. Her son will be a father, whether he wants to be or not. And apparently, according to Kiya, he does not. Maddie wonders if Peter has a problem with the idea of being a father, or of being involved in this life-long way with Kiya—or with anyone. He has no memories of having a father or even a real father figure; perhaps that plays into his aversion. He doesn't know how to be a father. She feels the old guilt rise up. She never gave him a father.

43

When Peter was little, he used to ask about his father. Maddie remembers Peter as a child, standing in the kitchen of their apartment in Illinois, wearing his striped sweater and corduroy pants. Maybe someone said something at kindergarten, asked him about his father, she doesn't remember. She told him his father loved him but lived far away, too far to visit. His father lived in Iowa then, and he didn't seem to want to visit. He had their phone number, but never contacted them. Several years later, Maddie heard Mark had died. He drove off the road late at night, no other cars involved. He was probably drunk. She didn't tell Peter. Mark had never come to visit Peter, never called. She thought Peter would probably rather think he had a father still alive somewhere than to know of his death. Avoiding the subject was made easier by the fact that Peter never asked again about his father.

She feels cool air thread its way through the open window, and remembers the moment of stillness and calm she felt on the lake earlier today. If Peter ever learned these facts about his father, she would like to tell him also the other things about his father—his kindness to Maddie when she was in a hard place, his shyness. His intelligence. His sadness he couldn't escape from, the darkness that haunted him. His strangeness that she'd fallen in love with, his oddness that was part of his brilliance. She'd watched for that sadness in Peter, wondering about genetics, and saw only a cheerful, thoughtful boy growing into a young man. When he told his mother he'd decided to major in philosophy, she blurted out in surprise, "Your father majored in philosophy!" Peter looked at her then and didn't say anything; no question, no response, not even a "Huh." He had to have heard her, yet it was as if she hadn't said anything at all.

Now he is going to be a father. The mother of this child will need some help, Maddie can see; Kiya is sweet, but her emotions are all over the place. She is a piece of glass, glinting and fragile. Maddie hears a loon call faintly from the far shore. She closes her eyes and there it is, before her, as if it were standing in the room: a child with curly pale hair, sturdy bare chest and arms. A child created out of passion and orgone energy; a child looking at her, waiting to be brought into this life.

＊ ＊ ＊ ＊

The day after Evie drove to Orgonon and talked with Wilhelm Reich, she walks to the end of the lane to get the mail. It is raining, and she wears her yellow slicker. Along with a flyer for the local hardware store, she receives two white envelopes. She puts them in her jacket pocket and waits to open them until she gets back to the dry camp. She shakes the water from her slicker on the porch and settles in the old rocking chair.

She opens the one from her parents first. Her mother writes that she is glad the trip went well, that Evie arrived safely and the camp is in good shape. She tells her to keep the door locked at night. This is followed by a scrawled note from her father. He writes: "We will arrive later than we thought. I got talked into attending a workshop in July, which ends the 20th. Your mother found it in her heart to forgive me. We'll take off right after that, in fact, the very moment it ends. I hope you'll be okay in holding the fort until we come." Evie smiles, remembering her father's rant against the impropriety of the common phrase "holding down the fort." She holds the letter to her chest in gratitude at this news. She can't imagine how she can explain her visits to Rangeley to them. This gives her nearly seven weeks before she has to try. Maybe the treatment will be done by then.

She puts her parents' letter down and lifts up the next one. It has no return address, but she recognizes Eric's handwriting. She is afraid to open it; what could he possibly want to say to her?

The letter is typed on thin parchment paper, mistakes erased and retyped in a few places. Eric couldn't just let those things go, even in a letter to her. "Dear Evie," he writes. "You said it would be impossible for us to be 'just friends' after all we've been through, and I respect that, but I can't just let you go with the thought of never speaking with you again. We went through a lot together, and you know I will always think of you." Evie smiles wryly at this, imagining Eric's gaze fixed on her as he wrote this; so earnest, so sincere. Such a *nice boy,* her mother always said, and Evie couldn't tell if there was a note of irony in her comment. At first, Evie had laughed at the force of Eric's naïve sincerity; it reminded her of the Bible salesman in a new story by Flannery

45

O'Connor. Eric seemed so sweet and naïve she didn't trust him, suspecting him of harboring evil depths. Gradually she came to realize that he was truly well-meaning, even if he didn't have always the self-knowledge to know what motivated him. And he was cute.

He writes, "I know you don't think I was genuine when I said I loved you. You thought I was [here something is erased and retyped over] just after one thing. Well, sure, I did like that one thing, but I also really did love you. Just because we turned out not to be right for one another doesn't mean I didn't love you." Here Evie feels the damn stinging behind her eyeballs again. She gives an exasperated sigh at herself, at her stupid girly emotions. "I just wanted to put that out there. I was thinking of buying you a ring and asking you to marry me, I was that serious about you. And I was broken up when it didn't work out. "

At this Evie throws down the letter. What? He was thinking of buying her a ring? This strains her faith in his sincerity. Why had he never mentioned anything like that? And where was that emotion when he was hanging around with Betty Thompson? And another thing . . . here Evie gets up and walks impatiently over to the window, watching the rain pour down on the surface of the lake. Eric and she don't have the same taste in many things; what if he'd purchased a ring and expected her to like it enough to wear it for the rest of her life? Just like him, she fumes, to assume if he bought a ring she'd love it.

Evie returns to the chair to finish the letter. "And I wanted to tell you one another thing," Eric wrote. "I got accepted into a graduate program in architecture at the University of Edinburgh (remember I said I was applying? I bet you don't remember, do you?)" He had her there; she did not remember. "It was when your grandfather got sick, so I don't blame you if you don't remember. Anyway, I was accepted, and my parents decided it was worth it to foot the bill. I think they're terrified of me living at home. So I will be leaving for Scotland in August. You remember I always wanted to study abroad, and this is my chance.

I know this means we won't see one another again for a long time, so I just wanted to let you know that I was going and that I have fond feelings toward you, and good memories of our time together. It was a growing time for both of us." Here Evie scrunches up her nose, makes a prissy mouth, and says in a high-pitched voice *it was a growing time for both of us.* He signs off "With affection always, Eric."

"All right, Eric," Evie says aloud to the letter, "you're getting a little carried away. Calm down." She picks up the letter again and reads his words: "I did like that one thing." She remembers him above her on the narrow bed in his apartment, his naked chest and shoulders, his grunts as he pushed into her. And the time she finally just, without any thought about it, pushed him off her chest before he was finished. He lay angled awkwardly against the wall, looking at her in complete amazement. "What? What's wrong? Did I hurt you?" All she could do was shake her head, mutely; how could she tell him that she didn't like this, that she didn't enjoy it, and didn't see how he could? It wasn't pain, exactly, that she felt, but it wasn't pleasure either. His question gave her an out. "I'm sorry, I have a cramp," she lied. "I think I'm starting my period and I'm worried about it. And it did hurt, a little." Eric was as inexperienced with women as she was with men, and he believed her.

She liked Eric, she really did, but after that time she felt like she was pretending with him—or maybe she realized she had been pretending all those other times when she acted as if she liked it, and she couldn't do it anymore. It wasn't too long after that Eric asked her about the mole on her back, and then her grandfather became ill, and she went home for his funeral, too late to say good-bye. Then when she returned to school it took her a long time to want to get together with Eric again, who seemed to be doing a lot of studying for chem tests with Betty Thompson, and she and Eric just fell apart.

Sure, Evie thinks, she was difficult and distant, but couldn't he have tried harder? I mean, if he cared enough to buy a ring? She imagines the ring, a simple diamond in a gold band. Maybe she would have liked that, maybe she would have liked being Mrs. Eric Lawson, but all she can think of now, as she stares out at the gray stippled lake, is that wedding rings are for someone else—someone grown-up.

Chapter Seven

Kiya pushes the door open gently. The curtains are drawn and the lights are off, but her mother is lying on her side in the hospital bed, looking at the door. She smiles, as if she'd been waiting for her, and Kiya smiles back in relief.

She sits in a chair next to the bed. "How are you doing?" her mother asks.

"How are *you* doing," Kiya says. "You're the one in the hospital."

Her mother tries to sit up higher, pushing a pillow up behind her; Kiya takes a hand to help her. "I don't remember how I got here," she says.

She looks better today, Kiya thinks; there is some color in her cheeks. "You called me, and I came. You were sick in bed. I called the doctor, and they called an ambulance. You weren't making much sense. You scared us," she says and bites her lip to stop a trembling she feels there. "Scared me," she amends, realizing that there is no "us" in this, apart from her mother and herself. Her father lives in San Francisco and doesn't know of her mother's illness.

"I'm sorry," her mother says, squeezing Kiya's hand. They are so intertwined, so tangled; her mother's illness hurts Kiya and Kiya's pain hurts her mother, which in turn hurts Kiya more. "I'm on the mend now, so says the Almighty Doctor."

"That's good," says Kiya. "Because we don't want you meeting the other Almighty, not just yet."

"No, I'm not ready for that." She laughs weakly, but she is herself again, it is her old, self-deprecating laugh. "I need to hang around longer to bother you some more."

And to see your grandchild, Kiya says to herself. She hasn't been able to tell her mother yet. She issues a fervent, silent prayer that this will happen: that her mother gets well and that this so-called child, this thing of imagination and morning nausea and a few extra pounds, this thing which will supposedly someday emerge as a living breathing human being, comes to pass.

Sitting on the bus, Kiya sighs deeply, feeling her muscles relax as she does so. She has been stiffened against pain, she thinks, for so long. She puts her hand on the softness of her abdomen, imagining the small being inside her, turning in unfettered joy. She must protect it; she must open herself to energy, to health, so that her child can be strong. Water is alive, and it's healthy to be near it. Kiya closes her eyes, remembering the way the lake looked the other day.

Visiting Maddie was a crazy thing to do, but she was drawn there. It was the memory of the lake, the brightness of the water pulling her there, and the thought of Peter's mother. She liked Maddie, and after that awful moment when her mother didn't recognize her, she needed to be recognized. And she wanted Maddie to know she was pregnant with Peter's child, that she was going to give birth. Now, as the bus jounces along, Kiya wonders if talking to Maddie, spending the night there with Peter's mother without him, will make Peter angry. She had never considered how he would feel about that. Telling his mother about her pregnancy, talking about her relationship with Peter. She clenches her hands together, feeling her muscles become tense again. Of course he will be angry; why doesn't she think of these things before she does them? She wants to stay together with Peter, yet she does things that she knows will make him angry, will push him away from her. She presses her fingertips against her eyes, feeling the darkness rise. It is hard to fight it, hard to remember her own goodness. She puts her hands down and turns to the day outside the window, forming a smile on her face to match the way she would like to feel inside.

* * * *

Oriental Bittersweet, Lambsquarters, Giant Hogweed. Crabgrass, Ragweed, Poison Ivy. Peter brushes his legs against all these plants except the last one as he walks by, naming them in his head. Some of the names are interesting for such boring-looking plants: Hairy Galinsoga. Shephard's Purse.

He is walking to his car, his skin dark with dust and streaked with sweat. They've been working on the grounds of a nursing home outside the city, near the ocean. Residents of the home watched him through the windows, some coming out in wheelchairs to look at him and Gary. It was probably the best entertainment they'd had all day. "This doesn't look like a bad place to live," he'd said to Gary.

Gary looked up at the two stories, the little balconies outside each room. "You and I couldn't afford it," he said.

As Peter walks, he considers the idea that he couldn't afford a nice nursing home when he's older. Are they that expensive, then? He supposes so, with all that care, and with the spacious grounds and that fountain out in front. This one is nicer than the one Alex lives in. Gary, who owns the business and makes more money than Peter does, couldn't afford to live here. There are so many things Peter hasn't yet considered, so many things he hasn't thought of. Mortgage payments, health insurance, retirement. And at the end of it all, a nursing home. He starts up his old Jeep. All that's in the future, right? He has a slightly queasy feeling in his stomach as he identifies another thing he doesn't want to think of: college costs. As a parent, not the one attending college. He's just two years into paying back his own school loans, and can't imagine paying for someone else to attend college in what, eighteen years.

He wonders if Kiya worries about things like college costs. She's never mentioned them; the few times they did talk recently, all she ended up saying was she was going to have the baby, she wants to have the baby. He doesn't understand the feeling, and she can't seem to explain it to him. Since she doesn't seem to want to involve him in this decision-making process, his inclination is to back away and let her take care of things. If it's her body, then what's inside of it can be hers, too.

A shiny pickup truck is parked in the parking area by their apartment, so Peter has to find a spot on the street. The truck has bumper stickers that read "Squirrels: Nature's Speed Bumps" and "Go ahead, hit my truck so I can try out my new gun," and "If you can't feed 'em, don't breed 'em." Ryan's father is visiting.

"Hey, the philosopher is here!" Peter hears as he enters. Cigarette smoker's voice, with an edge of joking belligerence. As he turns into the living room Peter sees the blue-jeaned legs and cowboy boots resting on the coffee table, beer resting on the belly named after it. "How's the philosophizing going?"

"Hello, Rick. How are you?" Peter knows that he should respond in kind to Rick; should yell at him to get his dirty boots off their coffee table, should say in response to the constant taunts about his degree in philosophy that at least he was smart enough to get a college degree, unlike some people he could name. That's what Ryan tells him to do, and that's what Rick wants him to do. Peter supposes this is the way fathers toughen up their sons, with verbal slapping around. He never had a father, he wouldn't know. He practices his own form of rebellion against Rick by insisting on being polite, not raising his voice. By treating the man as if he deserved respect.

"Well I'm just doing fine, thank you. And how are you?" Rick imitates Peter's tone by lowering his voice exaggeratedly, enunciating carefully. Just in case Peter doesn't get the joke, Rick lifts his pinkie in the air as he brings the can of beer to his mouth.

Peter looks around. "Where's Ryan?"

"He's changing his clothes. We're goin' muddin' and he had to get out of his fancy pants."

Ryan comes out of the bathroom, zipping up. "We are not going mudding. We're not going anywhere. He's just dropping off some stuff for us." In the kitchen, Peter sees a small table and a bookshelf.

"I guess you don't need that bookshelf, huh Rick?" Peter knows it's a pathetic excuse for a joke, and he hopes Rick gets it, but Rick just shakes his head.

"Nah, and I don't need that guitar anymore either." He points the beer can at a guitar Peter hadn't noticed, leaning against the kitchen wall. "Ryan says you play good, and you can use it."

"I didn't know you played guitar," Peter says.

"I don't. Once I thought I would learn and someone gave me this."

Peter picks the guitar and holds it, turning it around. "Oh

51

no, you can't do this. This is a Gibson. You can't give this to me."

"What's the matter, not good enough?" Rick looks offended, though with him, it is impossible to tell.

"No, it's too good. You should sell this." It looks like solid maple on the back and sides, probably spruce on the top. He sits down and strums; out of tune and needs new strings, but this is one beauty of a guitar. He's never owned an instrument this nice.

Rick puts his feet on the floor and leans forward. "I would sell it, but I can't. It was given to me, see, by an old friend." Rick lights up a cigarette, and Peter is not going to tell him, this time, to take it outside. "He told me it was mine to have, mine to play, and if I ever wanted to get rid of it, see, I had to give it to someone who would play it. No sales."

"It's true," Ryan says, flopping into their old recliner. "I wanted him to give it to me, but he said I had to learn to play first. I never did learn to play, so he won't give it to me. He thinks I'll just end up selling it for rent money."

"The thing is, that's the deal." Rick puffs on his cigarette, eyes squinted. "You can't ever sell it. My friend gave it to me when he was going off to Vietnam, see. In the 1960's. He was my next-door neighbor, a guy older than me but we was friends. He told me to keep it for him, and when he came back, he'd get it from me. If he didn't come back, I had to play it, or give it away to someone who would play it. No money changing hands." He shrugs, taps his cigarette ash into the empty beer can. "He never came back."

Peter doesn't know what to say. The wood is smooth to the touch under his hand. "I will play it, you can bet that. I won't sell it. I'll play." Then, he says, "Thank you."

Rick stands up, brushes ashes off his shirt onto the floor. He points the cigarette at Peter. "No money changing hands over that guitar. Just play it good." Then he's out the door, and they hear the roar of his pickup starting up.

* * * *

Monday morning, Maddie walks up the stairs to her office.

The hallway is quiet and empty at 8:00 a.m. In her office, she opens a window part-way to bring in the feeling of the outdoors, which she won't see again until her lunch hour. She stands for a moment at the window, leaning her forehead against the cool glass. In the mornings she is aware of the days of her life passing, turning into months and years. She remembers being in this office ten years ago, and fifteen; she is growing older. For this quiet moment, the glass cool against her forehead and the sunlight bright on the parking lot and trees outdoors, she reaches into herself to find out what it is she should be taking from this day, what it is she should be understanding. She finds something, but could not put it into words if she were asked to.

At her desk she looks at the framed photo of Peter, eight years old, grinning into the camera with the lake behind him. She looks at the dried flower arrangement on top of the shelves, which Ron gave her for Secretary Appreciation Day, and which has lasted several years. Finally, she takes a photo from her wallet, pulling it out of a pocket to hold below her desk and look at. It is a snapshot of Alex she had printed, taken just months before he became ill. They were in London on a vacation, but all that shows of London in the photo is a gray sky and a bit of the River Thames flowing behind him as he stands on a bridge by the railing. He is laughing, the wind blowing his gray hair back. The photo always makes her smile. He was a sweet man. Is a sweet man, she supposes, though she's not sure of that. The photo reminds her of the way she loved him, and it reminds her that he is still alive. She tucks the photo back in her wallet and turns to her computer, ready to start the day.

Late in the morning, Ron comes to her office to talk about the department budget. He pulls a chair next to hers, so they can look at her computer screen together. He leans against her to point at figures on the screen. "There, this . . . that is just wrong." Maddie tries to concentrate on the figures but for some reason she thinks of her father, leaning against her mother as they sat on the couch in the evening. It was a comforting gesture, even to Maddie, who sat on a chair across the room, reading. She thinks Ron is not conscious of how close he is, so Maddie tries to pay no attention to it either, shifting away to take notes on a piece of scratch paper. She suddenly remembers where the discrepancy came from. "We haven't gotten reimbursed yet for photocopying. That's it."

Ron sits back. "Ah! You're right! I forgot about that." He slaps a hand on the desk, and puts his other hand on Maddie's shoulder, shaking it gently in delight. "You're a genius." Maddie smiles, but his gesture pains her and she wonders, briefly, if Ron is conscious of his gestures at all, but knows exactly what he is doing, and just what effect they have on her.

She eats her lunch with Susan from History on a picnic table outside the Student Union. Susan takes a sandwich from a plastic bag, holding the plastic on the table so it doesn't blow away. "So Jane is asking me what she should wear to the dinner."

"Really." Maddie takes a bite of her salad.

"Yes. She actually took pictures of two dresses and showed them to me on her phone."

"She must be excited about it."

"I think she is," Susan says. She makes a wry face. "I didn't really like either of them, but I couldn't tell her that."

"Yeah? What are they like?"

"Really, they are exactly what a history professor would wear. Conservative, business-like. Unsexy." Jane tends toward nylons and low heels.

Maddie considers telling Susan that she is going to be a grandmother. That would change the subject of conversation away from Jane and Ron's incipient (or perhaps actual) love affair, but she's not ready to talk about it yet. It's too fresh, too uncertain, too fraught with danger. Peter hasn't even told her yet himself. She wonders when he plans to bring it up, and wonders if Kiya will tell him she already told his mother. Maddie decides not to mention it to him, just in case.

After work, Maddie stops at the nursing home. It's not Tuesday, her regular day, but she didn't make it last Thursday, and she wonders if Alex missed her. She wonders if he noticed at all that she wasn't there; wonders if Tuesday and Thursday are substantially different for him than any other days.

She pushes his door open. "Hello there!" she sings out. Alex is in his reclining wheelchair, set in front of a television which is turned on. Maddie pulls a chair up beside him and looks for the remote. She turns down the program, a cooking show. Alex's eyes follow her movements. She sits still, looking at him. He looks at her, at her eyes. He makes a grimace which is perhaps a smile, then his gaze wanders away. "Alex . . ." she says softly. His eyes are on the window, the fading light beyond the curtains. "Alex . . ." she says again. He looks her way again, and for just a moment she thinks she sees the old Alex there. A slight shift of expression; a ripple across his features. She puts her hand on his clenched hand, feels the human warmth there. "Do you remember London?" she says softly. His eyes half-close, in a dreamy way, and stay like that.

✳ ✳ ✳ ✳

Evie wonders how one dresses in order to sit in an orgone accumulator. She thought she had caught a glimpse of it the other day, a large rectangular wooden box in the corner. Comfortably, she supposes. The day is cool, so she wears long cotton pants, a button-up blouse, and a light sweater. Looking in the mirror above the dresser at herself, she buttons up all the buttons, then unbuttons just the top one, so she looks more relaxed than she feels. She turns on the radio on the way to Rangeley and is surprised to hear a snippet of music coming through the static: "Secret Love," by Doris Day, a song that was popular last summer. Before she can consciously identify where it comes from, Evie feels a pain so real it is almost physical, starting somewhere in her center and moving up to her eyes. Last summer she and Eric had sung along to this song on the radio on a car trip they took to visit her family. It was a fun trip, and they had been in love; how could that have all fallen apart? How could she have let it all slip away? Because it was her fault, she knew it was her fault even at the time, though there was nothing she could do to stop it. She squeezes her eyes shut briefly, and reaches in her bag for a cigarette.

When she parks and walks up to the house this time, no one comes out to greet her. She stands on the porch and looks through the front door screen, tapping gently. The house seems empty and quiet, until she hears a door closing, and a shadowy figure comes

towards her. It is the man she'd caught a glimpse of the other day
when she was talking with Dr. Reich. He is a solidly built, middle-
aged man with thinning hair. "Hello," he says, opening the door.
"He's expecting you." The man has a gruff Maine accent. Evie
follows him through the room she'd been in before, into a smaller
room that looks like an office. It has a desk, covered with books
and papers, and two chairs. "He'll be right in," the man says, and
leaves.

She takes in the book-lined walls, the large window overlooking the woods. And she cannot help but notice—though she
tries not to look—the large painting that takes up one entire wall
of the room. It shows a human figure, roughly painted, a leaping
naked man, arms and legs outspread. The figure is indistinctly
painted but its gender is impossible to mistake, as pushing ahead
of it is an enormous penis, longer than the length of the figure's
body.

Evie knows that sexuality is important in Reich's work, that
he believes a healthy attitude toward sex is the basis for healthy
living. She doesn't think she is a prude, but she argued with a
friend of hers who said that Reich was sex-crazed, sex-obsessed.
She had pointed out his ground-breaking work in psychoanalysis,
in the importance of the musculature, and the effectiveness of
some of his experiments with orgone energy. "It's not all about
sex," she'd said; "and seeing it that way is just our American Puri-
tanism coming out." But now she cannot deny that the painting
makes her uncomfortable, very uncomfortable, and she is reminded that in spite of everything she said back in Illinois, she
knows that sexuality is a very large part of Reich's focus, and she—
for some reason she is no longer sure of—has sought him out.

She hears footsteps in the hall and turns to see Reich approaching, wearing a white lab jacket. She is glad to see it; the
jacket reminds her that he is a professional, a doctor, not some
backwoods sex fiend. She stands up, happy to turn away from the
painting, but Reich walks past her to sit at his desk, next to the
wall with the painting. "So," he says, and just sits there looking at
her. Evie feels he is taking her in, observing her; it is as if he sees
her discomfort, and guesses its source. Again, there is a small smile
on his face. "How is . . ." he thinks for a moment, remembering,
"Evelyn today?"

She gives him a determined, cheerful smile. "I am fine, thank you."

"Are you ready for treatment?"

"Yes, please. I would be very grateful." She will be grateful to get into the box, to see what she experiences there, and to walk away from this office.

"I need to make some things clear before we begin," Reich says in his accented voice. He leans back in his chair, his wide face serious now. "We are doing these treatments to help build your strength so that you can better fight off any cancer still in your system. I make, however, no promises about the effectiveness of the treatments, and they will not necessarily cure any cancer you may have. Do you understand?"

"Well, yes, but . . ." She hesitates. "You do feel this is a good idea, right? You think they may help me?" I'm not just wasting my time here, she is thinking.

He leans forward, his gaze full upon her. She feels heat, rising up her face, from the intensity of his look. "I am quite sure it can help you. But orgone treatments are not a cure-all, and I don't want you angry at me if things don't go as you would hope."

She nods a brisk, affirmative nod. Already she feels a new energy, just being around the man. "I understand."

He then stands and politely takes her elbow to escort her out of the room. At the doorway, he pauses, and looks at her. "You haven't told me," he says, "what you think of my painting."

For a brief, horrible moment Evie does not know what to say, then Reich lets his head drop back with a full-throated, hearty laugh which echoes around the room.

Chapter Eight

Kiya pulls up outside Umojo on her bicycle and unhooks her helmet. The fresh air this morning feels especially good, as earlier she had been hit with a bout of nausea. The air makes her feel alive again. She locks the bike in the rack next to the salon, wondering how long she will be able to continue biking. Maybe she can bike straight on through her pregnancy, and then after get one of those baby bike seats to hook on behind her.

Clyde, at the coffee machine, sets down his cup when he sees her. He turns to give her a hug, then pushes her away, holding her shoulders to look in her face. "How are you doing, my peanut?"

She has told Clyde, and no one else at work, of her pregnancy. Now he glances at her loose shirt and murmurs in her ear, "You look great, but you can't keep it hidden forever." Looking around to make sure no one is in earshot, he says, "You know they won't fire you because you're pregnant. They can't do that."

"Shh," she says. "I know." She smiles at him, at the concerned look on his sweet face. "Why don't you and I get married, Clyde? You would be such a wonderful father."

"Well yes, honey, I would love to. But what about the real father, what's his name. Peter. Wouldn't he have something to say about that?"

"I don't think he'd mind. He doesn't have much to say to me these days about anything at all."

"Oh no. Loser boy." He looks up to see Jeny, another stylist, push through the door to the coffee room. She's wearing a colorful close-fitting dress Kiya hasn't seen before. "Beautiful girl!" he says, turning his smile on her. "That is one hot dress."

Feeling small and deflated, Kiya slips out. She sets up her tools at her station, pausing to look at herself in the mirror. Her hair could use a color touch-up, she supposes, and she doesn't think she could get away with wearing a dress like Jeny's. She wonders if being abandoned by her baby's father makes her a less-than-desirable property all around: not only as a girlfriend, but even as a friend. She wonders if she can even claim to be abandoned by her baby's father. They weren't living together, just hanging out, and now Peter hasn't called her in two weeks and (she counts) two days. Does that qualify as abandoned?

* * * *

At the grocery store fish counter, waiting to place his order, Peter becomes aware of a low-grade, steady headache. It's been building since he entered the store. Maybe Kiya is right, and it's due to fluorescent lights.

She'd shown up yesterday at his apartment after work, carrying a pan covered in aluminum foil. Vegetable lasagna, which she'd made herself. Kiya, who likes to cook as much as he does, which is not at all. He wasn't expecting her; he'd just gotten out of the shower when he heard the doorbell ring. There she stood, wearing a pink cotton dress that, with her tousled blonde hair, made her look about five years old. She held out the pan, a look on her face both hopeful and contrite. "I made this for you."

They sat on the old leather couch in Peter's living room. "What would you have done," he asked, "if I wasn't home?"

"I was going to see if I could leave it for you."

"That's nice of you," Peter said. "But why?"

"Why would I leave it?"

"I mean, why did you make it for me?"

She sat primly, ill at ease, and looked down at her hands in her lap. "I wanted to say I'm sorry."

He waited to see what she would say next, and when nothing else was forthcoming, he asked, "Sorry for what?"

She looked at him then, and he was reminded again of how pretty her eyes could be. "I'm sorry for not talking about this . . ." she gestured toward her midsection, "with you more. I'm sorry for making my decisions without seeing what you wanted to do first."

"Okay," Peter said. "Thank you. And does this mean that you're open to changing your mind about what you will do? Is that what this 'sorry' means?" He knew he sounded harsh, but what else could he say? Oh good, now everything will be fine and we'll move in together and be happy forever?

Kiya sighed, and leaned back on the couch. Her eyes caught

something in the corner of the room. "Hey, where did you get that guitar?"

Peter went over and picked it up. "From my roommate's father. Isn't it nice?"

"You're kidding me." She touched the wood gently. "It's beautiful. Can you play something?"

"Well . . ." He'd been practicing, teaching himself. He picked out a new song he was working on. With good strings and a tuning, his playing didn't sound half bad.

"That's beautiful," Kiya said, and he thought maybe she meant it.

They ate lasagna, and she told him about the book she was reading about Wilhelm Reich, about deadly orgone radiation, or whatever it was. Peter remembered that his grandmother had been treated by him. "You know," Peter said, "My grandmother had cancer when she was young, and she went to his place in Maine to see if she could get it treated. He had all these theories about sex, you know, about how we shouldn't block it. What if he didn't block it with my grandma?"

"Yes, well." Kiya seemed uncomfortable again. It couldn't have been his comment about his grandmother and Reich; she wasn't prudish. "There's something else I need to apologize for also."

Peter paused, fork in the air. "Yes?"

"Your mother." Kiya looked around the small kitchen, the beat-up linoleum floor as if searching for words. "I visited her."

She then told him then about her mother's illness. "She didn't even recognize me one day. I went into her room and she didn't know who I was."

"Is she all right now? Your mother, I mean?"

"She's getting better. She's much better than she was. But I was so upset, I just got in my car and drove to your mother's."

Peter took a moment to think about this. "I'm surprised you remembered where it was." Then, "Wait," he said. "Wait. Did you . . ." He looked at her belly.

"Yes. I told her." Kiya sat up straight in her chair, hands in her lap, like a child about to take her punishment.

Peter's reaction surprised himself. He slammed his chair back from the table and stood up, stamping a foot on the floor. Kiya flinched. "You *told* her?" he said.

Kiya's voice was small. "Well, I wouldn't just go and spend the night and not talk with her about it . . ."

"Spend the *night?*"

There was no answer to this. Kiya's head was bowed. Finally, she said, "It was late, and she invited me."

His mother, that canny soul, had not mentioned this. The fact that his mother knew that Kiya was pregnant seemed to put it in a new light for Peter; it made her pregnancy real in a way it hadn't been real before. He knew then, without a doubt, that Kiya would have a baby, would do nothing to stop the pregnancy. There would be a—impossible as it was to imagine—baby. And his mother knew. He felt as if he were a high school student again, and his friends had narced him out, turned him in to the authorities. His mother was the baby-making authority in his life, and she knew he'd been making one with this woman.

After that, the evening had not gone well. Peter couldn't get over the fact that Kiya was going ahead with this pregnancy, with or without him on board. He didn't invite her to spend the night. At the door, saying goodbye, she'd wrapped her arms around his neck and kissed him gently on the cheek. He felt the softness of her cheek on his, the faint scent of her cologne—something sweet and spicy, something familiar.

"Goodbye," he said. "Thanks for the lasagna."

At home now Peter puts his food away. He starts to unwrap the fish he bought, then remembers there is leftover lasagna. He heats a piece in the microwave and takes it over to the table, along with a book from his bookshelf—*Being and Time*. He has been missing the seriousness with which he used to read, the sense he used to have of knowledge building inside him, piling up piece by piece and gaining its own momentum, its own life. "Thus to work out the question of being means to make a being — one who questions — transparent in its being." He puts the book down and stares out the window, unseeing. A being is being made inside Kiya, "transparent." He pictures the small gelatinous thing letting light shine through it, its budding organs visible, delicately sucking its infinitesimal thumb.

* * * *

Maddie stays home the night of the faculty/staff dinner. She usually enjoys the drinks and food, the chance to dress up and celebrate with her colleagues at the beginning of the school year. She tells herself, and she told Susan, that she isn't in the mood this year; she's been to enough of those dinners to last her a lifetime. Susan had nodded thoughtfully. "I think I'll go, though," she'd said. "I'll fill you in on things." Susan lifted an eyebrow, suggestively.

Maddie takes a sunset walk after dinner, watching the sky change colors above the trees. She used to take her dog Bruno for a walk every evening. When he died a couple of years ago, she decided that she was done having dogs. Too much work, too much like having a child. Still, she misses, sometimes, the companionship, the sense of another someone close by. Back at home, she listens to a radio program on extra-sensory perception while she cooks her dinner. The radio host describes early experiments in the 1930's, using cards. Maddie stands still in the kitchen, the knife she'd been cutting carrots with in her hand. She is thinking of Mark, remembering a discussion they had about extrasensory perception, a long time ago. Mark believed it was possible; he thought, in fact, that he could see right through people, could see what was in their minds. It was ridiculous, Maddie thought, but didn't say so.

That night, though, as they made love on the mattress on the floor, Maddie was thinking of women they'd seen at a rock concert; beautiful women, one in particular, who had full breasts under a halter-top that swayed when she danced. Maddie wasn't beautiful like that; flat-chested and lean, she was just average. That night in her jealousy it seemed she had nothing, really, to recommend her. Why was Mark with her?

They began to quietly make love. As Mark hovered above her, Maddie could not get the images of women at the concert out of her mind. Women dancing, women singing, women he would rather be with . . .

Mark suddenly stopped, and whispered close to her ear, "No, Maddie, it's you. It's YOU I want to be with. No one else."

Maddie turned back to the carrots. She'd never told anyone about that night because she didn't want people thinking she was crazy. But after that, she recalled, she often felt uneasy being with Mark—if he could read her mind, did she have *any* secrets from him at all? She and Mark broke up just before she learned she was pregnant. He'd offered to marry her when he learned of the pregnancy, but he was drinking a lot then, and their relationship had already ended. It would have been a disaster, Maddie thought, to take him up on it. He seemed relieved when she declined his offer and said she would raise their child alone.

She wonders what Mark would be like now if he were still alive. She thinks he would have eventually contacted his son. He wouldn't have wanted to die without having talked with him.

After dinner, Maddie hears sounds again from the house next door. Anguished noises, and thumping, followed by the sound of someone crying—a high, childish sound. She puts her book down and moves closer to the window, listening. She hears a pounding sound, as if someone is hitting someone or something, and more crying.

Maddie wonders if she should call the police. No, she should check it out herself first. But what if something violent is going on, and he turns the violence on her? She tries to remember what her neighbor's face looks like, tries to remember if he seems as if he could be violent. He has that edge, that Maine gruffness; maybe it can quickly turn into rage, she doesn't know. She puts on her jacket and slowly zips it up, gathering her courage. It's something she must do.

The wet grass squelches under her sneakers. She sees through the darkened porch of the house next door to a lighted room, probably the kitchen. She walks up the steps and knocks on the outside door. There is the yelling again, louder now, coming from inside. She's sure they can't hear her knock; she's going to have to go inside the porch.

Maddie opens the unlocked porch door and stands in front of the door to the house, looking through the glass window. She sees her neighbor standing with his back to her in the brightly lit room. Facing him is someone she can't see well—a child, a boy probably. It is he who is doing the screaming, as her neighbor holds the boy's arms. Feeling as if she is entering a scene in the kind of movie she doesn't like to watch, Maddie knocks on the door.

The boy yells just as she knocks, and the man seems not to hear her. He holds the boy's arms down, and the boy quiets for a moment, perhaps to take a breath. Maddie knocks again. This time the man hears her, and jerks around. She sees surprise on his face, and confusion, but he does not let go of the boy. "Come in," he shouts.

The boy starts yelling as Maddie enters, thrashing around wildly. The man puts both his arms around the boy and holds him tightly, rocking slightly from side to side. In a confusion of emotions, Maddie sees that the man is trying to help the boy, who is out of control. "Can I help?" she says above the boy's noises.

The man shakes his head, continuing to hold the boy. "He'll be . . . all right," he says, breathing hard. "Just wait."

Later, after the boy falls asleep, the man—his name, he reminds Maddie, is Jack—brings two beers to where she sits in a wooden rocker on the porch. She retreated here when the boy calmed down, and stayed, listening to the sounds quiet down, the yells turning into quiet sobs, then silence. Jack lowers himself, groaning, into the rocker next to her, popping open a beer can as he does so. "So there you have it," he says and puts the can to his mouth for a long drink. "That's my grandson, Paulie. He's a sweet boy, sometimes."

"Is he . . ." Maddie pauses, uncertain, not wanting to say the wrong thing. "Autistic?"

"You got it. Autistic as hell. Other problems, too. It's tough

64

for his parents. They do their best, but they need to get away sometimes. I help out. Usually, Paulie likes it here, but sometimes he loses it."

"Sorry I couldn't be of help," Maddie says. She takes a drink of beer, bitter and cold and frothing.

"That's all right," Jack says. "There's not much to do but ride it out, make sure he doesn't hurt himself. At least that's all I know how to do."

"It must be hard," Maddie offers.

"Yup," Jack says. Again she thinks he is parodying the Mainer, parodying himself. "It ain't easy."

"Is his father your son?" Maddie asks, remembering the young man she occasionally sees here.

"Yes. He lives in Augusta, with his wife." Jack takes the last drink from his beer and gets two more from the refrigerator in the kitchen. The house, as far as Maddie noticed when she was inside, is comfortable, cozy. Overstuffed furniture in the living room, wool rugs on the floor; things, she thinks, that speak of a woman's touch, but she's never seen a woman with him. Now they sit in semi-darkness on the porch, lit only by lamplight coming through the windows of the house. She sees the lake through the dark trees, glimmering. "How about you?" Jack asks. "You have children?"

"Yes, a son. Peter lives in Portland. Works on trees there."

"That right. I could use some tree work done around here."

Maddie is suddenly aware that she is sitting in darkness, with a man who apparently has no wife, drinking, and looking out at a lake quiet in the moonlight. This, she knows, could give someone the wrong idea. She hands back the second can of beer, unopened. "Thanks, but I better be going. I didn't mean to barge in on you tonight. I just thought, you know . . ."

"Thought I was abusing someone, didn't you?" Jack grins at her, his teeth white in the darkness. "No, I'd be more subtle about it if I was doing that."

* * * *

Evie sits gingerly on a wooden folding chair in the accumulator. Dr. Reich had her take her sweater off and laid it over a nearby chair. "Are you comfortable?" he asks. She nods. "You should feel something soon after I close the door; a kind of warmth or tingling. Don't worry, it will not hurt you. We'll keep this first session short, just maybe fifteen minutes. All right now?"

"Good," Evie says. He closes the door gently, and she is alone in the darkness. A faint line of light comes from around the edges of the closed door, and for a moment she feels alarmed, panicky; is she trapped? She closes her eyes and takes a deep breath. She has asked for this, it was her idea; it will be fifteen minutes only, and will help her. Or at least, a small voice says inside her, it won't hurt her.

She begins to feel warm, but maybe it's just from being in an enclosed space. The warmth seems to come from inside her and is comforting, not frightening. Sitting in the small dark space reminds her of something from her childhood, being enclosed somewhere dark. An old memory; she thinks it was in her neighbor's house, a closet. Maybe she was playing hide and seek? A sense of excitement, of being hidden away and triumphant, pride at hiding so well from the older kids. Then a door opening, light coming in—a sense of air—then the door closing again and Rickie, her friend Alice's older brother, there in the enclosed space with her.

Evie, sitting on the folding chair, twists uncomfortably at this memory, at its unpleasantness. Did something happen in the closet at Alice's house? Why does she remember this, her childish excitement turning to fear, and then anger and shame, if it didn't happen? But why hasn't she thought of it before this moment?

The door opens then, light and air flooding in, but instead of an adolescent boy, it is Dr. Reich standing there, looking at her.

She thinks on the drive home about what it was like, being inside the accumulator. She had been expecting physical sensations, and that's what Dr. Reich asked her about after she got out of the box: yes, a little sensation of tingling and warmth; no, she didn't have any unpleasant sensations; and yes, she could make it back for regular treatments. They agree on three or four times a week. But she hadn't expected a memory dredged up out of nowhere, or the feelings associated with it.

In the memory, if that's what it was, Rickie seemed to be about twelve years old, which would have made Evie just eight. Alice, a year older than her, was Evie's best friend throughout her childhood. They played together nearly every day. They drifted apart in high school, and Evie hasn't seen her for years. Though she hasn't thought of him in all that time, Evie remembers hearing that Rickie enlisted in the Army after graduating from high school. It was 1947 then, the war well over, but he still wanted to see some action. She'd never liked him, always found him unpleasant; was this why? Did he hurt her when she was a kid, and she forgot about it until today? She hasn't consciously remembered this moment before but something about the memory feels familiar, feels well-used, as if it's been stored somewhere and hidden, but not really forgotten.

Evie shakes her head and rolls down her window more, letting the cool mountain air whip through her hair. She thinks of the house painting waiting for her. If she is to drive to Orgonon several times a week, it's good the old car is still chugging along.

Chapter Nine

"I like Montessori daycares and schools," Kiya says. She is blow-drying Jeny's hair after work in the salon. Clyde has just given Kiya's highlights a touch-up and is sitting next to Jeny, listening. The salon looks different at night, with the bright lights inside and the darkness outside through the tall arched windows. "I mean, don't you? Aren't they the best?"

"I guess so," Jeny says.

"Oh sure," Clyde says. "But . . . money? Those places cost, you know. Will the father pay for that?"

"Well, I'll work . . ." Kiya says, uncomfortably. She twists Jeny's hair vigorously around a brush, aiming the hairdryer with the other hand.

"Oh honey, you are so sweet," Clyde says, wrapping his arm around Kiya's shoulders. Kiya hears the condescension in his tone, and stiffens. "No, I mean it, you are," he says. "Well, I need to go now, beautiful girls. Take care, don't go overboard." He kisses Kiya's cheek, says, "Remember I love you."

When he is gone, Kiya styles Jeny's hair in silence for a time. They are alone in the salon. She fluffs Jeny's hair in her hands, holding them on either side of Jeny's face, then drops it. "That looks fantastic," Jeny says. "You are so talented. You are the best stylist here, you know that? Better than me, better than Jacques. Better than anyone."

"Thank you, sweetie," Kiya says. "But do you think I'm nuts? For wanting to have this baby, for having these plans?"

"Oh my god, no." Jeny stands up, brushing hair from her skirt. "Maybe you aren't the most practical person in the world, but I admire you. You have so much courage." Yup, Kiya tells herself; she thinks I'm crazy. Everyone knows now, everyone is being super kind and positive and Kiya can't stand it.

She takes the push broom and begins sweeping up the bits of hair. "Do you know why my parents named me Kiya?" she asks.

"No, why?"

"Because it's the sound a seagull makes. My mother liked the sound that much." Whenever she remembers that, Kiya has an image of a gull, wheeling above the waves, and it calms her.

At home, Kiya lies on her bed with the lights on. She feels a deep weariness, a kind of groggy tiredness she didn't know before she became pregnant. She glances at the framed photo of Andrew on her dresser. He had just finished playing a game of tennis with their father, back when their father was a presence in their lives. Andrew is sitting on a bench in the sunshine, his forearms resting against his knees. He is wearing a white shirt, looking up into the camera. He is laughing and looks happy but there is just a trace, in the shadows of his face, of the darkness that consumed him later.

Kiya knew something was consuming him, something was making him sick and angry and not himself, but she didn't know what it was. No one knew. He sat in his room for months on end. Their mother was worried and tried to help, but didn't know what to do. Kiya first tried to help Drew, then she got irritated at him. She tried so hard to keep herself stable and happy, put so much effort into it, and it seemed that Drew was just letting things slide, throwing his life away. Their mother finally made an appointment with a counselor for him, but Drew died before the first appointment. Their father had quit his law practice months before then and found himself another job on the far end of the country, in San Francisco.

Back home for his son's funeral, her father took Kiya out to dinner. It was one of the worst meals Kiya ever had. She doesn't remember what she ordered, because she couldn't eat it, and she and her father couldn't find any way to talk with one another. He had a little beard, which he'd never had before, and it made him look like someone else, someone she didn't know. They moved silverware around on the table like people on the worst kind of blind date. She knew he had a girlfriend in California, and she wouldn't ask about her, or his life there. At the funeral the next day, she remembers how her father put his arms around her mother, and how her mother stood stiff and unyielding in his embrace.

69

Kiya turns on her side, cradling her full stomach. She wonders if her father thinks it was his fault that his son killed himself. It's true his abrupt departure didn't help with Drew's depression. She wonders if the thought torments him. Maybe she should make more of an effort to communicate. He sends a check on her birthday and on Christmas; he calls on those days, and they have stilted conversations. Kiya finally emailed him to tell him that her mother had been ill, but she was better now. He wrote back "Give her my love." Kiya stared at those words for a long time. At the next visit with her mother she thought about bringing it up, but couldn't.

A month out of the hospital, Kiya's mother is still recovering. She walks to the nearby market for groceries and exercise most days, and Kiya picks up anything else she needs. Her mother used to work in their father's law office, but hasn't worked in years. Before she got sick she spent some of her time painting watercolors. On nice days she walked down to the water and painted there, sitting on a bench. Her painting style is unschooled but energetic, with surprisingly vivid and dark colors, not the pastel colors one might expect. Kiya has one of her mother's portraits of flowers hanging above her table. They are riotous, angry slashes of color.

Kiya didn't know what to expect from her mother when she told her she was pregnant, but she wasn't expecting her mother to burst into tears. She hadn't seen her crying like that, really sobbing, since Drew's funeral. Alarmed, Kiya couldn't tell if the tears were from happiness or sadness.

"It's both," her mother said when Kiya asked. "I don't know, really. It just strikes me so." Her face was red and blotchy, her face wet. Kiya brought tissues from the bathroom and handed them to her.

"You couldn't tell?" Kiya asked, looking down at her belly.

Her mother shook her head, then nodded, laughed. "I wondered what was going on. Maybe it crossed my mind to wonder if you were pregnant, but thought surely you couldn't be, or you'd tell me."

"You were sick," Kiya said. "I didn't want you to worry."

"Telling a mother not to worry is like telling the rain not to fall." Her mother dabbed at her eyes. "What does Peter think of this?"

Kiya hesitated. Her mother had met Peter once briefly when Kiya brought him by to say hello. She couldn't lie to her mother, not about this. "He's not sure what to think," she said, and her face gave the rest away.

"I see." Her mother reached across the table and took her daughter's hand. "Are you sure you want to do this? With or without Peter? It will be so hard."

"I'm sure. I'm very sure." She rubbed her stomach gently, feeling its soft fullness. Every time she told someone she was pregnant, she felt as if she was giving the little one inside her more energy, more love, more of a chance at a life. "I'm happy," she said, and smiled at her mother, and for the moment, that was not a lie.

❋ ❋ ❋ ❋

Peter thinks maybe the guitar has magic properties. How else to explain how good it is starting to sound as he plays it? He took piano lessons when he was a kid, then picked up the guitar and the banjo, but wasn't ever really serious about them. On this guitar, his playing sounds like music, real music. Home from work, he picks up the guitar and plays before even taking a shower. His fingers are becoming more agile, more flexible.

He doesn't think of Kiya, doesn't think of the future. It will take care of itself. He rides the waves of autumn energy, the air crisp and colorful, the sounds of music hanging in the air, waiting for him to pick them out like ripe apples hanging from a tree. He is young and he is healthy, and he likes the way Toni looks at him when he sees her working behind the counter at a coffee shop in the Old Port. She wipes her hands on her apron and sits beside him in a booth on her break. She has dark shiny hair pulled back, and a dimple on one side of her face. She likes him, he can tell, but doesn't want to get close to him. She is keeping her distance, and that makes sense to him. He's a person one should be careful about, after all; he's not trustworthy. She's from far northern Maine, from "the county," and is a down-to-earth, sensible girl. She doesn't say why she won't go out with him, but it probably has to do with what he told her the first night he met her, the night he learned Kiya was planning to have a baby. He can't think of it as "his baby," and he can't think that he is going to "be a father." Those are words for other people, other places; he doesn't accept them.

Toni is telling him now about something new the coffee shop is doing. "They have this lower level, a cellar really, but they're fixing it up to be very cool, and they're going to sell wine there. By the bottle, that is; nice wine, at reasonable prices. Once they get it fixed up, they will have wine-tastings. And I think they should have someone play music. You should see if they'd hire you. You'd be perfect; sitting on a high stool in a corner, with this little light shining on you." She creates the scene with her hands in the air. "By yourself, wearing a flannel shirt and blue jeans—the earthy look—playing guitar and singing songs you wrote. Simple, the perfect backdrop to tasting wine."

"Yeah, that would be great," Peter says. "But Toni, you never heard me play. How do you know I'm any good?"

She fixes him with a look. "I know some things. I just know. I can tell. Don't doubt me on this."

She does know things. He says, "You should at least come over to my place and hear me play before you promote me to your boss. You don't want to embarrass yourself."

"Sure," she said. "I'll do that. Oh, look at the time. I'm late." And she slides out of the booth, slips away.

Peter finds a scrap of paper in his pocket and writes down his telephone number. He stands at the counter, waiting to catch Toni's eye. When she comes over, he gives it to her. "Come on by sometime," he says.

Without a woman to fill up his free time, Peter doesn't know what to do with himself. Work makes his arms and shoulders tired but leaves him with another kind of energy, a jittery, diffuse feeling that he should be doing something. He's wasting his time. Tree work is good, and it pays the bills, but he doesn't think he wants to be doing it when he turns thirty, or forty. He's not sure what he would like to be doing. The only thing besides sex that soothes this feeling, that makes him able to forget about it, is playing the guitar. The strings crossing the frets are a grid, the longitude and latitude of music. He practices finger-picking patterns, plucking out chords and melodies. In the absorption of using his hands, of learning how to create sounds that make sense, he forgets his anxiety, his feeling that he should be doing something else. The chords are mapping some territory inside himself, and that is enough.

When the phone rings and a number comes up he doesn't recognize, he almost doesn't answer it. He finally puts the guitar down and picks it up, and hears Toni's slightly husky voice. "I didn't think you'd call," Peter says.

"If I'm telling the boss she should hire you, I thought I better take you up on that offer to hear you play."

⁎ ⁎ ⁎ ⁎

On the Monday after the faculty/staff dinner, Susan leans close to Maddie in the small lounge, as Maddie pours coffee. "Ron and Jane were sitting together," Susan says, "but it didn't look like they were having a good time. They didn't talk much, you know?"

"No? No holding hands? No kissing?"

"Eww!" Susan says, laughing. "Can you imagine?"

"I'd rather not," Maddie says. She takes her coffee back to her desk. She sits in front of her computer, checking email absently as Susan follows her in, still talking. She doesn't want to tell Susan about her own Ron and Jane sighting over the weekend.

She had gone to the gym for yoga, as she does on some Saturday mornings. She prefers to use a public gym downtown rather than the university gym, as it is less crowded and has fewer young students. She likes being surrounded by older, softer bodies, by the character that shows through the lines of peoples' faces. She was warming up on the stationary bicycles that faced the street through one-way glass when she saw Ron and Jane. The view was perfect; they were directly across the street, and she could see them, but they couldn't see her. They paused at the sandwich shop, hesitated, and sat at a small table outdoors. The day was overcast but warm. Ron went inside, while Jane waited for him at the table. As she waited Jane's shoulders slumped, and she gazed unseeing at the street.

73

After a moment Ron returned carrying two takeout cups. Jane sat up and smiled, but to Maddie, she looked strained. It was 9:30 a.m.; had they spent the night together? They sipped their drinks—Maddie knew that Ron's would be black coffee—without speaking. After a short time, they stood up. Ron glanced around, probably to see if anyone was watching them (if only he knew, Maddie thought), and put his arms around Jane for a brief hug. A goodbye hug, she thought, as they smiled at one another, then went in opposite directions.

Maddie had pedaled slowly on the bike, thinking. She was glad that wasn't her down there; glad she didn't have to deal with the awkwardness of dating, of spending the night together (which, if she had to guess based on what she saw, did not turn out all that well), of saying goodbye, and the tired, confused day which would follow.

Maddie doesn't tell Susan about what she saw; she will give Ron and Jane that little bit of privacy. Instead, she tells her of her experience at her neighbor's house. "I'd been hearing these noises and really thought someone was being abused. Screaming, shouting. It was his grandson making the noises. Autism, I guess. Just a kid having a tantrum."

"Aw." Susan's face grows soft in sympathy. "It must be hard having a child with problems like that. I mean my kids had tantrums, god knows, but they fell in the normal range. At the time, though, you feel like the world is falling apart."

Maddie remembers the expression on Jack's face as he looked over his shoulder to see her there; it was anguished and afraid. By the time he'd joined her on the porch, he was his calm and sardonic self. In control.

Maddie doesn't remember Peter having tantrums. He was a quiet, solitary kid, but maybe that was because of where they lived. He finally found a friend who lived close enough to visit, but he still spent most of his time alone. She is about to answer an email when a memory surfaces: Peter, around six years old—not long after they moved to Maine—closing himself in his bedroom and crying. Was that a tantrum? It went on for a long time, she recalled. What was it about? Something to do with the move, she thinks, with all he missed back in Illinois. She remembers standing outside the door, asking if she could come in. He must have said no because she didn't. She wishes she were there again. She'd open that door; she'd go inside the room and take that little boy in her arms.

That reminds her of an earlier memory, when Peter was born. Maddie was living alone in Chicago, taking college classes. When she started labor, she didn't want to call Mark. She called her mother instead, but her mother couldn't get there until the next day. Maddie had arranged to have a friend come with her for labor, but they wouldn't let her go into the delivery room with her—that was only for the baby's father, she was told. The friend, Ellen, stayed until after the baby was born, and when they took the baby away, the friend also left for home.

In the hospital, Maddie lay in a room all by herself. She was alone and empty, and the parking lot outside the window looked unbearably sad. Her sobs brought in a nurse, who asked what was wrong.

"I want my *baby*," Maddie cried, embarrassed at her sobs but hurting and alone.

The nurse had laughed, twitching the blanket on Maddie's bed. "You'll get him soon enough, don't worry." By the time someone finally brought Peter to her arms, Maddie felt irrevocably changed, convinced of the sadness of the world in a new way.

She finds it comforting, sometimes, to visit Alex. When she is troubled by memories, such as the one of Peter crying in his room, or her crying alone after his birth, it soothes her to give Alex his hug, to massage his hands. She lifts one of his arms above his head, stretching out the muscles for him in a way he can't. Tired of reading picture books, she starts reading Roald Dahl's *The Witches*. Perhaps she is living through Peter's childhood again, she muses, by reading these books. If she is, she guesses there is no problem in that. She reads the book's first line: "I myself had two separate encounters with witches before I was eight years old."

* * * *

When Evie nears Mt. Vernon, rain is spattering the windshield. Mt. Vernon is a tiny town, with houses and a few local businesses lining the road next to the lake. She decides to treat herself to a café meal. She parks beside the road and enters the small, cheerful diner. A waitress carrying a tray waves her into the room, where she sits at a table at the back, with a view of the lake. She orders a cheese sandwich and vegetable soup and eats them slowly, looking out the window.

The waitress stops to chat when she brings Evie her check. She wears a white and yellow checked apron around her waist and looks harassed, with hair loosened from a ponytail falling in front of her face. She pushes it back, and refills Evie's coffee. "Sorry it was so slow coming," she says. "We're short on help because the girl who was supposed to work with me just up and quit this morning."

"Is that right," Evie says. "It's no problem. Do they need someone to work here, then?"

The waitress looks at her, assessing. "Maybe. Talk to the owner." She points to a gray-haired man, standing behind the cash register.

Evie is making good headway painting the house; it is scraped, primed, and she is ready to begin the first coat. She thinks she can finish the first coat with just a week's work, and be done with the second before her parents arrive. Why not find a job? It would make her parents happy, and make her feel better about filling up the car with gas money from her bank account. She brushes crumbs off her lap and stands up. The man at the register looks at her, unsmiling, over glasses pushed down on his nose as she approaches.

"Hello," Evie says. She flashes her confident, midwestern smile, the one she learned to use while working at the Crow's Nest Café in Urbana. It helped convince her customers, and herself, that things were under control, and now she sees it thaw the man's expression, though he doesn't go so far as to return her smile.

"Yeah?" he says.

When Evie first visited Maine, this kind of response—unsmiling, gruff, laconic—convinced her that New Englanders were unfriendly and rude. After a time, however, she came to see that the gruffness was a cover, sort of like the door to a house, that when opened revealed a friendly garrulity. "I wonder if you need

76

someone to work here," she says. "I live nearby, and I have experience."

"Huh," the man grunted. "What kind of experience?"

After a short conversation, the man asks for the name and phone number of Evie's employer at the Crow's Nest. Evie digs in her handbag and is grateful to find the small, beat-up leather address book with the information. The man tells her to stop by the next day. "We'll see if we can put you to work."

Chapter Ten

Kiya, small round belly pushing out her sweater, walks past a cathedral on her lunch break. Impulsively, she turns in on the sidewalk toward the door. Autumn flowers in yellow and rust colors line the walk. The heavy doors are locked, but she stares upward, at the circular stained-glass image above the door. It is the Virgin Mary, in white and deep blue robes, looking down at the child she holds. He sleeps against her chest, his gold halo sparkling like ancient jewels. The Virgin's halo also is elaborate and sparkling, but not as bright as the halo of the child. It's only right, Kiya thinks, and whispers it: "It's only right." She's not sure what she means; she is transfixed by the image. The beauty of the young mother, the purity of her expression, the roundness and sweetness of the small infant create a sensation inside Kiya which is somewhere between beauty and pain. While she is staring upward at the image she feels something move deep inside her, something small and tentative, gentle tappings like butterfly wings in a place where no other person has ever touched her before. It could be gas, but she doesn't think it is; it is a message, like radio waves from another universe.

She walks away slowly from the image, head down. She has been spoken to, she has been blessed. An angel has come to her, bearing good tidings. The child has been gathering universal energy and growing stronger and more powerful with every minute. It is not an accident that the first time she felt the baby move, she was staring at an image of the Virgin Mary holding the Savior of the World. As Kiya walks down the street she feels surrounded by light.

Her boss had called her into his office earlier this morning, for a "chat." Nick had asked her how she was doing. He said she looked great. "You feeling good?" he asked.

"Fantastic," Kiya said. She smiled and twisted her fingers, wondering what he was going to say.

He leaned back in his chair, swept his dark-blonde hair back with his fingers and looked at her through thick-framed rectangular glasses. He finally got down to it. "You can work as long as you feel comfortable working. And you can take an unpaid leave for as long as you want, before or after the baby is born. We'll try to keep your place for you. I can guarantee you can have your job back if you take a ten-week leave; after that, we'll try, but there's no promises."

Kiya nodded, slowly. A ten-week unpaid leave. She has $1200 in her checking account. Rent, due in two weeks, would be $900. And if she went back to work after the baby was born, there would be—she supposes—daycare costs. Or babysitter, or whatever. Maybe there are government programs to help out.

"Do you know yet how long you'll want to take off?" Nick asked. "I mean, I know you can't really tell, but what are your plans?" He and his wife have a three-year-old son. He looked at her as if she would have an answer.

"Well, I don't know yet," Kiya said. "I'll let you know."

Now, as she walks slowly on the Portland sidewalk, feeling the sun warming a cool breeze, Kiya lets the stained-glass image fill her thoughts, replacing Nick's words. From somewhere—the times she went to church as a child, maybe—a bible quotation comes to her. "Consider the lilies of the field, how they grow . . ." They don't work, they don't toil or spin, yet are beautiful. Life will provide. She imagines white lilies blowing sideways in a spring breeze, in the sun.

When Kiya checks her cell phone between haircuts that afternoon, she finds a message from Sarah, her psychiatrist. She had canceled her last few appointments with Sarah, leaving messages that she was sick, then said she'd call her when she wanted to make an appointment. Sarah doesn't know she is pregnant. Now Kiya hears her cheery, calm voice float over the phone. "Hey Kiya, I've missed you. Just checking in to make sure things are well with you. If you've switched to someone else, that's entirely cool. I've just been thinking of you and hope you will call back and let me know what's up. Thanks!" Kiya pictures Sarah's short, rather scraggly blond hair, her wire-framed glasses, her big smile. She likes Sarah. Sarah has always been good to her and has tried to help. But Sarah doesn't understand that Kiya can survive quite well without medications; Sarah is too connected to the medical/pharmaceutical industry. She sucks on the teat of the industry. Kiya laughs, picturing Sarah hanging from a large, robotic tit, her mouth clamped to it while her feet dangle in the air.

After work Kiya finishes the tofu/kale sandwich she brought for lunch and gets on her bike. She has a doctor's appointment in an hour, but she doesn't want to keep it. She feels fine; she feels more than fine. She's eating well and taking her vitamins, and she felt the baby move today. The doctor said something about a sonogram, and Kiya doesn't want a sonogram. There's no reason for it; it's unnecessary, and more medical intrusion. She doesn't want to know if the baby is a boy or a girl. It's a special baby whatever it is.

Kiya pulls into a little park by the side of the road and gets off her bike. She calls the doctor's office and tells them she has to cancel her appointment for later today. The receptionist asks if she wants to reschedule; Kiya says she will call back. Feeling airy and unencumbered, she gets back on her bike and pedals toward her apartment. The light follows her, wrapping her and her baby in warmth and protection.

✢ ✢ ✢ ✢

"That's good. That's really good." Toni, sitting on the floor listening to Peter play his music, nods to her words. "I was right, I could tell. You'd be perfect for that gig. She was asking me for suggestions, and I'll give her your name."

"I'd be cheap," Peter says.

"Not too cheap. I'll see what she's offering and let you know."

Peter puts his guitar back in the case he bought for it. "No, cheap. I'm not experienced. I'd do it for free."

"C'mon," Toni says, sitting on the couch next to him. "Have some self-respect. You're better than a lot of people out there."

"Okay, okay." He goes to the refrigerator and brings an open bottle of white wine along with two glasses to the coffee table.

80

"How are things going with your baby momma?"

Peter shakes his head slowly. "We don't talk. I don't see her anymore."

"Yeah but . . . what will happen after the baby is born? Will you be around?" Toni sips from her glass, looking at him over the rim.

"She seems to want to do this all by herself. So that's probably what will happen."

"Did she *say* she didn't want you involved?"

Peter looks over at Toni, not speaking.

"Sorry," she says, taking the hint. "I'm just curious. It's a big deal, you know?"

"Babies get born and grow up without fathers around all the time. It happens. I don't remember my father at all. I turned out okay."

"Yeah, but didn't you want to know your dad? Wouldn't you have been happier to have him around?"

Peter shrugs. He is beginning to feel that anxiety again and needs to do something with his hands. Since Toni seems to be in no mood to let him put them on her, he picks up the guitar again and starts picking something soft. "I don't know. Sometimes kids are better off without their dads around. What if their dads are no good at being a dad? Better he weren't there, right?"

Toni leans back on the couch. "My dad isn't perfect, but he's such a part of who I am. I can't imagine growing up without that. I'm kind of like a clothesline, you know? Strung between two poles? My mom and my dad. Without one of them, I'd just be flopping around."

"And no one could hang any clothes on you."

"Right. They couldn't pin anything on me." She smiles at him, her dimple showing. Peter thinks maybe she might let him kiss her, after all.

The wine cellar is chilly, but two lights aimed at the little stage where Peter plays keep that area warm. Jasmin, the manager, has set up a microphone for him, set on low. She wants the crowd to be able to talk about the wine, and to buy it.

He flexes his fingers to warm them up. Toni, sitting at a little table to the side, gives him a smile. She looks pretty in a black dress, with her hair tied up. He has kissed her, many times, but that's all. He finds himself strangely shy about going farther, and she doesn't encourage him. Besides, kissing is fun.

He strikes a chord, then another, and begins to pick the melody. The group quiets for a minute, listening, then starts their conversation again, at a lower pitch. Another couple make their way down the narrow twisting stairway; this is not an event for the handicapped. He keeps the music quiet, playing instrumental for a while. He begins to sing when people seem to be feeling comfortable, when they have a glass or two of wine in front of them. They continue their conversations, but there is light, scattered applause at the end of songs. Peter likes the applause, but he is really playing for one person, who is wearing a black dress with some little things in it that sparkle when they hit the light, someone who smiles in a certain way when she hears something she likes. Someone who doesn't know, yet, that Peter does not have what it takes to be a father.

* * * *

There were no lakes in Maddie's childhood. Maddie's mother and father had a small dairy farm in central Illinois. There was a small pond, however, on the farm, and it was her favorite place. In winter her father shoveled it so they could ice skate. It was too muddy to swim in, but in summer she would take a book, a blanket and an apple through the fields to sit under the trees by its edge, reading.

The farm wasn't a great success, but they managed. Her parents worked all day, and in the evenings the three of them would curl up on the couch, eating popcorn popped on the stove and watching "Gilligan's Island" or "Gunsmoke." On Sundays, her mother would make a picnic in a basket, and they would take it out to the pond. Her parents were happy, she thinks; they argued, but they laughed, and at times they would cuddle with each other on the couch.

Maddie wonders what her life would be like now if Alex were still well. She would have moved in with him. They would have gotten married; she thinks they would be happily married, cuddling on couches, watching movies together. But what if it hadn't worked out, their living together? She wonders what made her think she could ever live with a man happily. Maybe she just isn't the type. She hopes that Peter manages to live with someone happily, hopes he gets married. She hopes she hasn't passed a curse on to him.

In October, the weather turns colder. Maddie builds a fire in the stove and contemplates bringing in the dock. It must be done before the lake freezes, but it's a heavy old wooden thing. She calls Peter and asks if he can come up to help. "You can bring Kiya," Maddie says, just to see what he will say.

"No, that's not going to happen." They have talked briefly about Kiya's pregnancy, but it's a touchy subject. "I'd be happy to come up and help, but not with Kiya. And not this weekend. I have a gig."

"A gig?" she says. The word is one she has not heard him use before.

"I'm playing my guitar at a café in the neighborhood. And singing."

"Peter. I had no idea."

"Yes, well . . . that's what's going on. Maybe next weekend. But Greg wants me to come in on Saturdays to do tree work for a few weeks, while we still can."

Maddie hates to ask her neighbor—first, she breaks into a family situation, then she has to ask him for help. But it's what neighbors do in Maine, right? It's the neighborly way. He offered. She tells herself she'd help him if the situations were reversed. His dock is a lightweight aluminum one; she's sure he can manage it by himself.

"Sure," he says. "No problem. I'll be right over." When he comes, he's wearing knee-high rubber boots over pants.

"You'll probably get those wet," Maddie says, gesturing at the pants. She is wearing shorts and water shoes.

"No problem," he says. "Now how is this thing put together?"

Maddie tries to unscrew the metal pieces holding the wooden sections together. After a moment, she hands the wrench over to Jack and lets him do it. Together they pull the heavy pieces up the rocky slope to the deck. Maddie drops an edge of the dock onto her foot, and lets loose a few choice words. Jack gives her a look, but when he slips on the rocks and bangs his shin, he does the same. "We're a pair, ain't we," he says with a grin.

Finally, the wooden pieces are upright, resting against the broad trunk of the white pine. Maddie covers them with a tarp, putting bricks on the edges to hold them down. "That's quite a job," Jack says. He is breathing heavily from the effort.

"It sure is. I keep saying I'll get a new dock, but never do." She looks at him; his pants are soaked above the boots, and his arms are smeared with dirt. "Why don't you change your pants," she says, "and come back over for dinner? It's the least I can do."

Inside the house, Maddie curses herself as she cuts vegetables for stew. What was she thinking? The words just popped out; she didn't plan them. Now he would think for certain that she had designs on him. In her frustration, she cuts a finger, and lets out a sharp cry.

As she wraps a band-aid around the finger, Maddie tells herself to calm down. Asking him over for stew is a neighborly thing to do, not a come-on. She'll be friendly, not seductive; he'll figure it out. He's not her type. And besides, she likes eating with someone more than eating alone. Food tastes better when it's shared.

Jack shows up at her door, cleaned up and carrying a six-pack of Heineken. "It's all I had," he says, as he sets it on the table.

"No problem," she says. "But I'll have wine. I'm just making fish stew. Nothing fancy."

Jack settles his bulk in a chair. "You don't know," he says, "how much I love fish stew. Especially when someone else is cooking it. Especially when that someone is a woman."

Here it is, Maddie thinks. She turns away to pour herself a

glass of wine, planning her speech, and when she turns back Jack speaks before she can. "And by that, I mean that women are just better cooks than men. Better cooks than the men I know, at any rate. Men are better at lifting docks, women are better at making fish soup."

Maddie considers. "All right," she says. "I don't know if it's true or not, but I'll drink to that."

As they eat, Maddie says, "My friend Alex made wonderful fish stews. He taught me how. So he proves you wrong."

"He's a great chef, then, and a good teacher. Because this is delicious."

"He doesn't make them anymore," Maddie says. Again the words came out without her thinking them or planning to say them. Having said that, she has to explain. "He's in the Lakewood Nursing home," she says. "He's not doing any cooking." She takes another drink of wine.

Jack nods, thoughtfully. They eat in silence for a moment. "My wife tried to teach me to cook," he says. "Before she passed away. It never took." He gives Maddie a quick, sideways smile. "I can grill burgers and put bagged salad in a bowl."

"Then you won't starve. I'm sorry about your wife."

He eats, takes a drink of beer. "Thank you." He looks out the window, points to where a small white sailboat floats silently on the lake in the fading light. "Nice, huh? Better than a noisy motorboat."

Maddie thinks about asking why, if he likes the silent sailboat, he insists on using electric weed-whackers and lawn mowers on his patch of grass, but she manages to stop herself.

※ ※ ※ ※

The next day when Evie steps into the accumulator box, she is wary. She wants to be open and comfortable so the orgone energy can work on her, but she also feels a deep, uneasy fear. She doesn't want any unexpected childhood memories rising up like monsters in the dark.

She perches on the chair in the dark, a book in one hand and a flashlight in the other. Dr. Reich has told her it would be okay, if she is bored, for her to turn on the light and read, but that it would be better to leave it off and just sit there if she can. She wants to be the good student, the good patient, so she sits still, head leaning against the wall behind her.

She waits to feel the warmth inside her but feels nothing. The darkness reminds her of the bedroom where she sleeps in the cottage; it is dark in there at night, but she hears noises from outside, calls of loons and swishing of trees and water. She remembers the moment, earlier today, when she walked along the shore and frightened a white heron, which took off close to her. As it flew above her head, great wings flapping in its ungainly rise, she saw one feather fall from its body. She tried to stay under it as it twisted, back and forth, in the air on its way down, until it finally landed in the water next to the dock. It seemed to mean something to her, some kind of message, though one she can't interpret.

At last, she feels a tingling, then a warmth, though not as strongly as she felt it yesterday. Maybe she is guarded, protecting herself emotionally, and it is hindering the energy from its work. She tries to relax. She thinks she feels an intensified sensation of warmth where she had the melanoma removed, the two-inch scar on her back. When she thinks of the mole, she can't help but imagine cancer cells from it racing through her body, stretching out irregularly like a spreading mole on her skin, reaching out for the lymph nodes, the holy grail. She thinks idly of holy grail; such a weird idea. It must have been sexual in some way, even to the knights who were searching for it, she thinks. Something ultimate . . .

Again, unbidden, comes the image of a door opening, a figure standing there. This time the figure seems enveloped in the light coming from behind it, like a magazine illustration showing a figure standing in the light at the end of the tunnel, or what someone sees as they approach death. "Oh for goodness sake . . ." Evie whispers. How ridiculous is that? Rickie Simon appearing as Jesus, welcoming her to the afterlife. She doesn't think so. If that's the best her subconscious has to offer, she is disappointed.

She can just make out the hands of her watch. She's been in here twenty minutes, just ten more to go. She opens the book—a collection of stories by J.D. Salinger, billed on the cover as "Explosive and absorbing"—but she can't see without the light. Sighing, feeling as if she is failing in some way, Evie switches on the flashlight and begins to read. "Just recently, by airmail, I received an invitation to a wedding that will take place in England . . ."

When half an hour has passed, Evie sits up straight, looking toward the door impatiently. Another few minutes pass; she hears voices outside, Reich's voice and another one she doesn't recognize. Footsteps finally approach, and Dr. Reich opens the door. "Sorry," he says. "You can open this yourself any time you need to, actually."

Evie steps out carefully, a bit dazed by the light. The air in the room feels cool and seems to move around on the skin of her arms and legs in ways she hadn't noticed before. She feels the small hairs on her arms lift, attentive. A tall young man with dark hair is standing next to Dr. Reich. "This is a colleague, Dr. Anderson." The man dips his head toward Evie and smiles. "How do you feel?" Reich asks.

Evie nods. Her cheeks feel flushed. "A little warm. But good," she adds.

"No headache?"

She shakes her head. "Evie suffered from melanoma," Reich says to Dr. Anderson. "She is healthy but concerned about the cancer spreading. I don't believe it has spread, but intervention in this stage can be an excellent preventative. It helps the body build its natural defenses." The dark-haired man nods. Evie feels observed, like their guinea pig. Then Dr. Reich looks at her, his eyes compelling and direct, and the feeling goes away. "Next Monday, then?" he asks.

"Next Monday." When Evie steps outdoors and walks to her car, the air is wondrously cool on her arms, and the trees' movement against the sky makes her feel something inside her chest, as if the world is moving inside her, as well as outside.

Chapter Eleven

At work, Kiya begins to feel strange. She feels suddenly as if the air has been let out of the day, the sunlight dimmed. She has trouble keeping up a conversation with her clients and cutting hair at the same time; she has to stop to think about what to say to a question and forgets where she was when she turns her attention back to the head of hair in front of her. A cold coming on, perhaps, or a virus. She looks out the window at the building across the street. It looks gray and bland, slightly malevolent. Perhaps something—the Deadly Orgone Radiation Reich wrote about, perhaps—is sucking all the juices out of the atmosphere, all the marrow from her bones. She shivers.

On her way to visit her mother, she thinks maybe it is a virus of some sort. She is starting to feel headachy and weak. Of course, she won't mention this to her mother. She freshens her lipstick and prepares a smile before she knocks on the door, and is rewarded by her mother's smile. "Kiya, sweetheart, come in."

When Kiya asks how her mother is, she says, "Oh, you know. Good enough." Kiya asks if her mother made it to her doctor's visit this morning, and her mother says "Of course. He says I'm doing well. So I guess I am. How are you doing?" She looks at Kiya, her face uncertain.

"I'm wonderful." When her mother looks unconvinced, Kiya tells her, "I got a thirty-dollar tip today." It's true; a woman who's been coming to Kiya for years always gives her a big tip. Her mother's expression brightens at the news. Kiya marvels at her power to make things all right for her mother.

After she finishes her tea, Kiya says she has to go. "I'm meeting a friend for dinner," she says. "Jeny, from work." It's not true, but she wants to go home, and she doesn't want her mother to worry.

At home, she lies on the couch, covering herself with a blanket. She is shivering. The flu, she supposes, but she doesn't want it to cross over to the baby. Can babies in the womb become ill? At the thought of her baby, feeling feverish and ill with no one to touch its forehead and talk to it, no one to kiss it in its prison inside her, Kiya feels so sad that she starts to cry.

Crying makes her head throb and her sinuses congested. Getting up, she goes to her bookshelf. She reaches down to a section of narrow books on the bottom shelf and takes one over to the couch. She opens it and, holding it on her lap, begins to read. "The night Max wore his wolf suit and made mischief of one kind/ and another/ his mother called him 'WILD THING!'/ and Max said, 'I'LL EAT YOU UP!'/ so he was sent to bed without eating anything." She rubs her stomach as she reads, and the words and gesture comfort her. She whispers, "I will never send you to bed without your supper. No matter how wild you are."

Kiya throws up during the night, and doesn't fall deeply asleep until light is touching the sky. She is dreaming of large warm but frightening monsters in some secluded place—an island—with no way to reach someone to help her. She is wondering if she can make friends with the monsters since they are all she has—but they are so warm, too warm—when she comes awake to her phone ringing its Umojo ring. "Oh my god," she mutters. She is sweating in her bed, clutching her pillow. It's ten thirty, half an hour after she was supposed to be at work. "I'm sorry," she says into the phone. "I'm sick . . . I got so sick I forgot to call in."

Nick says they can find ways to cover for her, and will reschedule appointments they can't cover. She can tell he is not happy. "I'm so sorry," she says. "I'll be in tomorrow." She tries to eat some toast but can take no more than a bit. She drinks some tea, and falls asleep again in the chair by the window, with the sun warm on her.

When Kiya wakes up, the sun is already low in the sky. She feels shaky and weak, but not feverish anymore, and she doesn't feel as if she's going to throw up. She is instead aware that her life is coming apart at the edges, that things are beginning to become deeply out of her control. She holds her right hand in front of her, watching it quiver, her muscles too weak to hold it steady. The light coming in from the window is gray. She thinks of the young woman who stood in front of the church, who walked away certain that she would be provided for and wrapped in a glow of light, as if she were someone else, someone Kiya cannot understand. That woman, Kiya sees now, is crazy. Thinking of her makes Kiya feel sick to her stomach again. It was a mistake, thinking she could have this baby, thinking she could be a mother. Everyone else knew it all along; Kiya just now sees it for herself.

❊ ❊ ❊ ❊

"Never gonna be a man, I won't! Like to see somebody try and make me!" Peter and Toni are curled up on her couch, watching the Mary Martin musical version of *Peter Pan*. He told Toni it was his favorite movie as a young child, and she had never seen it. "Oh, that's so . . . obvious," Toni says.

"What?" He shifts his arm around her shoulders, feeling the comfort of her body leaning into his.

"That this was your favorite movie. And your name. I mean it's great, but it does say something about you that the boy who never grew up is your favorite story."

Peter pauses the computer and looks down at her. "Is that an insult?"

Toni sits up straighter, laughing. "Sorry, I don't mean it to be."

He starts the movie again. "I just wanted to fly, and live on an island with pirates. You can't blame me for that." His phone buzzes, and he takes it out of his pocket to look. He sees a message from Kiya. She writes: "I can't do this."

He stares at the screen for a moment, then leans to one side to put the phone back in his pocket. "What was it?" Toni says, her eyes on the screen.

"Nothing," he says.

She turns to look at him. "It is not nothing. Nothing is ever nothing. Why don't you want to tell me who it was?"

This is the kind of thing that always bothers Peter about relationships, this sense of ownership. Privacy goes out the window. "It isn't important," he says. "Whatever it is, it's an intrusion on our time together."

90

"Peter." Toni stops the movie and sits up. They are in the combined living room/bedroom of the studio apartment she moved into. The scent of curry lingers in the room from the dinner Toni made. She runs her fingers through her hair, letting it fall around her face. "I don't need to know everything about your life, but there's no reason for you to keep things from me. If you feel like you have to hide things, then there's something wrong with our relationship."

Peter didn't know they had a "relationship." To him, the word means something specific, something like "going together," rather than any two people simply being   friends with one another, spending time together. He's not sure of how Toni uses it, but since she is a young and unmarried woman, he suspects she means it in the first way. Toni is steadily watching him.

With a sigh, he pulls the phone out of his pocket and shows it to Toni. "It's from Kiya. I haven't talked with her in ages, I don't know what she means when she says, 'I can't do this.' In order to find out, I'd have to call her and have a long and painful talk, and you and I are together now. This is our time."

Toni pulls her legs up on the couch. The couch is soft and over-stuffed, with a slipcover that wrinkles under her when she moves. "Okay, it makes sense why you wouldn't want to answer that just now. I appreciate that. But there's no need to hide it from me, unless you want to keep having a relationship with her while you're in a relationship with me."

Peter throws his head back on the couch. "This *relationship* stuff . . ." he murmurs.

"Yes?" Toni tilts her head sideways to look at him. Danger, he thinks. "Are we not in a relationship?"

"Toni, you know I'm crazy for you. You also know that I'm not into this people-as-property kind of thing. I don't own you just because we're sleeping together; you don't own me. Right?"

Toni is silent for a moment while Peter wonders what's brewing inside, and if it will erupt. She looks at him directly then, and there is something in the force of her eyes that gives him a jolt. "No, I don't own you, and you don't own me. But I have a responsibility to you to be fair and kind, and you have the same responsibility to me. You don't get intimate with somebody just to pretend that you have no connection to them. Right?"

Peter has the uneasy feeling that there is going to be no winning this type of argument, not with this woman. "Right," he says, and glances at the phone in his hand again. "I haven't talked with her in a couple of weeks."

"I think you should call her," Toni says. "She might need help."

Peter puts on his jacket and steps out onto the small back porch of Toni's apartment, leaning against the railing. He texts back. "Can't do what?" There is the "swish" sound of text delivery, and very quickly the response. "Can't be a mother to this baby." He sighs in exasperation and gives in, jabbing at the phone to call her.

Kiya answers right away. Her voice is faint, uncertain. "Hello?"

"This is Peter. So what's going on?" He tries to keep his voice friendly but cool, uninvolved.

"Um . . ." There is a fumbling sound. "I'm thinking I can't have this baby after all. I mean I'm not a mother, I made a mistake thinking I could do it."

Peter walks out onto the grassy patch of lawn, away from the house. A fence surrounds the yard, with houses close on all sides. The night is chilly, stars faint in the sky above him. "So are you thinking of getting an abortion, then?"

"Oh, no I can't do that . . . I don't mean that."

She sounds confused. "Kiya, are you all right?" There is he, getting involved; he can't help it.

"Yes. I've been sick." She sighs. "I missed some work, I'm afraid of losing my job. If I can't keep a job, I can't take care of a baby, right?"

Peter doesn't know if the two things correlate, but he's willing to agree. "Well, what are you thinking of then? If you don't want to get an abortion?"

"I guess . . . I guess I should put the baby up for adoption. Some other parents can do a better job with it than I can."

Peter glances back at the house, at the upper story window where the warm light shines out. He wishes he were up there, still watching the movie; wishes he'd never looked at the text. He wants a beer. But remembering the way Toni looked at him, remembering her expectations of him, he says, "We should talk, right?"

    ✴ ✴ ✴ ✴

In a way, Maddie knows she is dreaming; in another way, it is entirely real. Alex is there with her, leaning back in his reclining wheelchair, but alert. His head is lifted slightly as he looks at her, and his eyes are awake and bright. He chuckles in his old way, the old Alex, so real that she can reach out and touch him. He is telling her what it's like to be the way he is. "It's not bad," he says. "I'm always with you."

"You are?" Maddie asks, surprised.

He chuckles again. "Sure I am. But don't worry, I won't hurt you. My job is to help."

Maddie understands then, in the dream, that Alex's job— and, he suggests, the job of others like himself, others who are alive but helpless—is to keep the world going. Their energy fuels those who love them; unable to use it themselves, their life energy is given as a gift.

The dream lingers at the back of her mind all day, giving her a little jolt when she remembers it. There is something creepy about it, vampire-ish or ghoulish, but in this case, it is the living who feed off the not-fully-living. Yet in the dream, Alex was offering his life energy to her, with love, and in gratitude for her love.

When she stops by after work, Alex seems more sluggish than usual, his eyes unfocused and dull. She massages his hands, watching how the muscles of his face relax as she does. Since he seems to enjoy it, she decides to do his feet too. She pulls open the Velcro bindings and takes his socks off. Sitting on the ground, she moves his feet gently, flexing them, and rubs the skin of his feet and his toes. Looking up, she sees an expression pass over Alex's

face, a ripple like the wind over water, leaving his face more peaceful than it was before.

The expression on his face stays with her, a warm spot to
touch on as she drives home, makes dinner, and sits out by the lake
after. The combination of the dream and the smile make her feel
as if she is close to Alex, as if he is, as he said in the dream, with
her all the time. It is cold, the breeze pulling leaves off the trees
and whirling them around the deck, but she wears a warm jacket
and watches the sky grow dark. Acorns drop occasionally from the
tree, making a "thunk" on the wood of the deck. The sun is setting
minutes earlier every day, bringing less light to the world, more
darkness as winter creeps nearer. She hears a door slam and footsteps on the grass. There is a rustle through the trees and brush
separating their property, and then Jack's voice. "Are you enjoying
your solitude, or would you like some company?"

"Sometimes I do want my solitude. But just now company
would be nice."

Jack settles himself in the other Adirondack chair. He also
wears a jacket. He looks out at the lake. "Before too long you
won't want to sit out here at all."

"I always do," Maddie says. "At almost any temperature, for
a few minutes, as long as it's not pouring rain."

"And you're not a Mainer. You're sounding like one,
though."

"Not a native Mainer."

"Then not a Mainer." Jack maintains that it takes more than
living in Maine for decades to be a Mainer. "It takes generations."

"I know, I know." She's heard this before. "How's that
grandson?"

"Paul's in school these days. Special Education classroom."
Jack shakes his head. "Doesn't learn anything there. He's brighter
than they know. He doesn't talk well, see, so they think he doesn't
think well. But he's smart."

Maddie remembers her dream and Alex's smile. "What does
he talk about when he's with you?"

"Well, he doesn't talk too much. But he communicates. He communicates without words more than he talks. But it's a language other people don't understand."

"That must be frustrating for him."

"Ooh, yeah."

They stare out at the darkening water. Maddie wants to ask something about Paul, but she doesn't know what it is. Something about the purpose of his grandson's life, something about what he or his parents think about this. It must be painful, seeing their son and grandson like that; what makes it worth the pain? *Is* it worth the pain? This is a question she can't ask, and if she did, Jack would have to answer her in accepted, conventional terms. They don't know one another well enough to tell the truth.

* * * *

Evie has been buying beer at the Mt. Vernon General Store. Every time she buys it the teenage boy with acne behind the counter asks to see her id, and every time she pulls it out of her wallet and shows him. She was 21 in May. The cashier looks at her insolently, as if he thinks she might sit right down in front of the store and drink the entire six-pack and then puke in the street. She buys Schlitz because that's what Eric used to drink. She doesn't really like the taste of any beer but likes the way she feels after one or two. One day it occurs to her she could try something else. It's legal, and she has money. She lingers in front of a bottle of whiskey, but is afraid to buy it. The cost puts her off--$3.85—and she's not sure she would like the taste. She's never had it. A bottle of red wine, "Burgundy," is just $1.25.

After a dinner of toasted cheese on bread, Evie pours the dark red wine into a mason jar and sips it. The taste is full and slightly bitter, but not as bitter as the beer. She takes a second glass and her cigarettes outside and sits on the end of the dock. The sun has set across the lake, and in the darkening light, she sees a small group of loons gathered by the island. She hears their warbling cries and once again wonders if they are called "loons" because they sound like crazy people, or if crazy people are called loons after these birds. She sips the dark wine and thinks maybe she will be one of those crazy people that are called loons. She has a good start on it; only 21 years old, and already she lives by herself, smoking and drinking, on a remote lake in Maine. Already she is alienated from society, already she is dealing with health issues, and lonely. Already she can't keep a boyfriend, can't understand how people are supposed to act in the world. She is a social isolate, a strange person. A cat lady without a cat. She breathes in deeply on her cigarette, and coughs.

She throws the cigarette in the lake and lies down on the dock, facing the stars. She feels a moment of calm. She *does* have a relationship, she is not alone; she is in relationship to the stars above her. There is emptiness now all around, and the pinpricks of light above flutter, communicating. It makes sense, somehow; it's all she needs.

When Evie wakes, she is still lying on the wooden dock, clammy and wet, covered in dew. It is still dark, but she thinks the sky may be lightening above her, the black shifting gradually into gray. She laughs at herself, at her neediness and dissolution, and pulls herself upright. It occurs to her for just a moment that this time at the camp may be valuable to her, may be special; a pause in her life, like after a deep breath is exhaled, when the emptiness floods in. She steps slowly up the dock toward the cabin, toward her waiting bed.

Chapter Twelve

Kiya is trying hard to rise to the challenges of the day. She remembers how she used to channel sunlight, bringing it inside herself to shine out. That was the "other" Kiya. This Kiya would like to feel that sunshine, but it doesn't reach her anymore. This Kiya tries to keep on an even keel, tries to turn away from darkness. This Kiya can't visit her mother as often as she used to, because she is afraid of bringing her down.

Kiya remembers to smile at customers, to talk with them about their hair. She tries to remember facts about their lives to bring up in conversation with them like she used to—how was that trip to France they took, how's their son—but bits and pieces floating in her memory slip away. Who cares, after all; what does it matter? It's play-acting, all of it. No one truly cares about anything. She sees that in their eyes in the mirror as they look at her, then look at themselves, their wet hair slicked back, the black robe tied around their necks. When their smiles fade, the emptiness behind the pretending is revealed. They look at themselves in the mirror and see their own lined, drawn faces, the shadows there waiting for them. There is really no denying it. Drew was in on that fact, and he gave into it. His was a selfish act, but she understands why he did it. Kiya knows the truth now, but she will never give in.

She is cutting the hair of a woman she's seen several times before. Caroline, her name is, and Kiya remembers that she works for the Mayor's office. Something to do with public relations. Kiya's hands perform their work; they have not forgotten how to lift and thin, to scissor and shape in a way that frames the woman's dark eyes and eyebrows. "How are things in the mayor's office?" Kiya asks. She makes her voice loud enough to be heard by Alice, the stylist working next to her, so she knows—in case she was doubting—that Kiya is still on top of things. Caroline smiles, murmurs, "Just great," then lifts up a strand of hair near her temple. "What do you think of getting rid of this gray?"

After work Kiya slips away quickly, without talking to anyone. She's afraid they will ask if everything is all right. They will be concerned, they will try to help her. They will try to buck her up, but she knows it's really because they want her to be more efficient, to be her old self, the one who brings in the customers. It's not, she tells herself, because they care.

She walks into the wind, holding her coat around her. She is to meet Peter in a coffee shop. She has no illusions anymore about Peter having feelings for her, or about them getting back together. She was in love with him, and he may have been a little in love with her, but he grew to hate her. What more is there to say or do about that?

As the weather grows cooler, she thinks of her brother more and more. She speaks to him in her head; they have little conversations. Kiya is early for her meeting with Peter, so she passes the door of the coffee shop, walking down the hill toward the harbor. Drew's voice is sardonic, cutting, and it sometimes fills her head. He says, *Why give that guy the time of day? Why even talk with him? He's not worth it.*

He's the father of this child, Kiya thinks. I have to. She hears her own voice answering inside her head, smaller than Drew's, less certain. But she is right. Peter does have some say, after all; she forgot about that before. She is more sensible now, less giddy. She sees things more clearly. Life is difficult, impossibly so, and she made a mistake in thinking she could do this by herself. But now the right thing to do is to consult Peter, consult the person who is the father of this child. No matter how hard it is to do, no matter how painful it will be to see his face.

She walks back, and slips into a booth next to the front window. She doesn't order; she'll let Peter do that. She rests against the padded back and holds her hands around her stomach, the small round warmth. She reminds herself that there is another life in there, a small and special life, one that deserves protecting. One that is of more value than hers.

* * * *

Peter enters the coffee-smelling warmth of the shop. He

brushes down his hair, tousled by the wind. He sees Kiya, her blond hair in a corner booth, and begins to smile in greeting, but his smile fades when he sees her face.

Peter lowers himself onto the bench next to Kiya, both of them facing toward the room. The window to the street is behind them, the sun fitfully coming through clouds. Kiya looks at her hands in her lap. "I'll get us some coffee," he says. "Café au lait for you?"

When he returns, Peter sits across from her. He picks his espresso up, blowing little ripples on the surface. Kiya sips the white milky foam he brought her, and as an afterthought says, "Thank you." She is pale, with circles under her eyes. He glances around; the shop is nearly empty. Peter says, "So, you are thinking of adoption."

Kiya nods. "Yes. I haven't done anything about it yet. I don't know who to call."

"I don't know either. There must be some information online."

"I haven't looked." She is still stony-faced, staring into her coffee, not looking at him.

"Kiya . . ." Peter can't keep the exasperation from his voice. She is like a child, helpless. "What is going on with you anyway? Are you serious about this?"

She looks at him then. "Don't get angry. I'm . . . I'm having a hard time."

"Clearly," Peter says. He's quiet, then says, "You said you'd been sick. And you said something about losing your job."

She shrugs. "They haven't let me go, but I think it's coming. And even if they keep me on, I don't know what to do with a baby. How to pay for it. I was being stupid, I guess, to think I could." She puts a peculiar emphasis on the word "stupid," as if she is something repulsive.

"Well, no," Peter says. "It's not really stupid, lots of people do it." He catches himself, and says, "Of course, I think the right thing to do is not to keep it. It would just be too hard. And it would have a better life . . ." He stops as he sees her face. She can't bear what he is saying; she looks as if she's going to throw up. "I'm sorry," he says.

"No," Kiya says faintly, waving a hand in front of her face as if to ward away a bad smell. "It's all right, you're right, I suppose."

Peter stares at his coffee, at the steam rising faintly from it. The sound system is playing Lady Day singing "God Bless the Child." Billie's voice rises and falls just below the chatter, the hissing of the cappuccino machine, a reminder of a world of struggle beyond the cheerful warmth of the shop. Kiya is suffering, he can see that, and he doesn't know how to help. She takes a deep breath, and says, "So I guess I needed to know if you think putting the baby up for adoption is . . . a good thing."

He nods. "Yes."

"So I have your permission."

"Yes. You do. I'll sign whatever." They don't speak, until Peter says, uncertainly, "It will be hard." He has a vague idea of adoption being difficult, but looking at Kiya makes him think of what a very, very hard thing it could be.

Kiya lifts her face then, and stares straight at him. Her blue eyes are wet and shiny, and as he watches, they fill. She blinks, but doesn't wipe the tears from her face. "Yes," she says. "I guess it will be."

* * * *

Maddie has learned to wait for her son to call her, rather than call him. She used to call him in the evenings but the times he answered, he always sounded impatient, as if there were other things he should be doing. Now he calls her every few days on his schedule. No matter what she's doing she tries to pick up. She also tries not to ask about Kiya, but it's hard. She is planting spring bulbs on the side of the cabin when her phone rings. The light on the lake is gray and subdued, with a fall chill. She sits back and pulls the phone out of her pocket. "Hi, Mom." His voice is quiet.

"How are things?" she asks. "How's the music coming?" She has guessed, from things Peter has said, that he's dating someone else already, but she doesn't ask about that. One thing she's learned in her quarter-century of mothering—except when she forgets—

is to stay out of things.

"Okay. Good, actually. Hey listen . . ." She hears the sound of traffic in the background; she waits. "Maybe I shouldn't tell you this over the phone, I don't know. Maybe I should come in person."

"Oh no, you don't, buster. If you bring something up like that, you have to tell me what it is."

"All right, all right. The thing is, Kiya is saying now that she wants to put the baby up for adoption."

Maddie holds her breath, is still. "Is she just thinking of this, or is she serious about it?"

"She sounds pretty serious."

She feels her heart do a funny fluttering kind of thing. She doesn't want to tell Peter that this child, the child of the future, has appeared to her, in half-sleep and on waking, several times. She can see the full cheeks, the tousled blonde-streaked curly hair, the way the child (male or female, she can't tell) looks at her seriously, then breaks into laughter. A droll child, with a sense of humor. How could that child now be taken away from her?

"Ma?"

"Yes, I'm here." She looks down, still kneeling on the grass. She stands up, knees aching, and limps over to the chair. "What do you think about this?" she asks.

"I think it's probably a good thing. Kiya isn't the greatest at keeping her life organized, you know? I don't really know how she could handle this mothering business."

"I guess . . ." Maddie marvels at how mature and reasonable her son sounds. He seems more reasonable than she feels. She remembers herself when she became a single mother, her own disorganized life. Dirty sheets, unpaid bills, tears at night. "I guess it's probably the right thing to do, then. Aren't you a little sad about it, though?"

"Sad?"

"About losing your child. About not being able to be a father to it."

The line is quiet for a moment. She no longer hears traffic noises. "Maybe a little, I don't know. I never felt connected to it, you know?"

"Yes, I know," Maddie says. "That would have happened more when it was born. That connection."

"I'll have other chances."

"Yes, you will." After they hang up, Maddie hears a calling sound and sees a group of five or six loons making their way somewhere out in the middle of the lake. She doesn't want to let her grandchild go, the child which is more thought than reality at this point, and tells herself to wait, just wait; maybe Kiya will change her mind.

* * * *

After an initial period of nervousness about waitressing at the diner—it's a "café," the owner says, not a diner—Evie enjoys going to work. Her only other human contact is her brief conversations with Dr. Reich at Orgonon, and she discovers that she doesn't feel like a weirdo talking with other people at the café; she feels like a somewhat normal young lady. They don't know about the scars in her armpit and on her back, they don't know about her bad habits or her strangeness; to them, she is a cheerful young woman with a blonde ponytail. She takes the early shift, setting her alarm for 5:15 a.m. and driving in the early, delicate light. When she enters, she takes a deep breath of the coffee-scented air, puts on the checked apron, and finds it easy to smile at customers.

Every morning, soon after they unlock the front doors at 6:00, an old man makes his way toward the café. She can see him through the front windows. He wears baggy tan pants and a dark blue jacket in any kind of weather, his cane helping him navigate the sidewalk. He reminds Evie of her grandfather, with his careful walk, his cane, and especially his slow, wry smile when he looks at her. "There's my girlfriend," he says this morning when Evie opens the door for him.

"She's too young for you, Frank," the cook calls out from behind the counter.

"Ah, what do you know," Franks shouts back. "These youngsters don't know anything. It takes a man with some wisdom to know how to treat a lady. Isn't that right?" he says to Evie.

"Absolutely." She pulls out the chair for him to sit at his favorite place, in front of the window. He lowers himself slowly down, groaning with the effort. "I'll get your coffee," she says. She brings it with sugar and creamer, on a small tray.

"Oh, you're good to me," Frank says. "You're a good girl, Evie."

"What you don't know," Evie says, "can't hurt you." Frank chuckles, but as she turns in Frank's order, the first of the day— two eggs over easy and toast with marmalade, same as always— Evie thinks that it's true; she carries with her, always, the sense that she is not a good person. She pauses at the window at the back of the café, looking out toward the lake. She's never realized this quite so clearly as she does on this morning, as the morning light creeps over the grass. She feels as if there is something wrong with her. Something she should be ashamed of, and something that Frank, if he knew, would think less of her for. His eyes would no longer be bright when they looked at her, and he would no longer joke with her so warmly.

After work Evie drives the Dodge to Orgonan. As she navigates the wooded country roads, Evie wonders what has she ever done so wrong that she should feel that sense of something bad about herself. She had sex, she supposes, and she wasn't married; but that was something that many of her friends did, and she doesn't think of them as bad. She didn't really want to have sex, but she was curious, and Eric seemed to think it was a big thing, something really important. Now that she thinks of it, Frank wouldn't think there was anything at all bad about that, either; he'd probably love to hear about it.

She just doesn't understand what all the fuss about sex is. It was about as enjoyable as washing dishes, and personally, she doesn't care if she never does it again. This, she realizes, is a wrong way to think, somehow; Dr. Reich would not approve. Maybe this is why she thinks she's bad. In one way, she'd think she was truly bad if she *did* enjoy it; in another way, she's bad if she doesn't. But this, she tells herself as she turns into Orgonan, is much, much too complicated to follow. She steps out of her car and smooths down her skirt.

Dr. Reich greets her warmly when she arrives. His friend, Dr. Anderson, is there again. Reich's cheeks are flushed, and he seems more cheerful than usual. While she sits in the accumulator she hears voices and the movement of feet. After her half hour, Dr. Anderson opens the door to the box. "Dr. Reich had to meet with someone," he says. He motions for Evie to sit at the table. "How was it today?" he asks. "Do you feel all right?"

"Yes," Evie says. In fact, she feels warmer than usual, and is perspiring lightly. "I feel fine." And she does; she feels a renewed sense of energy lately, or at least less fear of the cancer spreading.

"Good," the man says. He speaks with an accent, but Evie can't identify where it is from. He is tall and blonde, Nordic-looking. "A young woman like you should feel good, should feel happy." He smiles at her, and Evie can't help but smile back. He really is handsome.

He leans forward on the table, with a quick look toward Reich's office. The door is closed. "Do you know," he says, "anything of the problems Dr. Reich is dealing with?"

"No," Evie says uncomfortably.

"The government is harassing him. They are burning his books." He leans back in his chair, looking at her. "You didn't know this? They are actually, literally burning his books."

She shakes her head. "I'm sorry. I don't follow the news." She remembers hearing something about this months ago, when she was in Urbana, but she thought it was a false alarm. Reich is a scientist, after all; this is not the Middle Ages, scientists are not persecuted for their research. "I hope he's not in danger?"

Dr. Anderson looks at her seriously. "He may go to jail."

"Oh, no. I'm sorry. I hope he doesn't."

"I didn't think he would talk about it with you; I just thought you should know." Evie doesn't know what to do or to say. "The FDA is paranoid," Dr. Anderson says. "They are opposed to the natural human life force. It frightens them. Although . . ." He leans forward, again with a quick glance toward the office. "Dr. Reich does not always act in his own best interests. He is not the most practical person." He leans back again and smiles at her. Evie is not sure if his smile is paternal and patronizing, or something else.

"Is there anything I can do?" she asks.

"Oh, no. No, I just thought you should know. Things are very hard for him now and yet, he continues to help people such as yourself." Evie is about to stand when the doctor suddenly reaches one of his hands out and covers her hand, which rests on the table. He gives it a sudden, forceful squeeze. "You should be grateful."

Chapter Thirteen

When she can't sleep, Kiya walks. Her small apartment is oppressive. Though it's past midnight and the air is cold, Kiya wraps a scarf around her neck, puts her coat on, and walks the streets. Dry leaves scuttle on the sidewalks in front of her; branches scrape above her head. In her bed, trying to sleep, Kiya thought of everything: Drew, her father, her mother (who calls often, her voice quavering with worry, to ask if Kiya is going to visit that day), where her good energy has gone, work and how she will manage to get herself there the next day. Her back aches when she walks, but when she walks she doesn't think of anything; she just feels her body, she breathes the air. Things she was thinking of drop away into the street, into the deep night.

A few cars pass, slowly. One weaves from side to side, bumping the sidewalk, then straightening out in the street. She hears noises behind her, footsteps. She doesn't turn. A voice from behind: "Hey lady!"

She finally stops and turns slowly. Two kids, high-school aged boys. Punks, wearing hooded sweatshirts and carrying skateboards, one kid with a tattoo on his neck. The other kid is heavier with a dull, aggressive look. Kiya doesn't say anything. The skinnier one says, "Got any change for us?"

She continues to look at them for a few moments, trying to focus. They are just kids. She shakes her head and turns around to continue walking.

They run in front of her, block her way. The skinny one is clearly the leader. "Lady, we SAID, do you got any change for us? And by CHANGE, I mean bills."

She left the apartment without a bag, without a wallet, with just her keys. Now she stands staring at the boys, hands in her pockets. She supposes she is in danger. "No," she says. The bigger kid approaches, staring at her aggressively. Looking at his face so close to hers, she sees undistinguished brown eyes and a line of blemishes across his cheek. She thinks, dispassionately, that he's probably not very smart. "I left my wallet at home." Her voice is flat.

The skinny kid pushes the bigger one out of the way. "Listen, what are you doing? You looking for trouble, walking around like this? 'Cause you're gonna find it."

"I don't care," Kiya says.

He shakes his head, staring at her. Kiya wonders if this will be her child, years from now; will he roam the streets, begging money, stealing. A runaway. This boy has some cleverness in his expression, some observation, and a quicksilver anger. Maybe someday her own child will kill her, not knowing who she is. "Lady," he says, the anger fading as he shakes his head, "you are crazy. Go to hell." He turns to the other boy. "C'mon, asshole," and they slap their skateboards in the street and push away.

Kiya listens to the sound of the skateboard wheels on the pavement. Several blocks away a police car drives across the street perpendicular to this, slowly. The boys continue to skate, she continues to walk. Her head throbs, and the night is depthless, two-dimensional. After a moment, she realizes that she must have been afraid, because her heart is pounding heavily.

The next morning she lies in bed, staring at the ceiling. She finally fell asleep when she got back to her apartment, and now she realizes that she forgot to set her alarm. She will be late for work again. She hears Drew's voice: *Way to go, loser.* He would tease her in the way brothers teased sisters, but the sound of his voice now is not teasing, it is serious. He almost sounds sad for her, for her being such a loser. "Do you think I care?" Kiya says aloud, to Drew and to herself. "Do you?"

She takes her time dressing. She is late already, and they will fire her today when she gets there, so why should she rush? She takes extra care with her eyeliner, drawing dark elaborate lines around her eyes, thicker than usual. She puts on green and pink patterned tights, short boots, a short tight dress that shows off her stomach bump. She mousses her hair so that it sticks up all around. She feels she has a date with someone, though she doesn't know who it is; something is finally going to happen. She's tired of waiting for it.

The sun on the street hurts her head. She can't bear to look at the faces of the people around her as she walks; they are so bland, so cheerful, so stupid. Either they are too stupid to know about the darkness and emptiness underlying everything, or they are liars, deceivers, pretending everything is great. She wonders about hell, about the idea of an afterlife of damnation. She watches her feet in her short boots, walking, as she thinks it over. It's not right; she doesn't believe it. She doesn't think that Drew is burning in hell. These people won't burn in hell, but perhaps they are, at this moment as they walk down the street, burning in some pain, something like she is, and hiding it from themselves, hiding it from everyone. Perhaps it is she, Kiya, who is at this very moment burning in hell.

Kiya steps from the sidewalk onto the street, still watching her feet and thinking of flames in the darkness, and then the on-rushing darkness is something real, something visible as it tears into her, with a blare of horns and a screeching of black, smoking tires.

✳ ✳ ✳ ✳

Peter is in the bucket working high in a tree when his phone rings. He feels it vibrate in his pocket as he lifts the chainsaw to a branch, and then feels the greater vibration of the saw cutting through wood. He finishes the tree and waits until he's safely on the ground to take his phone out of his pocket and look at it. Maine Medical Center, and they left a voicemail message. Kiya was in some kind of accident, and—for some reason—she gave them his name.

He takes the elevator to the fifth floor, like the woman at the Information desk told him to. He gives Kiya's name to a woman behind a counter. She stares at her computer screen, clicking and tapping, then says, "She's still in surgery. You can sit over there if you want." She points to some nearby chairs and tables. Peter takes a seat, picks up a magazine, and puts it down. He is missing work for this. Gary had to let him go early, and he's not getting paid for sitting here.

After half an hour Peter approaches the woman behind the desk. "How long do you think it will be before I can see her? I'm supposed to be working . . ." He feels lame, thinks that the woman behind the desk sees him as a husband who doesn't care about his pregnant wife, or something. He wants to tell her *See, I'm not her husband, not even her boyfriend, and I don't know why I was called instead of someone else,* but he doesn't. He waits until she makes a phone call, then she turns to him and says, "You can see her in a few minutes. Her doctor would like to speak to you first."

Peter is reading a *Sports Illustrated* when a doctor approaches. "Peter?" He holds out a hand. "I'm Rich Randall." "Peter King," he says, shaking the offered hand.

"We called you because Kiya gave us your name before the surgery. We found your number on her cell phone."

"I wondered," Peter says. "I'm not a family member or anything. We aren't that close . . ."

"Does she have a family member we can call?" The doctor, a stocky, gray-haired man, peers at him over reading glasses.

"Well, her mother, yes." Peter remembers Kiya's mother, her flustered manner, her reliance on Kiya. Remembers that she'd been sick recently.

"She suffered a concussion and a broken fibula," the doctor says, "along with some scrapes and bruises. We set the leg; it will be fine. The pregnancy is still viable. Her injuries didn't affect the fetus as far as we can tell. Is there anyone who can help her when she is released?" He looks at Peter, waiting. "She'll need some assistance for a time."

When they finish talking, the doctor points to a room down the hall. "She should be just coming awake," he says. Peter walks over to the door hesitantly. He hasn't spent much time in hospitals and doesn't know the protocol. His mother, that healthy soul, has never been hospitalized except when she gave birth to him. Once he visited a high school friend who was hospitalized after a car accident that killed a mutual acquaintance of theirs. That was depressing.

He leans his head around the door; if she's not awake, he will just leave. He sees the bed, the white sheets, and blanket, and there is Kiya, her blonde hair sticking up around her head on the pillow, except for the part of her head that is covered by a bandage. She is opening her eyes, which at that moment seem to focus on him.

He steps in. "Hello there."

She looks confused. She doesn't say anything. "How are you feeling?" Peter tries again.

At this, she gives a little chuckle, a sarcastic sound. Then he realizes, with alarm, that she is crying. She turns her head to the wall, away from him. Fun times, Peter thinks and sits on a chair next to the bed. He sees her hand lying on top of the blanket, white and helpless-looking, and picks it up to hold in his. It seems the thing to do.

"The hospital called me," Peter offers after a moment.

"I'm sorry," she says, and he doesn't know if she's apologizing for having them call her, or for crying. "I am so small." She must still be drugged, still out of it. "I thought I had a baby inside me, but I was wrong. I think it was a dream." She suddenly is still, and her eyes open wide. She turns to him. "The baby?"

"It's okay. The baby is fine. You still do have a baby inside you."

She relaxes. "You have a broken leg," Peter says. "And a concussion. You'll be fine."

Her eyes fix on him; they are, at this moment, an impossibly light blue. "No, I won't," she says faintly. "But thank you."

"What happened?" Peter asks. The doctor said just that she was hit by a car. He wonders, suddenly, if that was her intention.

"I don't remember too well. A car, I guess. I didn't see it."

He decides to just ask. Maybe, in her impaired state, she will tell him the truth. "Did you do it on purpose?"

"I don't think so." She doesn't sound too sure. "I was on my way to work. I didn't care, though." She stares at the ceiling, and her eyes close.

Peter calls Umojo, talks to someone named Lily. "Did anyone tell you that Kiya was hit by a car? She's all right, but she has a broken leg and a concussion, and she won't be able to work for a while."

"Oh, I'm *so sorry*," Lily says, her voice tragic. "We wondered. I'll pass it on. Give her our love, if you talk to her."

"They send their love," Peter says after he hangs up.

"I'm sure they do. They love me so much they can't think of anything else; they love me all night and all day." She pulls herself up on her elbows. "Ouch!" she says, wincing. She takes a drink of water from a glass on the bedside table, a tiny sip from the straw, and settles back down again. "And you love me too," she says, her voice small and raspy. "And I love you, and I love myself, and Drew loves me, and Daddy loves Mommy, and everyone loves everyone, and everything is lovely." Her eyes close again, the lids pale blue and flickering, and then still.

*　*　*　*

When Peter called his mother to ask if Kiya could stay with her, he said that his girlfriend Toni suggested it. "Can't Kiya stay with her own mother?" Maddie asked. "I know she and her mother are close, and her mother has an apartment in Portland." She's not keen on the idea of having a depressed, perhaps suicidally depressed, young woman with a broken leg on her hands. A young, depressed, pregnant woman.

"Yeah, but her psychiatrist said it wouldn't be a good idea." Apparently, the psychiatrist, who Kiya had stopped seeing, talked with her in the hospital and said it would be better for Kiya if she didn't stay with her mother if it could be helped. "Kiya doesn't want to stay there, either. She says her mother's not up to it. And her mother doesn't have an extra room."

"And she can't stay alone?" Maddie asked. "Because to be honest, I don't know if I'm up to it, either."

"The doctor said she should be with someone. And I think actually that she has to give up her apartment, too. She can't work anymore . . ."

"Oh, gawd," Maddie said. "I'll think it over." As she hung up the phone, though, she knew she would say yes. What choice did she have?

Now she stands in the doorway of her second bedroom, Peter's old room. It could use a new paint job and new curtains, but she's not going to stress over this. She already replaced the poster of Johnny Cash giving the finger with Van Gogh's "Starry Night;" that's good enough. She's putting herself out to take the girl in, after all. Maddie starts to walk away, then turns around. Well, new curtains wouldn't cost that much. And they would brighten it up.

When Ron hears that an ex-girlfriend of her son is going to move in with Maddie until after the baby is born, he is amazed. No one, Maddie thinks, does amazement like Ron does; he is astounded. "You have to be KIDDING me," he says. "You must be INSANE to let this happen." His eyes are round behind his glasses; his hands spread out in bafflement. "You finally have privacy, you finally—after years of rearing your child by yourself— have peace and quiet out there in your little haven by the lake, and you're going to take in an emotionally disturbed, pregnant woman. Not only that but an emotionally disturbed, pregnant woman who is a former GIRLFRIEND of your son's. Who probably has all sorts of mixed-up feelings about your son. Who is carrying his child. Maddie. Maddie. Maddie." He puts a meaty hand on her shoulder; she feels its warmth through her thin blouse. "Think this over, Maddie. It's not too late to say no."

He's putting on a show for Maddie and for Jeff and Susan, who are in the office and laughing at his antics, but he is also serious. When his ex-wife's son wanted to move back in with them for a while after college, Ron would have none of it. "It would wreck our love life," she remembers him saying. Apparently, something wrecked their love life anyway, as it wasn't long after that they started divorce proceedings.

Maddie defends herself. "She really has nowhere else to go. And she is pregnant with my grandchild, even though she's going to give the child up for adoption."

"You said she was disturbed, right? Depressed, mentally ill or something?" Jeff says. He is chewing on a celery stick.

"Yes, she has issues. But she can be sweet, too. I like her. You guys just can't understand."

"I understand," Susan says. "You want to help her out, you're able to help her out. You have an extra room, she needs it. It's only for a limited time, then she'll be on her feet. You're doing a good deed."

"Well, Maddie is a saint, and I'm not. It comes down that that, I guess." Ron shrugs.

"That's ridiculous," Maddie says. "I'd rather you call me a sucker than a saint, if that's what you mean."

"Sorry, Maddie, you're not a sucker." Ron comes over and puts his arm around her shoulder, in a jocular hug. "You're just a better person than the rest of us, you can't deny that."

Then they are gone, and the office is empty again. Her shoulders still feel the warmth of Ron's arm. Maddie tries to picture the empty lake with the sun shining on it. It's an image she turns to for peace and serenity. Today, though, what comes unbidden to her is the image of Peter's room when he lived at home as a teenager: the mess the room was then, not a spot on the floor visible, drawers always open, the bed never made. She thought the mess reflected his teenage anger, the confusion inside him. It had made her feel angry and confused just to look at that mess, helpless and not able to help her beloved son. This will be different, Maddie reminds herself; Kiya is not her child. She is helping the girl out, and maybe in some way helping out what will be her grandchild also. She turns resolutely to the computer, to the papers on her desk, away from the thought of that kernel of life which she can help, but will not be able to know.

* * * *

Alone again, drinking red wine at the camp, Evie piles brushwood for a campfire in the fire pit. Once the small branches are cracking, she puts a log from the woodpile on it. Her grandfather had a fire going every evening when they were here, even on warm nights, and in the smoke she smells him, feels him close to her. He would sit with the breeze to his back so the smoke blew in the other direction, and pull his harmonica—his "mouth organ," he called it—from the front pocket of his overalls. When he played "East of the Sun and West of the Moon," her grandmother would sing along: "I wish that we could live up in the sky, where we could find a place away up high, to live among the stars, the sun, the moon . . ." Sitting on the ground next to his chair with her arms wrapped around her skinny legs, Evie used to ponder the lyrics. It was clearly a love song, but if this "house of love" was built in the sky, east of the sun and west of the moon, did this mean that it could not exist on earth? Did this mean it was just imaginary? If that was so, why did her grandmother's face look so sweet when she sang the song?

Evie's favorite song was "Will the Circle Be Unbroken." She knew the words and could sing along. Again there was "a better home awaiting in the sky." The song promised they would meet again in heaven. Now, poking a stick into the fire, she thinks about the blue sky, and heaven. Orgone energy is supposed to be glowing blue; do people's imaginations put heaven in the sky because that's where they will reside blissfully, floating on waves of blue orgone energy? She pictures her grandfather waiting for her there, arms outspread. The idea is creepy and makes her shiver. She'd rather have him here.

She sits down on the picnic bench. She and Eric went camping last summer and built a fire at their campsite. She remembers his arm around her, his whisper in her ear, "This is romantic, isn't it?" She enjoyed cuddling, and the warmth of his body, but did romance always have to lead to . . . that? It seems to Evie that romance and sex are two different things; one is warmth and affection and laughter, the other is grunting and sweating in a dark room, people sounding as if they are in pain. She pokes a long stick gloomily into the fire, wishing she had some marshmallows.

In the morning Evie feels clean, washed by sleep, her body fighting off all the bad things. In the early light, she is capable of anything. This morning Frank doesn't show up until nearly 9:00, but when he does walk down the sidewalk toward the cafe, other people are beside him: young healthy people, spilling off the sidewalk onto the street, laughing. "You got room for us?" he shouts as he enters, his face wreathed in a smile.

Evie pushes two tables together. A young man steps up to help. "This is my grandson," Frank says. The man holds out his hand for her to shake. "Mike. And these are his sisters, Alice and

Fran. And their parents, my son John, his wife Eloise." The girls take their grandfather's arms, to help him into his chair, but he brushes them off. "I can do this. Isn't that right, Evelyn?" He looks at her for confirmation. "I do this every day of the week."

"He does," Evie says. When they are seated, she takes their orders. Frank's grandson, a man around her age, is a younger version of Frank, with the same broad smile. He orders two eggs over easy, with toast. "A chip off the old block," Evie says to Frank. Something about the family, the way they nudge each other and jokingly complain, feels familiar to her. They remind her of home, though she is an only child.

Later, as Evie is picking up the empty plates, she asks where they are from. "From a small town in Illinois," John says. "South of Chicago."

Evie stops and looks at him. "Where?"

"Near Kankakee."

"No. I know that place. I grew up in Decatur. I graduated from Champaign/Urbana." There are crows of recognition.

"Fran is about to start her senior year at Champaign/Urbana," Eloise says.

How strange it is to meet these people with their midwestern accents, their familiarity with her home, here, so far away. Looking at their cheerful faces around the table, their bright plaid shirts, Evie misses her home and her family. "You should come over for dinner," Eloise says, and her voice makes Evie think of hot sun on straight green rows of corn.

Chapter Fourteen

Kiya thinks of the place she goes to as a cloud. A whitish-gray cloud, smooth in consistency, with no turmoil. She doesn't float through this cloud; it is as if she doesn't really exist, and this cloud exists instead of her. It is not unpleasant. Because of the cloud, she doesn't have to answer when someone speaks to her. Because of the cloud, there is nothing she has to do. When discomfort intrudes, or pain, some noise or disturbance arises from somewhere within the cloud—it just happens, not really coming from within herself—then someone does something, and the cloud is smooth again.

She opens her eyes to see her mother standing beside her bed. Her mother attempts to smile at her, but her mouth quivers instead, and a groan rises from within Kiya. It is a groan not of pain but of disappointment. Her mother is here, and Kiya cannot stay in the cloud any longer.

"What?" Her mother's voice is frantic, her hands fluttering helplessly toward her daughter. "What's the matter? Does it hurt?"

"No . . . no. I'm all right." Kiya is herself again, regretfully. Her lower leg hurts inside its stiff white house. She takes a breath and pulls from somewhere—the sky, the cloud, herself—a smile. A smile, for her mother. "I may not look it," Kiya says, "but I'm all right." Her mother's eyes are still anxious. When Kiya says "I'm all right," she is telling her mother she is not following Drew's path, she is not like Drew.

Her mother sits in a chair by the bed; she lets her body release into it with a sigh. "Kiya, I don't know . . ." She pulls a tissue from her purse and wipes her eyes with it, her nose. Kiya longs for the white safety of the cloud. Her mother says, "I've talked with your psychiatrist."

"Oh?" Kiya summons up a memory of *psychiatrist:* friendly, glasses, hair that needs a trim.

"She hasn't talked with you in quite a while."

A nurse walks by the door, shoes making a swish-swish sound. "I guess that's right." Kiya closes her eyes, just for a moment. Finally, she says, "I'll talk with her again."

"Good, honey. You have to take care of yourself." Her mother looks at her handbag, resting on her lap. "So you're going to stay with Peter's mother for a while."

Kiya doesn't know what to say. She hasn't thought through how she would talk with her mother about this. She just knows that once Peter mentioned her staying with his mother, that was the only thing she could think of to do. Maybe the lake would help her feel better. "I didn't think I could stay with you," Kiya stammers. "I mean, I knew you'd let me, but it would have been too much. I would have been there in your living room all the time, in the way with my foot up . . ."

"But you know you can stay there if you need to, right?" Kiya sees that her mother needs confirmation that she is reliable, that she is able to help when needed. That she is a good person.

Kiya reaches for her hand. "I know you will always be there for me. And when I get through this, I'll be there again for you, too."

While she waits for Peter to pick her up, Kiya trims her bangs with tiny nail scissors she found in her bag. A nurse took the bandage off her head and washed her hair this morning, then put a clean bandage on. Her hair feels silky now. Hair has always been something she can manipulate, can work with. She doesn't have any products, but is able to give the fine strands some lift and shape with her fingers as it dries. She can angle the small hairs just so and doesn't have to think about anything else for that moment except their pale silkiness and shape against her skin.

Jeny and Clyde have already gone to Kiya's apartment and moved her stuff out. Kiya can't bear to think of them sorting through her dirty clothes, her journal scribbles, her half-used, pathetic makeup bottles. She tried to tell them to throw everything away, none of it was worth the trouble, but they wouldn't. "We're saving it all for you, sweetheart," Clyde had told her blithely over the phone. "That way when you're yourself again, you won't be angry at us for throwing away that art award you got in eighth grade."

"I did?" Kiya doesn't remember any award.

"You did," Clyde said. "And it's in one of the boxes in your mother's garage. Talented *child,*" he said, and for just a moment she'd thought maybe they could be friends again, someday.

And now Peter is here, handsome Peter in his brown denim jacket, brushing his hair to one side. "How ya doin'?" he asks. "Ready to go?"

For that moment it seems that he is her Peter, her boyfriend once again, and they are off on an adventure. The sky outside the hospital window is blue, he is smiling at her . . . Then he looks around the room, finding the suitcase Jeny had brought, and the nurse is there with a wheelchair. The nurse is smiling and Peter can let his fade, as if she has taken on that duty for him. He can hoist Kiya's backpack and pull her suitcase as the nurse helps Kiya, ungainly stupid Kiya, into the chair. "Silly me," Kiya breathes, settling into the chair. Silly, for pretending even for a moment that Peter could care for her. She closes her eyes as the nurse pushes the chair down the hall.

* * * *

On the drive Peter attempts, once or twice, to make conversation, then lets it drop. The seat is pushed far back so Kiya's leg has room to be out straight in front of her, and she rests with her face turned away from him.

Peter knows he is doing the right thing by helping Kiya, but he is struggling. He has always believed in personal freedom to make his own decisions, decisions not bound by what other people say is right or wrong. He has a hard time determining how much he needs to care. Toni told him to ask his mother to take his ex-girlfriend in; a weird situation, but she convinced him it would be best. He knows his own self-interest needs to sometimes take a second seat to the interests or needs of others, and he thinks that this is probably one of those times. But why, he wonders, does doing the right thing feel so wrong? Isn't there supposed to be a feeling of contentment at helping people, at doing what is right? Maybe the good feeling will happen later, but right now he feels just uneasy, uncomfortable with Kiya, and uncomfortable at the thought of his mother taking Kiya in.

He glances over at Kiya, seeing only the back of her blonde head, the white bandage taped to the side closest to him. He thinks her eyes are closed. He supposes this is difficult for her. Thinking how hard this may be for Kiya makes Peter feel more uncomfortable than ever; it's as if he is slipping outside of himself, like a part of his essence is being pulled from the center of him, where it belongs, and is falling into the black hole of another human being. It doesn't feel right. He wonders if this is what Sartre meant when he wrote: "Hell is other people."

Kiya stirs and turns to look at him. He glances at her, then back to the road. Her mouth twitches, as if she is thinking of speaking, but she doesn't say anything. He remembers when that face did nothing but smile at him, and he remembers how happy he used to feel when he was with Kiya. There are dark half-moons under her eyes. Finally, she says, "Thank you for taking me."

He shrugs. "Not a problem."

"Your mother is very kind to take me in. Like a wounded puppy."

"It's okay, she loves puppies." He looks over at Kiya. "Kidding!"

Kiya barely smiles, but she does smile. Peter takes that as a personal achievement. "Seriously," he says, "she has room. It's all right."

Kiya shifts in her seat, making a face from the movement. "I can't pay much," she says.

"She understands." He glances at Kiya's midsection, the roundness there pushing out her shirt. "She's helping out the next generation." At that Kiya turns her head again in the other direction, quickly. She stares out the window as if there is something out there to see. Peter turns on the radio and hums along. He gives up trying to talk and lets himself think of Toni's face, her laugh.

When they arrive, his mother helps Kiya out of the car while Peter gets her suitcase and bag. When Kiya is standing up and has her crutches under her arms, Maddie reaches a hand out as if to help her. "I'm all right," Kiya says. "I can make it." She clumps ahead of them to the house, and Peter looks at his mother. She shrugs, and they follow.

Peter is happy to leave the house, to leave Kiya in the care of his mother. He is happy to drive away a little too fast, the window open just to let the cool breeze rush through the car. He puts a cd in and turns it up loud, singing along to The Talking Heads. There's nothing more you can do, Pete, he tells himself; you got your mother to take in an ex-girlfriend who's in trouble. Remember to be nice to your mom for the rest of her life (but you'd do that anyway, he tells himself, right?). Visit sometimes, but not *too* often—too often would be bad, because it might give Kiya the wrong idea about things. Reassured that he has satisfied his duties, Peter allows himself to look forward to that night. Toni and he are going to hear some music at the club where they met. She wants him to be good to Kiya, as if it's a character test. And he does care about her approval.

✻ ✻ ✻ ✻

All the rest of her first afternoon Kiya stays in the bedroom with the door closed. She is settling in, Maddie thinks; making herself at home. Still, there are no noises, no opening and closing of drawers, just quiet. Maddie decides the girl must be sleeping. She looks rough, with the dark circles around her eyes, with the head bandage and the crutches. Maddie makes a dinner of chicken and vegetables and knocks hesitantly at the door. "Kiya?"

There is no answer, and for a moment Maddie is afraid. Then she hears a rustle and a voice. "Come in." Kiya is lying on the bed, hands folded on her stomach. Her suitcase is beside the bed, unopened. "Are you hungry?" Maddie asks.

"Oh, sure," Kiya says, and swings her legs slowly off the bed. Her right leg is in a cast to the knee. Maddie hands her the crutches.

At the table Kiya picks at her food, moving it around on her plate, finally eating some. They are silent until Maddie decides she can't take it any longer. "So Kiya . . ." The girl's head jerks up, as if Maddie has yelled at her. "I'm just wondering what our arrangement will be here."

Kiya swallows, and says, "I don't have much money. I'm sorry . . ."

"No, that's not what I mean. I know that. You don't have to

120

pay for your room or food. If you want something special, you can buy it. What I mean is, what will you be doing with yourself."

The girl looks at her, mute. "Do you have any ideas about how you'll spend your time," Maddie asks, her voice gentle. "Until you're able to go back to work?"

"Um . . ." She looks at her plate, unhappily.

"Okay," Maddie says. "We'll look for work you can do from home. Does that sound good?" It is like talking to a five-year-old.

Kiya nods. "Sure," she says.

After dinner, Maddie sits on the couch with the laptop in front of her, looking for work Kiya could do. One website has positions with start-up costs ranging from $100 to $10,000, and they all look shady to Maddie. "Can you do web design?" she asks Kiya, who sits across from her in the stuffed chair. Kiya shakes her head no, and Maddie goes back to the computer.

"It's not the money," Maddie says to Susan the next day at work. "Sure, money would be nice, but I can feed her. It's just that I can't have her sitting around all day, getting more and more depressed."

"People need to be working," Susan says, nodding her head so vigorously that her curled bangs bob up and down. "What's she good at?"

"Cutting hair," Maddie says. "And styling hair."

"I'd pay her for that," Susan says. "I need to do something with this. Is she good?"

"She must be. She worked at an expensive salon in Portland."

Susan looks uncertain at that. She dyes her hair at home and has a basic bob cut. "Well, I'd be willing to give her a try. As long as she doesn't do anything too fancy. Why don't you get a cut?"

Maddie touches her hair; it is parted on the side and cut straight across at chin length, as always, and is beginning to show the gray. "You think I need one?"

"A new style is always fun," Susan says, and Maddie wonders if she's being diplomatic.

When Maddie mentions her hair-cutting idea to Kiya, Kiya shrugs. "I'll cut your hair anytime, or your friend's hair," she says. She's sitting on the deck, her leg in the cast stuck out in front of her. As far as Maddie can tell, Kiya sits in a chair or rests on the bed all day. She took the bandage off her head earlier today to reveal a red bloody scrape surrounded by black-and-blue. "Ouch," Maddie said when she saw it.

"I'm going to leave it off," Kiya said. "I think it's all right now to do that, so the hair can grow back." Now the spot draws her attention, and Maddie wishes Kiya would cover it back up. Her hair sticks out oddly around it. "I won't charge anything," Kiya says. "I'm grateful to you for taking me in." The girl is still pale, and looks thin, except for her small stomach bulge in front of her. She stares out at the lake.

"I don't know what to do with her," Maddie says to Jack. She slipped over to his house after dinner and is sitting with him at the scratched wooden kitchen table. "She watches tv, she stares at the computer, she sleeps, she sits and stares at nothing. She needs antidepressants but won't take them because she's pregnant. She thinks they'll hurt the baby or something."

"They might." Maddie is surprised to hear this from Jack, who doesn't seem as if he'd be an expert on depression, antidepressants or pregnancy. "Maybe she's doing the right thing there."

The next night Maddie is sitting on the deck after dinner, wrapped up in her warm coat, when she hears a rustling in the leaves. Kiya is inside the house. It must be some small animal, a chipmunk perhaps. Sometimes she sees weasels out here. The deck is on ground level and animals can easily get on it. One summer night after she had eaten fish for dinner, she was dozing in her chair with one hand hanging over the edge of the chair when she was awakened by something licking her fingers. Looking down, she saw what looked like a large weasel; it was a fisher, which can be aggressive. She held herself still until it waddled away, then she ran into the house.

Now something small and white and wriggly runs from the trees, toward her chair. She stands up, giving a shriek. The animal turns around and lurches in the other direction, toward Jack, who is making his way towards her. He reaches down to pick it up. Holding the animal close to his chest, he walks over to Maddie.

It's a dog, a white puppy. "You scared the shit out of me," Maddie says to the dog. It tilts his head to look at her and tries unsuccessfully to wriggle out of Jack's arms. "Is he yours?" Maddie asks, rubbing the little dog's head. She looks at the dog's belly, between its legs. "She. She's adorable."

"Well, she could be mine." Jack nuzzles his cheek against the dog. "But it's more likely that she's yours."

They hear a noise inside, and the door opens. Kiya stands in the doorway, supporting herself on her crutches. "What's this?" she says. "Who is this little guy?" She looks more interested, more awake, than Maddie has seen her looking since she arrived.

"My son's neighbor had these puppies," Jack says. "They are just about ready to leave their momma. Labrador mix. And I was thinking, you need a guard dog. These places get broken into sometimes. A guard dog is what you need, to scare those bastids away." He lowers the puppy onto the ground. It runs over to Maddie, its stomach swaying from side to side, and plopping down beside her, starts gnawing on the toe of her shoe.

Kiya starts down the stairs to the deck, crutches clumping. Jack reaches out a hand to steady her at the last step, but her eyes are on the puppy. "I could help take care of it," Jack says. "Take it over to my place and drop her off if you needed to go somewhere. Cute, isn't she?" Kiya, sitting on the edge of one of the wooden chairs, doesn't answer. She leans down to pick up the puppy, holding her against her face, then resting her on her stomach. The puppy jumps up to lick her face.

*   *   *   *

Frank's family visits every summer, driving from the Midwest to fill all the corners of his old house. When Evie is invited to dinner for the following night, she puts on new red pedal-pushers she bought in Augusta. She wears a cotton, flowered button-up blouse, and tries to make the hair around her face curl becomingly. She wets the strands and wraps them around her fingers, but

123

they flop down as soon as she lets them go. She doesn't know why she cares—except it's the first time she's been invited anywhere except Orgonan since she arrived, and the first social engagement of any sort she has had in months.

Frank's house is an old Federal style in the center of Mt. Vernon. She knocks on the heavy front door, feeling as if she should have brought something with her—but what? Flowers, maybe, but now it's too late.

Slow footsteps approach the door, but when it opens it is not Frank, but one of his granddaughters. "Hello, Evelyn," the girl says. "I'm Fran. Come on in. We're happy to have you." She glances to the side, shyly.

"You can call me Evie. Thanks for inviting me." As Evie follows the girl down the hall, she sees that she holds one leg out to the side as she walks, the foot at an angle, which gives her a slow, lilting gait. *Polio,* Evie thinks. She hadn't noticed it at the café.

Alice is setting the table, and Eloise stands at the stove over a steaming pot. She wears an apron tied over wide hips. She says to Evie, "We're just having spaghetti; hope you don't mind."

"Mind? I love it," Evie says. "I'm so glad not to cook by myself and eat by myself for once." Remembering her manners, she asks if there is anything she can do to help.

"Oh, goodness no," Eloise says. "Have a seat. I have plenty of hands to help." The kitchen does seem to be full of bodies milling around, of voices and confusion. Evie tries to remember who is who: Fran has the limp, Alice is wearing the pink dress, and their father's name is . . . John, she thinks. Dinner at her parents' house is a different affair. Her mother is usually in the kitchen cooking alone, often holding a book in front of her face while she stirs. Her father is usually in his office, reading or grading papers. Evie would sometimes cook dinner for her family when she was home, but the kitchen was a silent place, one person toiling away there with only the company of her thoughts.

Here there is clatter in the steamy room, the sound of voices overlapping one another: Eloise shouting at John to get his fingers out of that cake frosting, John asking Fran to bring the salad to the table. Eloise calls out "Frank!" and waits for an answer. When none comes, she tells Alice to go get him.

Mike sits down next to Evie. She has no problem remembering his name. He is lanky, with dark hair combed back from his face. He smiles and says, "This place is a madhouse."

"I like it," Evie says.

When Frank finally shuffles in, he looks surprised to see Evie sitting there. "What is this, a new grandchild?" he asks. He is seated at the head of the rectangular table. Evie unfolds her napkin on her lap and waits for a signal to begin eating. Instead, she sees heads bow, and Eloise murmurs, "Bless us, oh Lord, in these thy gifts, which we are about to receive through thy bounty, through Christ our Lord, amen."

"Amen," the voices of those around the table echo. Frank leans in over the rising chatter to say, "Father, Son, Holy Ghost, who eats the fastest gets the most." He follows this with a wink in Evie's direction and reaches for the bowl of spaghetti.

Evie learns that Eloise and John have a farm outside Kankakee. Mike lives there and helps them, and also works at a construction agency in town. "I'm saving money," he says, "for my own farm." His parents exchange looks.

"We're not in favor of that," John offers around a mouthful of spaghetti.

Eloise wipes her mouth. "Farming is a hard life. And here is Mike, with a degree in mechanical engineering. . ."

Mike shrugs. "I thought I wanted to be an engineer. That was before I realized I really wanted to work with animals like my parents do, on the farm. I want to grow things."

"Well, we can't live our children's lives for them, can we?" Eloise says to John. He doesn't answer, just keeps eating. "We have to let them make their own mistakes."

"I'm studying literature," Fran says. "I want to teach English in high school."

"And don't ask me what I'm going to do," Alice says. She shakes her head, making red curls swing. "I'm just sixteen and I don't have to grow up yet. But how about *you?*" she asks, pointing a fork at Evie. "What are you up to?"

"Alice!" her mother says. "Don't point, and don't be rude."

125

"No, it's fine," Evie says. "I just graduated with a degree in psychology. Eventually, I might work for a social agency, or maybe go into counseling. Right now I'm staying at my parents' cabin on Parker Pond until they come out next month. I'm repainting the exterior."

"You're what?" Frank shouts from the end of the table. He leans in, left ear cocked toward her.

"She's painting her parents' cabin," John says loudly.

"By herself?" Frank says. He looks angry. "Mike, you have to go help her there, for chrissake. That's no job for a girl by herself."

In the silence and darkness of the accumulator, Evie goes into a kind of dream state. A waking dream, in which the darkness takes shape in front of her. This time it is not frightening, however; the close warm darkness reminds her of what it was like to sleep next to Eric. His breathing next to her, his solid reliable warmth. It had been nice to come awake in the night and realize she was not alone. The dark inside the box has the warmth of a person; she has the sense of someone next to her, the air his breath, and it is comforting.

Chapter Fifteen

Kiya napped during the day, out of boredom. This made the nights in the small bedroom impossibly long. She didn't want to walk around the house or go outside, afraid the clunking of her crutches would wake Maddie. She had pain pills which helped her sleep, but often she would awake again when it was still dark. The cloud of comfort was dissipated by then, leaving only a few streaks of fog and a headache. Kiya pushes open the window by her bed looking out on to the lake and leans her head out. It helps to breathe the cold air, to see the stars burning in the sky. She can see the darker shadow of Spruce Island outlined against the faint light of the sky, and she hears the sound the water makes as it touches the shore below her window. The surface of the water catches glimmers of the stars and the light of the moon, and holds them, trembling. She thinks she sees streaks of light in the dark sky, like in Van Gogh's painting hanging above the bed. Kiya sits on the bed, leans her head on her arms on the windowsill, and watches the light shift over the surface of the lake as the moon rises and sets, as clouds cover and uncover its light. Sometimes she dozes off like that, and wakes with her leg and her head hurting, her back aching.

The break in the fibula is a clean break, "uncomplicated," the doctor said, but it hurts. At night when it wakes her, she will sometimes find herself wondering how much it hurt Drew when he died, or if it hurt him at all. She thought it must have. She wonders if, as he stepped off the side of the tub, he regretted what he was doing and tried to make his feet find his way back behind him to the tub. She wonders if he grabbed at the rope, if his legs waved wildly, until they went still.

She never told her mother or her father or even her psychiatrist about the night before it happened. She and Drew were supposed to meet after he got out of work. They were going to have dinner together, a sister/brother date. He was trying to figure out what to do with his life, he'd said; he didn't know what he should do. He hadn't applied to colleges, was wondering if he should. Kiya knew she should be the big sister and advise him, but she wasn't feeling good that night. She called him and canceled. She was tired, she had a cold, she wasn't up for it. She was impatient with Drew and didn't want to spend the evening, when *she* didn't feel good, listening to his problems. She knew he was going through a hard time, but his self-centeredness irritated her. They made plans to do it a few nights later. Kiya knows that if she told someone about that night, that person would tell her she shouldn't feel bad about it, that it wasn't her fault. Kiya also knows that person would be lying, and they both would know it. Drew's death was, at least partly, her own fault.

When Kiya sees the puppy, she wants it. The desire is irrational and overwhelming. She knows she can't keep it, she knows that when she looks for an apartment in Portland it will be even harder to find one with a dog, she knows she doesn't have any money to take care of it. She knows she can't ask Maddie to get it and take care of it when she is already taking care of Kiya. She just wants it, that's all. Her desire reminds her of the way she felt when she first learned she was pregnant, when she knew she wanted the baby and nothing else mattered. Her desire for the puppy makes her miss that feeling, that desire for her baby, the feeling that nothing could possibly stand in the way of achieving that desire.

Maddie says she'll think about keeping the puppy. She says, "I haven't had a dog for years. It's a big commitment." Still her face goes soft when she looks at the puppy, and she smiles.

"It's not ready yet to leave its momma," Jack says. "You have a week to think about it." The puppy spreads its little legs and lets go a stream of yellow water onto the deck. Jack grabs it up, too late, and moves it onto the grass.

"Then there's that," Maddie says.

"I'd be here all day," Kiya says. "If you wanted to get a dog, this would be a good time. I could help train it."

Kiya knows she is helpless; she is like a puppy herself, as she said to Peter. Maddie takes an afternoon off work to drive her to

Portland for appointments and drop her off, like a package, at her mother's. Kiya didn't want to make the appointments but it seemed she had no choice. She is like a child again, doing what the adults tell her to. Her mother, wearing her red wool jacket and leather gloves, drives her carefully to the gynecologist. She waits in the outer office, her face smoothing out when Kiya tells her the gynecologist says she and the baby are both fine. Then her mother drives her to the orthopedic surgeon for her check-up. They have an early dinner, then her mother drops her off for one more appointment, a late one with her psychiatrist. Peter is to pick her up—Kiya the parcel-person—and drive her back to Maddie's.

Sarah's office is in her small house in South Portland. Kiya lets herself in by the side door. She is ten minutes early for her appointment. The inside door to Sarah's office is closed, so Kiya settles in a chair, her cast stretched out in front of her. She is so anxious about seeing Sarah again, she feels as if she might throw up. She thinks Sarah must hate her for not showing up, for not calling her or telling her anything.

When the door finally opens and Sarah comes out, however, she is smiling, and greets Kiya warmly. "I missed you!" she says. Kiya smiles, guiltily, and wonders if she should say she missed Sarah also. But it would be hypocritical to say she missed her when all she had to do was call, so she says nothing. They sit in their usual spots, Kiya on the soft reupholstered couch, Sarah in her rocker across from her. White Christmas lights, up all year round, are strung across the bookshelves, twinkling. Sarah takes in Kiya, looking at her cast and crutches, at her swollen belly, at the healing scrape on her head, the purple bruise around it. "So how have you been?" she says softly.

When Kiya walks outside, it is completely dark. She waits by the curb for Peter to pick her up, leaning against her crutches. Somewhere inside her is a calm place, a circle of peace in the midst of chaos and pain. She focuses on that small calm place, as she leans into the wind. If she pays attention to it, maybe it will remain, it won't disappear. The world is broken and imperfect, she herself is broken and imperfect, but for the first time, she thinks that if she waits, if she is just patient, some of the broken pieces may knit themselves together.

* * * *

Back in Portland, Peter walks alone along the Western Promenade. It is November, and the nights are dark early now. Snow is forecast. The houses by the shore are big old gorgeous things, light shining through tall windows. Through them, he sees chandeliers, arched doorways, the flickering light of a fireplace. They always remind him of fairy tales, of stories his mother read him when he was small. How, he wonders, do people manage to live in these houses? He's heard that many of them are condos, but what do they do with their lives that makes them able to live in houses like that, with a view of the water? At these moments he wonders why he majored in Philosophy; he wonders if it's too late for him to study something else. Business or maybe law, except those fields don't interest him. Sticking his hands deeper in his pockets, Peter tells himself what his professor used to say: the study of Philosophy will allow him to understand his life better. And to understand, he thinks now, the big difference between his apartment—which he doesn't know how he will pay for next month—and those houses.

Gary told him yesterday that the work was drying up, that he was going to have to lay him off for the winter. Peter has been expecting this, but still, it came as a blow. Last winter he found a part-time job at a restaurant that barely carried him through until March, when Gary hired him on again. He doesn't want to have to do that again, but what else is there? He is finding music gigs once in a while, and they are fun, but they don't pay his rent.

Toni quit the coffee shop because she found the kind of job she was hoping to get when she moved to Portland; a firm hired her to do web design and graphics. It's what she got her degree in, and she's good at it. She goes to work every day excited to prove herself and is full of conversation about it when they're together. She doesn't want to go out as much in the evenings, because she has to get up early for work. They see each other only on weekends these days. Peter wonders if there is someone else at work, someone more dynamic than he is. Someone with a career, and with more of a chance of someday living in one of those houses on the Prom.

At home in his apartment, he picks up his guitar and strums. Toni thinks he should make a cd of the songs he wrote, but even she doesn't push it; she knows as well as he does how unlikely he is to make money on a project like that. He sings, "The road is here, and it's a long ways away." The sound of the music gives him a strange satisfaction, almost a shivery feeling.

Peter remembers the day his mother told him his father had majored in Philosophy. What he didn't tell her then, couldn't tell her, was that he knew this about his father. His father had told him.

Peter had been twelve and hanging out at his friend Adam's house. Adam had just gotten a new computer and Internet connection, which Peter and his mother didn't have yet. Adam said, "I could look up people on here." He found a site that gave basic information about people, like how old they were and where they lived. Adam looked up his parents and his grandparents but grew bored when he didn't find anything interesting. Peter told himself he didn't care about his father but typed in his father's name: "Mark Greenleaf." Several came up, but only one in Chicago, born in 1958. And there was his phone number, right there.

Peter called one afternoon when he was home alone. His mother had started letting him stay in their house alone after school until she got home from work. He was amazed when someone actually picked up the phone, and said, "Yep, this is Mark."

Peter had planned out what he was going to say, but it took him a stunned minute to get the words out. "This is Peter. I'm your son."

It was a very weird phone call. Mark—his father—talked and talked, and didn't want to hang up the phone when Peter said he should get off. After just a moment of conversation, however, Peter started thinking that his father's voice sounded strange. He giggled, like he was giddy or a child, and sometimes his voice would dip down as if he was really tired. He said he was sorry that he didn't help raise Peter, but that he wouldn't have been a good father. He said Peter was better off with just his mother, that his mother was a fine woman who he knew would take good care of Peter. "Was I right about that?" he asked.

"Yes, she's fine," Peter said. Then he said what he'd been waiting to say. "But I need a father too. You're my father."

Mark had made a strange sound at that, halfway between a groan and a sigh—or maybe a yawn. Then he said, "Aw, kid, you don't know, but you're better off without this father." That's when Peter asked his father to tell him some things about himself, and his father told him that he had a degree in Philosophy from the University of Chicago. When Peter asked where his father worked, he said: "At home."

"What do you do?" Peter asked.

"I read and study and write." Peter thought then that his father was a writer, maybe a famous writer, until his father said, "I don't really have a job. It's one of the reasons I wouldn't have been a good father to you." Then Mark asked him things about himself; what he was interested in, what he looked like. Peter said "Hockey," and "Normal. I just look normal. My hair is light brown." It was almost 4:00 by then, and Peter said he had to hang up. His father asked if he could call him some time; Peter said sure and gave their phone number. "Maybe we can get together and meet sometime," Mark said. "I don't drive but I can take a bus."

"Yeah, okay. Sure."

That's when Mark said the strangest thing to Peter. He said, "You know, I'll be thinking of you. I'm connected to you, and always will be. You don't know me, but I think I know you, and in some way, I will always be with you."

"Okay," Peter said.

"I don't mean for that to creep you out," his father said, though it did. "I just mean I'm there for you even if you don't know that I am."

"Okay," Peter said. "I have to go now."

After that call, Peter thought his father was probably a hippy, someone who tuned in and dropped out or whatever people did in the 70's. He would have been too young to go to Woodstock, but Peter pictured him with long hair, smoking dope and reading philosophy in some dark apartment. He wondered what philosophy was, exactly. He was careful not to bring up any mention of his father to his mother. He remembered the shadow that used to cross her face when he asked her about him. Then when he was older it became a matter of pride; his father never did call, and so that man didn't matter to him anymore. His mother started dating Alex when Peter was a teen. Peter didn't have any problems with Alex; he grew to like him and thought he'd be someone he might develop a relationship with. He was a nice guy, friendly but not pushy, just willing to talk to him and joke around. Then Alex got sick all of a sudden, and that was that.

Peter types "Craigslist Maine—jobs" into the search bar of the computer. Maybe someone needs an unemployed tree-worker philosopher with musical talents. When summer comes, he can be employed as a tree-worker again. Peter hears a faint tapping. He lifts his head and looks out the window, into the darkness. Thin flakes are swirling, hitting the window. When summer comes, the baby will be born. He will be a father, but not really a father—a father not in name, but biologically. An unemployed father, in a sense. He smiles faintly and looks down at the list of jobs available. Any of the ones he is qualified for look unappealing to him. He closes the computer and picks up his guitar. Strumming, picking, he makes sounds, matching the faint tapping of snow on the windows.

* * * *

Maddie pulls on Alex's fingers gently, working them with her own fingers and then rubbing his palms. When she's done with the hands, she moves up to his arms, rubbing his forearms. She always liked his forearms, the way the muscles there, covered in fine brown hair, tapered down to his wrists. Now the arms are white and soft, but still, they are his, and his eyes half-close as she touches him. "So Ron has been dating Jane, the history professor," she tells him in a low, intimate voice as if he can understand her. "They don't talk about it, of course, but everyone knows." She imagines Alex's voice saying to her *Everyone knows? What does President Obama think about it?* That's something he would have

133

said. "Well, everyone who works in the two departments, that is. President Obama has more important things to think about." She massages his shoulders gently, the thin unused muscles under the knit button-up shirt. When Alex became sick, George Bush was still President. When the tv news is on, Maddie imagines that Alex's face shows interest when Obama appears.

"Well, I hope that they make each other happy," Maddie says. She sits back in her chair and picks up the stack of books. "What next? What looks good to you?" His eyes focus on the wall as she asks. "Maybe I'll just talk to you. This business about Kiya . . ." Alex's eyes wander over to her. "It's hard. She's planning to put the baby up for adoption. I suppose that's best, but . . ." She picks up Alex's hand again and begins rubbing. "I could have put Peter up for adoption. I knew he didn't have a responsible father, and I wasn't the most responsible person in the world. I certainly didn't have much money. But I made it work." Alex's hand jerks slightly, as if to pull away; maybe she's working it too hard. "Sorry." She sets it down again, gently. "If she didn't want to be a mother, that would be one thing. But I think she wants to be a mother to this child. And when she gets herself back on her medication, after the baby is born, I think she could be a good mother. She was doing fine until she went off the medication."

Maddie leans back in the chair. "Oh, don't listen to me." Alex's eyes begin to close, as if in obedience. "I don't know what I'm talking about. I don't know this girl. Maybe I should get together with her mother and talk this over." The idea dawns, bright within her. They could have coffee, she could find out what Kiya was like before she got pregnant, when she wasn't depressed and crazy. They could set this thing on the right course. "But wait . . ." She sighs. "I suppose it isn't my decision to make, is it?" *That's right,* she imagines Alex saying as if she's just figured out the answer to a puzzle. *It's not up to you.* "Well, you can't blame me for trying, can you?" she says lightly. She puts her palm on his cheek gently, feeling the warmth of his skin. His eyes stay closed, but the lids tremble at her touch.

Maddie pulls the orange dog vest over Sadie's head. Sadie is restless, trying to twist away like a toddler, but Maddie manages to fasten the Velcro closing under her belly. Jack brought the vest over for Sadie, said she needed to wear it all hunting season. Maddie grabs her coat, hat and gloves and heads out for a quick walk before dark. Halfway down the lane, she hears the rumble of Jack's truck behind her. She steps over to the side. The truck slows, and Jack rolls the window down and leans over toward her. Maddie leans in, smiling, then sees his face, hears his tone, and her smile disappears. "You care more about that dog than you do yourself," he says. "A white hat and gloves and a dark coat. I can't imagine." He sounds outraged.

Maddie turns away, facing ahead, and keeps walking. He lets the truck inch along beside her. "I mean really, Maddie, what were you thinking?"

She decides he's not going to go away until she says something. "Okay, I suppose I should be grateful to you for pointing that out to me so kindly. Thank you." She turns away again and tries to continue walking. If only he knew how rude he sounded, she thinks.

He pulls the truck over, parks by the side of the road, and joins her. He is wearing his fluorescent orange jacket and cap. "I'm just trying to save your life," he says. "You'd rather not get shot, I take it."

"Right. Point taken. I thanked you, didn't I?" After walking for a moment, she says, "Not everyone is a hunter, you know. Not everyone likes to go around killing innocent animals for fun. So not everyone knows what *hunters*"—she puts a certain emphasis on the word— "look for."

"Well, let me tell you. This is what they look for." He points to her hat. "Just that color, walking along through the woods. White-tailed deer. Bam."

"You know," Maddie says, "there are ways to say things, and there are ways to say things. So I don't know about hunting. But I do know about common politeness. And rudeness." She glances at him, tugs at Sadie's leash as she scrambles, belly low, after a chipmunk.

"What? That was rude?" Jack looks truly baffled.

"The tone, yeah. It's this Maine thing . . . this making fun of

135

the flatlander thing. It's a Maine sport, along with killing gentle, vegetarian animals."

Jack turns his head to the side away from her, and she thinks he is angry until he turns toward her again and she sees he was hiding his smile. "I didn't mean to make fun of you for being such a flatlander. Though you make it so easy . . . I can't help the way I talk, can I?"

"Yes, you can," Maddie says.

"What should I say, then? How should I tell you that you're endangering your life?"

"You could have simply said 'You should wear some orange. You could get shot.' And you could use a polite tone. I would have said 'thank you,' and worn orange next time." They walk, their shoes crunching on the gravel. "Why don't you try it now," Maddie says.

Jack makes his voice high and exaggeratedly polite, with his Maine accent exaggerated. "Maddie deah, you might think of wearing some orange the next time you go out in the woods in the middle of hunting season. I mean, if you want to continue living for a while."

"Better," Maddie says. "You need more practice, though."

"I guess I wasn't raised well," Jack says. He is amused. "I'll just keep walking beside you," Jack says, "so those rude hunters in the woods know you're not prey."

* * * *

Evie waits in line at the General Store, holding a basket full of cheese, apples, eggs and a bottle of Chianti wine. The man in line in front of her is talking with the teenaged boy behind the counter. Evie stands back half-listening, looking at the packs of chewing gum to the side so she will not appear to be impatient, but when she catches part of what they are saying, she holds very still. "Yeah, up at *Organan,*" the customer is saying, drawing the word out in a sarcastic manner. He leans over the counter to speak in what he probably imagines is a low voice to the clerk, his flannel shirt stretching across a wide back. Evie can clearly hear him say

"You know what they do up there?" The boy mumbles something in response, and the man says, "Yeah, but it has to do with sex. Healing with sex. Sexual energy. In some kind of a box. You oughta get yourself on up there."

The boy makes a faint, embarrassed reply, kind of a whinnying laugh, and the customer steps toward the door. He glances back at Evie, his face full of merriment. He is a middle-aged, cheerful-looking man. He stops to add, "And he makes rain fall too. With his cloud-buster." He pronounces this *bustah,* taking emphatic delight in the word, in the idea. Holding a paper bag in one hand, he slaps the other hand flat on the wooden counter. "Hah!" He points toward the boy, glancing back toward Evie, including them both in his delight. "You take care now," and he is out the door, into the sunshine.

This time when Evie puts her food and wine on the counter, the boy rings them up, takes her money and gives her change all without looking at her, his cheeks tinged red with embarrassment. She feels almost sorry for him. Driving home, she remembers the conversation she had with her friend in college about Reich. "Crackpot" was the word he'd used. She thinks of the painting behind Reich's desk, and of Reich's ferocious intensity; then she remembers Dr. Anderson telling her the F.B.I. was "paranoid," and squeezing her hand. Walking up to her front door, she pauses to wonder if she is in danger, if she is being naïve and susceptible. Then, she shrugs, in the patterned light falling through the branches above her head. What great danger is she in, after all? No one is forcing her to get in that box, and no one—yet—is trying to take advantage of her. She enters the cool shadowy house, looking forward to her dinner alone, watching light move across the water and fade away.

Chapter Sixteen

Sometimes it seems to Kiya as if she is in a dream, half-awake and half-asleep. She wonders if she has done embarrassing things in this state, like in dreams where she goes to work half-naked. When she sits in Sarah's office on her weekly visit, and Sarah is asking questions in her gentle way, it feels sometimes as if she is waking up. Or as if she has just woken up in a strange house, a strange country. She feels a sense of alarm then: what has she been doing? What's going on? Then Sarah smiles, and Kiya carries on the conversation as if she were not slipping in and out of states of consciousness.

She felt almost like herself again, the old Kiya, when she was cutting the hair of Maddie's friend Susan. Susan sat last weekend on an ottoman in front of her in Maddie's kitchen so Kiya could sit in a chair and still be higher than her as she cut. During the time when she felt Susan's hair in her fingers, when she combed and snipped and thinned and made conversation, she was reminded of how time used to pass at Umojo, of how the sun would shine through the tall windows all day long. When Susan looked at her blow-dried hair in the hand mirror, Kiya could tell that she was pleased. "I like this," Susan said, her cheeks pink in self-conscious pleasure. Susan has a round face, and Kiya had given her side-swept bangs to create angles. Kiya told Susan her hair would look good if it were longer, to lengthen her face, and Susan said she might let it grow. Susan curled one of the loose curls Kiya had given her around a finger, feeling its softness. She said, "Maddie, you should have her cut yours. Doesn't this look nice?" Susan had marveled at herself, standing with the hand mirror in front of the wall mirror in Maddie's entry.

"I'm too old a dog for new tricks," Maddie had said, leaning against the kitchen wall with her arms crossed in front of her. Looking at her then, Kiya saw Maddie's good cheekbones, her square face and strong jaw, how her eyebrows were dark and full.

"Maddie, your hair would look great in layers," Kiya said. She could picture it, picture Maddie looking beautiful. She would like to make her that way.

Another time Kiya almost feels like herself again is when she is playing with Sadie, the puppy. When Kiya gets down on the floor with Sadie, her cast out in front of her, when she strokes Sadie's short, smooth white fur and her soft tan ears and the dog nuzzles her, she is brought back to her childhood, to their dog Ginger. Drew, when he was little, would fall asleep on the floor cuddling up next to that dog. She remembers Drew's sweetness as a boy, how he loved Ginger, and the angry voice she sometimes hears or imagines coming from Drew fades away. She doesn't know why she hears his voice so mean sometimes, saying awful things to her; he never talked that way. He loved Kiya; he used to cuddle up next to her on the couch when they watched movies together.

Sadie tries to bite her fingers, and Kiya holds Sadie's head to discourage her. Sometimes, when Maddie isn't looking, Kiya will kiss Sadie, right on her puppy lips. Maddie agreed to get the puppy if Jack would promise to help take care of it. "When you move, if you're able to have a dog, maybe you can take her if you want," Maddie said, almost shyly, as if she were offering Kiya a great gift. Which she was, Kiya thought, though Kiya didn't know how to handle it. "Thank you," Kiya said after a moment.

Kiya's leg is growing stronger, the pain diminishing. She still gets headaches and still has sleepless nights. "What are you thinking about, at night when you look at the water?" Sarah once asked.

Kiya would often think about Peter, but she didn't want to tell Sarah that. It was a hopeless thought, but one she couldn't give up. "The sound of the water soothes me sometimes," she said, and that was true. "It's whispering. And I like the way it's always moving, just slightly, like it's alive." Another thing Kiya couldn't say was that sometimes that sound and movement were terrifying to her in ways she didn't understand. The water was alive and judging her. It had unseen depths, and it was angry.

Jack comes over to help her train Sadie. They take her out in the little yard next to the house and Jack tries to teach her to sit, to come when called, to relieve herself on the grass instead of in the house. The snow has mostly melted, and the yard is covered with last year's brown, flat grass. Jack is a tall man with a belly that pushes out his tee shirts. He has graying hair that falls over his forehead, and metal square-framed glasses. He is remarkably patient with Sadie, who gradually figures out what "sit" means. Kiya sits on the deck chair, watching. Jack motions her over to the grass. "You need to be in on this," he says. "She might end up being your dog, and she has to learn to listen to you."

"Uh, I don't think so," Kiya says, not moving.

"And why not?" He looks at her. Kiya sees the sky blue through the bare trees behind him.

"Most landlords don't want their tenants to have dogs. Cats, maybe."

Jack picks up a stick and throws it. Sadie sits and looks at him, looks at the stick, then trots over to see what she can do with it. She picks it up, shaking her head with it in her mouth, then brings it back to Jack. "That's why you have to train this dog well. So that when that landlord sees Sadie, he knows right away that this dog wouldn't ever mess up his nice floors. C'mon now, get over here. It'll do that leg good."

Sighing, Kiya pulls herself up and hobbles over to where Jack stands. She has been walking a bit without her crutches; the freedom feels good, but frightening, as she imagines herself tripping, falling into a dark, timeless hole, like Alice. "Atta girl," Jack says, taking the stick from Sadie's mouth. Kiya doesn't know if he's talking to her, or to the dog.

When Sadie brings the stick to Jack, he takes it from her mouth, then takes a dog treat from his coat pocket. "Sadie, sit!" Sadie paws his leg. "Sadie . . ." He pushes her small rear end down with one hand. "Sit." Sadie sits, then jumps up again, trying for the treat. He repeats the maneuver until Sadie sits for a few seconds, and he gives her the treat. "Good dog!" He takes another treat from his pocket and hands it to Kiya. "Now you try."

Kiya positions herself in front of the dog, as Jack did. "Sadie, sit." Sadie stands looking at her until Kiya leans down and pushes Sadie's butt down to the ground. "Sadie, sit!" When Sadie stays for a few seconds, Kiya gives her the treat.

Jack looks down to Sadie, nuzzling at his hand. "You know," he says, "you're doing a good thing for that little one there." He points to her belly.

"What do you mean?"

140

"I mean bringing it into the world like you're doing. Eating well, taking care of yourself, all the other stuff you're doing. You're helping that person have a good start in life. You should be proud of yourself."

Kiya feels suddenly shy. She looks down at the small mound of her belly, smoothing her sweater over it. The granola she ate for breakfast is feeding that little person in there, right now. She is not taking her antidepressant medication, she reminds herself, for a reason; it's for the one inside her. Her actions affect someone else directly; she is extended into the world, no longer alone and isolated. "Thank you, Jack." In the sky beyond Jack, she sees small pulsing streaks in the pale blue.

* * * *

Matthew and Peter are playing their music on a small raised stage in the corner of Local Color, a natural foods restaurant. While people eat cranberry/roasted squash sandwiches and drink hard cider or herb tea, Matthew saws a fiddle and sings while Peter plays guitar and sings harmony. At the end of each song, some people applaud; others continue eating and talking. Their pay is a free meal and a beer.

The manager approaches them after the show. "You guys sound great," he says.

"Thanks," Peter says and asks if he has any other work available.

"You mean, like kitchen help?" the man asks. "Not now, but I'll let you know if I do."

The next week they play at a club called the Blue Moon, and Peter asks the same thing. Toni is sitting beside him then by the bar after the show, the manager standing behind the bar, and after Peter makes his half-hearted request Toni says energetically, "He's a super cook. Really top-notch. He's great to work with too—I met him at a restaurant—and did you know he has a BA in Philosophy?" She cocks a thumb toward him. "Smart guy, this one."

"Is that right," the manager says, smiling. "Well, drop a resume off."

When the man walks away, Peter looks at Toni. "That was

something," he says.

"Hey, it's what you have to do." Toni sips from her beer nonchalantly.

"Yeah, but . . . you lied. I'm not a great cook, I barely know how to cook. And you never worked with me at a restaurant."

"Peter." She turns on the stool to face him. "You are smart enough to be a great cook if you put a tiny portion of your brain power toward it. And if I'd worked at a restaurant with you, you would have been a great guy to work with. That is not a lie."

The next week, when the bar manager calls Peter and says he wants to hire him, Toni says "See?" Peter doesn't point out that, if he isn't up to the job and gets fired, it will be her fault. Luckily the cooking he is required to do turns out to be uncomplicated, and he discovers that the small experience he's had working in a diner for a month helps him pretend he knows what he's doing. He assists another cook in the kitchen and moves to the bar to help out when the kitchen closes.

Late one night, when Peter is washing glasses in the bar sink, the manager, Eddie, says, "You know, you and Matthew can play here any time. We just can't afford to pay you much. Well, technically we can't afford to pay you anything. But you can have all the free drinks you want."

"Thanks, Eddie. But I'm afraid that might turn me into an alcoholic."

"Okay then, you can play for free, with no drinks."

Every week he drives to his mother's house, picks up Kiya, and takes her back to Portland. Kiya's mother drives her around to her appointments and has dinner with her, and then Peter usually takes her back home—an hour's drive each way. Four hours a day sitting in a car with an ex-girlfriend, something the younger Peter could never have imagined himself doing. Something the younger Peter's former girlfriends would never have allowed. Toni, however, encourages it; she says he owes it to Kiya, and it's only until her leg gets better. Sometimes Peter doesn't mind; he is reminded of the way he used to enjoy being with Kiya. There are still days when she sits sullen and unspeaking in the passenger's seat, her belly in front of her and the seat pushed back so her leg in the cast can have room, but he has learned to pay no attention to her during those times, put in a cd, listen to the music. Other days she seems to forget her unhappiness and talks to him. She tells him about Sadie, his mother's dog, about the tricks Sadie has learned, how sweet she is. She asks Peter about his work. About his music. About his mother. "You know, she's really a nice woman. And attractive. She's been alone for so long."

"Well, not alone . . ."

"Alone except for her boyfriend in the nursing home. How strange is that! How sad! Did you know him?"

"Yes, I *do* know him. He's still alive. I visited him in the nursing home." It was last year, but he needs to let Kiya know Alex is not dead yet.

"That is so romantic. She must have loved him so much." Kiya sighs and leans her head back on the seat rest.

He supposes it's true that his mother loved Alex a lot, but Peter saw them more as friends. It is impossible to imagine his mother in a romantic relationship. His mother was just his mother, always around, sometimes irritating, usually pretty nice. "I guess so," Peter says. "I think she also loved my father too, though. According to what she said."

"Yeah? You never met your father, right?"

"Right." He taps a finger on the steering wheel.

"Do you know anything about him?"

"I know he got a degree in Philosophy. I know he doesn't have much of a career."

Kiya is silent a moment, looking out the car window. They are passing a lake, flickering blue on her side through the trees. "Maddie has never talked about him to me," she says. She turns her head to look at Peter then, and her blue eyes are alight. "Peter," she says, "you told me that your grandmother, Maddie's mother, knew Wilhelm Reich."

"Yeah, Evelyn. I guess she thought the orgone box healed her cancer."

"And you mentioned that you thought your grandmother and Reich may have been . . . intimate?"

Peter looks at Kiya, one eyebrow raised. "Are you thinking about my grandmother's sex life? Whoa, you have way too much time on your hands."

"It's important because of this." She points to her belly. "I looked up what Reich looked like, and it's possible that he could be your mother's father. Especially when he was young, his mouth looked a lot like hers. And they were close. Her mother thought he was wonderful, Maddie said."

"But she was married to my grandfather before my mother was born."

"I know. But just six months before. Your mother told me. She thought it was funny."

Peter thinks of Grampy, a man he hardly remembers. Flannel shirts, the smell of pipe smoke. He was a farmer. "My mother said her parents had a good marriage. They loved one another."

"They could love one another, have a good marriage, and Reich could still be Maddie's father."

"Kiya, that's pretty far-fetched. You could never find proof of it, and I hope you don't mention it to my mother."

"Oh no, I never would. It might upset her." Kiya looks satisfied, as if she's convinced Peter.

"So have you contacted an adoption agency yet?" he asks.

"No . . . no, not yet." Kiya pulls her cell phone from her pants pocket and starts tapping the screen.

Too busy thinking about my grandmother's sex life, Peter thinks. "If you need help with that," he says, "let me know. I can research, or whatever. We want to find somebody good, right?"

"Right," Kiya says, and subsides into silence.

✻ ✻ ✻ ✻

On the day before Thanksgiving, Kiya and Maddie make pies and bread together. Kiya sits at the table and makes bread, while Maddie makes the pie crusts. "This is always what I imagined having a daughter would be like," Maddie says. "We'd cook together." She lifts the crust from the bowl, patting it flat onto flour sprinkled on the counter, then rolls it out carefully with the rolling pin. "It's what my mother and I used to do." She rolls up a small ball of dough and lets it drop for Sadie, who sits beside her. The dog licks it up and sits, waiting for more.

Maddie has asked Kiya's mother to dinner, and Peter. Peter said, "I will come to your house for Thanksgiving dinner, because you're my mother and because I love you. And I will put up with having dinner with my ex-girlfriend and her mother because you want me to. But I don't want you to get in your head anything like us all being one big happy family. Because that is not going to happen, ever. Kiya and I will never be a couple again. You know that, right?" Maddie had marveled at his tone, so firm and grown-up.

Now Kiya, adding cups of flour to the large bowl in front of her, asks, "What was your mother like?"

"She was a sweet woman. My parents were farmers. But they both liked to read. They'd go out dancing on the weekends in Galesburg."

"Do you have any photos?"

Maddie wipes her hands on a towel and goes into her bedroom. She brings out two photos in small frames. "This is my parents' wedding photo, and this one is my mother." The wedding photo is a headshot of two young people. Maddie's mother is wearing a pale-colored suit, and her father a dark suit and tie. Her father is grinning in the photo. "They were married at a Justice of the Peace, so my mother didn't bother with the white dress." In the other photo, Maddie's mother smiles into the camera, head turned to the side. "This is her senior picture."

"She was so pretty," Kiya says. "And your father so handsome."

"I was their only child. So I got all their attention." She wipes the photos carefully with a corner of the towel and returns them to her room.

"You must miss them, now that they're gone." Kiya is kneading the bread dough thoughtfully, deliberately.

"My mother has been gone a long time. She died before Peter was born. But yes, I miss them." After a moment, Maddie says, "And you must miss your brother."

Kiya, kneading the soft brown dough, doesn't speak. Maddie thinks she didn't hear her, but the look on Kiya's face, closed and inward, tells her she did.

The next day Sadie begins to bark, and Maddie looks out the window to see a Honda parked out front. After a moment, a woman steps out uncertainly as if she doesn't know if she has the right house. Maddie pushes open the door and waves. "You found us!" The woman looks relieved and smiles when she sees Kiya. Kiya lifts up her crutch to wave it at her mother.

Judith is about her age, slim, and gives an impression of fragility. Her hand shakes slightly as she hands Maddie a bottle of wine. "I didn't know what to bring, I hope this is all right . . ."

"Oh, this is lovely, thanks. Come in, sit down."

Though it is barely past noon, when Maddie offers to open the bottle of wine, Judith accepts. "You don't want any, right?" Maddie says to Kiya.

"God no," Kiya says. "I'm just glad to see my mommy here." She puts an arm around her mother affectionately. "Isn't the lake beautiful?" Kiya asks. She looks out the windows to the lake, the water turbulent, glinting in the sunlight.

Peter shows up just before dinner. "Have you met?" she asks Judith as Peter says hello.

"Yes, we have," Judith says. She is more comfortable now. "Good to see you again, Peter."

"You too, Judith." He sits awkwardly on the couch next to Kiya. Poor Peter, Maddie thinks; always the only man around. She excuses herself to check on the turkey, and to put vegetables in the oven to roast.

After dinner, Maddie takes Sadie outside. The small dog squats and pees, then sniffs around the dead leaves. It feels good to get away from the over-heated kitchen, from the closeness of people and light and conversation. Maddie stands on the deck, looking over the lake in the early darkness. The air is cool, the quiet soothing. She hears voices from inside but doesn't have to answer, to be responsible. Kiya has been quiet since Peter arrived, answering questions when asked but not contributing anything else to the conversation.

Maddie isn't sure what she was hoping for by inviting Judith here; she did it to be nice to Kiya, she supposes, and to let her mother see where her daughter was living. She wanted to get to know Kiya better by getting to know her mother. She is aware at this moment, however, that none of these efforts have a future: Peter and Kiya will not be together, and the child Kiya is carrying will not be a part of their lives. She may never see Judith again, so why is she bothering to develop this friendship? Why didn't she reserve a room for herself in Boston and go to a nice restaurant?

The door opens, and Judith steps out. "Would you like company?" she asks. "Or would you rather be alone?"

"No, please," Maddie says, and gestures to a chair. "It was just a little close in there."

"Yes," Judith says. She takes a cigarette from a leather case and holds it up. "Do you mind?"

"No, not at all."

"I smoked for years," Judith says. She lights the cigarette. "Then I managed to quit but smoked a few when my husband left us. Then after Drew died, well . . ." She makes a helpless gesture.

"Oh, I can imagine." Maddie wraps her coat around her more tightly. "I can just imagine."

"You and your husband divorced? Peter's father?"

"Yes. Well, we never married, actually. Peter never really had a father."

Judith takes another puff of her cigarette. "I was married to Kiya's father, but he was never much of a father to the two of them. Oh, he tried, I suppose . . ." She trails off, looking at the lake.

"Some men just don't have a talent for being a father," Maddie suggests.

"Yes!" Judith looks at her. "It's true, isn't it?"

"Peter thinks he wouldn't be a good father," Maddie says. She motions her head toward the kitchen, where they see the figures of their children moving around in the brightly-lit kitchen. "But I think he would. I really think he would."

"The same is true for Kiya. She thinks she can't be a mother, she's not able to. I admire her for thinking first of the child, but . . . she's a loving person. She'd be a good mother, I know she would." Judith looks at Maddie, and on her face, Maddie sees her own longing reflected.

"Wouldn't it be nice to have a grandchild," Maddie murmurs.

"Yes, wouldn't it," Judith says. They both look out toward the lake, the rough slate-colored expanse moving restlessly, soon to be still and frozen. Sadie climbs up the steps, and whines at the door to go in.

* * * *

This time, the half hour in the accumulator is up before Evie is ready for it to be. When she arrived, Dr. Anderson was there. He told her that Dr. Reich was gone, visiting his lawyer, dealing with the legal issues threatening him. Now Dr. Anderson opens the accumulator door and looks at her. "How was it?" He takes her hand and Evie steps out, shaking her head slightly. "What?" Dr. Anderson asks.

Evie's cheeks feel warm. She smiles at Dr. Anderson. "It just felt good," she says. "I felt happy. I don't know why." It's a sunny day, and light slants into the long room in a way that is soft and welcoming. She laughs lightly, over nothing.

Dr. Anderson chuckles with her. "It's the orgone energy. It is making you strong, making you happy. You should always feel this way. It makes your cheeks pink." He had dropped Evie's hand but now he picks it up again. "It makes you look even more lovely." With his other hand, he caresses Evie's bare forearm. She inhales sharply and involuntarily jerks her arm away. "What's the matter?" he asks. "I won't hurt you." He steps closer to her.

The caretaker isn't in sight, and the house is quiet around them. "I know you won't *hurt* me," Evie says, and can't say more, because she doesn't know that, not really. She feels very young and uncertain. He puts his hands on her shoulders and looks at her face. He is much taller than she is; his hands feel warm and heavy. "Do you want me to kiss you?" he asks. He is standing very close

148

to her. She smells the starch of his shirt, and something beneath that—a piney, masculine smell.

She shakes her head *no,* mutely. "Then I won't kiss you," he says. He runs his hands down her arms, slowly. "But I think you might like it."

On the way home, Evie wonders if she might have liked it if Dr. Anderson had kissed her. She imagines his face, smooth-shaven, coming close to hers, his mouth open slightly, pressing against her mouth. The thought makes her shiver. She did not want Dr. Anderson to kiss her, and she still does not want him to kiss her and doesn't think she ever will, but he was right: she might have liked it.

Chapter Seventeen

The day Kiya gets her cast off, she asks her mother to drive her to Umojo. She brings thick tights along, to cover up her leg after they take the cast off. Getting the cast cut off is terrifying, with the noisy round saw cutting so close to her skin, and her fear of what her leg will look like beneath it, but it is also liberating. "I'm shedding my skin," she tells the doctor over the sound of the saw. He is a man she's never seen before; youngish, kind of cute, with shaggy brown hair. "I'm becoming a new person. A stronger, better person."

"I've never heard anyone say that before," he says, smiling at her. "But it's true your life will be easier now than it's been the past few weeks." He finishes sawing and, with both hands, pulls apart the cast. Kiya leans over, peering at her leg. The skin is white and pasty. "Use a loofah on that," the doctor said. "It will perk your skin up."

"I need my life perked up," Kiya says earnestly. "Will the loofah help with that?" She is flirting with the doctor, she realizes.

"It might," he says, smiling back.

Kiya tells her mother she is going into Umojo by herself. "It would just look weird," she says, "for me to go in with my mother, you know? Like I'm not independent. I mean I know I'm not, but I want to look like I am." She touches up her lipstick, looking in the mirror in her mother's car. She has toned down the eye makeup, which pleases her mother greatly. She touches the hair on the side of her head, grown over the spot where it was shaved. "I'll be right back." She steps carefully from the car, taking the crutch from the back seat.

She's not sure what she hopes for from this visit, but she feels the need to show herself to the people here, to let them know that she isn't totally over the edge. She pushes open the door and steps in, and the smell and feel of Umojo rush over her: the sunshine through tall windows, the smell of scented hair products and cologne, the attractive, smiling faces turned toward her. The relentless cheer of the atmosphere, welcome now to her. "Kiya!" The hugs, the voices, everyone acting happy to see her. "You look wonderful!" Jeny holds her at arm's length, looks Kiya up and down.

"Oh no. I'm fat from both the leg and this," she says, pointing to her midsection. "Not a lot of exercise going on here."

"Lovely little baby bubble," Clyde says, patting Kiya's tummy gently. A young woman Kiya doesn't recognize continues cutting a woman's hair, smiling vaguely in her direction.

"Thank you, I missed you guys. I just needed to stop in. I needed to see your faces." She feels more like herself, the old Kiya, just seeing them. Nick comes out of his office in the back. He has a new small beard.

"Kiya!" He hugs her. "You look wonderful."

"Can we talk for a moment?" Kiya asks. This is the hard part.

"Come on in." He pushes open the door to his office and motions for her to sit.

Perched on the edge of her chair, Kiya says, "I'll just take a minute. I wanted to say that I know I wasn't responsible toward the end when I worked here, and I'm sorry about that. It was a rough time, but I'm better now. I'm wondering if, in the future, you would consider hiring me again, or if I blew my chances for that. I really, really love working at Umojo." Her words are true to her as she says them; achingly true. If she doesn't keep this child, and if she can't go back to work at Umojo, she has nothing, absolutely nothing, in her life.

"You're doing better, then?" Nick asks, and Kiya nods. "I'm glad to hear that. We were worried about you, both before the accident and after. We all like you here, Kiya, and know that you are a very talented stylist." Kiya looks down at her hands, twisted in her lap; she's not sure she likes the tone in his voice. Soothing her, as if she were a child, and he is telling her why she can't have a popsicle.

Kiya looks up and tries to keep the pleading out of her voice. "Working here is my first priority. I'm not ready yet to stand on my legs all day, and won't be for a few months yet. But after that— definitely after the baby is born—I would love to come back to work if I could."

"We'll see if that can happen," Nick says. "We did have to

hire someone else, but people come and go, and we know you do good work. Your clients miss you, have been asking about you."

"They have?"

"Oh, yes." Nick nods. "Very much. So let's just see what happens." He stands up. "Your phone number is the same, right? I'm glad you came by, Kiya."

She smiles, thanks him. She walks through the salon using the crutch, the dark-haired woman she doesn't know casting her a sidelong glance, and as Kiya smiles and waves at her friends and limps to the car, she doesn't know if has just been let go definitively, or re-hired.

"I'm worried," Kiya tells Sarah, "that the stress or depression hormones in my body are going through the placenta, and are messing the baby up." She leans back on the couch, hands cupping her abdomen.

"What can you do about that?" Sarah asks.

"Hmm. Not much. Be less stressed, I guess."

"You know what strikes me?" Sarah asks. "How concerned you are for your baby. How much you care about him or her. Every time you talk about the baby, you are concerned for its future."

"Yes, well . . . isn't every pregnant woman that way?"

Sarah smiles. "It would be nice if they were."

"So that's good, right?" Kiya looks uncertainly at her.

"Yes, it's very good. It speaks well for you as a mother if you decide you want to be one someday."

"Oh, I do," Kiya says. "I really do."

Sarah is silent for a moment. She asks, "Have you thought more about contacting an adoption agency?"

"No," Kiya says. "I don't think about it."

"I wonder what keeps you from thinking about it." Sarah's voice is soft, and Kiya wants to ask her why *she* thinks it is, but knows that Sarah would just answer her with a question of her own.

"Because I don't want to do it?" Kiya asks, uncertain. "When

I'm feeling down, I don't think I should keep the baby. When I'm feeling better, then I want to. It's like I'm two different people." At least two, she thinks.

"It's hard, isn't it?" Sarah says. "Both of the people you feel like you are probably each have something to offer. Both deserve to be listened to."

Kiya agrees, but privately she thinks that there is one voice she should not listen to, and that's the voice of her brother when he's being mean. Every now and then he still speaks up, his voice angry, hurt and mocking, reminding her of all the pain it is possible to feel in this life.

✻ ✻ ✻ ✻

"So you talked with your father just that one time." Toni's eyes are wide and shining in the dark of Peter's bedroom. She loves a good story.

"Yup, that's all." He holds her closer, tracing with the finger of one hand the tattooed words on her arm; *Life is a luminous halo*, the black words partially surrounded by a golden cloud-like halo. She told him Virginia Woolf wrote them. "He never called me back."

"Why don't you try to visit him?" Toni props herself up on one elbow.

"Why should I?"

She lays the palm of her hand flat upon his chest, on the thin hairs there. "So that you'd know more about him. So you'd know where you came from."

"I don't need to. I came from my mother, from Illinois and from Maine. I came from the earth. And I'll return there."

"Poetic," Toni says and kisses him quickly. "Except I still think you should try to contact him again. Give him the chance to explain himself, now that you are an adult."

Every now and then Toni brings up his father, suggesting that Peter should try to contact him again. He wishes she'd leave it alone. She has two sturdy, affectionate parents; she doesn't understand his feeling that he is better off not traveling down that particular pathway.

Peter offers, instead, to take Toni to visit Alex in the nursing home. "Are you sure it's all right if I go?" she asks. "I mean since I don't know him or anything."

"It's fine," Peter says. "They like for their people to have visitors. Cheers everyone up." It's been a long time since Peter visited.

When Peter walks into the nursing home he approaches the desk and asks a woman there if he can visit Alex Murray. The woman points to the center of the room, where several people in wheelchairs sit in front of a television set.

Toni takes Peter's hand as they approach. "Alex," Peter says. "How are you." Alex's head turns vaguely in his direction, and an expression Peter can't read makes its way across his face; a smile, a grimace of recognition, perhaps? Then it is gone, and Alex is looking vacantly at him, and at the young woman standing next to him.

"Alex, this is Toni," Peter says in a loud voice. Toni, to his surprise, leans down and lifts one of Alex's hands from his lap. Holding it carefully between her two palms, she says clearly, "Pleased to meet you." This time Peter is certain that a look passes over Alex's face; he is trying to smile, to say hello. Toni continues to smile at him, holding his hand.

They push Alex's chair to a corner, where Peter and Toni can sit down. Alex gazes at them abstractly. "How long has he been here?" Toni asks.

"It's been more than six years now."

Toni smiles at Alex, as if he can understand. "Long time, eh?" To Peter, she says "And your mother visits every week."

"Twice, usually."

Toni watches Alex. "How much of what we say do you think he understands?"

Peter shrugs. "Some, Mom thinks. I'm not sure. She reads children's books to him."

Toni nods. She takes Alex's hand again, and to Peter's surprise, begins to sing a Beatles song in a low, crooning voice. "Oh yeah I, tell you something I think you'll understand." It's the first time Peter has ever heard her sing. Her voice is husky and breathy, appealing. When she ends with "I wanna hold your hand," Peter applauds. He hears a murmur of approval from the cluster of wheelchairs behind them. Toni looks embarrassed. "I don't know what prompted me to do that," she says. "I just thought maybe he would like it." It seems to Peter that Alex looks more alert, aware than he did when they first said hello.

"I think he did. That was very nice."

Peter tells Alex, "Next time, I'll bring my guitar. We'll make some music in here." They push him back in front of the television, and Toni leans down to give him a hug when they say goodbye.

Another person Toni wants to meet is Kiya. Here, however, Peter has drawn the line. This is why he hasn't taken Toni yet to visit his mother, where Toni would also meet Kiya. He can't imagine sitting at a table with his current girlfriend beside him, his ex on the other side of the table. Toni insists it wouldn't be weird. "You said yourself that a relationship is not the same as ownership. I don't own you, and Kiya doesn't own you. The two of us could be friends. You'd be surprised."

Peter actually could see Toni getting along with Kiya. "In another life," he says, "you two can be friends. Not this one, if I have anything to say about it."

"Uh oh," Toni says. It is early evening, and they are walking along Commercial Street in Portland. "I'm thinking maybe somebody still has some romantic feelings for someone he doesn't want this someone to know about."

"Because I don't want you two to hang out together? That's crazy."

"I'm just saying, if you were truly detached emotionally from Kiya it wouldn't matter to you if we hung out."

"Kiya's a friend. I'm happy we're not going out together anymore, and I wish our situation didn't require that we spend so much time together. She's crazy, to tell the truth. I'd worry about that baby if she decided to keep it."

Toni wraps an arm around his and matches her steps to his. She wears black tights and suede booties, and tries to step around the puddles. It snowed earlier in the day, but a change in temperature turned the snow into melted water. "I feel for her," she says.

"I thought maybe I could help her somehow, that's all. I don't have any devious schemes or anything. I just thought I might be able to be a friend."

Their footsteps crunch on the sidewalk. They hear a foghorn, low, from the water; cars swish by on streets wet from melted snow. Finally, Peter says, "The problem is really that Kiya didn't want to break up with me. It would be hard for her, not for me, to get together with you." There, he's said it.

"Okay, that makes sense. She was in love with you. She still is in love with you."

"Maybe, I don't know. Yeah, I guess."

"All right. Hey . . ." and Toni is off on another topic, this time talking about some guy she works with. "So Sean is doing this advertisement package, and he's looking for someone who knows something about music. It's not really his strong suit. I mean he thought he could handle it, but enough people told him that he really couldn't, so he's seen the light of day and is looking for someone. So I told him about you. He wants somebody to write some music for him. Okay if I give him your phone number?"

"Sure," Peter says, "but I can't imagine he'd want to actually pay me money."

"Maybe not much," Toni says. "But something. You might be surprised."

"Talk about surprise," Peter says. "You can sing!" Toni laughs, holding onto his arm. Peter, trying to identify what it is he is feeling at this moment, decides it is happiness.

✵ ✵ ✵ ✵

"Oh, this is going to be more than wonderful." Kiya's hands take on a life of their own as she works with hair; it's as if they belong to someone else, a confident and accomplished artist who is just distantly related to the Kiya that Maddie knows. They are in Maddie's kitchen again, Maddie on the ottoman this time and Kiya on the chair. Kiya's leg is well enough that she can stand on it now for short periods of time. Susan has come over to see the transformation, and to advise. The scene reminds Maddie of times when her mother's friends would get together in the kitchen of the farmhouse in Illinois and do one another's hair. She remembers the small pink plastic curlers, the papers wrapped around each curler for the perms. The strong smell of ammonia mixed with cigarette smoke.

Now her kitchen smells of coffee, and lemon juice mixed with a conditioner that Kiya sprays on Maddie's hair. "You're supposed to sit in the sun for a couple of hours, for the full lightening effect," Kiya says. Snow has been falling softly all day, covering the pine branches in a coat of white. "But I think sitting under the sun lamp for a bit will do the trick." Maddie had purchased a sun therapy lamp because she thought it would help Kiya, but she herself has been sitting under it while she reads the newspaper in the morning before work.

Kiya lifts the sides of Mattie's hair, showing her what the cut will do. "You'll have more body and shape, and this texturing around the face will highlight your facial structure."

"Sounds like magic," Maddie says. "Kiya the magician." She closes her eyes and lets her work. It feels good to have someone's hands on her head, to be fussed over, to be touched.

"So have you noticed what's been going on between Ron and Jane?" Susan asks.

"Besides their love affair, you mean?" Maddie asks, her eyes still closed.

"No, I mean the fact that they haven't been speaking to one another."

Maddie opens her eyes to the room's soft light, the snow falling silently outside the windows. "They haven't? How do you know?"

Susan shakes her head. "I heard it, but didn't believe it until Jane came into my office. Richard— "a sociology professor— "mentioned asking Ron something, and you should have seen the look on Jane's face. She said, 'You go ahead and do that,' in a way that left no doubt about how she felt."

Kiya brushes away some hair clippings from Maddie's cheeks. "Maybe she's just mad at him," Maddie says. "Lovers' spat."

"What's this?" Kiya asks, interested. "Someone you work with?"

"Nothing important," Maddie says. That's all she needs, Kiya thinking that she has a love interest. "I love the feel of that belly of yours against my back," she says.

"Oh, oh, Maddie's changing the subject," Kiya says. "It must be serious." Kiya smiles at Maddie in the mirror propped in front of them. Kiya's cheeks are full and pink, and Maddie can't help but smile back.

Maddie warms her head under the sunlamp for ten minutes, then lets Kiya blow dry her hair. She tries not to look until Kiya says "There." She lifts the mirror to her face and looks. "What do you think?" Kiya asks.

"I . . . don't know." It isn't that she doesn't like the way she looks—she does like the hair shorter and shaped around her face, the bangs cut unevenly and brushed to one side. The lemon juice has brightened her hair, made the gray less noticeable somehow. "I like it, but I look like someone else," she says. Someone younger and more stylish, she thinks. "I look like someone who lives in Boston. Or Portland, at least. Not someone who lives on Parker Pond."

That evening Maddie goes through her clothes closet. It seems wrong to wear her same clothes with this hairstyle. She doesn't want to buy new clothes; she just wants to wear something different, something she doesn't usually wear. She pulls out a navy belted jacket, a crisp white blouse. Too severe, she decides. A short jean skirt with this dark cardigan—why not? She hasn't worn that skirt in years, but it still looks good on her. She can wear it Monday, with her leather boots. And the fringed scarf Peter gave her for her birthday. She puts her jeans and sweatshirt back on.

Kiya is sitting on the couch, Sadie beside her. Kiya looks guilty when Maddie comes in. She had at first tried to keep Sadie from getting on the couch. "Oh, never mind," Maddie says, waving her hand toward the dog. "I give up on that." Sadie grins at her, as if in victory.

"You look wonderful," Kiya says.

"Thanks." Maddie touches her hair self-consciously.

"You should go somewhere to celebrate the new 'do.'"

"I'll stay here, thanks." She sits on the couch and looks out the window. "Still snowing." The branches of the white pine are heavy with white.

"That tree looks so beautiful," Kiya says. "I really love it."

"You're feeling better," Maddie observes. Seeing beauty in things is something Kiya couldn't do when she first arrived.

"I like it here. I'm grateful to you. I hope I can pay you back somehow." Kiya looks earnest in the lamplight.

Maddie pats Kiya's leg gently. "No need for that. You gave me a free haircut. I am enjoying having you here." And she is, now that the girl has cheered up somewhat. She just doesn't know what will happen when the baby is born. She's afraid that the birth, and the loss of her child, will throw Kiya even more deeply back into her depression.

"I know I can't stay forever," Kiya says, thoughtfully. "I may need to stay until after the baby is born. Then I'll see about getting another place. Is that okay?"

"Of course. Stay as long as you need to." Maddie goes to the kitchen. She means to start cooking dinner, but she stands at the window for a long time, staring out at the snow.

✳ ✳ ✳ ✳

On Saturday morning, just as Evie is setting up her ladder, a car pulls up out front. Mike steps out of the car and gives her a half-wave. "I came to give you a hand," he says. "Unless you'd really rather do this by yourself."

"No, no. I'd love help." He is wearing Bermuda shorts and a faded plaid shirt. Evie is aware of her faded, ill-fitting painting clothes; she wishes she hadn't tied her hair up in the stupid bandanna. "I just didn't know that you would really show up."

"Oh, you don't know my grandfather very well," Frank laughed. "There is no denying him. And actually, I like to paint." He looked out at the water. "Especially with a view like that."

There is only one ladder. Mike climbs that to paint, and Evie

159

stands on the ground. She works to one side of him, so she doesn't get dripped on. The June air is warm, a few cumulus clouds in the mild sky. Mike asks if they can listen to the radio while they paint. "We don't get reception here," Evie says. "We'll have to listen to the silence. Or ourselves talking."

"That's okay with me," Mike says. If they turn their heads to the left, they see all the way across the lake. From a distance, they hear the sound of splashing and children's voices, calling across the water. "Kids and camps," Mike says. "A good combination."

"I always liked it here," Evie says. "But I never had anyone to play with like those kids do."

"That's too bad," Mike says. "The downside of being an only child, I guess."

They brush in silence for a few moments, until Evie says, "On the other hand, I got all my parents' attention."

"I bet you always got to sit on your mother's lap when she read you a story."

"Yes. Why? Doesn't everyone?" She smiles up at Mike, who shakes his head.

"Not after my little sister was born. Then it was as if she owned that lap."

"Sad," Evie says. "Poor, lap-deprived Mike." There is something easy about being with Mike; she feels as if she's known him for a long time. Maybe it's the midwestern accent, the way of talking which makes her feel that she's at home. Or maybe it's his manner, his open friendliness. When they are silent, it is a comfortable silence.

He asks her why she came out so long before her parents. "Aren't you lonely here?"

Evie thinks about this. "It's a little scary at night sometimes. It's so dark, and the only sounds are the loons, or little animals rustling outside the camp. Once I heard coyotes."

"So why are you here? Just so you can paint the building before your parents come?" He is reaching up to paint the top boards, next to the eaves.

Evie remembers her need to fix herself, physically and mentally. "I wanted to be alone for a while. I needed to, I guess. I had some things I was dealing with."

"You're brave," Mike says. Then they paint in silence. Evie supposes that she is brave to be alone out here; either that or she is a coward for not wanting to be close to people. She thinks, for no real reason, of Grandpapa, sitting on the rocker inside the camp. It's as if he is there now, as if she could hear the creaking of the rocker if she would stop and listen. The scraped clapboards are bare and dry in places; it feels good to mend that, to cover it all with the thick, white paint.

Chapter Eighteen

After the holidays, the days become long and dark, the nights longer and darker. Kiya encourages Sadie to sleep with her in the bed so she won't be alone, but still, she wakes and spends hours staring at the ceiling. She strokes Sadie's fur, listening to the dog's faint snores. Kiya gets up after Maddie leaves for work and limps around the small house, drinking tea while staring out at the lake. She has every intention of contacting an adoption agency—she has found several possibilities online—but the thought makes her unhappy, and right now she needs to find things to make her happy.

Her mother has found a box of Kiya's art supplies, unused for years. "You used to be such a good artist," her mother said. "You never thought so, but you were." Now Kiya sits at Maddie's kitchen table and pulls out brushes, tubes of paint, oil crayons, pastels, pads of thick, creamy paper. The afternoon outside the windows is gray and leaden, the lake, a sheet of paler gray. Kiya feels a deep hunger within herself for color. Where did autumn go, with its brilliance?

When the afternoon light dims, so early now, Kiya turn on lamps and keeps on drawing. At first, she is hesitant and afraid, not wanting to make something ugly. Then she remembers that what she wants to see is just color, healing color, so she begins to layer oil crayon on the page. It's for her, she reminds herself; it's just to make her feel better. It does, and when she looks up at the lake again later she sees colors there she couldn't see before—lavenders and pale green, yellow and brown.

Before dark, Kiya takes Sadie out for a walk. She puts on boots and uses the crutch. The air feels good, but as she makes her way down the quiet, empty country road and the pale light fades, she begins to feel sadness descend upon her again. She's getting better, Kiya knows that, but she can't pretend that life isn't sadness. She can't pretend that it's not all about loss: her childhood; her brother; the father who used to love her. Her father used to play with her and Drew when they were little, running around their yard in the fallen leaves. He would take them sledding in the winter, hunched up on the sled behind them, yelling as they slid down the hill. In summers he taught both Drew and Kiya to play tennis. He'd play tennis with friends from his office on weekends. He would be careful about his appearance, wearing only crisp white shorts and matching shirt, checking his collar and sunglasses in the mirror before he left. Then they moved to Maine and he was gone from home more often, then he was gone for good.

She and Drew had been best friends. When they were small, they would paint themselves with mud after it rained, chasing each other around their small backyard. Drew and Kiya got drunk for the first time together when a friend of Drew's gave him a bottle of Schnapps. They saved it until their parents went out and they were home alone together, two goofy teenagers dancing to The White Stripes and getting sick on stuff that tasted like cough syrup. No one could make her laugh like Drew could.

Now she walks down this empty road, alone but for a dog that doesn't belong to her, and a baby who will soon be someone else's. She knows it's melodramatic to feel this way, and knowing that makes her even sadder; she wants to cry but thinks crying is indulging herself. Finally, on the way back home as Sadie gambols beside her, a feeling of pure sadness makes its way through, and she feels the welcome, forgiving rush of tears.

At the house, Kiya unhooks Sadie from the leash and lets her run. Sadie's legs are longer now, her body leaner and more confident. Kiya sits in the deck chair and closes her eyes. She hunches inside her jacket against the cold, remembering the warmth of sunshine on a still summer day. She thinks of her father again, of playing tennis with him on a summer day. She pictures him wearing his white shorts, self-consciously adjusting his tee shirt as people pass by. What was he so worried about? And why did he move so far away from home? Why San Francisco? When he called for Kiya's birthday last summer, he told her she should fly out to California to visit him. He'd buy her a ticket, he said. Maybe she should take him up on that offer. She pictures herself sitting in an airplane, thin again, looking out the window as the earth rushes by. She is content, but then, in a half-dream state, she realizes that she's missing something very important; something is lost, something flying by her in the blue sky outside her window.

* * * *

Toni's friend Sean is a small, energetic guy younger than either Peter or Toni. He didn't finish college, he said; it bored him, and he got a job offer without a degree, so why bother? Peter visits him at the office where Sean and Toni both work. Toni is in design, and Sean is on the tech side of things. They are looking at Sean's laptop computer on a high desk with stools in front of it, but Sean is in constant motion around Toni and Peter, dipping and shifting and turning and jiggling; the guy just can't stand still. The office is white and open around them, brightly lit and stylish. Peter sits down on a stool, feeling old next to Sean's incessant energy. Sean says, "Toni tells me you write music, play music. She says you're really good on several instruments."

Peter glances at Toni. It's true he plays banjo and guitar, and he took trombone lessons for a year in high school. "I didn't major in music in college, though," he says. "I minored in it. And I do play, and write music, so yeah . . ."

"Listen, I don't care about academic credentials. At all. At all. I'm just looking for someone to write little songs. Jingles, you know? I'm doing it for a package that will include SEO, and I need music for some interactive ads."

"Okay," Peter says. He doesn't know what Sean is talking about, but he'll go along. "I can do that."

"Just give it a try, we'll see how it works out. If you like it, we can work together. It wouldn't be a lot of money, but something." Sean tells him to try it out by writing a song for an imaginary client. "Say this person is . . . oh, I don't know, say it's a company that sells coffee. Yeah, try that. Should be fun, huh? Write me a song for someone who sells coffee." Sean, tapping his foot in its pointed boot, seems like an advertisement himself for coffee.

"Lyrics, or just music?"

"Just music for now. Yeah. And it doesn't have to be an entire song, either. Just a part of one. A few bars, just to pull someone in."

In the elevator on the way down, Toni says "He seems off-the-wall, but he's really good at one he does. He makes more money than I do, that's for sure." She leans her body against his; he can feel her warmth through both their winter coats.

"Sure," Peter says. "Coffee, coming right up."

At home Peter picks his guitar up and starts fooling around, picking a jazzy melody. But remembering Sean's round eyes and intense expression, remembering the way his boot tapped under those tight jeans, he reaches for his banjo instead. Songs about coffee float through his head; he remembers a hard-driving song from his youth called "Percolator," but he wants something lighter, with a brighter tone. He picks out a tune on the banjo, and imagines a light, bopping sound to go along with it—mallets on wood, or something like that, like that old coffee commercial, but updated. He slaps his desk with his fingers, then digs into his closet for the bongo drums he's had in there forever. He picks out the banjo tune that came to him and imagines someone bopping along on the banjo. This Sean guy may be full of shit, but writing a little tune suggesting coffee is something Peter can do.

※　※　※　※

Ron has been reserved with Maddie lately in some ways; no more sitting close to her at her desk and putting his hands on her shoulders as they talk. Yet she feels his attention in different ways. His eyes linger on hers longer, for example. Even when other people are in her office, even when a small group of three or four are discussing the tricks the new campus president is up to, Ron's eyes slide over to Maddie's as he talks. He looks first at her to see if she laughs at his joke, if she gets it. When he comes into her office and she is alone, he is almost shy.

Ron calls her on the phone one day. "Just checking to see if you're in your office," he mutters.

"What? Are you checking up on me?" she laughs.

"No, I mean . . . I'll be in. I just didn't want to walk down the hall if you weren't there." His office is three doors down from hers.

"Sure, I'm here."

Ron pauses at the door and glances down the hallway both ways before entering her office. The hallway is quiet. He looks down at the stack of folders in his hands, then up at her. Standing across from her, he drops the folders on her desk. "I don't know what we do with these," he says. "They all graduated."

She looks at the pile of folders and holds out her hands. "Give them to me."

He hands them to her. "I mean, do we put them in a folder graveyard somewhere? Do we keep them forever?"

"I keep them for four years in that file cabinet." She points to the back of the room. "Then I shred them. Why?"

"Because I'm curious," Ron says. "Because . . ." He stares at Maddie, mournfully, then abruptly turns and walks out of her office.

Maddie sits at her desk for a long moment, tapping a pen on its surface. She hears the dinging sound that means she received an email, sees it is just a listserv announcement. Finally, she gets up from her desk, and steps out into the hallway.

She pauses at the half-open door to Ron's office, hesitates, then taps. "Hello?"

"Hello!" Ron pushes his chair back from his desk, gestures at her. "Come in."

Maddie stands hesitantly just inside his office. She rarely comes in here; they usually talk in her office. His office is a mess, as always; papers piled in stacks on his desk, on top of file cabinets, and on chairs. He motions to the one empty chair beside his own. "Sit down."

She perches uneasily on the edge of the chair. "I was just wondering if everything was all right."

Ron sits in his chair, looking at her. She can't tell what he's thinking. Finally, he stands up, closes the door to his office, and turns to face her. He is wearing his baggy khaki pants, his khaki safari vest over a button-up green shirt, and his hair is jutting out at all angles as usual. He stares at Maddie gloomily through his wire-framed glasses. He says, "I was trying not to ask you to go out for dinner with me."

"I thought I'd done something wrong," Maddie says. They are sitting opposite each other in a corner booth in a small, dark restaurant.

"No, I'm sorry, I just didn't know what to say. I'm awkward about these things. I apologize." Ron had suggested this place, in the next town over.

Maddie looks down at the plastic-covered menu placed in front of her. "I've never been here before."

"The haddock is good," Ron says, not looking at the menu. The waitress, when she seated them, said hello to Ron as if she knew him.

After they order two haddock dinners, Maddie and Ron sit looking at one another. "I wanted to ask you out," Ron says. "I just didn't know if it was a good idea. In fact," he says, "I know it's not a good idea. We'll go into the office tomorrow and see one another."

"Right," Maddie says. She looks up and smiles at his obvious discomfort. He is really so cute. "Still, I'm glad you said something."

His expression lightens then, and he smiles back at her. "We've been working together for how long? Since I became chair."

"Two and a half years," Maddie says.

"I've always liked you."

"I've always liked you, too," she says. "Surely you could tell that." She pauses, looks around her. Most of the tables are empty, and she doesn't recognize anyone she knows. "You're right, though, it's probably not a good idea for us to go out together. The job thing."

"Right," Ron says, as he reaches across the table. He touches Maddie's fingertips with his, tentatively, then holds her hand in his. She is reminded of a dream she must have had; a dream of Ron touching her, caressing her. "It would be a very bad thing to do," he says. "We couldn't concentrate on our important work."

"Well, it's not that . . ." Ron's hand moves past her wrist, pushing up her sweater to stroke her arm. "It could be very awkward at work, that's all," she says.

Ron slowly removes his hand and picks up his fork. "No, you're right. You're absolutely right. It could be very awkward. And probably more awkward for you than for me."

Maddie is glad he recognizes that. He is her boss after all, her supervisor, the one who writes her performance evaluations. She thinks there is a written policy somewhere about relationships like that. She has had a crush on Ron for years, but she is past the heady compulsion of youth to procreate, to push someone into bed. She moves the conversation to other topics. "How was the conference?" Ron had recently returned from New York City.

"Oh, fine. I met with some old friends there. That's always worth the trip." He pushes food around on his plate, head down, and orders chocolate cake for dessert. Maddie smiles; there is something about Ron that is childlike, and she resists saying he can't have dessert because he didn't finish his dinner. She also resists the temptation to ask about Jane. If Ron wants to pretend that no one on campus noticed the relationship, she will go along with that. "How are things going with your ward?" he asks.

"Kiya, you mean? She's doing all right. I think living in the country is good for her."

"Living with you is good for her, you mean."

When they leave, Ron walks Maddie to her car. Their footsteps echo in the night air, in the empty car lot. At her car door, Ron takes her hand again. "Thanks, Maddie, for being your kind and sensible self."

"Thank you for dinner," Maddie says. "And for your friendship." Something more seems needed, so she opens her arms for a hug. A friendly hug, she thinks, one that will represent their friendship and respect for one another.

After a moment of surprise, Ron takes her in his arms. She feels him push her back against her car, and his body and his lips press against hers, hard.

* * *

The next time Evie goes for her accumulator treatment, she is relieved to see no sign of Dr. Anderson. Tom, the caretaker, lets her in when she knocks. After a moment she hears footsteps on the stairs, and Dr. Reich is there. She is reminded of the power of his personality, the force behind the look he levels at her. He asks her how she has been. "Good," Evie says. "I've been healthy. I have an appointment with a doctor in Farmington for a check-up."

Dr. Reich nods, and his face looks suddenly heavy and distracted, as if something dark has swept across it. He has pouches under his eyes. Remembering what Dr. Anderson said, Evie blurts out, "And you? I hope everything is all right with you . . ."

"Everything is not all right with me. The plague that is growing everywhere in the world is trying to consume me." At Evie's alarmed look, he says, "Not a physical illness, but an emotional one. There are small people in the world, who are afraid of anything they cannot understand." He is angry. "They will not believe the truth if they are confronted with it."

Evie thinks of the cloud-busters, long silver tubes pointing at the sky, which Dr. Reich uses to cause rain. It is no wonder, she thinks, that people are suspicious of his work. It sounds crazy. She stands awkwardly, one hand leaning on the table, feeling tongue-tied and awkward. "I believe," she says. "I believe the accumulator is helping me. And I am very, very grateful to you for everything you do for me, and for other people." It's true, she realizes; she is not saying this just to please the great doctor. "You are giving me hope for my future."

Dr. Reich's face softens when he looks at her. She is reminded of how a face can mirror internal weather: she sees the clouds calm, peace spread as if over water. "Thank you, Evelyn," he says.

That evening, Evie stands in front of the old mahogany dresser with a mirror arching above it. She has closed the bedroom curtains. She pulls her shirt off, unhooks her bra, and turns on the overhead light. She has been undressing in the dark without looking toward the mirror to avoid doing this, but it's time. She twists

169

around, looking over her shoulder to see the scar on her back. It's been nearly three months, and the stitches, which were raised and red before and surrounded by purple bruises, have faded. The skin there is smooth and nearly level. She reaches one hand back to touch them, feeling their slight bumps. She steels herself and lifts an armpit to look at the longer scar there. It curves around from her back to her breast, a wicked smile. The scar is clearly visible, but the breast it curves onto is intact. The bruising and swelling are gone, the stitches still a lurid pink against the lighter skin. Their lines remain, crossing the initial cut like giant thread marks.

When she puts her arm down and faces forward, nothing shows; she is a completely normal young Caucasian woman, smooth-skinned and slim-waisted. She smiles at herself, cheerful and perky-breasted. It's only when she lifts her arm that her illness is revealed, her secret trauma exposed.

Chapter Nineteen

Kiya's mother has offered to go with her to talk to people at the adoption agency, but at the last minute, she decides she'd better not go in. Kiya actually decides this, as she stands outside the building looking at her mother's pale face, her trembling lips. "You know," Kiya says, "I think it's probably better for me to go in by myself." The sun is bright on them and on the other people on the sidewalk, who veer around the pregnant woman and the gray-haired, shaky woman.

"Well, all right, if that's what you think is best," her mother says, relief clear on her face. She looks around. "Is it all right if I wait in that coffee shop over there?"

"That's fine," Kiya says. "It's the best thing."

She is brought into a room more like a living room than an office, with upholstered chairs and framed art reproductions on walls painted lavender and pale green. The woman across from her, Adrienne, says, "This is a hard time for you, I know. Deciding that you're not ready yet to parent is a decision that you make for the child's best interest, and you deserve nothing but praise and support for that decision." She speaks precisely, and Kiya envies her ability to put such things into words. If she tried to do that right now, Kiya would cry.

She looks around; not a paper or computer in sight. "Um . . . do I sign some papers or something?"

Adrienne smiles. "This meeting is just to get to know you, and to help you understand the process." The adoption can be either closed or open, Adrienne says; if she chooses open, she can get to know the adoptive parents before the birth, and they can get to know her. She tells Kiya that she will be able to choose the parents of her baby, and may request pictures of the baby and updates from the adoptive parents if she wishes. Profiles of prospective parents, people who hope to be parents, are online. Adrienne asks Kiya how she's doing financially, and if she has medical insurance.

"MaineCare and my mother have been paying for my medical costs," Kiya says, "and I live with a friend." She tries not to listen to the little voice inside her, a familiar male voice, that says *Loser. Freeloader.*

"It's good you have that support," Adrienne says. "You need it emotionally as well as physically now." Adrienne then tells her that the adoptive parents, through the agency, would be able to help her financially when she is pregnant if she decides to place her baby.

Kiya has not considered this idea. "You mean the adoptive parents, the ones I would choose to give my baby to, would pay my bills while I was pregnant?"

Adrienne nods. "Yes. And medical bills, if you needed them. Prenatal vitamins, things like that."

"Wow." She is afraid to ask her next question; what would happen if she changed her mind when the baby was born. It would make her sound indecisive, weak. "That's great," she says instead.

Back at Maddie's house, Kiya looks up the agency online and finds profiles of couples who want to adopt. One couple shows photos of the two of them—both beautiful and athletic—posing in a variety of places, including in front of the Eiffel Tower and Big Ben. They seem a little too perfect to Kiya. Another couple has two children already, both adopted, two little girls shown hugging one another. Another couple are both women, smiling into the camera. They look like people Kiya would be friends with.

The lovely smiling people in the photos should make Kiya feel cheered at the prospect of two of them welcoming her baby, but instead, she finds herself angry. What makes them think they would be better parents than she would? She stands up to look at herself in the full-length mirror hanging on her bedroom door. She is six months along now, her belly round in front of her. She thinks it looks beautiful, because it holds her baby. She feels its movements deep inside her. The would-be adoptive parents are married, are doctors, lawyers, stay-at-home mothers. Does that automatically make them better parents than she would be? She looks at her defiant face in the mirror and hears the small, sure voice inside her, saying *Yes. Yes. Yes, it does,* and then hears Drew's sarcastic voice adding to it: *Duh. Duh, you dweeb, what do you think?*

* * * *

On busy nights at the Blue Moon Peter is officially a bar-back. He washes glasses, refills the ice, gets wine and beer and liquor from the basement, and changes the kegs. Occasionally he pours beers, but usually, the bartender serves the drinks. The bartender is either Eddie or Jake. Eddie is easy-going and older, with a good sense of humor. Jake is younger, and he takes pills. He is fast behind the bar and has a way of joking with customers that verges on sarcasm or rudeness, but customers love him. Peter doesn't know how Jake does it. Peter has always enjoyed going out and having a few drinks but is learning what it's like to be sober around drunk people. He wonders if people are more stupid than he thought they were, or if they just sound that way when they are drunk. Tonight, two heavy guys wearing tee shirts are leaning on the bar, glancing over at a table where three young women sit. "No tits to speak of on the one in red," the guy with the beard says.

"Yeah, but that one next to her . . . she's got 'em, ain't afraid to show 'em."

"Tit's ain't all she's got. Got a big round ass, too."

Peter feels sorry for the women, who don't know that their bodies are the topics of conversation, if it can be called conversation. Toni was supposed to come in after work tonight, but Peter is almost glad that she has not shown up yet. He doesn't want to hear his two companions comment on the various parts of Toni's anatomy. He checks his phone, and sees a text: *Sorry I don't think I'll make it in tonight. Too tired. Tomorrow maybe?*

As he walks home after work, Peter thinks of Toni. She gives him his freedom, his space, which is what he always wanted in relationships, but for some reason, he's not happy about it. Is it possible, he wonders, to have space and freedom and still be in love? Maybe asking for both is asking for the impossible.

The fact that there will be a child of his somewhere in the world is always in the back of Peter's mind. He is not proud of his early reactions to the news, the way he rebuffed Kiya. He couldn't help it, though; he was overwhelmed by the thought, and by the way she dropped it on him. The wind picks up as he turns the corner to his street, and blows a few wet flakes in his face. Maybe he should write a song for the child, for his child he will never see.

Hunched in his jacket against the wind, Peter imagines a boy running around on a green lawn. A young boy, just five or six years old, running through the grass.

When he was little, Peter went through a period of wanting a father; he didn't have to have HIS father, just a father, just someone to call "Dad." He didn't remember his father, and so it was as if he never had one. He remembers quite vividly now, saying to his mother "I just want someone to call 'Dad'." He feels sorry, not for himself, but for the little kid he was then, as if he were someone else. The poor kid! Just wanting a dad!

As he unlocks the door to his apartment, Peter reminds himself that Kiya is planning to put their baby up for adoption. This means that the baby, his son or his daughter, will have a father, a present and loving father. Someone financially secure, someone ready to be a father. They are making sure of that, by putting the kid up for adoption. Why, Peter wonders as he turns on the lights in the empty apartment, does this not make him feel happier than it does?

✻ ✻ ✻ ✻

The kiss is always on Maddie's mind. At work, she thinks of it whenever she sees Ron, whenever she talks with him. She knows he is thinking about it too, or something like it; knows it in the way he looks at her, in the way he, again, lets his shoulder brush against hers as he leans down. Sometimes when no one else is in Maddie's office, just the two of them, he will look her full in the face with a half-smile, a look that suggests they share something secret. The look Ron gives her makes her stomach twist in a way she remembers from high school. She was outside raking leaves one day, fifteen or sixteen years old, when a boy came walking down the road and stopped to talk. He was from a neighboring town and had come to visit his grandparents, who lived in the house next door. As they talked, he and Maddie walked behind the barn. There he suddenly pulled her to him and kissed her hard. She remembers the electric feeling she got in her stomach then, excitement heightened by a touch of fear. It was a feeling she thought she was all done with, and she feels it again now when she thinks of Ron's kiss.

She didn't mean to respond to his kiss. She thought it was rude of him to lean into her like that when they'd decided not to see one another, when she'd reached out for a friendly hug. His mouth had been hard and slightly wet against hers, his beard bristly, but Maddie had—without thinking about it—found herself responding. She let the kiss go on too long, and she kissed him back. She can't blame Ron, she is guilty.

It had been so long since she kissed someone. Really kissed someone, when they kiss back. She kisses Alex every time she leaves him, but him kissing her back belongs to memory.

Lately, Alex has been appearing in her dreams. He is healthy, and loving. Often she dreams that he is lying next to her in her bed, spooning up against her back like he used to do. He reaches out to stroke her hair, and she wakes with the feeling of his warm hand upon her head. His presence next to her is so real when she wakes up, she has a hard time believing he is not there. She feels like a widow, but she is a widow who was never married, and whose husband is still alive.

Maddie stands at the photocopier making copies, listening to the humming and thumping as the machine does its work, when she feels something warm on the back of her neck. She jumps, and turns; it is, of course, Ron touching her, his hand gently cupping her neck under her hair. He is grinning impishly, like a naughty child. He keeps a hand on her shoulder, lets it drop down her arm, brushing casually against her breast. Maddie gasps, and turns back to the machine; the door to the hallway is wide open, anyone could walk by and see them.

Susan and Maddie eat lunch together in the cafeteria. Maddie is quiet, paying attention to Susan. Does she suspect anything, has she noticed anything? It doesn't seem so; Susan chatters away about nothing, about school gossip and her family, as usual. The historians are doing a Program Review, she says, and Jane Dougherty is "going crazy" with it. "I gather all the information, and send it to her."

"Is it a lot of work?" Maddie asks, interested now that Jane's name has come up. "Is she a pain to work with?"

"Not more than anyone. She's around a lot, staying late to

work on it. No social life, I guess," Susan says, raising an eyebrow at Maddie.

Maddie takes a bite of her tuna sandwich. She is thinking of a way to change the subject when Susan asks about Kiya. "I need another haircut," she says. "I love the last one I got. Can she do it again?"

Maddie reads to Alex just before dinnertime, when food smells are reaching down the hallways, into his room. They make her hungry, and she wonders if Alex gets hungry too, wonders if the food smells good to him. His food is brought into his body through a tube going into his stomach. Such a mechanical way to live, she thinks; is it worth it for him? She holds his face between her hands before she goes, his loose skin warm beneath her palms. She looks into his eyes. He looks back at her, and she kisses his forehead. She feels him with her, feels his presence.

On days when Maddie visits Alex, Kiya has dinner cooking by the time she gets home. Maddie told Kiya she doesn't care what she cooks, anything is better than Maddie doing it herself. Lately, Kiya has been trying new recipes, roasted vegetables, and soups. Healthy meals, to help her baby grow strong, she says. Today when Maddie enters the kitchen, she smells something good. "Is that bread?" Sadie jumps from the couch to say hello, tail wagging.

Kiya turns from the counter, smiling bashfully. "Well, yes. I tried out a new recipe. Walnut buckwheat. Hope it's edible."

"Oh, I can't believe it. You ar e too wonderful." How sweet Kiya can be, Maddie thinks, the girl's cheeks pink from cooking, her belly round and lovely under an apron. How pleasant it is to come into a house full of good smells, of bright lights, of creature warmth. How different it will be—how lonely the house will be, how quiet and dark, after the baby is born and Kiya leaves.

* * * *

Evie has brought copies of her x-rays and doctor's reports along with her to Maine and dropped the folder off at the doctor's office a week ago. Now a nurse in a white dress tells her to undress— "Just take off your shirt and bra, dear, and put on this johnny." She hands her a cloth gown.

"Why do they call it a johnny?" Evie asks, holding it up.

"I don't know, dear." The nurse takes her temperature, then leaves her to undress and put the light cotton gown over her top, tying it loosely closed in front. Evie sits on the edge of the padded table, waiting. She tries not to think of the fact that in a few minutes, a man she's never seen before will be looking at her naked breasts.

"Evie Russell," the doctor says when he enters. He is smiling and gray-haired. "Are you related to Edward Russell?"

"Yes," Evie says. "He was my grandfather."

"I knew him. He was a friend of mine, actually. I have a camp on Parker Pond. He was a great man, a wonderful guy. Irreplaceable."

"Yes," Evie says. Keeping the sharp pricking in her eyes from turning into tears, which would spill over her cheeks, gives Evie something to concentrate on as she opens her gown to show the doctor her scar. He touches the scar, as she had done the night before, but his fingers prod forcefully into the skin. He pushes into her armpit, then asks her to raise her other arm and pushes his fingers there also. He is checking for lumps, she realizes. He feels her neck, then asks to see the scar on her back. He listens to her lungs and asks her how she's been feeling.

"Good," Evie says. "Fine." She considers telling him of her orgone treatments, but decides against it. He takes his stethoscope from his ears, and she waits for his pronouncement.

"Everything looks fine," he says.

Evie has read enough of the works of Wilhelm Reich to know that he would think her attitude toward sex is unhealthy. She herself thinks maybe it's not healthy, but she doesn't know what to do about it. It's not like she can just make herself like something she doesn't like; she's never liked beets, for example, and she can't just talk herself into thinking they're delicious. She suspects that the failure of her relationship with Eric was due at least in part to the fact that she never enjoyed sex with him. Surely he could tell? She learned in her psychology classes what psychotherapy can do, but doesn't want to attempt it; she doesn't think she's crazy. And she can't imagine what her parents would say if she told them she was seeing a psychiatrist. Why, they would ask; to benefit my sex life, she would reply. Sure.

She wonders what it would be like to stop into a bar some evening, say the one in downtown Farmington, where she would know no one. Maybe she could enjoy sex if it were with a stranger, someone she would never see again. She drives slowly past the bar, trying to peer in its darkened windows, then turns onto Route 27 and speeds up out of town. She knows she will never stop at the bar by herself, will never have sex with a stranger.

At home, the sun is warm on her shoulders, the lake water still. Evie changes into her swimming suit and steps slowly into the water, which is still cool, and ducks under quickly. She swims away from the dock, her body becoming used to the water until it doesn't feel cool anymore. She feels the ache where the doctor prodded under her arm, but she is healthy, she is healthy. She is strong. Her legs scissor in the water, her arms reach above her head. She thinks maybe sex—good sex—would feel something like this: the water surrounding her body, her breasts lifting inside her suit, an energy coming from inside her and spreading out to her fingertips. She stops a distance from the dock, treading water, and lifts her face to the sun.

Chapter Twenty

Kiya's father is flying into Portland the following week for business, he says, but wants to see her. He seems to think she still lives in Portland. She calls her mother when she gets the email. "Does Daddy know I'm pregnant? Because I haven't told him."

"No," her mother says. "I haven't told him either. I thought you could do that yourself if you wanted to."

"I guess he'll find out," Kiya says, "since we're having lunch."

Kiya arrives first at a café in the Old Port. She wonders whether to leave her coat on or to take it off; wonders how to reveal herself to him. Should she stay seated and tell him, or stand up and let him see for himself? In the end the decision is made for her, as she goes to the bathroom and on the way back to the table sees her father coming through the front door. She stands by their table and waves. He still has that silly mustache, but he's added a small neat beard, which makes the mustache less obvious. He is wearing a stylish trench coat she hasn't seen before. His eyes travel over her, registering. He blinks.

"Kiya." When he reaches her, he puts his arms around her and holds her tight. "Kiya. My baby." His voice is muffled against her shoulder, and Kiya finds herself squeezing her eyes tight to keep in the tears.

"Daddy," she says, and then the tears can't be held, are rolling down her cheeks. "I missed you." Having him hold her, smelling his smell of shampoo and the faint men's cologne he always wore, hearing him say her name all remind her that she did miss him, she does miss him—misses the dad she used to have, the one who would hold her and call her his baby. Not this mustached, bearded imposter.

They sit down. Kiya, fishing in her handbag for a tissue, says, "So you see what's going on with me." She wipes carefully under her eyes.

"I see you're pregnant. Congratulations, I guess? Isn't that what one is supposed to say?" He smiles, and she sees his uncertainty, his desire to please her.

"Sure, you can say that," she says. "You can say whatever you want." She picks up a menu and pretends to study it. "I'm not keeping the baby, by the way. I'm putting it up for adoption. Or 'placing it,' as we're supposed to say. It's more gentle, or something."

"Oh, Kiya. I'm sorry. Is the baby's father . . ." He doesn't finish.

Kiya shrugs. "We're not seeing one another anymore. He doesn't want to be a father. He's around, though, and he's been helpful. In fact, I'm living with his mother now. She's more or less supporting me."

"Is that right. The things I don't hear." He sounds vaguely irritated at his lack of information. He glances down at the menu. "I'll have the veggie wrap."

"It isn't like we keep in constant touch, though, you and me. Anyway." She looks at him, tries to smile. "How's your life in the Bay Area? How's your girlfriend?"

"Life is good. Work is going well. Sophia and I broke up."

"Oh. Sorry," Kiya says, though her voice comes out sounding not sorry at all.

"It wasn't a good relationship," her father says. "I rushed into it, as an excuse more or less to get out of the marriage to your mother. I know that's hard to hear, and will make you respect me less than you probably already do, but it's the truth."

"Was it so bad, then, being married to Mom?" Kiya feels pain somewhere around her heart as she thinks of her mother, her pale face and anxiety, her sadness.

"Your mother is a wonderful person. I meant it when I said I loved her. But we shouldn't have been married. *I* shouldn't have been married. Kiya . . ." He straightens his shoulders and looks Kiya in the face. "I'm in a new relationship now, and I want you to know about it. It's the first honest relationship I've had in a long time. My partner's name is Elliot." To Kiya's questioning look, he adds, "Yes, Elliot is a man."

Kiya feels as if a new building, in a new city, is being constructed around her. The shapes of her world are rearranging themselves as she sits on her chair, trying to take it in. Her father?

Yes, her father . . . it starts to make sense. Her father smiles at her confusion, with pain in his eyes. It is as if he is changing before her eyes into a different person; not the person she thought he was, but perhaps the person he really is.

"But why did you get married in the first place?" Kiya asks. "Why didn't you just accept that you were gay?" They have been talking for some time; the afternoon light is low in the sky, as they sit at the table in the same café. Kiya orders more hot water for her tea, her father another Sam Adams.

"It's hard to explain. I was attracted to both men and women, and I thought I'd have a better life if I married your mother. She was a good friend, and I wanted children . . ." He shrugs. "I wanted *you*. And your brother. I didn't think I have could have that otherwise. I just didn't know. I was stupid, I didn't know."

Kiya's father, at this moment, looks younger and vulnerable to her, like someone she could be friends with. "But why then did you take off with a woman? With Sophia? Why not just get divorced from mom and then be your gay self?"

He smiles at her and wipes a hand across his face. "That would have been the smart thing to do, wouldn't it? I can't tell you. I liked Sophia. May`be I thought it was more understandable that I take off with a younger woman than that I got divorced because I was gay. Maybe I thought it would make me happy." He leans forward over the table. "I was hiding, Kiya. I had my mother's voice in the back of my mind. She was the original homophobe, and my father wasn't far behind. And I thought I wouldn't find love with a man. I had a . . . an ugly idea of what love with a man would be like. I didn't know it could be like it is with Elliot. It took me a long time to learn. I have to apologize to everybody. You and your mother. And Drew. Maybe Drew most of all."

"I wish he were sitting here," she says. "Listening to this. He would have been very interested."

"I do too. I wish I could have talked to him. In a way, his . . . his death made me finally get honest with my life. I knew I couldn't wait any longer."

Kiya stretches back in her seat, twisting to relieve an ache in her back. She listens for Drew's voice, for a tone, wondering what he would say, but all she hears is a faint hum, blood running through her veins like air rushing through a shell.

* * * *

Sean likes the coffee tune Peter came up with and gives him a real assignment, a paid one. Peter writes a tune Sean will use in ads for a Portland-based business with branches throughout New England. The work takes Peter two days and Sean pays him $250. When the ad is complete and Peter looks at it on the business's webpage, it gives him a thrill to hear the tune he wrote. He lets Sean know he is available anytime for this kind of work, and Sean says he will call him again. After three weeks, Sean texts him that he has another job for Peter to consider. The next day, Sean texts again and tells him to never mind; the company didn't want to pay extra for original music.

Peter and Matthew are playing occasionally in clubs, where they do covers as well as their own work. The income from these jobs is small. On nights when Matthew finds them a gig and Peter has to work, Matthew has other friends who take Peter's place. At The Blue Moon Peter chops vegetables, cooks French fries, washes dishes, and replaces beer kegs, all the time wondering whether this is really what his life is all about.

Peter knows that his worth as a human being isn't based on his job or the money he is making, but there are times when he can't remember what, exactly, it is based on. He thinks of volunteering at a local soup kitchen. He makes a call, and a woman tells him to fill out a form online, but somehow he never gets it done. He's not sure they need him. And he feels pretty sure that the soup kitchen will continue operating more or less as it has been if he doesn't show up.

Peter would say he's having a mid-life crisis, only he's not old enough. Toni is caught up in her job, which is more and more demanding, and they go out just once or twice a week. When they are together Peter sometimes falls quiet and lets the quiet extend until Toni says something. What does he have to talk about?

There is an emptiness in his mind, a place of wonder which could be beautiful, but now just seems empty.

One afternoon he does what Toni has been suggesting he do. He opens a browser and types in his father's name: Mark Greenleaf. Maybe it's time for him to give the man a call, see what genetic material he himself has come from. He adds "Chicago" to his father's name, but still comes up with an intimidatingly long list. He guesses his father would be around the same age as his mother, but Peter doesn't have his father's middle name or place of employment. He doesn't want to ask his mother, but after a fruitless hour or two on the internet, he gives in and calls her.

"So that's when she told me that my father was dead." Peter is talking in a low, even voice close to Alex's ear. Alex seems to be leaning toward him in his reclining wheelchair, as if to hear him better. "She said she never told me before because I never asked. Makes sense, I guess. Right?" Alex's body shifts slightly in what Peter can imagine is silent agreement.

"She was surprised to hear that I'd called him. She didn't know that. Yes, I did," Peter says, as if in answer to a question. He looks behind him to make sure that the door to Alex's room is still closed, that no one is listening in on their—his—conversation. "I was a kid. I found his number and talked to him. In my memory, he sounded kind of out of it. High. Maybe he was on pills, pain pills or something. He said something weird to me. Said that he would always be with me." Peter laughs, and is surprised at the way it sounds: scornful, scoffing, hurt. He didn't know he had that bitterness in him. "As if. I mean, if he were going to always be with me, if that's something that my father wanted, then all he would have had to do would have been to pick up the phone. Make an airplane reservation, come visit. Send me there on the airplane, whatever. Right?" Peter stares at Alex, but this time gets no reply, not even a shift in Alex's posture. He remains looking straight ahead.

"Maybe I need to be understanding, maybe the man had an addiction or something and couldn't do anything. All right, I get it. That's what my mother said; she said my dad was a smart and talented man. But he struggled with addictions. I don't know how much he struggled, or how much he was just addicted. But anyway."

Peter stares through the open blinds out the window. A rectangle of yard covered by crusty snow, a parking lot where he can see his old Jeep next to a dirty white car. He turns back to Alex. "Why am I telling you all this, you ask? Because you were the only father I had. I bet you didn't know that, did you? Because you and I didn't have that kind of relationship, not really. We didn't know each other well enough." Peter looks down at the water bottle he holds in his hands. He unscrews the cap, lifts it up to his mouth, takes a drink. He hears voices go by Alex's door, from the hallway, louder then fading. Women's voices. "But I just wanted you to know that you could have been that father to me if anyone could have. You were good to me. Bratty kid that I was then, you treated me well. Better than I deserved. You talked to me." Peter remembers sitting on the front steps with Alex, talking about school. He said he didn't think his teacher liked him, and Alex laughed at that. Alex said, "Who wouldn't like you? They'd have to be crazy." Simple, but it was a nice thing to say. "Remember that?"

Peter rubs a palm across his face, looks around. He puts a hand on Alex's shoulder. "So, thanks. I guess I'll go now. I'll be back again. You take care." He hesitates, then leans forward and places an unmanly, gentle kiss on Alex's cheek, feeling the softness of old skin beneath his lips.

* * * *

On a bright Saturday morning in late February, Maddie hooks the leash onto Sadie's collar and walks with her down the lane. Yesterday there was a steady sleet, which froze solid as the weather turned colder overnight and remains frozen this morning. All the tree branches are covered in a glittering, clear sheath of ice that catches the early sun. Low tree branches are bowed even lower by their weight of ice, nearly touching the ground. The electricity went out in the night, but came back on this morning. Sadie prances happily ahead of her, long legs jerking the leash ahead, then backtracking to sniff something by the side of the road, then jerking ahead again.

Maddie has a memory of a morning like this back in Illinois when she was a girl. It was some holiday, perhaps New Year's Eve, and she was in the back seat of her parents' car as they drove to Grandma and Grandpa's house. The sun shone through ice-covered tree branches, as it is doing today, and Maddie remembers feeling that this was the most beautiful thing she had ever seen. She told herself then, ten years old and sitting in the back seat of her parents' car, that she must remember this sight for the rest of her life. And she has, she thinks; it is still with her, the flat white fields, the ice coating all surfaces like it was made of jewels instead of water. There the land was flatter and more tended; here it is more overgrown, more varied but catches the sun in the same way, a bright gift.

Maddie remembers her mother and her father sitting in the car seat in front of her. She can visualize her mother's brown hair, falling in curls onto her neck. Kiya had asked about the relationship her mother had with Wilhelm Reich, wondering if it was a romantic one. Kiya's eyes lit up at that idea, the possibility that her baby's grandmother had a relationship with a famous person.

Maddie stops suddenly in the lane, forcing Sadie to stop with a jerk also. She wonders if Kiya was suggesting that Maddie herself was a love child of Reich. Now that she remembers the conversation, she thinks that is what Kiya was suggesting. Maddie laughs but then wonders. Her mother was certainly infatuated with Reich and his ideas, and she was pregnant when she married Maddie's father. Maddie remembers her father, his full lower lip, the way he would look at her over his glasses. She tries to remember what Reich looks like from the photo on the back of the book Kiya was reading. Vaguely similar in appearance to her father, as she remembers, so who would know?

When did Reich die? She walks again down the lane, Sadie skittering back and forth ahead of her. She'll check it out when she gets back home. A truck approaches; Jack, with his grandson in the passenger's seat. Jack stops beside her, rolling down the window. "Hello there," he shouts. He's wearing sunglasses and grinning, and he almost, she thinks, looks handsome.

"Hello," she says. "And how is Paul today?"

"He's just fine," Jack says. "We have some ice fishing to do today. Right, Paulie?" The boy returns his look blankly, his mouth slightly open, but begins to bounce on his seat. "Yessir, better get moving here," Jack says.

"Have fun," Maddie says. "Be careful."

"Always." He waves at her, and drives away, his grandson now bobbing up and down beside him.

She finds the book by Wilhelm Reich in the bookshelf and opens it. He died in 1957. Maddie was born in 1961. He isn't her father, isn't Peter's grandfather, the baby's great-grandfather. Kiya will be disappointed.

Maddie puts a log into the wood stove and watches it crackle and ignite. She leans back on the couch and remembers how Ron looked at her when he came in the office yesterday. He sat in a chair next to her behind her desk as they discussed the budget, and leaning against her, rested his hand on her thigh. When she caught her breath and moved his hand away, he wasn't abashed at all, but instead gave out a great roar of laughter. He enjoys this, she thinks; he likes upsetting her, embarrassing her. He teases her by doing those things, teases her like Joey Meester used to do in junior high school when he would snap her bra strap. In a way, it makes her excited and giddy, makes her feel young and desired again, and he knows that. He can tell by the flush of her cheeks, by her embarrassed laughter. When she looks in the mirror she sees a pretty woman, someone who can still turn a man's head. But his behavior worries her, and as she sits on the couch she feels a sick, gnawing sensation in her stomach. What will be the outcome of this; what can possibly happen? Outside her window, the sun has been covered by clouds, and the ice bowing down the branches has lost its glitter, looking merely cold, and dangerous.

* * * *

Evie stands outside the front door of Orgonan, waiting for someone to answer her knock. Through the screen door, she hears distant voices somewhere inside. She knocks again, loudly, and Tom is at the door. "Hello there, young lady; no need to break down the door." She follows him down the hall, into the room where the accumulator is.

"The boss says I'm supposed to let you in." Tom opens the door to the accumulator and points to the box with exaggerated politeness. "So here you are. He'll be by when you're done." Evie steps in and sits down. Tom stands for a moment holding the door, looking at her. "So this thing works for you?"

"Well, yes. Yes, I think it does."

"You feel something in it?"

"Yes, certainly."

He shakes his head. "I didn't feel a damn thing when I tried it." He grins at her. "But good luck to you, young lady!" He shuts the door.

Evie leans back against the wall and closes her eyes. After a moment she feels the warmth, then the slight tingling on the bare skin of her arms. There *is* something, no matter what Tom says. She imagines the healing working its way inside her, gently pushing aside obstacles to health and letting the energy within her run free. Her thoughts are looping and flowing now, untethered as she feels herself grow sleepy. *Anything is possible,* she thinks; she doesn't know exactly what she is thinking of, what she hopes for that she might consider, but it seems right to tell herself again, *anything is possible.*

From somewhere in the house Evie hears footsteps, voices. A door closes. A man's voice—Dr. Reich's—and a woman's. They pause in the next room, and Evie can just make out Dr. Reich saying: "So we agree on that, then," and a woman's voice, light, lilting: "Yes. Oh yes, that would be just right." There is silence then, and Evie opens her eyes, listening. She can't tell if their conversation is muted and quiet, or if they are not speaking. She hears a woman's laughter then, bursting out but quickly restrained. There are firm footsteps, and the door opens to a smiling Dr. Reich. "Well, Evelyn, how are you doing in there?"

She steps out carefully. Standing behind Dr. Reich is a young woman, probably in her early 30's. She has dark hair and is very attractive. "I'm feeling well," Evie says.

Dr. Reich stands looking at her, hands in his pants pocket under his white lab coat, but Evie gets the sense he isn't really seeing her. His attention is distracted, pulled back to the woman behind him. The woman smiles at Evie, rather distantly; she too is distracted. Dr. Reich speaks over his shoulder to the woman. "Evelyn has been in orgone treatment for the past month. She looks healthy, does she not?" He looks at Evie again, smiling, she thinks, as if he has just won some secret prize.

"Oh yes," the woman says, looking somewhat sympathetically at Evie. She must know how uncomfortable it is for Evie for her general health—probably her sexual health, too—to be observed and speculated on in this way.

Evie speaks up. "Well, I'll be on my way, then." She makes her way out the door and down the drive, hearing their voices start up behind her. Dr. Reich is separated from his wife and son, Evie has heard, so there is certainly no reason he shouldn't be taking up with another woman. Still, the woman is so young, and Evie can't help feeling irritated as she drives away.

She stops at the General Store for milk, eggs, and cheese, and the sun is low in the sky when she pulls up in front of the cabin. The small building looks welcoming to her; she feels protective of her little home. The new paint brightens it. She looks forward to sitting on the dock and contemplating the day, smoking a cigarette as she ponders her future, her strange and interesting life. She unlocks the front door. Through the window in the door, it seems as if the light inside is strange: reflected, wavering somehow. She pushes the door open and stops herself. Over the wooden floor, reaching under the couch and kitchen table, even touching the far wall, is a sheen of water, rippling and shaking like a small lake.

Chapter Twenty-One

"Do you remember how Drew used to color fake tattoos on himself with markers?" Kiya rubs her forearm, remembering. "Some of them were so funny."

"He was good, wasn't he? He spent a lot of time with them; they looked real." Kiya's father is sitting in the armchair in his hotel room, Kiya stretched out on the bed.

"Remember how he got you with the first one he did?" Kiya asks. "You really thought it was real."

"Yeah, it was a naked woman on his arm. It looked professional. I yelled at him."

Kiya laughs. It feels good to be talking of Drew, to be remembering him with her father. "He bought himself a set of good markers for that. Thin point. He had me help him."

"You did?" Her father looks at her, in astonishment.

"Yes. You didn't think he could do that all by himself, did you?"

"He never said anything."

"He wasn't a snitch," Kiya says.

"If he put half as much time into his schoolwork as he put into getting into trouble, he would have been valedictorian."

"He was smart, wasn't he."

Her father is drinking brandy. He lifts the glass to his nose, sips it. "And you," he says.

She looks at him. "What about me?"

"You are just as smart as Drew was. Just as talented."

"Yes? Your point?"

"I just want you to realize it, that's all. I want you to take your life and make it something. Something wonderful and truthful. Fulfill your dreams. Don't wait, like I did."

They had gone out to dinner with Kiya's mother. Kiya had insisted that her father tell her mother what was going on in his life, that he had a boyfriend. Once they ordered, Kiya kept giving her father significant looks, indicating this was the time; now or never. Still, he continued asking Kiya's mother about her life, about her health, about her painting, until the poor woman would have been excused for thinking he was interested in getting back together again with her. Finally, Kiya interrupted him, asking, "So Dad, how is *your* life? Anything new with you?"

"Yes," her mother said. She sipped from her glass of pinot. "What's going on with you? How is Sophia?" She grimaced slightly as she said the name, as if she were making an unpleasant joke.

"Actually," Kiya's father said. He told Kiya's mother he and Sophia had broken up, that the relationship had never been a good one. He said, "I have a new relationship now. With a man. His name is Elliot."

Kiya watched her mother, ready to offer support. To her surprise, her mother, after a moment of silence, began to laugh. It was helpless laughter, which grew. She rested her forehead on her hand. "Sorry," she said.

"Yes, well—what's so funny?" Kiya's father asked.

"Oh," her mother sighed. "It takes me by surprise, because I never guessed such a thing. But in another way, it *doesn't* take me by surprise. In another way, it seems right. Actually, I'm wondering why I was so dense, why I didn't see. And why our marriage lasted as long as it did."

"Well . . . I did love you." Kiya's father stared gloomily into his beer. "In my way."

"Yes, and I loved you too, but that's not enough to keep a marriage going, is it?"

Kiya's father shook his head and looked at her mother. "Apparently not." He smiled, a certain amount of relief on his face. "So you're not angry at me?"

"Of course I'm angry at you. I will always be angry at you, I think. But not because you're gay. I'm angry because you couldn't be honest with me. With us. Because you made everything so difficult."

Now Kiya says, "You want me to fulfill my dreams. It would be easy enough if I knew what they were."

"No, it wouldn't be easy." Her father puts his brandy glass

on the table. "It's never easy. We avoid letting ourselves know what those dreams are because we know it won't be easy."

"I can see how that applies to your situation," Kiya says. "But it may not be the case with everyone."

Her father says, "I think everyone knows, in some part of themselves, what they really want or need to do. All decisions are already made somewhere within us; we just have to open ourselves up to that, to stop denying it."

"Ooh, mystical," Kiya says, grinning up at her father. She rubs the taut skin of her belly, feeling the baby shift against her hand. "Here," she says, and walks over to stand beside her father. She takes his hand and holds it against her. "Feel."

Her father presses his hand against her and looks up at her when the baby moves. "Wow," he says. Kiya smiles at her father. She is happy to, for once, not be alone in her awareness of the person inside her.

"Are you sure you don't want to keep it?" her father asks.

* * * *

It comes to Peter just like that, a certainty that swoops down from somewhere and leaves no room for doubt: he and Toni should get married. He is walking home from The Blue Moon on a cold midnight, the streets black, cold and empty. He isn't wondering what to do, hasn't thought before of proposing to her, but in the space between one step and the next, he knows they should be married. He sees a wedding, white dress and all; he sees a house. A small house, but charming: maybe shingles. He stops himself from wondering how the house will get paid for. They will manage. People do manage, and he and Toni are as smart as the next couple. Smarter.

He thinks on this over the next few days. How to do it, how to ask? Should he mention it to her casually, or should he make a big deal of it? Is he supposed to buy a ring first, then pull it from a pocket and offer it to her on bended knee? Or should he, over pizza some night, ask her what she thinks of the idea? This last idea sounds more like him, more like him and Toni, and yet . . .

191

he wants it to be special. Not proposing-at-a-Red Sox-game special, but more special than asking her what she thinks of it over pizza and beers. He knows that everyone their age lives together first, for years usually, before they get married, but he doesn't want to do it that way. If you love someone—and he loves Toni, and is pretty sure she loves him—then why not do it? The grand gesture, the ceremony, seems the brave and elegant thing to do.

He invites Toni to dinner at a new restaurant he's heard about. When she says, "So expensive," he says not to worry; it's on him. "Let's dress up," he says.

He goes into a jewelry store and looks at diamond rings. He's not sure Toni is the diamond-ring-type of girl. She has her own style, and he doesn't think it goes with the traditional diamond ring. Besides, the only diamond he can afford is tiny. He decides to hold off on the ring.

"How does this look?" He puts on the navy sports coat he got from the thrift store, modeling for Ryan.

"Lovely," Ryan says. "No, seriously, it looks good. Kinda hip."

"I don't need a tie, do I?"

"God no, don't wear a tie. Here." He pulls one of his scarfs, a striped woolen one, from a drawer and wraps it around Peter's neck. "And you should wear a dark shirt. What's the occasion?"

Peter looks at Ryan, considers telling him what his real plans for the evening are. Ryan, holding a beer in one hand, belches. "Just a date with Toni," Peter says. "I want to look good."

He is nervous as he rings the doorbell. Usually, he texts her to meet him. But he wants to do this right; he wants to be a gentleman. There's something formal and old-fashioned about ringing a girl's doorbell, wearing a suit coat.

"Wow," Toni says when she opens the door. "Look at you, Mr. Fashionable." She is wearing black nylons, heels, and has a sparkly scarf draped over her coat.

"Look at you," Peter says, suddenly shy. "You look so pretty." And she does, with her shiny black hair curving around her face and her lips red and glossy. At the restaurant, he takes her coat and pulls out her chair. "Listen," she says, "I don't know what's going on, but I like it. I just don't know how long you can keep it up."

"What, is this so different than how I usually act?"

"Well . . . yes."

"I'll try harder." Peter studies the menu, trying to act casual.

"No, seriously, I don't know if I could handle it if you always acted like this. It's just not the Peter I know."

After they order, and after their drinks are served, Peter decides it is time. He lifts his glass of red wine. "To us," he says.

"To us." They clink glasses. "No, really, what's up?" Toni asks.

"Okay." This is it, he thinks. "I was just wondering what you'd think about the idea of . . . of us, um. Getting married. Someday." He adds the last word to soften the suggestion, to make it less real.

Toni's eyes open wide, and for a moment he can't help but see that she looks alarmed. Then she puts a hand to her mouth, covering up, rearranging herself. "You're serious, right?"

He feels a sudden flash of anger. "Yes, what do you think?"

"Just checking, just need to make sure." Her face looks flushed. "Wow, you surprise me, Peter King. I had no idea."

"Well, we've been going together for a while . . ."

"Five and a half months."

"Okay, five and a half months. But we're of a good age to get married, and . . . and I really like you." He knows it sounds lame. He reaches across the table for her hand.

She squeezes his hand in hers. "Peter, that is so *sweet.*"

Peter realizes, with a sudden, sinking feeling, that he hasn't adequately considered the possibility that she might say no. "I didn't say it to be sweet," he says stiffly.

She smiles at him, and he sees a tinge of sadness in her smile; he thinks, for one awful moment, that she is feeling sorry for him. Their food comes.

They eat. Toni asks him how his scallops are. "Good," he says. "But scarce. Hard to find." He pushes the last one around his bare plate. "How is your dish?"

193

"Mmm. Exquisite. So good."

When Toni finishes eating, she moves her plate away and leans back. "Peter . . ."

He stops himself from asking if there is someone else; that would be too cliché, too pathetic. "It's sudden, I know," he says. "But I love you and I think you're the right person for me. Everything about you is good for me. You make me want to be a better person. I just see no reason for us . . . not to get married." His voice drops at the end because he knows, if he took the time to think of it, he could probably find some good reasons for them not to get married. Or for Toni not to marry him, Peter.

"It's just too soon," Toni says, and her voice is decisive. She sounds absolutely, heart-breakingly sure. "I care about you, I respect you . . ." She stops, and Peter knows, as if she'd said it aloud, that his future is too uncertain. His career prospects are bleak. "It's just too soon." Her face is soft as she looks at him across the table. A group at a table next to them bursts into sudden, raucous laughter, and she leans forward. "We don't even know if we can live together. You don't know me as well as you think you know me," she says. "I need to know you better, and you need to get to know me better. You might find things about me that I've kept hidden."

Peter considers this. He remembers her openness with him about her former boyfriends, he remembers how she always—so far—has told him the truth. He remembers how she made him help Kiya when he didn't want to. "No," he says. "No, I don't think that would happen."

Peter kisses Toni good night at her door, like an old-fashioned date. "What, you don't want to come inside?" she asks. "You can. You're invited."

He shakes his head. "Thank you, but not tonight." He holds her, feeling her small sturdy body against his. "Maybe some other night."

"Okay, then." Peter is halfway down the block before he hears Toni open her door to go inside. He walks on, trying not to see himself as the rejected suitor. He tries to console himself with the fact that she still wants to see him; she invited him to her room.

But he knows that something has changed in their relationship. No matter what happens, he will always remember the look of sadness on Toni's face, and his sense that she was feeling sorry for him.

✳ ✳ ✳ ✳

As Maddie sits reading in her recliner, Kiya comes out of her bedroom and stands in front of her. Her hands are behind her back and a look of suppressed excitement is on her face. "Yes?" Maddie says. "Something up?"

Kiya pulls one hand from behind her back and waves a small piece of paper. "Ta-da!"

Maddie reaches. "What is it?"

"A check, made out to you. For $2000."

It's from Stan, Kiya's father. "He thanks you for taking care of me," Kiya says. "I was planning on paying you back after the baby was born, but he's helping me out."

"That's generous of him," Maddie says. "This is great, but I like having you here. You don't need to pay me anything back, this is plenty. Tell him I said thank you." She holds the check in her hands, looks at it. She has held off asking Kiya about her plans, letting the girl have her space, but now she says, "So, what's next for you? What will my favorite young lady do in a few months?"

Kiya sinks down on the couch. She looks embarrassed. "Well, I did talk with people at the adoption agency."

"Did you find prospective parents?" Maddie leans forward.

"I . . . held off on that. I looked at the files; there are wonderful people." She twists her hands in her lap. "I just couldn't do it yet."

"So you haven't signed anything yet?" Maddie feels an unreasonable surge of hope.

"I signed some papers, but there is no commitment yet. They're very good about that, about respecting my need to go at my own pace." Lines tighten around Kiya's mouth and between her eyebrows.

"I don't mean to pressure you, either. You can stay here as

195

long as you want."

"Thank you." Kiya looks toward the door. Darkness has already fallen, but she says, "I think I'll take a walk. I need the exercise." She takes Sadie with her on the leash. Kiya still limps slightly as she leaves, favoring the healing leg.

"It's a beautiful night," Maddie calls after her, and it is, the sky a clear indigo with Venus bright on the horizon. She thinks of the young couple who want Kiya's baby, who hope for it. She imagines them waiting at a window, the husband's arms protectively around his wife. It's pure imagination, she knows, but what else does she have to go on? She was never married, she never had a husband to wrap his arms around her protectively as they waited for their dream to come true. She did have love, though, she reminds herself; love with Alex, love with Mark before that, and the love of her son. She thinks of Kiya walking alone with Sadie in the night, and she wishes, in a way that is almost a prayer, for her to know love.

Maddie has to talk to Ron. Things can't go on as they are. She leaves him a note, asking to meet her after work sometime; she is reminded of junior high school, of slipping notes in a boy's hand as they walk from class to class. She feels that uncertain, that vulnerable. They meet at the place where they met before, and this time Maddie orders a gin and tonic. She doesn't know what will happen, but needs some courage.

"How are you, Maddie?" Ron asks as he sits at the table. He leans over to give her a friendly kiss on the cheek.

"I'm all right," she says. "I just thought we should talk, again."

"Any time," Ron says. "I'm always happy to talk with you. Or do whatever else you want to do," he says, his teeth gleaming in a sudden smile.

"Okay," Maddie says, and just like that, she knows what to say. "Okay, if you want to hang out, then let's hang out. If you want to date, let's date."

"That's interesting." Ron sips from his drink, a scotch. She can see the gears working as he thinks this over. "Do you mean it?"

"Sure. Only if we're going to do it, I don't want to be secretive about it. If we're going to sleep together, then you're dating me, and there's no need to keep it secret. Right?" She spreads her hands open on the table. "Nothing to hide. Neither of us is married, there's no law against it."

"No, there's no law," Ron says, and Maddie thinks he looks uneasy. "But you were right when you said it could cause problems at work."

"Well, if we're dating, we're dating. If we don't deny it, then people won't gossip behind our backs."

Ron nods, and nods some more. He leans back in his chair, hands in pockets, and looks around. "They still would gossip, though. You know that."

"Well, screw them then. Right?" She takes another drink of her gin and tonic. Maddie is playing a role, a female pirate role, hijacking the conversation. She is putting Ron's flirtation to the test.

Ron looks at her. "This is a side to you I haven't seen before, Maddie. I didn't know you could be so . . . aggressive."

"I'm not, normally. But what we have going on at work, while fun, is really uncomfortable for me, and makes it hard to get my work done. I like you. I really do." She decides not to mention that she's had a massive crush on him for years. "But this secret flirtation is getting hard for me to take." There, she said it.

"Okay. That makes sense. I'm sorry."

"No apology necessary. I am flattered, I really am. You make me feel attractive, and that's a lovely thing."

"You ARE attractive. Believe me. I don't lie about things like that."

"See, that's what I mean. You're nice, and make me feel like a woman. But when I'm working . . . like I said, if we want to date, we should date. If not, then we should forget that stuff, and be professional."

"Professional." Ron looks glum. "I guess you're right. But what fun is that?"

She smiles at him. He's such a boy. "Not much fun, you're right. But it's the grown-up thing to do."

"Grown-up," he says, and sighs. "Boy, you sure know how to pop someone's bubble, Maddie King."

※　※　※

Evie stands at the doorway, frozen. What to do? The cabin's central room, the combined kitchen and living room, has water covering the entire floor. She makes herself step inside, feeling the water soak her sneakers. She walks toward the sink and faucet against the right wall, her footsteps squishing. The sink faucets are turned off, but in the cupboard below them, water is running from one of the copper pipes in a steady stream.

Evie has no idea how pipes work, what makes water come into the house, or how to stop it. She wonders if the phone and electricity still work, or if the water has somehow ruined them. She wonders if she is in danger of being electrocuted as she stands here. She walks carefully over to the phone and picks the receiver up, holding it away from her ear. There is a dial tone. She dials the operator and asks her to call her parents' phone number. It rings seven, eight, nine times. The operator comes back on. "Ma'am, there is no answer at this number. Would you like me to keep trying?"

Evie tries to think of who else she can call. She has numbers in her little book for her next-door neighbors, but they are gone this week. She doesn't know the people at the end of the lane. She has Frank's number, taken when his family invited her to dinner. She dials it, her fingers shaking slightly and having trouble making it around the circle. On the second ring, Eloise answers.

"I have a problem," Evie says. "I don't know what to do." When Evie describes water all over the floor, Eloise says, "Here. I'll put John on the phone." John tells Evie to turn the water off. "There should be a valve somewhere." Evie puts down the phone, checks the back room, and finds a valve. It is rusted and corroded; she pushes hard until it is almost closed. "I couldn't get it all the way," she tells John. "It's still dripping under the sink."

"I'll send Mike out," John says. "He's our engineer. He

198

should be able to help you."

When Mike drives up, Evie is sitting on the front steps smoking a cigarette. "I'm sorry," she says. "This isn't your problem. I feel like a baby."

He walks toward the house, carrying a large metal toolbox. He grins, and pats her gently on the head. "Don't worry, little girl. The big strong man is here now."

Mike opens the toolbox and takes out a wrench, with which he tightens the valve in the back room. Bending down, he shines a flashlight under the sink. He reaches inside and pushes at the pipes. "The joint has given way."

"Ew," Evie says, noticing the smell for the first time. She looks down at her feet. "Is there POOP in this water? I mean sewage?"

Mike looks down. "I don't think so. It's just fumes." He looks in the metal toolbox. "I think Grandpa Frank may have what we need here . . ." He pulls a wood-handled wire brush out. "You could shine the flashlight in here," he says, handing it to her. She takes it, and reaches to turn on the overhead light. She pauses. "There's no problem with the electricity, is there?"

"There shouldn't be." Evie turns the light on and pulls a chair next to where Mike is kneeling on the floor, reaching into the cupboard. His cotton shirt pulls tightly around his shoulders. She hadn't noticed before how broad they are, how like a man's, rather than a boy's. She leans down next to him, shining the light on the pipes.

He works without speaking, and Evie watches. After cleaning the pipes, he puts some stuff—soldering compound, he calls it— onto the pipes from a small tin box. He takes out a metal container, with a nozzle. He leans away from her. "Watch this," he says. Flame shoots out. He leans back in, aiming it carefully at the pipes.

When the pipe is fixed, Mike and Evie clean up the floor. They push the water outside, using brooms and buckets. The water didn't reach high enough to touch the furniture. Using all the towels available, Evie and Mike wipe the floor down. They wring the towels out and wipe again. "I think that will have to do," Evie says.

"The floor should dry soon," Mike says.

Evie turns off the overhead light and switches on a table lamp. It is late, and they are both wet and disheveled. "I don't have any more towels to dry us off," she says.

Mike says, "The pipes need to sit for a while, then I'll turn the water on to see if it's fixed." They stand facing one another. Mike's hair is sticking up on his head and his skin is wet with sweat; Evie doesn't even want to think what she must look like. Through the open windows, a loon calls its high, warbling sound. "Since we're already all wet . . ." Mike says, and looks toward the lake.

Chapter Twenty-Two

Kiya is enormous, a slow-moving, full-bellied pod. She is nearly eight months along now and doesn't know how she can get any bigger. It seems as if there is no more room in her body. Maddie is kind to her, her father writes and her mother calls, Nick says maybe she can come back to work, and Sadie lies next to her in bed, but she knows she is truly alone in the world. At night she wakes, afraid of the future. She is afraid of the pain of labor and afraid of what will happen after that. She wonders what it would be like if she were married and pregnant, or if she were living with her baby's father and they were planning on keeping the child. Would she turn to him for comfort; would he stroke her shoulder and say, "Don't worry"? Would they make quiet jokes, in the middle of the night? Or would they argue, would it be worse with someone than it is alone? When she wakes, she pats Sadie, who doesn't move. She pulls the blanket over her mid-section and lets the warmth seep in. She reminds herself of what Jack said to her once: she is doing a good thing, letting this child within her grow strong. She is bringing something good into the world.

In the mornings, she lies in her bed looking at the print of "The Starry Night" hanging on the wall. She thinks the painting was an accurate reflection of the inside of Van Gogh's mind. It is how he really saw the night, full of that charging, shifting energy, not just the way he put paint down on the canvas. It is painful for her to look at, but she stares at it every day.

She thinks maybe the painting is painful for her to look at because though it is similar to how she sees the world, it is someone else's reflection of the world, not her own. She sees the sky through her eyes something like that, but different. The evening sky, when the sun is going down and there is still light in the world, can be so painful. Just the way the light runs from the sky, the grief as it leaves.

She sets up a canvas and opens new tubes of paint. She will do this; she has all day today, tomorrow and the next day too. She will make her own. She begins to paint the morning sky: blue and gray and yellow, the light jagged and swooping, not smooth. She will make the lake have a deceptively smooth surface, but suggest turmoil just beneath it, trying to break through. This is the way she feels: as if her body were a thin skin trying to contain the chaos. She holds it together for the sake of the baby. She has a vision of large marine animals, just below the quiet, frozen surface of the lake, bumping their smooth skin against the bottom of the ice, trying to break through.

Jeny from Umojo calls. She says she just wants to see how Kiya is doing. Kiya doesn't trust Jeny's innocence; she listens carefully for tones in her voice as Jeny tells Kiya they still miss her at work, that Clyde has a new boyfriend. She thinks Jeny is trying to gather some kind of information about her, she is just not sure for what purpose. "I'm doing well," she says, looking down at her rounded belly, the paint-splattered tee shirt. "I've been painting. Yeah, acrylic, just getting into it, nothing special. Feeling good. Heavy as a cow!"

"I bet you look beautiful," Jeny says. "Bet you are one beautiful pregnant woman." Her voice is almost wistful. "No, I'm not seeing anyone," she says in answer to Kiya's question. There is a moment of emptiness hanging in the air between them, and through it, Kiya almost feels a connection with Jeny, as if Jeny has emptiness in her life, which corresponds to Kiya's. Then Jeny's voice picks up, assumes cheerfulness as she says "Give me a call if you get to Portland sometime, okay? We can have lunch or something."

Kiya goes back to her painting, dipping the brush into yellow, smearing it across the sky. The sudden lift in Jeny's voice reminds her of how she used to channel sunlight and use it to cheer people up, her customers, her mother in particular. She used to gather it like paint, spreading it around the world. Who was that person? *Little Miss Sunshine,* she hears Drew's voice say. *Pollyanna.* The voice is not mocking, but sad, as if he, too, misses what was lost.

* * * *

Peter picks out a silver bracelet for his mother's birthday present and drives up to the house on the lake. The March day is cloudy and heavy with moisture, a restless wind tossing bare branches. The ground shows through the snow cover on the lawn outside his mother's house, and the ice over the lake is softening, with patches of water on the surface. Jack, his mother's neighbor, has brought a cake. His mother and Jack have a kind of weird friendship, Peter thinks; Jack bought her a dog and he visits, and she makes fun of his Maine accent. Peter is glad she has a neighbor nearby, someone to call on out here in the country in case there is a problem. The cake is a round layer cake with chocolate frosting, resting lopsided on a plate. "Jack," Peter asks, "where did you get this cake?"

"What do you think? I made it."

"No. That's not possible."

"What you think just because I have a Y chromosome that I can't bake? Just because I have a—excuse me, ladies—a penis I can't bake? That would a great mistake." Jack looks at Peter from under the gray hair falling over his forehead. "I'm not a great cook," he says, "but I learned how to make cake from a box. It was my job when my wife was alive. The rare times we needed a cake, usually birthdays, I would make it. She would frost it and decorate it, which is why this one— "He points to the cake. "Looks so pathetic."

It's true, the cake leans to one side and the frosting is on the plate as much as it is on the cake, but "It looks delicious," Peter says. "Or at least edible."

"That's funny," Maddie says. "Alex would make me a cake on my birthday, too. Only he loved to make cakes, and he was so good at it. He would make a tiramisu cake . . ." She stops when she sees the look on Jack's face. "Oh. Sorry. Thank you so much, Jack."

"You're welcome," he says. "If no one else will eat it, I'll give it to Sadie." The dog leans against his thigh, head to the side in pleasure as he rubs her ears.

Kiya hasn't said much since Peter arrived. She stands by the stove, stirring. He walks over to stand beside her. "That looks good," he says of the fish stew bubbling on the stove.

"I hope it will be." She looks down at the pan.

"How have you been?"

She shrugs. "All right. Growing." She rests a hand on her belly. "You?"

"Well enough." He hasn't mentioned Toni to Kiya—why would he? —but figures she must guess he's not staying celibate. "Any news on the adoption front?"

"I talked to people at an agency." She says no more on that, stirring the stew and looking down, so he lets it drop. "I've been painting," Kiya says.

"Really? Anything you can show me?"

She shrugs. "Sure, all right," she says, wiping her hands on a dishtowel. "Promise not to laugh." She turns the stove down and leads him into her room—his old room—and turns on the light.

Leaning against the bed, facing the door, is a painting of the lake. Peter recognizes the view from the living room window, but the lake, the sky and the island all look fluid and moving. The painting is rough, not trying for accuracy, but there is something disturbing about it, something powerful. It gives Peter a sense of unease.

He can't say that, though. Can he? "Wow, Kiya. It's good. I didn't know you painted."

"I used to, a long time ago. I took art classes. My mom bought me some paints and supplies." She turns away.

Peter stays for a long look at the painting. Kiya hesitates in the hallway. "No, I mean it," he says. "There's something powerful about it. Almost disturbing."

"Yup, retired for seven years now." Jack and Peter are walking along the lane. "I worked for the Museum there for twenty-five years. Got into it because I liked history."

"Did you major in that in college?"

"Oh, yes. Sure did." They see the lake through the trees, the sun appearing and disappearing behind scattering clouds. "Your mother says you majored in Philosophy."

"Yes." Peter guesses something more is needed. "I was interested in it. Still am. But I'm just not sure what next, you know? Tree work is starting up again now, but those winters are long."

"And you play music."

"Yes. Actually, I'm looking for something new."

"And what would that be?"

"I don't know. Something I enjoy and can make money at." And can impress Toni with, he thinks somewhat bitterly. It's hopeless, is how Peter feels; all of it, the crazy idea of a career, the quest to get Toni to love him enough to marry him.

"Those things don't just drop in your lap, you know." Jack's voice sounds scolding. "You have to go after them."

"I suppose . . ."

"No, I mean it. You want something, it takes a lot of effort." Jack looks straight ahead as he talks, studying the way the road ahead of them dips and turns into the trees. They hear birds chirping in a tree they pass: "Tufted titmouse," Jack says, then "Nothing is easy. It's all hard work."

"Well, yeah, but it would help if a person knew what it was he was going after. Job-wise, I mean."

Jack glances at him, his eyes shrewd under his wool cap. "There's good work all over the place. Even now. You just have to go after it. Work for it, you know?"

"Work for work," Peter says and laughs. "Will work for work."

"Right, you got it." Jack is warm again, as if he's made his point. "Find what you want to do and go after it. Not too late, you know. You're still a youngster."

"Okay, *Dad*," Peter says, hoping Jack will catch his sarcasm but not take offense.

Jack bends down to scoop up some soft snow in the bank by the side of the road and tosses it into a tree. A group of small birds scatter, fluttering into the sky.

* * * *

Ron had decided, as Maddie predicted he would, to not publicly date her. She feels only a twinge of sadness at that; she had decided by the time she asked that his main motivation was the thrill of illicitness. She'd looked up the University's "Guidelines to Consenting Relationships," and found a passage that read: "Consenting relationships may constitute sexual harassment under this policy," and "Faculty and staff members are strongly advised not to engage in such relationships." She'd learned also that, if they were publicly dating, Ron could not supervise or evaluate her. She couldn't quite imagine how that would work, but was afraid that it might involve her losing her job.

Monday after they talked, Ron came into her office with his hands in his khaki pants, whistling. He'd always been proud of his ability to whistle complex tunes. He stood just inside her door, finishing a bit she recognized as part of the "Ode to Joy."

He smiled at her, she applauded, and they were back to their old selves at work.

Ron behaves himself, with just one exception: he has a habit of occasionally, at unpredictable times when the two of them are alone in a room together, fixing her with a come-hither look so exaggerated, so like Groucho Marx wiggling his eyebrows, that she has to laugh. She is glad Ron is not offended by her laughter and feels free to joke with him. She is able to do her work, which is a huge relief. And when Susan tells her, one day over lunch in the snack bar, that Ron and Jane are dating again, she is able to act casual about it, as if she doesn't care. "They are?" Maddie asks. "When did that start?"

"Oh, I don't know," Susan says. She picks a tomato slice out of her salad with a plastic fork and puts it beside the salad bowl. "I forgot to have them leave the tomatoes out. I talked with Fred about it." Fred is an older professor in Susan's department who likes to gossip.

"What, about the tomatoes?"

"No, about Ron and Jane. He says he thinks they never really stopped dating."

Maddie looks at Susan, quizzically. "Yeah," Susan says. "Maybe they had a lovers' spat or something when Jane was mad at him. But he saw them together soon after that, he said."

"Is that right." Maddie continues to eat, continues to pretend this doesn't matter to her. So far Susan hasn't seemed to notice anything odd about her behavior in regard to Ron. Of if she has, she is even sneakier about hiding it than Maddie is. The way her eyes glance sideways up to Maddie now, then slide back to her salad, makes Maddie wonder just a bit.

"And I saw them too," Susan says in an offhand way.

"Really? Where?"

"Oh, downtown. A while ago. Maybe three weeks ago, or something. They were at the coffee shop one weekend morning."

This would have been at the time that Ron was touching Maddie in the copy room, rubbing her thigh under the desk. Maddie is sure now, by the way Susan doesn't look at her—and by the fact that she didn't mention, then, that she saw Ron and Jane— that she knows something. Perhaps she thinks that Maddie has an unrequited crush on Ron. Perhaps, Maddie thinks, she did have an unrequited crush on him. But no longer, as she feels the warm rage course through her body.

Back at her desk, revising minutes she took of a meeting, Maddie still feels the warmth of her anger. She remembers seeing Jane in a new short skirt and boots lately, smiling, her hair in a looser style, her color high. Maddie is worth more than this, she wants to tell Ron; more than something you play around with in the down times of your relationship with someone else. Your *real* relationship. She even thinks, briefly, of how easy it would be to sabotage Ron. She could drop hints of what had happened, doing it in a way that would present her as the victim. As, perhaps, she was, or would have been. It is a small community; word would get around. It would be so easy to do. She checks the minutes over once more and prints them, hearing the printer start up behind her.

Maddie takes the papers from the printer and slams the stapler on them. She is wounded, but has her self-respect, she reminds herself; she didn't give in. She would feel worse, much worse, if she'd slept with Ron, then discovered he was still seeing Jane. She takes a breath and walks down the hall toward his office.

She taps on his door. "The minutes," she says, holding them out. He likes to review a paper copy; says his old eyes can't read the computer screen well enough.

"Thank you, Maddie," he says, turning from his desk to take them from her. He smiles up at her: a kind, tired smile. "You're wonderful."

"Yes," she says. She nods. "Yes, I certainly am," and turns back down the hall. Of course, she won't say anything. She looks out the window at the pale blue sky, the earliest beginnings of spring, and feels her spirits lift unaccountably.

✳ ✳ ✳ ✳

The air outside is still warm and humid, though it is close to midnight. Evie changes into her bathing suit in the bathroom, leaving her wet clothes on the floor. She steps out onto the dock. Mike is still wearing shorts but has taken his shirt off. She sees his body at the end of the dock, standing outlined against the starry sky. Evie feels suddenly anxious, and because she doesn't understand why she feels that way, she has to shout. "Get in! What are you waiting for?"

He turns around to watch her come down the dock toward him. "You get in," he says, "if you're in such a rush."

"You first." Their voices reach out over the water, but no one is around to hear them; it is dark all around the lake. The windows behind them send faint light onto the dock, but Spruce Island is just a greater darkness against the sky.

"All right," Mike says. "But then you better get in." He jumps in, knees held to his chest, splashing water that reaches Evie on the dock. Mike shakes his head, wiping his face. The water reaches his chest when he stands by the dock. "It's nice," he says. "Come in."

She sits on the wood, her feet in the water. She likes being here, part in the water and part out, looking at Mike in the darkness. The air is warm, and the house plumbing is fixed. Mike says they need to check the pipes later, but she feels sure he fixed it; she has trust in him. She reaches her hand down to the water. It is cool and feels good. She splashes him. It is a mistake, as he splashes her back, forcefully. But she wanted to splash him; wanted to lift water and throw it at him. She wants to do it again, and she does. This

208

time he doesn't splash her back, but stands next to her, and puts a warm hand around her ankle. He tugs it, gently. "Come in," he says again, his voice soft.

Evie lets herself slide into the water, and it's as if she is in a lake she has never been in before. The water, the air, everything feels different in the darkness. The dark lake might be full of danger, of things she cannot see, but she feels protected and taken care of. She is both afraid and strong, soothed and excited. She feels more alive than she has ever felt before. It must be the orgone accumulator, she thinks, that makes her feel this way. It must be . . . she wishes Mike would touch her again, would come nearer to her. She takes a deep breath and lets the water envelop her. She swims underwater, toward the warmth of his body.

Chapter Twenty-Three

In the morning, after breakfast, Kiya paints. This is her unconscious time. She lets whatever is inside her mind rise up and take form on the canvas. Often her painting is influenced by dreams she had; not the literal story-aspect of the dream, but the mood, the feeling, the things the dream was telling her. Her dreams, since she became pregnant, are wild and crazy: talking tortoises metamorphosing into angels of doom; snakes crawling from a burning fireplace; Drew. Sometimes she dreams of his body swaying, his face about to come into view, and she awakes with a start before she can see it. Other times he is alive, sitting on the couch at Maddie's house, talking with her. In one dream she was angry at him, yelling and screaming, trying to get him to come around. In that dream he just sat there, glassy-eyed and laughing at her, as if what she said were funny.

This morning she feels a strange sense of light within her, entering her. Maybe it is due to the increasing light in the world, the sun rising earlier dispelling the cold darkness of the Maine winter, melting the snow. The ice on the lake sometimes lets out a loud cracking sound, as it begins to break up. She dreamed of Drew again last night, but it wasn't painful or frightening. He was sitting on Maddie's couch, smiling. In the dream, he was happy to see her. "Kiya!" he said, looking at her with love. That's all it was, she thinks as she paints: love in his eyes. Then he said something like "I missed you," and "Where have you been?" As if *she's* the one who was gone, who was missing from this world. So like him, she thinks and laughs. She hears the sound of her laughter in the quiet, empty house; Sadie, lying at her feet, lifts her head inquisitively. "So like him," Kiya says to Sadie, "to ask me where *I've* been."

After painting, she eats an orange. She thinks of it as feeding the child inside her, filling out its limbs and making them strong. She doesn't know if the baby is a boy or a girl, doesn't want to know. It is genderless now, and she will allow it to stay that way as long as possible. She won't pick a name or concern herself about what will happen after the baby is born. Those concerns are for someone else, not her. She has not visited the adoption agency again or called them but has looked online again, and has picked out a couple she likes. They are in their 30's, and though attractive, they are not perfect-looking; the man is a little plump, with a beard and tangled, curly hair growing over his collar, and the woman has long smooth hair and a round face. They run an organic farm and have animals. They are leaning against one another, comfortably. The man has one arm around the woman, and another resting on the head of a friendly-looking dog. They both have white teeth and big, uninhibited smiles; it looks as if they are always smiling. She looked at their picture once, and read what they wrote, committing it to memory. They want to make the world better. She thinks they are waiting for her baby, waiting to give it a good life, a better life than she could. She imagines their arms outstretched longingly, and sometimes that frightens her, as if they are reaching, reaching inside her body to rip some part of her out, some part not ready yet to leave.

On the lane, Kiya lets Sadie off the leash, as no one is around for her to bother. She noses in patches of gray snow by the side of the road, then bounds ahead. Suddenly, from the brush around her on the side of the road, there is a flutter and a flapping, a swooshing noise, and a flock of wild turkeys rises into the air. Kiya guesses there are ten or twelve of them. They rise into the trees, their wings flapping hard to lift up their ungainly, heavy bodies. Most go deep into the woods, but one sits on a tree near them, looking down at Sadie, who stands legs spread, barking excitedly.

Just before the birds rose up, Kiya had been thinking of the other thing that made the light brighter today, that small nugget of hope: Peter had liked her painting. Peter had asked her how she was doing. Peter still cares.

* * * *

Gary calls Peter in to do tree work with him as the weather warms up. Last year, this was the time when Peter dropped the winter job he'd taken—working in a call center, a job he hated—but he thinks this year he might stay on working nights at the Blue Moon. He gets home late and has to rise early to work with Gary, but Peter has a plan. He's looked at the course catalog for the University of Southern Maine and discovered that if he takes a few Education courses, he can get a certification in teaching Classics to high school students. He would need just six more courses, he thinks. If he continues working two jobs all summer, he can save up enough money to go back to school and finish this second degree in a year or two. He will be a high school teacher.

When he gets up in the morning, Peter looks at his guitar, sitting propped against the wall in the corner of his bedroom next to his banjo. When he gets off work he takes a quick nap, then goes into the Blue Moon. The next morning his guitar is resting in the same place, still untouched, and the same the following morning. Peter feels sad about that, but he remembers the look on Toni's face when he asked her to marry him, and he remembers Jack saying, "You just have to go after it."

Peter hasn't mentioned his plan to Toni, or to Ryan, or to anyone else. Ryan might say if he's not going to play that guitar, he has to give it away. He doesn't know what Toni would say. She is still preoccupied with her job, but they've been together every weekend. They've been staying in more, rather than going out; he wonders if that's what happens when couples stay together. Other times he wonders if it is what couples do when they are tired of one another, when one or both of them is thinking of breaking up. He is wary with Toni, cautious, always looking to see if she wants to dump him, but so far she doesn't seem to. She calls him, she makes sure they have plans every weekend. They cook dinner, they watch movies, and sometimes Peter brings out his guitar and plays it.

His fingers, stiff at first, remember how to play after a while. Toni leans back in her chair, listening; sometimes she reads a book or a magazine while he plays, her foot tapping in rhythm. When he plays something she knows, she will sing along, in that surprising voice of hers. She says she doesn't know how to sing, doesn't know how to harmonize, but she stays on tune, and he loves the way her voice sounds.

Tonight, Toni is knitting as Peter plays. Her fingers move quickly, creating a thin tail, the beginning of a sweater. "How did you learn how to do that?" Peter asks.

"My mother taught me when I was sixteen."

"You actually let your mother teach you something when you were that age? Most kids don't want anything to do with their mother when they're sixteen."

Toni is silent, and Peter thinks she is counting stitches. After a moment she says, "I got over my rebellion early, I guess."

"So what, you were a wild sixth grader? A wild middle-schooler?" Peter laughs at the thought. "Toni Dubay, middle-school wild girl out of control."

Toni looks at him, and she's not smiling. "What do you know, Peter? Just what do you know about me?" She ties a knot in her knitting and stuffs it back into its bag.

"What, Toni? What? I'm sorry." She is standing. He stands and tries to put his arms around her.

She pushes his arms away. "You just don't know as much as you think you know, that's all. You assume I'm a certain way because that's how you see me."

Peter doesn't know where this anger has come from. "Sit down," he says. "C'mon, sit down, let's talk. Let me get you another beer." Toni is at the door with her coat on, her face red. "Please, Toni," he says. "I don't know what I did but I'm sorry. Don't leave like this. I'd just have to chase you down. I wouldn't let you just walk away. Right?"

She stands still facing the closed door, thinking. She tightens her lips and swings around to face him. "You see the person I am, and you assume I was always that way. You never ask anything about me."

"I don't?" Peter thinks. "I asked you what you wanted to do tonight. I asked what you wanted for your birthday."

Toni shakes her head and sits on the couch, still wearing her coat. "Get real," she says. "You don't know the first thing." She sinks back and unbuttons her coat. "Get me that beer."

"That first night I met you," Toni says, and takes a drink of the beer. Peter is sitting next to her. "You'd just learned Kiya was pregnant, and you were running from it. I wanted to make you stay and face it, I didn't want you to run away from Kiya. I knew she needed you. I knew because I was pregnant once too, when I was

213

really young. Yeah, just out of middle school."

"Oh, Jeez, I'm an idiot," Peter says.

"Yes, sure. We agree on that. And the guy—the baby's father—wouldn't even talk to me. Wouldn't even return my calls, once I told him I was pregnant, with *HIS* baby. I didn't want you to be that asshole."

Peter picks up Toni's hand from where it lies limp in her lap. "I'm sorry." He holds her hand, caresses it, feeling the softness of her skin. "What happened?"

"I had the crazy idea of wanting to keep the baby." Toni laughs a sharp, mirthless sound. "That was a terrible idea, but I didn't see it that way. I thought I was grown up enough. I was such a little girl. I ended up having an abortion."

"I'm sorry," Peter says again. He is abashed. "But of course you couldn't keep it," he says finally.

"No, but I could have given birth to it, put it up for adoption. That's why I admire Kiya for doing what she's doing. That's why I want you to help her."

"Wait," Peter says. "You mean you got together with me just because you wanted to get me to help Kiya? That was your motivation?"

"I got together with you because I was attracted to you." Her head is down, looking at their joined hands. "You were cute. Or something more than that. But yeah, I also thought I had a perspective that might help." She looked up at him. "I liked you. In spite of how you talked that first night. I knew there was more to you than that person."

Peter isn't sure, at this moment, that there is more to him than that person. "I've been self-centered. I'm sorry. You should find somebody better."

"You think so? Like who?" Toni looks up at him, all mock-innocence. "Any suggestions?"

Peter wraps his arms around her. "Me. A better version of Peter." He strokes her smooth dark hair, touches her cheek with the knuckles of his hand. "So tell me," he said, "what it was like to be a kid, how old? Fourteen?"

"Fifteen."

"And pregnant."

"Oh, you know . . ."

"No, I don't. I don't know anything about it. Tell me."

* * * *

At dusk, Maddie pushes through the door of the nursing home. As she passes the desk, Sharon, one of the nurses, calls her over. "He's had a rough night," Sharon says.

"Really. What's wrong?'

"Chest congestion. You can hear it when he breathes. The doctor was in this afternoon and prescribed antibiotics."

"Poor guy," Maddie says.

"He's lucky he has you," Sharon says. His brother living in Florida has visited just once, three years ago.

She can hear Alex's breathing as soon as she pushes open the door. When he breathes out through the tracheostomy, there is a sighing, wheezing sound. He is lying on his bed, which is raised in a half-sitting position. "Aw, poor baby," Maddie says. She picks up a hand and massages it, then takes the other one. Alex opens one eye, seeming to watch her. "Do you want me to read to you today?" His eye closes. "Maybe I'll just sit with you for a while." By pulling her chair close to the bed, she can lean her head gently against his shoulder. She puts his hand down and puts hers on top of it.

Maddie lets her eyes close. Leaning this close to Alex, she feels the warmth of his body, the steady rise and fall of his chest as he breathes. It has been a busy day, and she is tired. Last night she woke in the night, hearing Kiya move around in the kitchen, and couldn't go back to sleep. "Do you remember this?" Maddie said softly. "The night Max wore his wolf suit and made mischief of one kind and another, his mother called him 'Wild Thing!'" Alex's breathing seems to change, his wheezing sound almost becoming plaintive, like the voice of a child. "You are my wild thing," she whispers. "Only I know how wild you can be." She is quiet then, and for a moment almost drifts off to sleep herself. She is thinking of Max, on his boat sailing to another land; she is thinking of her and Alex, on a sailboat in the bay. They went sailing a few times. He is leaning over to coil a rope around something, and turning back to smile at her. " *You're the wild thing,* " he says, and his teeth are gleaming white in the sunshine. *"Always the wild thing,"* Alex says to her, and in this dream—or whatever it is—he is coming close to her, to kiss her, to hold her. *"Stay that way,"* he murmurs into her hair. He is starting to say something else when she wakes with a start.

Alex's eyes are still closed, his breathing still making a sound through the tube in his throat. "This is a first," Maddie says and sits up. She touches her hair, as if someone were watching. "Falling asleep in your room." In her dream, Alex was talking with her, flirting, calling her *wild thing.* He was about to say something else—what was it? His eyes were glancing away, he was about to say it was time to go back to shore.

She looks at Alex. It's been a long time since they slept together. His mouth is turned downward, as if he is struggling with his thoughts. "Stay strong," she murmurs into his ear, and is rewarded by seeing his eyelashes flutter.

As Maddie drives home she wonders how much Alex is aware of what's going on around him. She knows he is aware of her when she's there; he looks at her, and she feels a connection. She feels HE is there then, the Alex she knew, and he knows she's there. She is seen. The nurses say he knows she is there, also, but she doesn't know how much to believe what they say. They want to encourage her to keep coming. She wonders if he has any thoughts when he is alone, when she's not there. Does he remember things? Does he remember when they met? It was at a party held in a private room of a restaurant in town; a local bank sponsored it, to strengthen relationships between business and the university. Maddie was holding a glass of wine and a plate of hors d'oeuvres. Making her way through the crowd she had bumped into someone, and her wine spilled on his gray sports coat. She had been overcome with embarrassment and apologies, but the man—Alex—acted as if it were a joke. He put her at ease, he was fun to talk with, and after that, they were together. He was her good companion, her tender lover, her best friend. She feels dampness seep out the corners of her eyes and run down one side of her face, as she drives along Lake Road.

Jack has said that his grandson, Paul, is very smart, but can't communicate what he knows. Maddie thinks maybe Paul's parents, and his grandfather, might need to tell themselves that in order to take care of the boy, in order to be patient with him and not give up. Maybe they all are fooling themselves, Paul's family and Maddie, by imagining what their loved ones know. Yet it isn't hard to visit Alex, Maddie thinks; she feels a warmth when she sees him, when she thinks of him. She feels a connection, a sense of purpose. There is something meaningful there beyond herself, beyond her own needs.

* * * *

At work, Evie is in a dream. She takes orders, serves coffee and eggs and toast and cleans tables and restocks supplies and makes fresh coffee and jokes with customers. All the while she is remembering the lake, the night air, and especially how Mike's body felt in the water against hers. He had come up from behind, wrapping his arms around her. He'd been laughing, and then he was still, and wasn't laughing anymore. She had leaned into him, crossing her arms over his. His body had been warm and strong against her. She wanted to remember that feeling: the warmth of his body, the coolness of the water, and the stars above them, watching.

She doesn't think she has felt this way before. As she tries to keep her attention on work, she is also remembering back to when she and Eric started dating. They went to movies on campus, they had drinks at parties, they kissed good night, then they . . . She'd liked Eric, she did, and she cared for him. They had fun. But she doesn't remember ever shivering, longing for his touch. It was probably the lake, Evie tells herself, that made things so special last night: the lake, and the stars. She had never seen them so bright.

On her next trip to Orgonon, Reich greets Evie at the door. Inside the main room, he pauses, then motions her to follow him

217

to his office. He closes the door, and sits at his desk, leaning his chair back against the wall. "You have lightened," he says. "You no longer look so dark."

"I feel stronger," Evie says. "I'm not afraid like I used to be."

"Cancer can be very frightening. Even the word is fearful," Reich says thoughtfully.

Evie had said the words without thinking, without premeditation, but now she realizes they are true. She had been so afraid— of her illness, of death, of many things. "Fear can spread," she murmurs.

"Yes!" Reich says, letting his chair down with a thump. "There is much to be afraid of. One can be afraid not only of fearful things like cancer and death, but of wonderful things. Life." His face is bright now, smiling, and he leans forward. "Don't let fear get in the way of wonderful things."

Just as Evie is beginning to feel uncomfortable with the fervor of the conversation, Reich sits back again. "All right, then. I am planning a conference for August and continuing my work with the DOR-buster. I am very busy. And I think that your health is on a good path. Am I right?" Evie nods. "So perhaps we come to the end of your orgone treatments."

In the box, Evie takes a deep breath and opens her eyes. She wants the full experience in this, her last time here. She is aware of the smell of wood, the light showing through the crack of the door. She hears a very faint sound of voices somewhere in the house, the closing of a door. Her feet rest on the floor of the accumulator box. Below that floor is a rug, then another floor, and below that, the earth. She has often imagined orgone energy in the sky, but now she thinks of earth's energy rising up. She sees it as a dark, solid energy, thick and meaty, as opposed to the clear airy energy from the sky. It has to do with death and with the body, because the body will go back to the earth, and the body always has to do with death. The body does die, there is no way around that. It will crumble into dirt.

Evie suddenly wraps her arms around herself and leans forward over her knees in the dark box. Her body will die, she will die; if not soon, then later. It will happen. She does not want it to happen. It's that simple, and that painful. She will die. She will.

She feels the grief rise up from inside her, a pure strong emotion. Sobs jerk through her, bursting from her mouth. She tries to keep them quiet but she doesn't really care—she will die! She is filled with that shocking knowledge.

Evie leans her head against the back of the box. The crying fades, except for a quiet sob still rippling up now and then. Her face is wet. There is sadness running through her, not only in her center but in her arms and her legs. It almost feels good, to feel such sadness; to feel so much. She will die, but she is alive now.

She sits in the darkness, knowing that soon the door will open, and light will flood in.

Chapter Twenty-Four

Dr. Wang stretches a flexible tape measure over Kiya's bare stomach, from below her breasts to her pubic bone. "Baby is growing fine," she says. She squeezes Kiya's ankles and her wrists. "Looks good, good. Are you feeling all right?" The doctor looks at her over her little glasses.

"Yes. I feel cramps a lot."

"Braxton Hicks," the doctor says. She reminds Kiya, again, of the childbirth classes the hospital offers. "I'll look into those," Kiya promises, but she pushes the idea away into a small, dark place at the back of her mind. She thinks about walking, by herself, into a class full of happy, expectant mothers accompanied by their baby's fathers, eagerly anticipating the births of their children, and knows she can't do it. To herself, she promises to read more about labor, to prepare herself in that way.

Dr. Wang puts the cool round part of the stethoscope on Kiya's stomach, moves it around. She stops. "Here," she says. Holding the instrument in place, she puts the earphones in Kiya's ears. "Hear it?"

Kiya listens, hears the wah-wah-wah sound, fast, like the wings of a small bird, flapping through the air.

In her bedroom at Maddie's house, Kiya has arranged some of her objects on the dresser top: dried skulls of small animals, found by the side of the road and boiled clean; a small enameled box for earrings; feathers; a dried gourd, painted and glazed; the framed photo of Drew. They remind her of her apartment back in Portland, remind her that she has a life apart from this one: apart from being pregnant, living in someone else's house. After the baby is born, will she have her own place somehow? Will she still be the person who collects feathers from the ground? She can't imagine paying that sort of light-hearted attention, picking up feathers as if they matter.

Above the dresser, she has tacked a row of postcards and photos. Reich, staring out at her benignly, his gray hair sticking up at odd angles—she could have helped him with that. A photo taken from a magazine of the Portland harbor, light shining on the houses rising above the water. And several postcard images of Van Gogh paintings: a self-portrait of him in a blue suit; a pair of boots; and one she particularly loves, of people walking by a river at night, lights reflecting in the deep blue of the water.

She has just finished a painting, inspired by Van Gogh's boots, of her own old cowboy boots. She kept the background simple, as Van Gogh did for his boots, and she worked at making the boots substantial, showing something of the life they have contained. They are worn and exhausted, like Van Gogh's boots, yet ready to serve.

She starts a self-portrait, standing in front of the mirror and sketching herself on the canvas. She draws the roundness of her belly pushing out in front of her and begins drawing her head, then throws the pencil on the floor. No, she can't do that. She doesn't know who that person is in the mirror, she can't characterize her in any way at all. Looking at her own eyes frightens her: there is something there, looking back at her. She looks wild and afraid, an animal trapped in a human skin.

On her cell phone, she finds a photograph of Peter. She stares at it for some time. He is leaning against a wall wearing a brown jacket, slanted sunshine on his face. He is squinting slightly, looking down at Kiya. The picture is filled with warmth and light and makes her feel good. She feels warm when she looks at the photo and thinks of Peter; in touch with something important. She doesn't want to question that feeling, think about it too deeply, or she will scare it away. She picks up the pencil again and begins to sketch.

* * * *

Peter King has discovered something new about how to live in this world. The sun looks new to him when he wakes up in the morning, as he runs down the stairs to begin his day. It is not totally due to Toni that he has this new way of seeing the world, but she has been instrumental. She'd been right when she said he never asked any questions of her, assuming he already knew who

221

she was. He set himself the task of asking her questions and listening to her carefully, actually listening, when she answered. It has become a game with them, something they do together; Peter asks Toni questions, and she answers them. The questions start out as important and profound ones: "Did you think you were in love with your boyfriend when you were fifteen?" "How did your parents respond?" "What did your father mean when he said that?" "Do you believe in the soul?" If Peter assumes too quickly that he understands the answer Toni gives him, and she can see that he doesn't, she stops him, saying "Whoa boy," and he knows to go back, to think again, to ask and listen again. Toni also asks him questions, but she's always been one to ask him questions, so there isn't so much of a difference in that. At times Peter catches Toni making her own assumptions, and he takes delight in calling her back, in pointing out that she wasn't really listening.

At times the questions become trivial: "Will you dye your hair when it turns gray?" "What color do you think looks best on me?" or even silly: "If you could choose a famous person to go to bed with, who would it be?" "Do these pants make me look fat?"

Peter's burst of energy came when he discovered that this approach of questioning, of thinking that he doesn't know the answer, could be applied to other situations, other people. He started at work with Gary. At lunch break, he asked him about his kids. He knew Gary had two kids and sometimes mentioned them, but Peter didn't think he'd ever asked about them before except in a very casual way. He didn't even know their names for sure, and had to ask, "How are the kids?" They had driven to a park to eat lunch near where they were working and were sitting on a bench looking at the harbor. The day was chilly, and they wore thick coats against the breeze. When Gary answered, Peter listened carefully, trying to fix their names in his memory: Amanda and Johann. He asked about Gary's son's name. This is when he learned that Gary's wife was from South Africa, and Johann was a family name. "Your wife is from South Africa?" Peter said. He'd met her a few times. "I didn't know that. She doesn't have an accent."

"She came over here when she was tiny. Her mother and father have strong accents. It's an Afrikaans name there." This led to a discussion of why her parents emigrated to the United States, and what their views on politics in South Africa were. Peter had these things to think on for the rest of the afternoon as he climbed, tying himself to the tree and working his way up.

He found it more of a challenge at The Blue Moon. The noise level was high, and people didn't go out to a pub in order to have serious conversations, at least not with strangers. When he worked in the kitchen, he was able to ask Nate, the chef, simple, non-threatening questions: "How long have you worked here?" "What do you like to do when you're not working?" He learned that Nate had been going to college, but had to drop out because his parents couldn't afford to help him. He was saving money to go back. "What do you want to study?" Peter asked, speaking loudly to be heard. He was chopping vegetables at one counter, while Nate cut up meat at another.

"Pre-med," Nate said, suddenly shy. "I want to be a vet."

Peter watched Nate's hands cut up a chicken, expertly, and knew he would not see Nate in quite the same way after this. "How about you?" Nate asked. "What do you like to do when you're not working?"

Peter told him that he was saving for school, also. "I have a degree in Philosophy, but I want to earn a teaching certificate." He saw Nate pause in his cutting, and look at him with interest.

One evening, Peter calls his mother. He's not sure how this questioning will work out with his mother, but he wants to try. He starts by asking her how things are with Kiya. "Is she doing all right?"

"She seems all right, but I don't know. She's very quiet, you know?"

"Is she?"

"Yes, well she is with me, anyway. Pleasant, friendly, just quiet. She's in her room a lot, painting. I don't know how she's doing, really."

"I saw one of her paintings," Peter said. "It's pretty good."

"Yes. Her mother paints. Maybe she inherited some talent."

"I didn't know that."

"How are you doing?" his mother asks. "How's work?" but Peter doesn't want to go there.

"It's fine. Hey, I have a question for you . . ." He's not sure, as he says the words, just what the question will be.

"Yes," his mother says, waiting.

It comes to him. "You and Alex were going out together for a long time. Right?"

"Nearly eight years."

"Why didn't you get married?"

His mother laughs, and when she speaks, her voice sounds young over the phone, almost girlish. "We talked about it all the time. We both liked the idea of dating, of being independent, but we were spending all our time together, so I decided to move in with him."

"You did?"

"Yes, and we were going to plan a wedding sometime after that. This was just before he got sick."

"Wow. I didn't know that. A wedding."

"Yes, it would have been my first. I don't know how I would have been as a wife. Difficult, probably."

"You would have made a great wife," Peter says. "Just like you were a great mother."

"Why, Peter. What a nice thing to say." She pauses. "Are you sure everything is all right?" and he laughs at the fact that when he says something nice to his mother, she thinks something is wrong.

"Things are fine," he says. "I just wondered about that, about you and Alex. He was a nice guy, you know?"

"Yes." She tells him then that Alex has been ill, fighting pneumonia. Peter listens to the intonation of his mother's voice as she says this, hearing her worry. He says he'll be up to visit again soon.

✻ ✻ ✻ ✻

When Maddie talks with Peter again, he asks if he can bring his current girlfriend, Toni, to visit. He asks when a good time would be; he particularly wants to visit when Kiya won't be around. "You know," he says to her over the phone. "Former girl-friend meets current girlfriend. Not something I would enjoy. Or anybody would enjoy."

Kiya is in her bedroom when Peter calls, with the door closed. Still, Maddie steps outside to talk on the porch. "I think she's going to Portland on Friday," Maddie says. "She has her regular appointment with the psychiatrist on Friday afternoon at 3:00. She usually is gone the entire afternoon."

"I work then, and so does Toni . . . Will she be gone on Saturday or Sunday sometime?"

Maddie considers this. "Well, I can see if I can find a way to make that happen. I'll let you know."

She puts on a jacket and rubber boots and makes her way across to Jack's house. The ground is wet and soft, mud season. His maple syrup evaporator is set up in his yard, with empty buckets and a pile of sapwood, thin long strips, on the ground near it. Smoke comes out the evaporator's chimney, with a faint smoky sweet smell. She steps around, walks up the steps to tap on the door, and when there is no answer, taps again. A light is on inside. He comes to the door, disheveled. "Sorry," he says, holding open the door. "I was taking a nap."

"Sorry to wake you." She steps inside, wiping her feet on the mat. "I have a favor to ask."

She explains the situation. "I would feel bad about it, going behind the girl's back like this, except I really think she needs to get out more anyway. It would do her good. And I agree with Peter that maybe it wouldn't be great for her to see his new girlfriend. You know, Kiya's not the most secure person in the world."

Jack thinks it over. "I could do that," he says. "I should be done boiling sap by then. I need to go to Augusta to pick up a few things; maybe I could take her with me, take her out to lunch too. There's a new café downtown. Would that work?"

"Perfect, that would be perfect." They agree that Maddie will speak to Kiya. Maddie calls Peter and tells him they can have their rendezvous in the late morning the following Saturday.

It is just a little less than three weeks until Kiya's due date, and Maddie hasn't heard anything of her plans. Kiya said something about maybe going to live with her mother for a while after the baby is born, but she sounded vague. Maybe Jack can get her to talk about the future.

On Saturday, Jack knocks on the door at 11:00. He steps inside, standing with his hands in his jacket pocket just inside the door. Maddie thinks he is trying not to look like an embarrassed suitor, picking up his date. She resists the urge to tell him he has to bring her back before dark. Kiya comes out of her room. She still limps slightly, and her bright blue jacket does not button across the width of her stomach. She has a big smile for Jack. Her face, alight like this, reminds Maddie of how she looked when they first met. "Hey Jack," Kiya says. She takes his arm. "Ready to be my date for the day?"

Jack smiles and tips his baseball hat. Maddie thinks they are cute, Kiya with her shy smile and Jack with his gray stubble and kind eyes. "Wait," she says. "I have to record this." She grabs her phone and holds it up. "Say cheese." Kiya smiles broadly, Jack gives his wry, embarrassed half-smile, and Maddie snaps the shot.

After they leave, Maddie puts out sandwich meats and cheeses, pesto, bruschetta, and tomatoes. She takes the sourdough bread she bought from the bakery and cuts it neatly into slices, laying them across a flowered plate. She is nervous about meeting this girl; it is yet another girlfriend, but her son might be serious about this one. He sounded different when he brought up the idea of bringing her home—nervous, as if it mattered. As if the visit was important.

Peter had said they'd be there between 11:00 and noon. Noon passes, it's 12:30, then it is approaching 1:00. Maddie combs her hair again, sits down, picks up a book. She puts the book down again with a sigh. It's after 1:00 when she finally hears a car in the lane.

"Sorry, so sorry we're late," they say, Peter's voice overlapping with the voice of the young woman beside him. Toni, it must be; dark hair slanting to the side of a smiling face, dark eyes bright, her voice cheerful, exuberant. "It's all my fault," Toni says.

"No, it's not, it's mine," Peter says. "The kitchen faucet started spewing water just before I left, Ryan was gone, and I had

226

to fix it."

"And I made him stop on the way to buy this, and it took a long time." Toni holds out a box. "Lemon bars for dessert, from this place in Portland. They are so good. I hope you like them."

"Thank you so much. I love lemon bars." She puts them on the table with the other food. As they sit at the table Maddie asks Peter, "Did you get a haircut?" When he says not recently, she says "You just look different somehow." It's his expression, she decides. His face is more open, and he looks at her directly in a way he didn't use to. He smiles more.

Toni makes a fuss over Sadie, who jumps up on her. "Bad dog!" Maddie says, but Toni just laughs. When she sits down, Sadie sits close beside her. When Toni stops petting her, Sadie puts a paw on her thigh. "Watch out," Maddie says. "She'll never leave you alone now."

Peter looks out the window. "The ice is out," he says. The white-topped waves are pushing the last few chunks of ice to the shore.

"The loons should be returning soon," Maddie says. "I watch for them every day."

"My mother loves loons," Peter says to Toni.

"Everyone loves loons," Maddie says.

"It's true," Toni says. "There's something about them. My parents live near a pond in northern Maine, and I would hear the loons all summer and fall every night when I went to sleep. I loved their sound." Peter reaches over and takes Toni's hand. *Uh oh,* Maddie thinks. Now she knows it's serious.

They make sandwiches, and Maddie serves the lemon bars. She asks Toni about her job. "What exactly does a graphic designer do?"

"I do whatever the firm comes up with me to do. Brochures, web design, whatever the client needs. I design brands for new companies, come up with ways to get their products out there in the media. It's a great place to work, and what I always wanted to do."

When they are done eating, Peter pushes his plate away. "Mom," he says, and Maddie's head lifts up. "I have some news for you."

"What? What?"

"Don't worry. I know it seems sudden to you, because you've just met her, but this is something I'm very sure of. We're very sure of," he says, looking at Toni, who nods and smiles. "Toni has agreed to marry me."

Chapter Twenty-Five

For some reason, Kiya finds Jack easy to talk to. Over a Thai wrap, she tells him about her father. "Just recently, he told my mother and me that he was gay. He's in a relationship with another man."

"Well, that's interesting, isn't it?" Jack chuckles. "What did you think of that news?"

"It made sense to me, once I thought about it for a while. Things started to come together."

"Like . . ."

"Like the way he couldn't seem to get happy. No matter what." Kiya thinks, now, of all the times, all the ways she used to try to make her father happy. Looking back, it seems that this was a major task of her adolescence. She was always trying to make him smile; if he smiled at her, she was worthwhile, and those smiles were a lot of work.

"Does he seem happy now?"

Kiya ponders this. "Well, there was my brother's death." She has told Jack about Drew, about how he died. "It's hard to be happy after that. But he seems more . . . himself. And he and I get along better. We hung out when he came back to Maine recently. We talked. It was good."

Jack nods, dipping a chunk of bread into his lobster chowder. "How's your mother? I heard she was sick."

"Much better. Much, much better. She's worried about me, but she's healthier." Kiya leans back, patting her round belly. "I give her a lot to worry about."

Jack wipes his mouth. "Not more than most kids. We have kids so that we have something to worry about."

"Your son didn't give you too much grief, did he?"

"Ha! That boy. Not unless you call phone calls from the police in the middle of the night, grief. Not unless you call bailing him out of jail, grief."

"No! Really?"

Jack nods. "And now he has this boy so he has someone to

worry about. But my son has grown up real good. He's a fine man now, a fine father and husband. Kids get through these troubles, they just need parents to keep hanging in there."

Unfortunate choice of words, Kiya thinks, as she sees Drew hanging there, above the tub, above their table. Her stomach lurches. "Well, not all kids get through their troubles."

Jack looks at her. "I suppose that's true. I'm sorry."

Kiya looks around. They are by themselves by a window overlooking the street; tables around them have emptied. She feels bold suddenly, and reckless. "I found him," she says.

"What? Who? Your . . ."

She nods. "My brother. Drew. I found his body."

Jack puts his spoon down on the table. "My goodness," he says. After a moment; "That must have been something." And after another moment, "Tell me about it."

Their lunch stretches into the afternoon. "I never told anyone that before," she says. "That I found him, I mean. Except for my parents and my therapist. No one else knew."

"Well, now I know too," Jack says. "Maybe it will be easier to tell someone else now. When you want to tell someone, that is."

Kiya cries silently, leaning over her empty plate. Jack orders dessert for them both and tea, without asking her. When she finishes crying, she eats every bit of the slice of apple pie. She wipes her eyes, says, "I think I feel better, having told you."

She does feel better, but she is also exhausted, as tired as she has ever been. She wants to lie down in the booth and sleep. She has been having cramps lately; the book she checked out from the library says early cramps called Braxton-Hicks can "mimic" labor cramps, and they are regular today, squeezing her uterus until it as hard as a rock. She had them in the night and wasn't able to get back to sleep for a long time. The tension of the contraction is almost painful, in her front and especially in her lower back. When she woke up this morning she had a small amount of blood on her underpants.

After lunch, Jack wants to take Kiya to the Maine State Museum. "I worked on a model of a three-story water-powered woodworking mill. It really works."

Jack seems excited by the prospect of taking Kiya to the museum, but she will have to say no. She puts on her blue coat. "Pregnancy makes me sleepy," she says, as they walk out the door. "And some nights I don't sleep well, for one reason or another, and I just have to take an afternoon nap. I really need to go home." Jack looks so baffled and disappointed, standing on the sidewalk outside the café, that she says, "I would really love to go there, though, another time. Maybe next week? Will you take me back?"

He shrugs and takes her elbow to help her into the pickup. "All right, can't argue with that."

Kiya feels safe and warm, riding in Jack's pickup. She looks over at him and smiles. He is a nice man, a fatherly kind of warm man. Maddie is like a mother to her, too, she thinks, growing drowsy. Jack listened to her story about Drew. She might even tell him the worst part, someday—maybe when they go to the Museum. She might tell him how she didn't meet with Drew the night before when he wanted to talk; how she could have saved him.

Jack makes a stop for gas on the way home. When he is inside she feels her stomach tighten again, harder than before. He is gone into the convenience store for a long time, but when he comes out he has only a bottle of water. "Looking for something?" she asks.

"What? Oh, yeah," he says. "Thought they might have this newspaper I was looking for."

"Mmm," Kiya says, settling into her seat again and closing her eyes.

Kiya is half-dozing, but she can feel when the truck turns into the lane, can feel when it pulls into Jack's parking space and stops. She opens her eyes. "Here we are. Thank you so much, Jack." She turns to open the door. There, in the parking space next to Maddie's, is Peter's red Jeep.

"Oh!" Kiya says. She can't keep the happiness from her voice. "Peter's here. I didn't know he was coming." She steps carefully down from the truck and walks toward the house. When she turns around Jack is standing there, looking uncertain. "Why don't you come in?"

When Kiya enters the kitchen, at first she can't comprehend what she is seeing. Peter is sitting at the kitchen table, and his mother is across from him, rising to say hello. The sun has come out through clouds and is shining on the lake behind them, making their figures in front of the windows dark and shadowy. Kiya is happy, the warmth of the car ride and the talk still with her, but between Peter and Maddie, facing Kiya, is someone else: a dark-haired, smiling woman. She is pretty. She looks nice, kind of; she has a good haircut. Sadie is standing beside the chair this woman sits in, and doesn't run forward to Kiya as she usually does. Kiya hears voices in greeting, and before their words make sense to her, she understands what she is seeing. She pieces it together. Peter looks embarrassed, and Maddie has a look on her face that Kiya can't quite understand. Concern, anxiety. This is Peter's girlfriend. There is no other possible explanation.

* * * *

Peter meant to leave his mother's house well before Kiya and Jack got back, but it didn't happen. He and Toni were late leaving Portland, and then Jack brought Kiya back earlier than he expected. Peter knows he has nothing to be ashamed of, nothing to be embarrassed about—he and Kiya are not together, he can have a girlfriend—but still, he felt bad when Kiya came in and saw them there like that, with no forewarning. She didn't handle it well.

They had told his mother their news and she needed a little time to process it, a little time to get to know Toni—her future daughter-in-law—before they just jumped up and left. He supposes they should have asked his mother to come to Portland. But he wanted Toni to see the house where he grew up, wanted her to see the lake. He has a right to do that, doesn't he?

They were just showing Maddie the ring. Peter and Toni had gone together to pick it out. It was not a diamond, but a delicate jade ring, in a silver setting. "I don't really like diamonds," Toni said, holding out her hand with the ring. "I like color. I love this."

Maddie had taken Toni's hand in hers, looking at the ring. "It's beautiful." It was just after that that Kiya walked in, smiling. She looked happy in her blue coat, pink-cheeked from the cold. She saw the three of them sitting there at the table, and her smile slowly changed. She looked afraid, her eyes darting from side to side. Peter didn't know what to do.

His mother walked over to Kiya and put an arm around her shoulder. "This is Kiya," she said. "Kiya, this is Toni." Kiya had pulled away from Maddie's arm as Toni came from around the table, walking over to the two of them. "Kiya. I've been wanting to meet you," Toni said. Kiya didn't return her greeting. After standing motionless for a moment, she had simply turned around and walked back out the door.

Now Peter stands in the kitchen with his mother, Toni, and Jack. Jack says, "I'll go after her."

Toni says, "I'm so sorry."

"No, I'm sorry," Maddie says. "It's not your fault."

"It's mine," Peter says, and though they both assure him it's not so, Peter knows it is.

When Jack returns, he wipes the mud off his feet and says, "She just wants to walk. Wants to be alone."

"Is she all right?" Maddie asks. "Do you think I should go after her?"

"I think she might just want to be alone," Jack says. "It won't hurt her."

Jack introduces himself to Toni. "Oh, sorry," Maddie says. "I didn't think. Jack, Toni and Peter are engaged."

A light dawns on Jack's face. He takes off his baseball hat and rubs his head in bemusement. "Is that right. Well, what do you know about that." He looks from one to the other. "Congratulations are in order."

"And . . ." Peter says. "I'm going back to school next fall. To earn a teaching certificate."

"Peter!" Maddie says. "You are full of news."

"It's all related to this lady," he says, patting Toni's arm. "And a little bit to this guy," he says, pointing to Jack.

"What, me?" Jack puts his hands across his chest.

"Yeah, you helped. You told me I had to work for what I wanted. So now I'm working two jobs, saving up money to go to school to work some more for what I want. But it's worth it." He leans his arms on the table, resting his head on them so he can look at Toni. She smiles down at him, that half-smile that says she knows him. It says she knows both his good and his bad, and she loves the good enough to put up with the bad.

* * * *

Alone in her house, Maddie puts away the lunch things, wrapping up the extra meat and cheese and putting them in the refrigerator. Peter and Toni have left to visit Alex. Two left-over lemon bars go into the refrigerator. She wipes down the table and counter, and wonders if Kiya will want dinner when she returns.

She sits in her chair, looking out at the lake. The nights are still cold, but the light lingers a little longer every day, the air becoming softer. Jack has finished tapping his trees and the snow is gone, except for a shrinking pile in the shadow of the garage. Kiya had seemed to be growing stronger, day by day; as her stomach grew, she seemed to be feeling better. Until today.

She likes the way Peter and Toni look at one another, the expressions on their faces. Marriage! A wedding! How does one get married, how does one stage a wedding? She's never done it. She has a vague idea that the bride handles most of the details. She hopes so, at any rate. She has no experience in such things.

Maddie looks up from her book to see the light fading, the sun down behind the trees. It will be dark before long. Peter and Toni have been gone for almost an hour. She picks up the phone and dials Kiya's number. It goes right to her voice mail.

Maddie sits looking out the lake, then calls Kiya's number

again. This time she leaves a message. "Kiya, it's Maddie. It's getting late and I'm worried. Come back; let's make something good to eat."

Maddie calls Jack. "Have you seen Kiya since she left?"

"She's not back yet? No." He had apologized for not keeping Kiya out longer, said he just didn't know how to do it. "She was so tired at the end of lunch, I thought she would be sleeping by now. She almost fell asleep in the car."

"I think I'll go look for her," Maddie says. "Wanna come along?"

"She can't have gone that far," Jack says. Maddie is driving the car down the bumpy lane, Jack beside her and Sadie in the back seat, her nose lifted and pressed to where the window is open a crack. "We should be able to see her."

"I just don't know which way she goes on her walks. I think sometimes she goes toward town, and sometimes heads north."

"Let's go north first," Jack suggests. "I bet she would go where there might be fewer people."

Maddie turns right at River Road, and drives slowly up and down the hills, on the black-topped road. The road ends in a T, and Maddie hesitates. "Which way?"

"Left," Jack suggests, and Maddie turns left, though she has no idea if that's a more likely direction than right. The road goes on for several miles. When they come to another "T," Maddie stops and looks over at Jack. "I'm turning around," she says.

She drives past the lane in the other direction toward town, which is five miles away. "How long is she usually gone on her walks?" Jack asks.

"An hour at most, usually," Maddie says. The road rises and dips, trees on either side deepening in shadows as night comes on. They pass a woman running, wearing reflector strips over her fleece jacket. They pass a couple walking briskly for exercise, their white sneakers glowing in the dusk. Then they see no other people except for the occasional car.

"How was your lunch?" Maddie asks.

"It was good. We talked about her brother and her father. She's a good kid, just has a lot to deal with."

"A lot," Maddie agrees.

Jack tries Kiya's number, and leaves a message as well. "Hey Kiya. Jack here. Give a call."

When they approach Mt. Vernon, Maddie looks at Jack sitting in the passenger seat. "She wouldn't have gone this far."

"She has to be somewhere, though. It's getting cold." It was in the 50's earlier, but now the car thermometer gives the outside temperature at 47 degrees.

"There are lots of side roads . . ."

Jack says, "Let's go back. Maybe she's home."

Maddie opens the door to her house. "Kiya?" she calls. She walks down the hall to the second bedroom, looks in the open door. The room is dark and empty, the bed neatly made.

Jack takes his car and Maddie takes hers, so they can cover more ground. Alone in the car but for Sadie, Maddie drives slowly, straining her eyes to see anyone by the side of the road in the dark. She pictures Kiya walking slowly, head down, huddled into her blue jacket. She was wearing dark leggings and a long tunic made of some kind of sweater material. Maddie hopes she is warm, wherever she is. She has only vague memories of what it was like to be pregnant, twenty-six years ago. She and Mark had broken up when she was pregnant, and she lived alone. She does remember swings of emotion, wild storms of grief, the intense emotions of youth compounded by the drastic physical changes she was going through. With her parents' support, she'd made the decision early on to keep the baby, with or without Mark's help. Even when she was most afraid, even when she didn't know what would happen for the rest of her life, she had the baby to look forward to, the knowledge that she would hold him in her arms, put him to her breast.

After an hour of driving, with no sight of Kiya by either of them, Maddie thinks she should call Kiya's mother. She knows Judith is not emotionally strong, and Maddie is afraid to tell her that her daughter is missing. Maddie feels responsible. *I lost your daughter,* she imagines saying. But no; Kiya is an adult, she walked away and is making her own decisions. Maybe Kiya contacted her mother, and Judith knows where she is.

Jack returns to Maddie's house soon after her. Maddie takes a beer from the refrigerator and hands it to him. He agrees she should call Kiya's mother. Call Peter too, he says, just in case he knows anything. "Okay, here goes," Maddie says, and taps in Judith's number.

Chapter Twenty-Six

When Kiya left Maddie's house, her brain was on fire. It was a white fire, a white heat, like a cloud that obscured everything around her. She knew there was a pain she would feel, though she didn't yet know what exactly it was from, or would be from. She just had to walk, walk away from it.

She remembers Jack coming after her, and though she doesn't remember what he said, or what she said, she does remember that she was able to step out of the white fire obscuring all sense in her brain for that moment. She was able to talk with him as if she was making sense, as if she knew what was going on and just needed a few minutes by herself. Whatever she said, it made Jack go away and leave her alone, which was what she wanted.

She walks until the inside of her thighs begin to hurt, along with the regular hard tightening of her belly with Braxton-Hicks. She turns around then, walking slowly back toward Maddie's. She knows she doesn't want to re-enter that house, but she has nowhere else to go. She steps into the woods beside the road, hiding behind a tree as she squats down to pee, and hears a car pass. The white cloud is calming down, and the outlines of her pain begin to be defined.

At the center of it are Peter and the woman, standing next to one another by Maddie's kitchen table. They obviously are together, belong together; obviously, the woman must be right for Peter in a way that she, Kiya, is not. Radiating out from this center are Maddie and Jack; Jack, her new friend. Jack, who took her out to lunch and listened to her so kindly, so intently, that she thought someone was finally understanding her. She gave him her greatest pain, her last image of Drew, and Jack took it in. He didn't try to tell her to feel better; he just listened. Kiya didn't feel alone anymore during the time she talked with him.

Then when she walked into Maddie's house a bright, horrible light was shining on her lunch with Jack, which after some time she was able to articulate to herself: Jack took her out to lunch to keep her away from seeing this, to get her out of the house. That's why he wanted to take her to the Museum. It wasn't so she could see the project he'd worked on. It was to keep her away longer, so Maddie could get to know Peter's girlfriend without Kiya in the way.

Maddie must have been in on this plan, and of course Peter also. As Kiya walks, as the light fades from the sky above her, she feels something creep over her, something dark and slippery. It is shame. It is unpleasant and stifling; it makes it hard to breathe. It makes her stomach tighten in embarrassment, the force of the contractions reaching around to her back. Did they think she couldn't handle meeting Peter's girlfriend; did they think she was still so in love with him that it would have driven her crazy? Did Peter think that? She feels the first touches of shame when she tells herself they were right to do what they did; they were right to hide it from her, to try to keep her away from the house. She couldn't have handled it, she couldn't have helped herself. She would have had to lock herself in her room, stay away. She was too weak. They must have seen that in her, and what she thought was Jack's friendship was, if anything, sympathy for the poor crazy girl. Pity for fucked-up pregnant Kiya. And Peter, too. She doesn't want to think of what Peter thinks of her.

She will stay away from them until this particular fever of her mind passes. The shame and embarrassment will go away. She will be able to be stand-up Kiya again, the cheerful sunny girl who can handle things. The one who cheers her mother up, who makes her father smile. The accomplished hair stylist, the Kiya people like. But not yet; she is not able to do that yet. She needs to be alone.

When she walks down the lane to the house, Peter's Jeep is gone. Kiya sees lights on inside, and the lights in Jack's house through the trees. For a moment, she is pulled toward their warmth, toward the comfort she would like to find there. The sky is dark, and the night is getting cold. They could cook together, chatting in the warmth and light of the kitchen. But at the thought of facing Maddie, of talking with her, Kiya turns away. Maddie's car is gone, and she doesn't see Jack's truck either. She walks to the shed by the lake, her boots squelching in the damp ground. Maddie keeps an extra key to the shed on top of the doorframe. Kiya reaches up, moving her fingers around on the rough wood until she finds it. She unlocks the padlock carefully and opens the door, trying not to make noise in case Maddie or Jack are around somewhere.

There is no electricity in the shed, but in the light coming in through two windows Kiya sees the kayaks, piled on top of one another. The paddles are leaning against the wall. She leans down, opening stuffed-full plastic garbage bags until she finds the one she is looking for, the one with the extra-warm sleeping bag. She helped Maddie put these away last fall. She ties up the bag again, and sets it on the ground near the lake.

In the shed, three kayaks rest together upside down on the floor. She pulls the orange kayak off the other two. It is light enough for her to carry. On the windowsill is a half-used pack of matches, which she sticks in her pocket. She lifts the kayak out of the shed, sets it on the ground, and pushes it toward the lake. She turns around and locks the door again, pushing the padlock closed. The sky is clear but for a few thin clouds, stars visible in the dusky sky. She will get away for a while, resting in silence on the island. She will be all right.

Kiya settles herself in the kayak. Her stomach nearly reaches the edge of the opening. She picks up the garbage bag and shoves it down beside her, into the space where her feet are, so she is able to paddle. Pressing the tip of an oar against a rock, she pushes herself onto the water. The boat rocks, then steadies.

※　※　※　※

"Your mother was all alone when she had you?" Toni is buckled into her seatbelt, her hand reaching across to rest on Peter's thigh.

"I guess so. She'd broken up with my dad, so he wasn't there."

"That must have been hard."

Peter shrugs; he wouldn't know. "She had me to comfort her, didn't she?" he says and smiles over at Toni.

They have left the nursing home and are driving back to Portland on a dark highway with pine trees thick on both sides. Alex, resting in his bed, had not opened his eyes during their visit.

Peter had put a hand on his shoulder, feeling the thin bone beneath the hospital gown. "Alex, it's Peter," he said. Alex gave no response. His breathing through the tube was noisy in a way Peter hadn't heard before. Toni had leaned over and put her hand on Alex's arm. "It's Toni," she said clearly into his ear. "We came to tell you that Peter and I are engaged. We're going to be married." Peter couldn't be sure, but he thought there was a change in Alex's breathing then, a quieting, a catch.

Toni sat next to Alex on chairs next to Alex's bed. She leaned close and sang, "I'm getting married in the morning, ding-dong the bells are gonna chime." She smiled up at Peter. "Sing with me?"

"I don't know that one. How about this one: 'Going to the chapel and we're gonna get married." Together they sang "Chapel of Love" to Alex. In the low light from the lamp on Alex's bedside table his face, half in shadow, looked craggy and noble; his white skin, the prominent nose, the lines around his eyes and his mouth timeless, as if carved out of marble. When they left, Alex was breathing deeply and slowly, a rattling sound with each breath.

They haven't yet talked about what happened when Kiya came in and saw them. Now Toni says, "I feel bad for Kiya."

"There's no need to," Peter says. "Our engagement has nothing to do with her. My mother is being nice to take her in; we don't need to let her make us feel bad. Our relationship is long over."

"Yes, I know. I know that's true. But still, I can imagine how she feels." She glances out the window, to where a break in the trees opens up to reveal a lake, shining in the moonlight. "There we all were, and no one told her we were coming."

"It didn't work out like I thought it would," Peter admits. He remembers their question game. After a moment, a question comes to him; "Do you think she knew we asked her to be kept away?"

"Yes, I would guess so," Toni says. "That's what would make her feel bad."

They are close to Portland when his phone, sitting on the dashboard of his Jeep, rings. He has programmed a ringtone of a squawking turkey, and Toni laughs at the squawking sound. It's his mother. "Kiya's not back yet," she says. "We can't reach her and don't know where she is. She hasn't called you, has she?"

* * * *

Judith doesn't know where Kiya might have gone. Maddie tries to be reassuring. "She often takes walks, long walks," she says. "She might even have gone to visit someone." Maddie is improvising now; Kiya never visits anyone near Maddie's house. "She knows people in the neighborhood. She might have just forgotten to call here or turn her phone on. I just wanted to see if she'd called you."

"No. She hasn't called me since yesterday." Judith's voice is rising in pitch, becoming breathless. "She usually calls every day. I wondered why she hadn't called today."

"Don't worry too much, okay? I'm sure she's fine. I'll be waiting here for her when she comes back."

"Oh . . . okay." Judith sounds as if she can't catch her breath.

"Do you have anyone you can talk to?" Maddie asks. Silence answers. "Why don't you call Kiya's father? She said she visited with him recently." She's not sure why she suggests this, but Judith sounds grateful.

"We did have a good visit. Maybe I will call him. He should know, shouldn't he?"

Maddie agrees, he should know. "I'll have her call you as soon as she shows up, or as soon as I hear from her, okay? And don't worry."

Maddie goes to Kiya's room again. She turns on the light. There are a few objects on the dresser and some photos on the walls, but otherwise, the room is much as it was when Kiya moved in, except for the canvases and painting supplies. Maddie has never snooped in Kiya's room before, but now she walks over to the stack of canvases leaning facing the wall. She turns one around, and Peter is looking out at her.

The painting glows with light coming through the paint strokes applied heavily, yet with a certain grace and confidence.

Peter's face, done in dabs of yellow, brown, tan and green, is angular, instantly recognizable. His hair is lit by yellowed streaks of the sun, and he looks out of the canvas with a slight smile on his face. He is painted with love, that much is clear.

It's ten o'clock. Jack leans back in a chair at Maddie's table. "She must be visiting someone," he says. "That's the only thing she could be doing. No way she's out walking somewhere in the night."

Maddie sits down at the table, heavily. She feels old, tired, confused. "You're right. But who?"

"Does she have any friends who live in this neighborhood at all?"

Maddie thinks, shakes her head slowly. "None that I know of. Only in Portland." She looks down at Sadie, lying on the ground near her with her head on her paws. "Sadie," Maddie says. "Sadie's her friend." Sadie's ears prick up, and her eyes look up toward Maddie. "Sadie, do you know where Kiya is?" Sadie lifts her head, staring intently at Maddie. "Sadie, where's Kiya?" Sadie lets out a low whine.

"It's worth a try," Jack says, taking Sadie's leash from the hook by the door. He pulls a flashlight from his coat pocket.

The night air is cool and damp, though the sky is clear. Maddie shivers. Sadie snuffles around eagerly outside the door, nosing a small wet patch of snow left under the trees. "Sadie, where's Kiya." Sadie pulls toward the lake, toward the shed. "Great," Maddie says. "She probably smells a chipmunk." The dog snuffles a pile of leaves and twigs beside the shed door. The moon, nearly full, is rising over the trees on Spruce Island. The sky is clear but for a few thin white clouds illuminated by its light. Sadie sits back on her haunches and lets out a short, loud bark.

"She's not in there, Sadie," Maddie says, but Jack asks if she has a key. Maddie puts her hand up on the frame, moving it around until she finds the cold metal key.

"Now you know our key's secret hiding place," she says.

"I won't tell anyone," he says. He points the light at the padlock so Maddie can see to unlock. It clicks apart, and she pushes the door open.

Jack's flashlight plays around the room. The plastic bags Maddie use for storage line one wall; lawn chairs are stacked on the floor. On the other wall, kayaks are stacked. "Wait," Maddie says, and grabs the flashlight from Jack. She aims it toward the kayaks. "Wait," she says again, not quite believing what she sees. "There should be three." She wonders briefly, wildly, if someone broke into the shed and stole one. Sadie, snuffling around the floor, whines, then paws something next to a garbage bag. Jack reaches down and picks up a small, black rectangular object. It's Kiya's cell phone.

Chapter Twenty-Seven

Kiya paddles slowly, steadily towards the island. Her hands are cold in her thin leather gloves, but the exertion makes her feel warmer. It's right for her to be alone; she's not able to be with people now. She will call Maddie and tell her where she is once she gets to the island. She will tell her she doesn't intend to spend the night; she just needs to be alone for a while. There is no place more alone than an island.

Away from shore, she stops paddling, catching her breath. The Braxton-Hicks contractions make it hard for her to breathe. She wonders if they are brought on by the stress of the day, wonders when they'll stop. The sky still holds some light in the west, but stars are appearing above her, small pinpoints growing stronger the farther she is from shore. Their beauty is hidden when she is back there in all the electric lights; she needs a time in nature to remember where the beauty is hidden, and where to find her strength.

She thinks of her mother, her dear frazzled mother. She used to think she, Kiya, was the strong one, but she doesn't think that anymore. Kiya pictures the two of them, her mother and herself, leaning against one another, holding each other up. They are equally fragile. When this is all over, after the baby is born, Kiya will go back to Portland. She will visit her mother again, will have tea with her, but everything will be changed. Kiya is a different person now than she was then, and she will be even more different in ways she can't foresee when she returns.

She allows herself to think, just for a moment, of what it would be like if she lived in Portland with her child. Her due date is only a few weeks from now. They would find a small apartment, maybe a one-bedroom. She pictures a crib next to her bed, a sweet lump in the middle of the crib under blankets. At night she would hear the baby's breathing, its small snores. Later, when it grew, it would call to her in the morning, like a bird. If she thinks of it like this, just the two of them, it seems entirely possible that she could make it work. It's only when she thinks of the world beyond the imagined bedroom, beyond the small apartment, that her breathing becomes tight and things become dark. Then she starts feeling sorry for the child, alone with her for a mother. She starts thinking that the baby deserves better.

She's never been on the lake before at night. The darkness is cold and rippling, shot through with thin streaks of light. The light in the sky and the water seems to move; to twist and turn like in Van Gogh's painting. She closes her eyes and rests, slipping into a dreamy, near-sleep state until her mid-section tightens, hardens, and she opens her eyes to take a deep breath.

At last, she is approaching Spruce Island. It is a small, uninhabited island, with a camping spot. Trees cover it thickly, the depths impenetrable in the night. As she draws closer the trees rise higher into the sky, blocking out the stars except for right above her head. She paddles around to the other side of the island. There is an open spot there, a little beach where she can lie down and see the sky.

This side of the island faces the open lake, the opposite far shore barely visible as a dark line against the sky. From somewhere Kiya hears a faint chorus, the high singing sound of spring peepers. She paddles close enough to the shore of the island so she can step out onto a rock and not get her boots wet. When she turns to pull the kayak up, she favors her bad leg and one boot, the one on the other foot, slips off a rock into the water. She pulls it out immediately but can feel the dampness seep into her socks, and her ankle is twisted. With her ankle aching, she is able to pull the kayak far enough onto the sand so that it won't float away.

She feels as if she's paddled across an ocean. She manages to untie the garbage bag, pull out the sleeping bag. She drapes it, open, over her shoulders. The warm weight is welcome.

The trees are thick and dark behind her but here, on the thin strip of sand between the rocks and the trees, she can see the sky, a darkening indigo. She fumbles in her pockets, looking for her cell phone. She finds the book of matches and a tissue, but no phone. She checks her pants pockets; not there either. Kiya stands, looking out to the water. She hears the spring peepers faintly, their small high voices rising and falling. She makes her way back to the kayak and checks under and behind the little seat, on the floor.

She leans as far as she can into the open front of the boat, where her feet go. Grunting and aching, she pulls herself upright again. Not there.

She sits down on a rock, the sleeping bag cushioning her. So she can't call Maddie to tell her where she is. Maddie will be worried. The night seems darker now that she knows she doesn't have her phone, the air chillier. She will start a fire if she can, warm up and rest, and then paddle back. Or maybe she will just warm up in the sleeping bag before she paddles back. She is tired and aching, and doesn't feel like getting into the boat again. She wants to lie down and let these Braxton-Hicks work themselves out. Sitting on the rock with the sleeping bag wrapped around her, Kiya pictures herself walking into Maddie's house. It's Sunday night; Maddie works in the morning. The house will be quiet, the light above the stove on.

On the rock, Kiya sinks deep into herself, focusing, concentrating on what is happening inside her body. The contraction is harder than she has felt before, harder than she can imagine Braxton-Hicks could be. Silly, silly, silly, she tells herself, hearing Drew's voice agreeing with her. She is breathing lightly, and she doesn't know what she is silly for. For her kayak ride, for her earlier despair. For losing her phone. For thinking some things were important when all that's important is this, the force and tightness in her stomach.

✳ ✳ ✳ ✳

When Peter enters his apartment after dropping Toni off, Ryan is sitting on the couch, hunched over his laptop. "Hey man," he says. "How'd it go?"

"Eh, okay. It went great with my mom—she loves Toni, who wouldn't? Not so good with Kiya."

"What! I thought you were going to sidestep all that."

"Didn't work out that way. She kind of flipped out. Now my mom says she's missing. She took off and hasn't come back."

"Doesn't your mother live like, nowhere?"

"Pretty much." Peter's phone squawks in his pocket.

"Hello?"

"Is this Peter King?" It's a woman's voice, careful and clear. "This is Jackie, from the Lakewood Care Center?"

"Yes?" Peter says, meeting her question with a question.

"I have your number listed as a contact for Alex Kimball, after Maddie King and Richard Kimball. I wasn't able to reach either of those people.

"Yes?" Peter asks again, more serious now.

"Alex's condition has changed over the past couple of hours. We thought we should let his loved ones know that the end may be near."

"I was just there . . ." Peter remembers the rattling breathing that started when he and Toni were there.

After he hangs up, Peter tries calling his mother on both her cell phone and her home phone. Maybe she's still looking for Kiya, but he wishes she'd take her cell phone with her. He leaves messages on both phones, telling her to call him, that the nursing home had called. "What am I supposed to DO?" he asks Ryan.

Ryan looks up at him. "Were you guys close?"

"Well, he was my mom's boyfriend. You know." Peter sits on the couch, heavily. "The thing is, he doesn't have anyone else." Peter tries his mother's cell phone again. He supposes she could have gone to bed, but usually, she gets up when the phone rings.

Ryan shrugs. "It isn't as if you can do anything, right? To help him? And didn't you say he isn't aware if you're there?"

"No, I think he knows when we're there. But you're right, I can't do anything for him. I'd just sit there."

"Well, then . . ." Ryan turns back to the computer as if the answer is self-evident.

Peter sits glumly, feeling himself sink into the couch. He remembers Alex's face, pale as marble, the way his breathing changed when Toni said they were to be married. He thinks of him smiling at Peter, years ago. He thinks how good a beer would be about now. "Fuck," he says, and gets up. "Fuck, fuck, fuck." He puts his coat back on, waves at Ryan's astonished face, and leaves.

* * * *

Maddie sees that the only thing to do, apparently, is to get in the two kayaks and go out on the lake looking for Kiya. "Do we need to bring anything?" she asks.

Jack pauses in his effort of carrying kayaks to the shore. "Are you warm enough?"

Maddie looks at her jacket. "I'll get my warmer coat. And maybe some snacks, in case we find her and she's hungry." When Maddie comes back out, she's carrying two life jackets and a blanket. She stuffs the blanket in her kayak. "Just in case we need it," she says. "Here." She hands the life jacket to Jack.

He looks at it in disdain, then, on seeing the expression on her face, takes it. "I'll take it in the boat," he says, "but I'm not wearing it."

"It might diminish your masculinity," Maddie says.

"Damn right." He starts to step into a boat, then looks back at Maddie, and puts his foot back on the rocky shore. "Here," he says, and takes her arm to help her in.

They push away from shore. Maddie sees the lights of her house grow smaller, sees the trees surrounding it reach up, darker than the sky. She hears a sound; *whoo whoo whoo whoo* coming from beyond her house, then the same sound repeated. "A barred owl," Jack says. He turns to look at her, his silhouette dark. "Where should we go? The island?"

"Yes," Maddie says. "We can start there." Maddie feels momentarily angry at Kiya; she would prefer not to be out here on the lake, late at night. She'd prefer to be in her house, getting ready to go to bed. But then she remembers the girl's face when she left earlier that day, and Maddie just wants to find her and help her. She asks Jack: "What if she doesn't want us going after her? What if she gets angry when she sees us?"

Jack is silent for a moment, the only sounds those of their paddles dipping into the water. "She's young enough yet that she doesn't know what she wants," he says. "Or what she needs. She'll be glad to see us, don't you worry."

Maddie shivers in a sudden chill. "Look." Jack points to the horizon, where Maddie sees the rounded edge of the moon rising above the trees. "The moon is almost full."

"Oh my god," Maddie says. "That is so beautiful." They pause to watch it inch above the trees on the far shore. The sound of the owl and the sight of the moon—its fullness becoming more apparent every second—make her feel reassured, as if in a world with such beauty, nothing can seriously go wrong. And suddenly she sees Alex's face in the sky, sees him smiling at her, his face taking shape around the stars. She catches her breath. "Strange," she murmurs.

Jack, paddling ahead of her, turns around. "Did you say something?"

"No." She paddles again but she still sees Alex. She feels him with her, the old Alex, before the illness. It's as if he's with her in her one-person lake kayak, sitting next to her, wrapping himself around her. She breathes him in, smiling with him at the strangeness of this night, at the beauty of that moon lifting up. She feels his arms around her, light as air. She takes in the scent of his being, and then she continues paddling.

As they approach the island Maddie hears something and stops. "Wait," she says softly to Jack, who stops also. There is nothing, just the sound of a breeze ruffling the water. Then she identifies a faint sound coming from the shore; "Peepers." They paddle again, drops of water from their oars catching bits of moonlight. They approach closer to the island's dark shore, and Maddie says again, "Wait. I hear something else." A sound rising up to the moon from somewhere on the island or beyond; "Is it a loon?" Maddie asks. "A dove?" She doesn't want to say what she thinks it really is: the sound of a person, crying and calling out into the night.

Chapter Twenty-Eight

Kiya knows she should get back in the kayak and paddle back
to shore. She stands up, slowly, and takes a step toward the shore,
then leans over with the force of the next contraction. It is unbe-
lievably strong. It takes her down to the ground, where she lies on
her side, her legs scrabbling under her. When it finally eases she
tries again, but the next contraction comes even sooner, taking her
to the ground again. She feels a sudden need to eliminate; she
walks a few feet into the trees, pulls down her pants, and squats.
The heaviness inside her is great. She uses leaves to wipe herself
when she finishes, and just as she stands up, she feels a warm wet-
ness seeping through to her pants. She can't control it.

Hands shaking, she unzips the sleeping bag. She pulls her
damp pants off and crawls inside. It is soft and warm, and the sand
is level beneath. She is warm in the bag, but shivers with emotion,
with fear. Is this it, then? How can that be? It's too early, she's not
ready. She's alone, it can't happen. No, no, no. She begins to moan,
her teeth chattering. No, it can't be. She tells herself she will get
up, put on her pants, and go to shore, but the sleeping bag feels so
good and then another contraction sweeps over and she becomes
animal, making inarticulate sounds.

She is alone in the night, like Drew was alone. No one is here
for her. When she opens her eyes, the stars swim above her, swirling in drunken circular patterns. Starry night, night of pain. Who
can she find to help her; what can she find in herself to help? The
energy is sweeping through her body now. She pictures it blue,
coursing like the lights in the sky, bursting inside her. Who knew
her body had this power, who knew it would feel like this? How
can she carry all this energy without exploding? She cries, soft
helpless sobs.

In the lull between the clenching pains, she hears a voice, as
if someone were lying next to her, speaking into her ear. It says,
"Kiya. Kiya. You can do this." She laughs, helplessly, at the ridiculousness of this voice she imagines. Another contraction, the
force of it like iron wrapping around her, inside her. The voice

tells her, "Be as strong as that. Stronger." Okay, she thinks, panting. Okay then, she'll do this. She doesn't have any choice. Another contraction makes her moan and her teeth chatter, but she no longer feels as if she will explode with fear. She will simply carry this child into this world. She will do this. A vessel, she is a strong vessel. She will not break.

She imagines she hears voices on the water, imagines other sounds: the scraping of boats on shore, voices calling her. She doesn't answer, just lets sounds escape with her breathing. A thin light flashes across her; it is starlight, the stars must be falling, and it does not surprise her that the world is ending. Through the end of the world she will continue, and when it is over she will be glad.

Then it is real, someone is here. Jack, leaning over her. His face, his voice is real. Maddie behind him, calling her name. "Kiya! We're here. We're here now."

They are outlined against the night, lit faintly by the flashlight, their faces concerned and kind. "Oh my god," Kiya whispers, "you are angels," and she lets out another sound, a groan which reaches into the night.

* * * *

Alex's passing is soundless, silent, nearly imperceptible; there is more and more space between his breaths, and then Peter waits for the next breath, and it doesn't come. A vein in Alex's neck flutters, then is still. Peter, sitting by the bed holding Alex's hand, slowly lets it drop. He pushes his chair back and is all by himself now. There were two of them a minute ago, and now he's the only person here. The noisy breathing has ended. Alex's face sags, his mouth hanging open. Without the noise of Alex's breathing Peter can hear the hum of the nursing home, the soft closing of doors down the hall, the whisper of footsteps. He looks at the bed and realizes Alex, whatever he is or was, is not there anymore, just this collection of flesh. Peter wonders, the question pure and strong and demanding of an answer: *Where is he? Where did he go?*

A woman opens the door and puts her head in. It is one of the women he saw earlier behind the front desk. She looks at Alex, lying on the bed, and at Peter sitting next to him. "It's over?" she asks. He nods.

The nurse asks if he wants to be alone with Alex. Peter nods, though he's not sure why. He thinks it's the thing to do, to give honor. He sits for a few more minutes, looking at the body that used to house Alex, then walks down the hall. The woman says she has finally reached Alex's brother and will talk with him about "arrangements."

"I'm glad you were here," she says. "I'm glad you were able to be with him."

Peter leaves the building and walks to his truck. The sky is bright and clear above him, with a round rising moon. He has never seen anyone die before. He has just been close to something tremendous. It wasn't sad, just—tremendous. The night is very still, the world more serious and more mysterious than he thought it was. The moon hangs solemnly, lighting up the sky around it in a white glow. It has seen all this before. Standing by his truck, Peter thinks of Toni, of her warmth and life.

Peter drives slowly to his mother's house. There are no cars. Once he sees a large animal at the side of the road—a deer, or perhaps a young moose. The animal pauses, looking at him as if trying to tell him something, share some wild knowledge with him. Its eyes glow in his headlights, then it passes into the woods and is gone. He slows down and looks into the trees where it has gone, but sees nothing.

His mother's car is parked in the drive and the house is lit up. When Peter opens the door, Sadie runs to him, pushes her body between his legs as she does when she is anxious, her tail wagging her entire body back and forth. "Mom?" he says softly, walking from room to room. "Mother?" The door to her bedroom is open and the room is dark. He turns the light on to see her bed, comforter pulled over it smooth and neat. It's past 2:00 a.m., and his mother hasn't been in her bed tonight. He checks Kiya's room and finds it empty also, the bed made.

Peter steps out the kitchen door, onto the landing. Jack's house next to him is dark. He looks around; after a moment, when his eyes adjust to the darkness, it looks as if the shed door is partly open. He goes down the steps, walks across the dock to the shed, pulls the door open. The kayaks are gone, all three of them.

Peter takes the down comforter from his mother's bed out to the Adirondack chair on the deck. Sadie scratches at the door and whines. He lets her out. She squats on the grass, then comes on the deck to sit next to his chair. Peter will sit in this chair until he falls asleep. He will sit vigil for Alex, and wait for his mother and Kiya (and Jack?) to return from whatever strange adventure they are on. If they haven't returned by morning, he will call the police. He pushes the comforter around him until he is enclosed in a soft cocoon of squishy warmth, and looks at the lake. The moon, now high in the sky, sends a bar of rippling light across the lake, like a lighted roadway reaching to him. He hears the odd call he recognizes as an owl from the woods behind his mother's house and hears it answered, from farther away. He watches the ripples on the water, thinking of how Alex's breathing died out. A faint sound comes from somewhere across the water; are the loons returned already? It rises and falls on the night air faintly, like a woman crying, or a child.

* * * *

When Maddie stepped onto the shore of the island with Jack, she thought Kiya was lying on the ground crying from sadness, a kind of emotional explosion. It was dark, and she could see the girl's face only when Jack shone the flashlight on it, the tears streaming down Kiya's cheeks catching the light. They would comfort her, Maddie thought; give her some food, and get her in the kayak to go home. Then she heard Kiya make a sound she'd never heard before, a groaning, animalistic sound and saw her pants balled up by the side of the sleeping bag. She felt something strange in her chest. "Kiya? What's happening?"

Jack seemed to catch on more quickly than Maddie did. "Are you in labor, sweetheart?" he asked, squatting down by her.

Kiya, through chattering teeth, said, "Guess so," with a little helpless laugh. "I'm sorry. So sorry."

"Oh wow," Maddie said. "Oh wow. Oh wow." It's all she could think of to say. Then, "Can you move? Any chance we can get you in the boat?" Somehow she knew the answer before Kiya said anything.

254

Now Jack is building a fire. He has gathered small sticks and leaves in a pile for kindling, a few feet from where Kiya lies, and holds a cigarette lighter to them until the leaves fire up, and a stick catches. Maddie sits on the ground next to Kiya. "When did you start feeling like this?" she asks.

"When . . . when I got to the island. I couldn't leave." Kiya sits up, and gets on her hands and knees, the sleeping bag falling from her shoulders. "Unngh . . ." she moans, and Maddie remembers the pressure of the body opening to let another body through. Maddie reaches over to massage Kiya's back, pushing up the tunic she still wears. Kiya is naked from the waist down, and unembarrassed. When the contraction passes, she pants and puts her head down, her rear still up in the air. Maddie continues to knead her back muscles gently. Kiya's skin is wet with sweat. "Does this feel good?" she asks.

"Yes," Kiya says. "It's . . ." And then she stops speaking, holding her head down in her hands as if in deep thought, eyes closed tightly as she has another contraction.

"It will be a natural birth," Jack says. The twigs have caught, and he lays small branches on top of them carefully. "Just like they used to do in olden days." Maddie looks over at him with sudden gratefulness. He is a good man.

The moon has crossed the sky, disappearing in the trees. Stars watch over above them. Jack feeds branches to the fire until it grows, casting a flickering orange light. Every now and then he gets up to find more wood, then comes to sit beside them, arms resting on his raised knees. Maddie massages Kiya's back, holds her hand, and pushes hair back from her face. Between contractions, Kiya covers herself with the sleeping bag to warm up, but throws it off again when the next contraction starts. Once Kiya looks up at Maddie, her face sweaty and fearful, and says, "Is it supposed to feel like this?"

Maddie's heart races as the list of things that could go wrong grows in her mind, but she smiles down at Kiya, squeezing her hand. "I think so. It seems normal to me."

Kiya takes a deep breath as another contraction shudders through her. "Breathe," Maddie says. "Deep breathing, that's the way. Everything is perfectly normal." After a time Kiya turns on her back, leaning against Maddie in a half-sitting position. Kiya's legs are trembling. "I think this is called transition," Maddie says, keeping her voice calm. She remembers the trembling legs, the feeling that whatever is happening is impossible, it cannot happen. She remembers feeling as if her body was not big enough to allow this other body through.

Kiya groans, and cries, and then makes a strange, growling sound. Her face is clenched. Maddie realizes she is pushing, bearing down. "Okay," Maddie says. "Okay, thatta girl. Push if you want." She has no idea if Kiya should push, if her cervix is dilated enough, but if she wants to push, she's not going to stop her. She couldn't if she tried. Kiya grips Maddie's hand and grimaces, pushing hard. Kiya stops, breathing deeply. Jack puts more wood on the fire, wipes a hand across his face, then comes around to Kiya's other side, to take her other hand. "You are strong," Maddie says to Kiya. "You are so strong." In the intermittent moments of quiet, through Kiya gasping to catch her breath, they hear waves lapping against the shore, and farther away, the sound of peepers rising and falling. Kiya groans again, pushing down hard, says *Oh my god oh my god* and between her raised knees Maddie sees something pushing out the skin around Kiya's vagina, making it bulge, the lips stretching wide and red. Another few pushes and something which is not Kiya appears, a small head, dark hair slicked down. The world holds its breath. Then a face emerges, eyes, a nose, all scrunched. "He's coming," Maddie says, and she doesn't know why she says "he." "He's coming, he's here, keep pushing." Kiya grunts and pushes, making a giant effort, then pushes again. A small shoulder slips out, then the other one, and then there is all of him lying in Jack's hands, stretched out and wet, tiny hands grasping for purchase in the unfamiliar air, squalling at the coldness, at the outrage of this new world.

Chapter Twenty-Nine

In the early part of her labor, when she realized it was actually going to happen here, on this island in the cold April night, Kiya was swept by an uncontrollable terror. She felt for a moment that she should have done what Drew did, should have stopped her life so none of this would have happened, but she wasn't strong enough to take that action, earlier or now.

Maddie and Jack brought light, brought warmth, took care of her. And after the incredible moment when she pushed the baby out, it was like the universe was singing to her because she had given birth to this child. It was all applauding her, the spring peepers and the stars and the lapping waves, all cheering for her. She had done it: they knew she could. She blazed with her own light in the night.

When the baby came out Jack held his small body in his hands and didn't know what to do. For a moment Kiya was afraid; was there something wrong with the child? Was the child dead, and Jack was afraid to tell her? Then Kiya heard a squall, a yell, and she started crying in relief. Maddie came up beside Jack and wrapped a blanket she'd gotten from somewhere around the baby. Jack and Maddie conferred in low voices, words Kiya couldn't hear for her own crying, then Jack pulled something small from his pocket. Maddie held the cord connecting the baby to Kiya, squeezing it gently. "You don't feel that, do you?"

"No," Kiya said. Jack did something at the water, and at the fire. It was a little jackknife he held in his hands, turning it over the fire. Then he came over and tied something around the cord at one end, then the other. He watched the cord—until it stopped pulsing, he later told her—and cut through, separating her from the child. "I used to do this for cows on my parents' farm," he murmured.

After that Jack took the edge of the blanket and sawed a cut in the top of it, then ripped it down, sawing off the bottom until he had a towel-sized piece. He went over to the lake, dipped it in the water, then held the wet blanket over the fire to warm it up. Maddie held the squalling blanket-wrapped bundle in her arms, looking down at it. She opened the blanket so Jack could wipe the makeshift towel over the baby's face and body, then she wrapped the dry blanket around him again and turned to Kiya. "Here," she said, and put him in Kiya's arms. "Your son."

Now Kiya holds him in her arms, looking at him. His face is small and perfect, eyes closed tight under damp strings of dark hair. A tiny hand works its way up his cheek, fingers splaying out and clenching. The skin on his hands is loose, like that of an old man. Kiya takes the hand in hers, letting it wrap itself around her finger. "He's beautiful," she says. The words are inadequate.

"He's perfect," Jack agrees. Maddie is making noises sitting on the ground beside him, soft snuffling noises in the dark. Jack puts his arm around her and squeezes her close to him, their shadows outlined by the fire. After a few moments, Kiya's pain is back. She feels the contractions again, squeezing, and something else comes out between her legs, something large, wet and warm.

"Oh—the placenta!" Maddie says. Jack holds out the wet blanket piece to Kiya and she wipes off her thighs and between her legs. Then Kiya is wrapped up again with her son in the sleeping bag. The trees stretching above them, the sky visible beyond them at the shore, the stars, the ripples on the water, the faint sounds of peepers—all are protective of Kiya and her baby, all conspiring to take care of them. "The universe won't let you down, little boy," Kiya murmurs to her son. "It will be there for you." He makes a grunting, squeaking sound of assent.

✻ ✻ ✻ ✻

Peter is sitting once again beside Alex, only when he turns to look at Alex to say goodbye, it isn't Alex's face he sees. It's the face of a stranger, a much younger man, with dark blonde hair dipping over his forehead in a style from decades ago. Peter pulls his hand away, then realizes the man on the bed must be his father. "Oh!" he says. "So that's it!" It's as if he has just figured something out, something put together for him as a mystery to solve. The clues have just led him to this.

The man's eyes open suddenly then, and he fixes them on Peter. He smiles crookedly, wheezing as he laughs—the sound is like the sounds Alex made, breathing his last breaths through the tracheostomy tube. The man—his father—is struggling to sit up, and Peter says "No, no, you mustn't," and takes his shoulders, trying to push him back down to the bed.

The man speaks somehow through the tube, words composed of the wheezing sounds. "Okay, you're right," he says, and shakes a finger at Peter, jokingly, as if Peter has just pulled off a good one. "My bad," the man says and lies back down. "You win."

Peter's eyes open wide. He is still sitting on the Adirondack chair, looking up at a sky lit by the pale colors of the dawn. He shifts, uncomfortable in the comforter wrapped around him, and turns to his side. Sadie, beside him, looks up. Her pale coat is almost pink in the color from the sky. Peter hears a crow call in the trees above, a loud cawing. It must have been that which woke him from the weird, weird dream he was having. He looks up, but can't see the bird.

Peter hears a sound he is sure must be a loon. He lifts his head and sees it, flapping its wings in the water halfway to the island, raising itself up. It calls again, the warbling warning call to a partner Peter can't see. Then something makes its way around the island in the distance: a boat, a kayak with one person in it, paddles lifting rhythmically against the pale water.

* * * *

Maddie puts another piece of broken wood on the fire and sits on the ground next to the sleeping bag. Jack has taken a kayak back to shore for help, and the two of them—the three of them—are alone on the island. Kiya holds her baby protectively inside the bag, one arm above his head, his small face open to the air. Both of them have their eyes closed, though every now and then Kiya's eyes open. She looks at her baby as if she can't believe it really happened. Kiya is beautiful in the pale early light, and Maddie wishes there were someone there besides her to note that beauty, to love her. *There will be,* she tells herself. Sitting on the ground in the cool morning, Maddie remembers the loneliness she felt when Peter was born, before they brought him to her. She has been pushing against that loneliness all her life, trying to pretend it wasn't there, or she didn't care if it was; trying to be independent, to be tough. Alex was finally her warm friend, her companion, and let her lean against him, but now he's gone. She remembers her sense of him last night on the way to the island. It was as if he was really there, but Maddie knows now that Alex has not really been there, not for a long time. It makes her sad, along with everything else that makes her sad, and she cries silently into her hands, the tears warm on her cheeks.

When Kiya was given her son to hold, after she said he was beautiful and that she loved him, she told Maddie that it would be other parents who would raise him, other parents who would be his mother and father. She had already picked them out. "I will always love him," Kiya whispered, the firelight shifting over her face. Maddie didn't know how, looking at her baby, the girl found the strength to do what she felt she needed to do.

Maddie hopes Jack hurries back with the motorboat he went to borrow. She doesn't know what babies need after they're born. Thank god for Jack, she thinks fervently. The shadows of the forest are becoming lighter, and Maddie sees through the trees to the glimmer of water on the other side of the island.

She walks on her hands and knees until she is right above the baby, looking down at his face. She reaches out a finger to touch his cheek, impossibly soft. His eyes open, slits widening to take in the brightness and mystery of this world. He looks at her face, close above him, with an intent squinting expression, as if he's trying to figure out what he's looking at. He looks intelligent and grumpy. Maddie smiles at him, memorizing his face. "Hello," she says softly to the grandson she will not watch grow up. "Hello, my darling. Welcome to the world."

Chapter Thirty

When they pull up to Maddie's house in the pale early light Peter is standing on the dock, waiting for them. Kiya steps out of the boat with the baby, Jack helping her. On the deck, she holds the blanket-wrapped bundle out to Peter. After a moment, he reaches out his arms. He holds the baby stiffly, looking at him intently, and then Kiya doesn't know if she can speak. Peter looks at up Kiya, his eyes searching hers. She sees the pain and confusion on his face, and she finds her voice again. She says, "He is perfectly beautiful, and we have made him for someone else to love."

Maddie fills the tub and Kiya bathes with the baby in warm water. She washes his pink wrinkled skin, his small tender body, carefully, and holds him on her soft stomach when he cries. These are gestures of love and farewell, the gradual detaching of him from her body. She will remember these moments all of her life: the way his legs look in the water, the feel of his soft small back on her hand, the skin loose and red.

She hears the voice again when she is looking at her baby, into his small grave face. It says, *You are strong.* It tells her, *You are suffering for this child; you are doing a good thing.* It sounds a little like Jack's voice, the time he told her she was doing a good thing by taking care of herself, staying healthy and bringing it into the world. He'd said, "You should be proud of yourself," and that's what the voice says to her now.

After the bath, she drinks hot tea, and Maddie finds a menstrual pad to catch her blood. Kiya calls her mother, tells her the baby was born and they are going to the hospital now, to make sure everything is okay. "I'll see you soon," Kiya promises. "Don't cry. I'm fine. We'll have tea together." She lays the baby on the couch, Maddie, Jack, and Peter gathering around it like the three wise people. Sadie noses between them to sniff the baby's face, his blanket, then sit back on her haunches.

Sitting in the back seat of the car with Maddie and Jack in front, Kiya holds her baby wrapped in the small clean blanket Maddie found. Maddie has called the adoption agency, and someone will meet them at the hospital. Kiya remembers the wind in the trees last night, the sound of the spring peepers rising and falling. What can she tell her son, these last minutes they will be together? She remembers the sky, the fire, and the stars. She whispers, "You will be loved and protected." His face scrunches at the sound of her voice, the feel of her breath against his cheek.

She will be torn with grief, she knows; she will cry in ways she's never cried before when she says goodbye to him for the last time. It will hurt, his absence an actual physical pain as if something is torn from her body. She will miss him all her life. She will let herself cry, and then she will remind herself that her suffering has a reason, and the reason is his face, the way it looked at her in the early light when they lay in the sleeping bag. He looked at her, and for that dimly-lit moment, she thought they communicated. She will never forget his face. She is doing this for him.

When they drive up to the hospital, the sun comes into the back seat where she is sitting. Kiya lets herself think the warmth is the presence of Drew, visiting. He would lean over to take the baby's finger in his; he would say, "Cute little dude, isn't he?" Then he would fade away, like the sun does as they pull under the entrance awning.

Jack opens the back door for Kiya and she scoots over, but can't stand up to get out of the car while holding the baby. Jack holds out his arms and Kiya gives him the child. "There's my little fish," she says, and she sees blue rippling water. She pictures her arms opening to set her beautiful fish free, letting him swim away in the shafts of light.

end

The author would like to thank Debbie Kinney, Shari Witham, Elizabeth Cooke, Kitty Burns Florey, and Gretchen Legler for their help in seeing this book through.

About the Author

Patricia O'Donnell is a Professor of Creative Writing at the University of Maine at Farmington, where she directs the BFA Program in Creative Writing. Her stories have appeared in *The New Yorker* and elsewhere. Her books include a novel, a memoir, and a collection of short fiction which won the Serena McDonald Kennedy Award. She lives in Wilton, Maine, with her husband.

About the Press

Unsolicited Press was founded in 2012 and is based in Portland, Oregon. The press publishes fiction, creative nonfiction, and poetry from award-winning authors. Learn more at www.unsolicitedpress.com.

CPSIA information can be obtained
at www.ICGtesting.com
Printed in the USA
BVHW032047090320
574291BV00004B/10

9 781947 021815